A SPARK IN THE BLOOD

Christophe Vallette—Driven by the death of one brother and the hatred of another, he created a new life in a new land.

Moira—Only one man could help her forget the violence of her past.

Brett—Wed to a perfect wife, ensnared by a bewitching wanton, he was torn between love and lust as the family was divided by the horrors of the Civil War.

Lionel—A genius in the laboratory and a misfit out of it, he knew one night of joy and a lifetime of anguish.

Barbara—She was beautiful, proud, and determined to prove she had equal rights with any man in public and in private.

Luke—His bold resolve and unrelenting determination were desperately needed if the Vallette dynasty were to survive the greatest crisis of all.

These were some of the Vallettes . . . men and women caught up in the mighty tides of history and the turbulent cross-currents of individual destiny . . . each adding to the greatness, reaping the rewards, and paying the price of—

THE VALLETTE HERITAGE

THE VALLETTE HERITAGE

LOUISA BRONTE

A JOVE/HBJ BOOK

Requests for permission to make copies of any part of the work should be mailed to: Permissions, Jove Publications, Inc., 757 Third Avenue, New York, NY 10017

First Jove/HBJ edition published August 1978

Library of Congress Catalog Card Number: 77-91250

Printed in the United States of America

Jove/HBJ books are published by Jove Publications, Inc. (Harcourt Brace Jovanovich) 757 Third Avenue, New York, N.Y. 10017

To the industrial families
That helped make America great

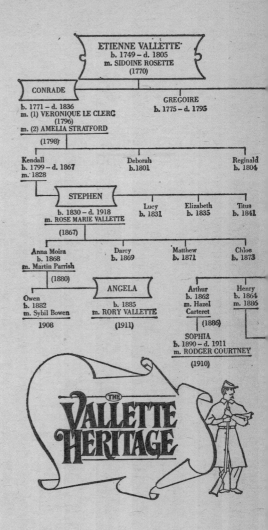

ETIENNE VALLETTE
b. 1749 – d. 1805
m. SIDOINE ROSETTE
(1770)

CONRADE
b. 1771 – d. 1836
m. (1) VERONIQUE LE CLERC
(1796)
m. (2) AMELIA STRATFORD
(1798)

GREGOIRE
b. 1775 – d. 1795

Kendall
b. 1799 – d. 1867
m. 1828

Deborah
b. 1801

Reginald
b. 1804

STEPHEN
b. 1830 – d. 1918
m. ROSE MARIE VALLETTE
(1867)

Lucy
b. 1831

Elizabeth
b. 1835

Titus
b. 1841

Anna Moira
b. 1868
m. Martin Parrish
(1880)

Darcy
b. 1869

Matthew
b. 1871

Chloe
b. 1873

Owen
b. 1882
m. Sybil Bowen
1908

ANGELA
b. 1885
m. RORY VALLETTE
(1911)

Arthur
b. 1862
m. Hazel
Carteret
(1886)

Henry
b. 1864
m. 1886

SOPHIA
b. 1890 – d. 1911
m. RODGER COURTNEY
(1910)

THE VALLETTE HERITAGE

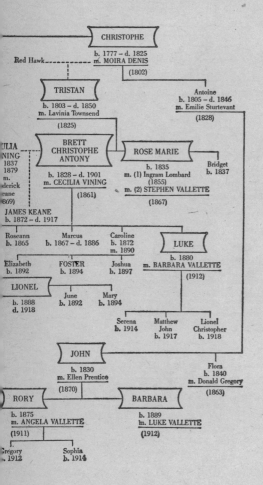

CHRISTOPHE
b. 1777 – d. 1825
m. MOIRA DENIS
(1802)

Red Hawk

TRISTAN
b. 1803 – d. 1850
m. Lavinia Townsend
(1825)

Antoine
b. 1805 – d. 1846
m. Emilie Sturtevant
(1828)

JULIA
VINING
1837
1879
m.
derick
eane
869)

BRETT
CHRISTOPHE
ANTONY
b. 1828 – d. 1901
m. CECILIA VINING
(1861)

ROSE MARIE
b. 1835
m. (1) Ingram Lombard
(1855)
m. (2) STEPHEN VALLETTE
(1867)

Bridget
b. 1837

JAMES KEANE
b. 1872 – d. 1917

Roseann
b. 1865

Marcus
b. 1867 – d. 1886

Caroline
b. 1872
m. 1890

LUKE
b. 1880
m. BARBARA VALLETTE
(1912)

Elizabeth
b. 1892

FOSTER
b. 1894

Joshua
b. 1897

LIONEL
b. 1888
d. 1918

June
b. 1892

Mary
b. 1894

Serena
b. 1914

Matthew
John
b. 1917

Lionel
Christopher
b. 1918

JOHN
b. 1830
m. Ellen Prentice
(1870)

Flora
b. 1840
m. Donald Gregory
(1863)

RORY
b. 1875
m. ANGELA VALLETTE
(1911)

BARBARA
b. 1889
m. LUKE VALLETTE
(1912)

Gregory
. 1912

Sophia
b. 1914

PART I
1795–1806

Chapter 1

Christophe Vallette sat at the library table, his light brown, curly hair gleaming in the lamplight, his eyes intent on the page before him. He had several open books spread around him, and from time to time he would glance at one or another of them. But always he would return to the page before him. He would study that open page until finally he understood the obscure chemical formula on it.

His mother stood in the doorway, unnoticed for several minutes, observing her youngest son. All three of her sons bewildered and surprised her; they were like strange chicks deposited in her maternal nest. Christophe, only eighteen years of age, was the most difficult to understand. He was as intense and quiet, as detached and absentminded, as his father, yet of a sudden he could be so harshly practical that he would shock all of them.

But Sidoine Vallette had no time to ponder this now. She rustled forward in her blue silk gown, shook back the lace of her sleeve, and gently laid her slim hand on Christophe's arm.

He started violently, as though wrenched from some strange world, and raised his face to her. His brown eyes, light, yet with depths in them, studied her face. He rose at once.

"Maman, I did not hear you come in. Pardon me."

He drew a chair forward, and she sank down into it, touching its rosewood arms nervously with the tips of her fingers.

"My son, where is your brother?"

The hint of caution that crept into his face might not have been noticed by any except a mother. All of the Vallettes had learned caution and reserve from the cradle. As devout Huguenots living in a harsh land of Catholic oppression and blind hatred, they had learned for generations that they must pretend to be what they were not—or suffer persecution, torture, banishment, even death. French they were, and devoted to their homeland, their manor house, their land. Yet they bitterly resented the horrors that tormented those Frenchmen who wished to follow the teachings of John Calvin rather than obey the Pope of Rome and the repressive Catholic churchmen of France.

Recently the Vallettes had been forced to withdraw to their country home, the last possession of a once-wealthy family. While in this house Sidoine Vallette sometimes felt surrounded by ghosts.

It was here in 1702 that a Vallette had been murdered: a Catholic neighbor had denounced him as a Huguenot, and he'd been run through with a sword. The victim's younger brother had hidden in the depths of the wine cellars, and later he'd escaped with his wife and two sons. They had lived in obscurity in the south of France until a change in the local climate of feelings allowed them to return.

The Vallettes were publicly baptized as Catholics—and privately as Protestants. Yet the violent eighteenth century had visited more bloodshed upon the Vallette family. Two cousins preaching the Calvinist doctrine were imprisoned and tortured, and they died in chains.

Etienne Vallette, Sidoine's husband and Christophe's father, had been stout of heart. He had gone to Paris and purchased a printing press, and with it he'd been able to publish the many pamphlets and books he'd written. His treatises on crop rotation, viniculture, and winemaking were welcomed, even by the Bourbons. And so Etienne rose in Court esteem—only to fall following the Revolution of 1789. Then his pamphlets on freedom of religion as well as of politics brought him unwelcome attention from the police. Paid toughs came and destroyed the press one night, and burned all of Etienne's carefully wrought pages denouncing oppression. Etienne had shot at them, wounded two, and been imprisoned for two months. He'd been released abruptly, with a stern warning against printing any longer.

So the Vallettes had fled again, to the uncertain sanctuary of the country home. Suspicious Catholic neighbors, the local authorities, and curious gossip combined to keep them aloof. They tended their vineyards, raised their sheep, and wrote and prayed in secret. Hopefully, since the spring of 1795 had seen a good rainfall, they would enjoy a harvest that would begin to restore their shabby fortunes.

Finally Christophe spoke, his voice soft and low for a man. His voice might lead one who did not know of his obstinacy and his brilliance to misconstrue him as gentle and easily swayed.

"Maman, I believe Gregoire is at his prayers—"

"I know he kneels in the chapel, my son! It is the vesper hour. And you know I do not speak of Gregoire, but of your hot-blooded, foolish brother, Conrade!" Her voice broke slightly, and he bent to her at once, placing his slim hand, so like hers, on her shoulder.

"Maman, I should not tease you! Forgive me. Conrade—" He hesitated. "He does not confide in me, I am too young, he says."

"Yet you know where he went. You know your brother."

"Oui, maman, I believe—he goes to see Veronique Le Clerc."

There was a brief silence in the dimly-lit library.

"Why—why must Conrade always wish what is forbidden?" Sidoine Vallette lifted her slender hand, and sorrowfully let it fall again to the arm of the chair. "He could court Angelica—or Bertha. Why does he seek after Veronique? Her father hates us—Etienne has clashed with him too often over land and politics. Oh, the politics . . . how I have come to detest them!"

"Conrade is so spoiled and headstrong, he has never learned not to chase forbidden fruit." Christophe's quiet voice deepened a little. "Maman, can you not see him for what he is? The more he is opposed, the more he must pursue his selfish desires, no matter who is hurt in the matter. He has hurt you and papa over and over again, and cares not what—"

"Enough! I have forbidden my sons to speak against each other! The times are difficult enough. The family must stand together." Etienne Vallette had entered the room unheard, and now stood at the head of the library table, his usually vague eyes brilliant with anger. "There shall be no war within the Vallette family. Remember our motto. *Together—Forever!*"

Christophe now rose and stood rigidly, his full mouth compressed against his anger. He raged helplessly inside at this dictate of his parents. Conrade was twenty-four, so handsome, so splendid, so intelligent, that he must be pushed forward. He must marry magnificently, preferably a girl with a large dowry to help the Vallette family. He was their hope—and so they spoiled the man who was lazy and all too willing to be ruined.

And all the time there was Grégoire, twenty, shorter, but still handsome, good, kind, gentle, unselfish. His deep religious feelings made the rest of his family, though devout themselves, vaguely uncomfortable, and so they scolded him freely, told him not to spend so much time at prayers, but to be more practical. Dear good Grégoire, who would sacrifice himself for any of them. He kept only his prayers and meditations to himself; all the rest he gave to them, his family. But the others did not appreciate him, no, not at all.

Etienne calmed down. "Where is Conrade now?"

Christophe looked at his mother. She said, with resignation, "He goes to court Veronique Le Clerc, I believe."

Etienne frowned heavily. "That is foolish. She must be encouraging him, begging him to come to her. She is a headstrong girl, a brazen one—"

"Not at all," Christophe said calmly. "She is quiet and

14

dovelike. It is because Monsieur Le Clerc has forbidden Conrade to see her that he persists. As I said—"

"Enough!" Etienne paced about the room, trying not to notice the shabby Persian rug beneath his feet. "Ah, that lad. What am I to do about him? My enemies are all about me, my friends will not pay their bills to me. What is to become of us? I wish we could start again somewhere else."

"Nonsense, Etienne." Sidoine was disturbed, and rose to take her husband's arm in her hands. "Do not speak so. This land has belonged to your family for three hundred years. So it has not produced well lately. Well, we have had rain and Christophe and Monsieur Lamartine have said there is some substance in the earth they can spread on the fields—"

Christophe nodded eagerly. His beloved master, Monsieur Lamartine, one of the foremost chemists of France, had spoken much of the earth, and the chemistry of it, and how it must be renewed in order to continue to produce. The grass must be better, to produce better sheep, and then they would have better wool, and that would make finer cloth—and so it would go. He was preparing a report for his father on what to do with the land.

Etienne paid no attention to his wife and youngest son. His thoughts had remained on his first-born, beloved son, Conrade. "He will get into trouble there. Le Clerc is no friend of mine. And I think he makes a match for Veronique with Hyacinth Mercier, the son of the pharmacist. The marriage of the doctor's daughter and the pharmacist's son—that is the way of the world, and we do well not to fight it." He sighed deeply. "She is a pretty one, though, I do not blame Conrade. He has my eye for the ladies." He gave a sad chuckle, not echoed by the others.

"It grows late, why is he not returning?" Sidoine glanced at the precious tall grandfather clock in the corner of the library. "I am worried about him. Etienne, we must send Christophe for Conrade, and urge him to return home."

15

Etienne frowned, but did not reject her suggestion. Christophe stirred uneasily. He did not like that errand at all. Conrade would resent it deeply, and more than likely send him on his way with a few angry words.

"Yes—yes, I think so," said Etienne finally. "Christophe, do go to Conrade. If he is in the house, and speaking in a friendly manner to Monsieur Le Clerc, let him be. But if he stands outside, and waits in the garden for that brazen young lady, tell him I order him—I, his father—order him to return home. We have serious business to discuss. Tell him that."

Christophe hesitated, then shrugged. "Yes, papa, I will go at once." The habit of obedience was strong, and he had great respect and love for his father.

He went for his cloak, and encountered Grégoire returning from the small chapel at the back of the first floor. Grégoire, roused from his meditations, gave his singularly sweet smile. "Well, brother, where do you go in such a hurry?" He closed the small prayerbook in his hands.

Christophe grimaced. "Chasing after Conrade, to order him to return home rather than court Veronique. He will thank me for that order, I assure you."

He went into his bedroom, and Grégoire followed him, his face troubled. "But Christophe, why do you do this? You know how Conrade will be."

"Father wishes me to go." Christophe picked his cloak from the wardrobe, slung on his wide-brimmed dark hat, and grinned at Grégoire. "Well, brother, wish me good fortune."

"I shall do better than that. I shall go with you," said Grégoire with calm decision. Though but two years older than Christophe, he had a quiet maturity which had been his from childhood. Some boys are wise beyond their years, and this was Grégoire. Perhaps it was from his philosophical studies, Christophe had thought, when he roused from his own scientific studies.

Grégoire went for his cloak and hat, and then met Christophe at the stables. They saddled and mounted. Christophe had brought his pistol and wore his short

16

sword; he did so automatically, as the countryside was uneasy from years of rebellion. He was surprised to see that Grégoire had done this also. "You go prepared, brother," Christophe said drily. "Do you not count on your prayers to keep us safe?" He was ashamed as soon as he had said it. He did not mean to mock his brother's faith.

Grégoire slashed him a smile from under his dark hat, and gave Christophe's arm a friendly squeeze. "Some ruffians do not know the language of prayer," he retorted. "One must speak to others in the language they understand."

Christophe chuckled under his breath as they started out into the darkness.

Conrade, standing in the dark garden of his loved one, grew more and more impatient. He could see movement within the elegantly appointed room, lit candles, footmen with trays of drinks, and graceful dancers moving to the sounds of violins. Several times he caught a glimpse of Veronique, a whirl of pink skirts, her sweet face glowing as she moved demurely in the dance.

It was maddening, maddening. Le Clerc was an ass. Conrade was as good a man, as marriageable as anyone Monsieur Le Clerc could find. He came from a long stock of sturdy landowners. True, he had no title, but the Vallette name was known throughout France for excellent woollen fabric and for the manor house where they had lived for centuries. Their wines graced many a table in the province. Just because Monsieur Le Clerc and Etienne Vallette did not agree on politics, and Etienne spoke rather too frankly in public places, was no reason to deny Conrade access to Veronique.

The French Revolution had turned everyone upside down and made enemies of neighbors. It did not need to be so, thought Conrade, with the impatience of youth and a shallow understanding. The Bastille had been stormed six years ago, to let forth some ignorant peasants. What was it all to do with Conrade and his love for Veronique?

17

The King and Queen had lost their heads to the guillotine. They had starved the whole country to pay for their reckless extravagances. Conrade felt some sadness, thinking of the gay Court. He had visited Versailles several times with his father, when Etienne had taken drafts of his books to receive the approval—indeed, the praise—of those who appreciated his efforts. Ah, those had been grand days! Conrade shifted from one leg to the other. If only the stupid revolt had not occurred, he might now be standing, in rose velvet and a powdered wig, bowing before a lady of the French Court. And now peasants in rags and red scarves led the government—or misled it.

The finances of France were in dire straits. The revolt had not increased the money supply. Christophe's master, Monsieur Lamartine, had been moved from the chemist's post at the Defense Ministry to head the Treasury. Rumor was that the authorities now grew more impatient with him. Did the stupid revolutionaries expect a great chemist to manufacture money out of air? Christophe had stormed, on hearing the news.

Oh, politics! Conrade was sick of the whole matter. Politicians snarled when everyone knew a path was made smoother with smiles and politeness. He enjoyed the diplomatic—ah, there was sweet enjoyment, and usefulness also.

The longer Conrade stood there, on one booted foot and then another, the more he fumed. He was not accustomed to being on the outside looking in, a child with his face pressed to the windows. He would see Veronique, and make it clear to her that he would approach her father for her hand. They would become engaged. Dear Veronique. He had kissed her twice, once on her arm and once on her sweet rosy mouth, and the memory burned in him.

The French windows opened to the cool night air. He stiffened. A couple came out, the girl in a red dress with a dark cloak about her shoulders. She hesitated, but the gaudily dressed man urged her forward to the gardens. Conrade caught his breath. That painted popinjay, with

18

the beauty marks on his face like a Parisian beau! It was Hyacinth Mercier, putting on airs because he had spent six months in Paris.

Conrade stepped further back into the shadows. Caution had been ingrained in him, for all his hot-blooded impetuosity. He would listen. Perhaps he would learn how much feeling Veronique had for him, or if she merely flirted with him. She was wearing her hair in the long curls he adored, with more short curls at her white forehead. She was but seventeen, slim at the waist, curved at the breast and thighs, a sight to catch at a man's heart. What large brown eyes she had, which danced when she was happy.

"Truly, Hyacinth, I must go no further." Veronique hesitated at the sundial. She glanced back nervously at the lighted manor house, at the sound of violins.

"Your father has given us permission to walk in the gardens, ma belle," murmured Hyacinth in the lisping manner he now affected. "Come, cherie. You must speak freely now. What do you think? How do you feel toward me?"

Her slim fingers nervously opened the fan, then closed it again. "I—I—my father likes you, but—"

"I am happy that your father likes me. But it is *your* feelings I would urge you to reveal. Ah, Veronique, you know I went away so that you might miss me more." At the ardor in his tone, Conrade frowned and scowled at him in the darkness. The young sprig! All knew he had gone to Paris to sow some wild oats before he settled down. The rumors that had trickled back had done him no credit.

"You are—most kind—but I—"

Hyacinth caught at her shoulders, pushing back the dark cloak. His hands caressed her bare shoulders—his head leaned so close to hers. Conrade stole forward, his hand on his sword. "Come, now, Veronique, no coyness. You keep putting me off. Your father has spoken to mine, it is all but set. Do you but say the word—"

She cried out as he clasped her roughly to him, and

19

pressed his mouth on her white neck. Conrade dashed forward, put his hand on Hyacinth's shoulder, yanked him from Veronique, and sent him spinning into a thorny hedge.

"How dare you accost her, you oaf!" Conrade raged, jealous at the sight of the girl he adored in the arms of his rival, and frustrated with longing for her himself. "Get away from her!"

"Conrade!" gasped Veronique, her eyes like stars in the night sky. "You came—you came—"

He caught her close, and settled her cloak gently about her chilled shoulders. "Of course, my little one, of course. Would I not be near when you need me?" All the chivalry in his nature rose up at the way she shuddered against him, and caught at him in her relief. "There, there, now, he shall not harm you."

Hyacinth recovered, and came forward. "Who is it? Who dares—ah, it is you, Monsieur Vallette," he sneered. "The man of many debts and many loves. Monsieur Le Clerc has forbidden you to come near Veronique. She is promised to me."

"Oh—that is not so," breathed Veronique, horrified. "Papa would ask me first. He swore he would never make me marry a man I did not love."

"But you are promised to me," raged Hyacinth, his hands on his hips, one hand dangerously close to the hilt of his short sword. "He waits only until you are ready to marry. He swore you would marry me. Get you to your crumbling house, your pigs and sheep, Monsieur Vallette. She wants none of you."

Hyacinth caught at Veronique's arm and roughly drew her to him. Conrade's temper flared. "Unhand her, you rogue! You can see plainly through your painted face that she does not like you. She shivers at your touch. She protests when you try to kiss her. She is not for you, and you must reconcile yourself to losing her to a better man."

"*You*, monsieur? How insane you are," Hyacinth said, then contemptuously spat just past Conrade.

The sword sprang into Conrade's hand. Veronique

squealed and fell back from the two men. Hyacinth too drew his sword.

"Is this what you want, you hothead? Do you not know I learned many a trick in the Paris studios of the fencing masters of the world?"

"So? Whose opinion do you ask? That of some fawning paid follower? Let us try each other—"

"No, no, I beg of you, please—I will call papa—" But Veronique's breathless voice was lost in the clash of swords. She scrambled further back, her hands to her heart, catching her breath, wide-eyed, thrilled that they would fight over her, yet afraid.

Christophe and Grégoire had left their horses tied at the end of the garden and had come forward on foot. In their dark hats and cloaks they came unnoticed, to stand appalled at the side of the hedge. The clashing of the swords, ringing through the darkness, was drowned out by the pianoforte and violins, and the laughter of those who danced, not knowing what went on outside.

Grégoire went forward quickly, to stand by Veronique. He tried to urge her toward the French windows; she shook her head until the curls danced on her shoulders. "No, no, you must stop them, Grégoire, stop them," she moaned.

His mouth tightened. "They cannot be stopped now, my dear," he said sadly.

Christophe watched, his sword out, keenly alert. He knew more of the reputation of Hyacinth than did his brother. He went quietly about the village, sat in cafés, intent over a game of chess, and heard much not meant for his ears. Hyacinth had been in Paris, and now, cocky and very much the man of the world, he longed to try his new-found skills on the females with loveplay, and on the males with swordplay.

The swords clashed, and parted, while the combatants stalked slowly around and around, watching for openings. Conrade darted forward, his sword slid over Hyacinth's arm, and there was a rending of the cloth. Christophe caught his breath—Conrade darted back as quickly. For all his height and quick temper, he was a formidable duelist. Conrade and Christophe and Grégoire had played at swords with each other and with neighborhood boys for many a year. But never in earnest, never like this.

Hyacinth dashed forward recklessly, and almost got inside Conrade's guard. Conrade fended him off, grew more cautious, circled his enemy again and again. The swords again met, slid down to the points, and off. The opponents circled. They watched, eyes intent in the semidarkness. Only the candlelit ballroom gave them light, for there was little moonlight that night.

The air was chill. The autumn scents of heady phlox and white jasmine filled Christophe's nostrils.

"Do you—surrender?" panted Hyacinth.

"Never!"

No more words, then. They resumed circling, the swords parried deftly; they were well matched. Then Conrade's sword flashed past his opponent's and plunged into his breast, past the embroidered vest, the white silken and lace shirt—to the heart.

Hyacinth momentarily hung on the sword. Then Conrade withdrew it forcibly, his face white in the night. And Hyacinth sprawled awkwardly to the ground, shuddered, groaned, and was still.

Christophe moved forward then. Conrade stood as though turned to stone. The youngest brother bent down and leaned to Hyacinth's face. He put his hand near the mouth. "He does not breathe," he said. "He is dead."

Conrade felt a surge of nausea. He was breathing with his mouth open, tense from his exertions. He turned his back, and plunged his sword into a flower bed again and again, to cleanse it of its bloody stains. Ever after, he would remember the scent of white jasmine, and the smell of the blood, and the sound as his sword left the body—like a stuck pig, he thought. Oh, God. He was going to be sick, and disgrace himself.

He had never killed a man before. Swordplay had been a deadly game, but never played to the end. Always there had been safety points on the ends of the swords, or there had merely been laughter at some especially skillful feint. Never this end—in the body of a man. A man had been alive but moments before, breathing, taunting, a cock of the walk. Now he lay dead, a grotesque heap on the stone paving by the fountain.

Veronique swayed, her hands at her mouth. "He . . . is dead . . . dead? Oh, dear God," she breathed.

Grégoire placed her gently on a bench, then went to kneel beside the fallen man. He felt the forehead and the hands, then folded the hands, closed the staring eyes, and began to pray.

The French windows opened again, and men began to come out. Foremost was Monsieur Le Clerc. "What is it? Someone said he heard swords! Who is there? Veronique, where are you, my darling?"

The others seemed unable to answer. Christophe said, "You must come here, monsieur. You see—there was a duel." He stopped, unable to continue, for behind Monsieur Le Clerc came Monsieur Mercier, Hyacinth's father. But he could not stop them. They came hastily, booted feet ringing on the stone paving, to stop aghast at the sight before them.

Monsieur Mercier knelt at his son's body, across from Grégoire. With shaking hands he reached for his son. "Hyacinth, my son, my eldest! What is it? What have they done to you? He is not moving, oh, my God, the blood!"

Monsieur Le Clerc turned on Conrade, standing sword in hand, his head erect. "It is your doing, I know it. Bully, bastard, you are trouble from your birth. Like your father, you must make horror for others. Like father, like son. Go, I will find you at the ends of the earth. Oh, my God, my precious Veronique. The man you would have married is dead, and at the hands of this enemy of me and of my house."

The guests stood stunned at the horror of it, and the sound of Monsieur Mercier sobbing over his son was all that echoed through the garden.

Chapter 2

The three Vallette brothers rode slowly through the night. Past the autumn fields, the orchards of apples and pears, the steep hillsides of grapevines they rode, conversing earnestly.

"I must go back, I must explain—" said Conrade over and over. "I did not mean to kill him, I never meant to kill him. But he was accosting Veronique—"

"Not tonight," counseled Christophe. "You know how Monsieur Le Clerc hates our father. And Monsieur Mercier will be in no mood to hear. Let us speak to some friend tomorrow, let him be the go-between."

"He swore revenge," said Conrade bitterly. "I will never see Veronique again."

Grégoire said gently, "Let us make haste slowly, my brothers. Time and patience, time and patience—"

But when they arrived home, they found their father and mother waiting impatiently, though it was long past midnight. Sidoine looked at their faces, and took Conrade's hands in hers. "Oh, my son, what horror has happened? You are white as chalk."

Etienne looked to Christophe to explain. He did, gravely, in a few spare words. "Conrade discovered Veronique in the gardens with Hyacinth Mercier. The young lout was attempting to force an embrace on her. Conrade challenged him—they fought. And Hyacinth died on Conrade's sword."

"Oh, my son!" whispered Sidoine, her hand to her mouth. She looked ill. Grégoire went for a bottle of brandy and snifters. He gave a small dose to Conrade.

"We must all keep our heads," said Grégoire sadly. "Monsieur Le Clerc swore vengeance, he is hotheaded. And Monsieur Mercier will go at once to the law; he is like that, and Hyacinth was his only son. We must plan immediately what to do. Shall we go to the South for a time?"

"Running away does not solve—ah," said Etienne, with a frown and a thoughtful look. He paced up and down the drawing room, pulling at his slight, graying beard. He studied the carpet without seeing it.

"I thought we might ask someone of influence to go to the families involved and explain our position," said Christophe, shaking his head at the offer of brandy. Grégoire studied his face thoughtfully and set the bulbous glass aside.

"Whom do you suggest?" asked Etienne sadly. "So many of our friends have gone by the guillotine. I myself am remembered for my politics, my closeness to the Bourbon court, and the time I spent in the prisons. Who will listen to us? The times are dangerous, everyone looks to his own safety."

"I thought of Monsieur Lamartine," said Christophe eagerly. "He is brave and good, highly thought of. He is fond of us, of me. He will do it, he will speak for us."

Sidoine made a little moaning sound, her face deadly white. Etienne went over to her, and put a comforting hand on her shoulder. "Easy, my dear. Christophe must learn of it. Christophe, I have received a letter from Paris. I was going to tell you tomorrow. Monsieur Lamartine has been placed in prison himself. His wife wrote in very distressed tones. She urges you to remain away from Paris, even to go into hiding for a time, as your association with the chemist is well known."

Christophe put his hand to his forehead. The shock was almost too much, coming after the events of the night. "But why?" he whispered. "He is good, kind. Why—prison? No, no, it must not be true!"

"He worked with Monsieur Tellier and both of them have aroused the suspicion of the government in power.

25

They are accused of stealing government funds. They are in prison for questioning—you know what that means," ended Etienne gravely.

Sidoine gave a choked sob. They all knew. Questioning was torture, sometimes on the rack, until a man would confess any crime in order to be free of it. And then death—by hangman or guillotine.

Grégoire dropped to his knees beside Christophe and clasped his brother's cold hands. "Oh, dear God," said Grégoire, "how long will it continue? Man against man, until all are animals! I have prayed mightily, and so have others, that this torment will end, and we shall live in peace with each other. Instead we go from horror to horror. Oh, my dear God—"

Christophe could not speak. His thoughts were with his dear good master, Monsieur Lamartine, his gentle face alight with some new discovery, his eyes intent as he studied the results of some chemical experiments. Oh, no, not him, in some grim chamber of torture, lying awake at nights on the straw unable to sleep for the pain of his questioning. Not Lamartine. If he were imprisoned, was anyone safe?

"I have had too much of this!" burst out Conrade, his face white, his brown eyes tormented. He strode up and down the room, much like his father at the moment. "This constant living in fear, this shabbiness and making ends meet, this wonder whether we will be next in prison. We should have left as soon as papa was released from the dungeons. We knew we had only a little time left. We should have left then!"

"Leave—our home?" whispered Sidoine. "The home of your fathers, these hundreds of years? Where would we go? Where would we be safe? And the land, we would lose the land—"

"To America!" declared Etienne, his gentle eyes aflame, standing with his hands on his hips, his face youthful once more. "To America! Where a man can be free!"

"America," muttered Conrade.

"America," murmured Grégoire with yearning, as a man might speak of heaven.

"America?" asked Christophe dubiously, his brow furrowed. "What would we do there?"

"What we do here! We would buy some land, we would raise sheep, hire workmen, build a textile mill, make woolens. Or any of a dozen schemes," declared Etienne. "There is magnificent land available for little more than the labor of a man's back. I have talked to men who went to America and returned to obtain passage for their families. They speak of miles and miles of green and fertile valleys, long rivers teeming with fish and leaping over waterfalls. They tell of opportunities for business beyond one's dreams—and a government that little interferes with people. After their revolution, they govern themselves. Each colony does as it pleases and makes its own laws."

"A chance to start again," murmured Grégoire thoughtfully. "No enemies, no fear, no prisons—"

"Oh, Conrade, do you wish to go?" asked Sidoine yearningly. "You are the one who would inherit the manor house, the land. Would you leave all this?" Her wave of the hand encompassed the drawing room with its shabby furniture, its torn carpet, the manor house itself with the leaking roof and streaming gutters. The land which much work might make well again.

"We could make our fortunes in America," declared Conrade, as glowing as he had been downcast. He went to his father, clasped his hand in his. "Father, are you willing to go and leave this misery behind us? Shall we set out together and make a new life for ourselves?"

"If you wish it, my son," beamed Etienne. He clasped Conrade by the shoulders. "I have thought of many schemes, many plans. We can—"

"First we had best away from here," said Christophe brutally, interrupting their dreaming. "What shall we pack? We have two carriages, and five horses. We must away, if we have no friends in high places who can help us against Monsieur Le Clerc and Monsieur Mercier. I

27

think the law officers will come for Conrade soon, without any protection of friends. What do you say?"

They gazed at him in bewilderment, but he had his way. Christophe was the practical one of the family, and Grégoire the dreamer was supporting him briskly.

They packed all during the remainder of the night. They had only a cook, a maid, and a groom in the stables. These were paid, and advised to leave quickly. Trunks and valises were packed with valuables which could be moved easily: the family silver, a few remaining jewels, furs, clothing, china, ivory, some gold coins.

They would leave behind the carpets, and the four-poster bed in which generations of Vallettes had been born. Sidoine shed a few tears over this in private, but wiped them away before any could see. Lives were more important than possessions, and she had known only cold fear since she had heard of Monsieur Lamartine that night. If he was not safe, then none of them were safe.

They filled the two carriages and hitched up the teams of horses. As they looked about for one last time before closing the door forever on the Vallette home, Conrade went to his saddled horse and said, "I must be off. I shall meet with you on the coast road to Le Havre."

Etienne, in his reddish brown greatcoat, large and loose, hanging to his knees, protested. "My son, we go together. There is safety only in our numbers."

But Conrade went off, galloping across the fields toward the village—or the Le Clerc home. Christophe shrugged, and helped his mother up into the first carriage. She was clad warmly in her cloak and woolen dress with fine black taffeta and wool trim. Her bonnet fit snugly about her worried face. He gave her a pat of the hand and a smile.

"He will join us, never fear," he said cheerily.

Grégoire came up beside her to take the reins. His face was grave, his eyes serene. He had his small prayerbook in his pocket, his case of books securely behind him in the carriage. It was just past dawn on that crisp October day as they set out in the two carriages. Christophe drove Etienne in the carriage behind Grégoire. They set out at a slow pace, so the horses would not tire. Christophe had one pistol in his belt, with his short sword, and a handkerchief full of bullets in his deep greatcoat pockets. He looked keenly back and forth across the fields as they drove.

They avoided the village, circling through the fields. The fewer who knew about their departure, the better. Christophe hoped Monsieur Le Clerc and Monsieur Mercier would not guess their plans; grief might paralyze their movements for a time. He noted the brown wheat fields, the redness of the apples in the orchards.

He would never see this land again, his France, his home. He was but eighteen; he tightened his mouth against grief and stared stonily to keep away tears. What had happened to his master, Monsieur Lamartine, was beyond grief. He would remember him always, with affection and love and devotion, and strive to remember the lessons in chemistry, and the lessons in scientific accuracy, and the lessons in friendship which the graying man had taught him.

They were into the main road before Conrade caught up with them. He rode swiftly across the fields, his huge stallion bounding with steellike legs—and before him in the saddle a girl.

They all stared. Veronique waved to them as they approached, her face excited and tear-stained. She wore a dark rose velvet gown and a heavy woolen cloak of the same shade.

Etienne motioned for the carriages to draw up. He leaned across Christophe to speak to them as they came. "What have you done, Conrade? Surely her father has not consented—"

"She came of her own consent," said Conrade confidently, with a grin at his father. "She loves me, she wishes to go to America with us. We shall be married in a free land."

Christophe bit his lips hard. His wild, hot-blooded brother had done it again. This would draw their pursuers after them surely. Abducting the only daughter of the wealthy Monsieur Le Clerc! Of all the foolish deeds. He looked at their radiant faces, as Conrade helped Veronique into the back of the carriage, her valise stuffed full of jewels and a few dresses. They had no thought to the consequences.

Christophe decided abruptly. He got down, handing the reins to Conrade. "You drive the carriage. I will ride, and remain behind when we are pursued," he said abruptly, and made Conrade take the reins against his protests.

"Pursued! We are not pursued," said Conrade, in bewilderment.

"We will be, now that you have done this," said Christophe grimly in his ear. "Go on, quickly. There is no time to be lost."

He got into the saddle and whipped the other horses so they started out with a jolt. While he waited for both carriages to start out, he looked behind them. No dust rose on the road yet.

Then he followed closely on the two carriages, turning back again and again to look. The stallion was fresh and eager. Christophe kept him severely to the back of the dusty path of the carriages, which the horse detested. He wanted to be out and running.

"Easy, my beauty. There will be time for that later," assured Christophe grimly.

It was about noon when he sighted the pursuit. He sighed. He had begun to hope that Conrade would be right. But someone must have gone to look for Veronique in her room, or perhaps her maid had discovered her absence when she came up with the morning chocolate. At all events, they were being followed.

The dust came closer, rapidly. The men following them were about five in number, thought Christophe, screwing up his eyes against the bright sunlight and the dust. And now they cut across the fields. At this rate, they would cut them off at the crossroads ahead.

He rode up to the carriages and gave orders curtly. "Conrade, draw off the road, see that Veronique is safe. Load your pistols. Have you your sword?"

Without waiting for an answer, he rode ahead to Grégoire, who was already pulling up and off the side of the road into the shelter of trees.

"Get maman to safety, Grégoire," he barked brusquely. "Your pistol? Good. Join me at the cross-roads. We must stop them from following us."

"Papa? Shall he go with us?"

"No, leave him to care for the women."

After tying up the horses, they stole ahead through the fields, arriving at the crossroads just in time to hide before the five horsemen swept up.

"Two men from the stables, and Monsieur Le Clerc and Monsieur Mercier, and Monsieur Le Clerc's brother," murmured Grégoire, studying them keenly. "Shall we let them go on?"

"To cut off our path? No, by God," said Christophe.

Conrade was white and angry. "She is promised to me, by her own promise! No one shall take her from me."

"I am more concerned that no one takes our lives from us," Christophe told him drily. Conrade gave him a startled look. "You did not comprehend? They hate us now. And since you killed Hyacinth, your life may be forfeit, and also ours."

"My God, they cannot—"

The men rode up, and Christophe called out, and stood. "You go no further, gentlemen! Turn back, on your lives!"

They did not. They dropped to the ground, and fired at them. Grégoire fired back, cool Grégoire with his excellent aim, and one of the stable hands dropped over with a cry. Conrade fired into the air.

"Go back! We will not be stopped!" he cried angrily.

"Give me back my daughter!" yelled Monsieur Le Clerc. "Have you not done our house enough damage? Give me my Veronique! I'll have the law after you!"

"She will marry me!" cried Conrade angrily. Christophe saw the sun gleam on the pistol barrel and fired. Monsieur Mercier yelled in turn, and dropped the pis-

31

tol, clasping his blood-covered arm with his other hand.

"You make yourselves outlaws! Are you not ashamed? Your father is wicked enough, but for the sake of your gentle mother, I will let the law only have its way," cried Monsieur Le Clerc, cunningly. "Do but surrender! You do not want to give up your land and your home!"

"We go—" began Conrade. Christophe clapped his hand fiercely over his brother's mouth.

"Will you give them leave to follow us to America?" he hissed furiously. "Close your mouth! Let me do the talking."

Conrade's eyes blazed at him, but he nodded. Christophe called out to the others.

"We go to find some friends of ours in Paris. They will aid us. It was an accident that Conrade killed Hyacinth Mercier. He is sorry for it—"

Conrade began to speak. Now it was Grégoire who clapped his hand over the eldest brother's rash mouth, and Christophe gave him a kick.

"He is sorry for it, and in time of calm we will sit down and discuss it!" yelled Christophe. "But first we must go consult with some friends. Let us go in peace. We will talk later."

There was some muttering among the others. Finally Monsieur Le Clerc called out, "Go ahead, then! We shall return home and await your return. Go in peace, but we must have a reckoning. The law will follow you if you do not return soon."

"Back away then, return home," called Christophe firmly.

They waited while the others mounted, helping the stable hand to his horse. They galloped off, and Conrade breathed freely.

"They are gone. You are clever, Christophe," he said, in admiration.

"Quickly, get the carriages on the way," said Christophe. "Bring up the stallion, Grégoire, I will ride for a time."

The others nodded, and went off. Christophe waited,

reloading his pistol, watching the retreating cloud of dust thoughtfully. He went on waiting, with cold patience, and then saw what he had feared. The cloud of dust had stopped.

They might be binding their wounds, washing them at the stream. Or they might be planning to return.

The carriages came up. The brothers mounted and rode on. Veronique babbled with fear to Conrade; Sidoine was white and silent. Presently, as Christophe looked back, he saw the dust cloud approaching them again.

He rode up to the first carriage. "Grégoire, they follow us again. Take maman and go ahead to the port, I will join you at Le Havre if I cannot meet you before. Go!"

Grégoire pulled up the horses and got down. They waited for the other carriage. Conrade got down, uneasily. "What is it?"

"We are followed yet again," said Christophe, with a calm he did not feel. "Do you go on. I will hold them off."

Conrade gave him a strange glance. "It is my duty, I am the eldest," he said. "And it is I who brought this trouble upon us by my rashness."

Grégoire smiled and put his hand tenderly on his brother's arm. "Do you go on, Conrade, and do not blame yourself. You love—that is no crime. And your loved one will need you. Do you go ahead."

They argued a little, but Christophe would have none of that. "We are wasting time. You must go on!"

Etienne called out, "They are closer!"

Grégoire pushed Christophe up into the carriage with their mother. "You must escort maman, Christophe. You are the practical one—they need you and your hard head, my brother. Go ahead, I will hold them off, and make sure they go home again. You know I have soft words of persuasion." He grinned up at Christophe.

"Perhaps that would be best," murmured Sidoine with resignation. "You are too quick with your pistol,

33

Christophe. Do you, Grégoire, persuade them that we will not remain to do them harm."

Grégoire nodded and waved them off. Christophe wanted to jump down and return, but someone had to drive the carriage. Minutes passed, then an hour. Christophe looked back again and again, but saw nothing. No cloud of dust, no stallion, no Grégoire coming to rejoin them with his gentle, confident smile.

It was evening when they stopped at a small inn just off the coast road. They had another day's journey before reaching the port. Christophe was very uneasy now.

Etienne settled before the fire, and comforted Sidoine. "Grégoire will rejoin us shortly, my love. You are not to worry."

Conrade was absorbed in making Veronique comfortable and happy again. It was finally dawning on her what she had done, leaving her family, her home, to go to a strange land with the Vallettes; she was inclined to be tearful and wavering.

"I will go back and see what is delaying Grégoire," said Christophe. He took a flask of brandy and some bread and cheese. Grégoire will be hungry, he thought.

The horse he took from the carriage was weary, and went slowly. It was past midnight when Christophe reached the crossroads, still finding no trace of his brother. He went back slowly over and over the ground. There was the acrid smell of black powder on the air, his own special black powder made in the laboratory of Monsieur Lamartine, the chemist, who was the finest chemist in the world—

A voice hailed him weakly. Christophe threw his reins over the head of the horse, dropped to the ground, and ran to a dark grove of trees. He found the stallion first, nibbling on the grass. Then he spotted the white patch that was Grégoire's shirt.

He dropped to the ground beside Grégoire. "Foolish lad, why did you not come on? We have worried—" He stopped abruptly, as his seeking hand found a wet sticky patch on Grégoire's breast.

"Christophe. I prayed that you would return. It is so . . . painful . . . to do this alone," murmured Grégoire, his voice weak and faint.

"To do what, my brother?" Christophe found the wound, a great gaping one in the chest; it sickened and terrified him. He looked about for water, but there was no stream nearby. Grégoire found his brother's sleeve and caught at it.

"Do not . . . leave me. It is . . . not long now. I have . . . made . . . my peace . . . with God . . ."

Christophe trembled, kneeling beside his brother, faint with weariness. He reached for the flask of brandy and gave a little to Grégoire, but the young man choked on it and turned away his head.

"No . . . need, my brother. Give me . . . your hand. They returned . . . I tried . . . to speak . . . with them. . . . Such fury . . . such rage. . . . God help me. . . . They finally left for Paris, losing your track," he said feebly, with one final gust of strength. "God go . . . with you . . . ever . . . my dearest, finest brother. Look . . . after them . . . all . . . for me and for . . . yourself. . . . You must have a . . . hard head . . . for them all . . . my brother . . ." He tried to laugh, blood gushed from his mouth, and he fell back against Christophe's arm.

Christophe could not believe Grégoire was dead. He waited for a time, chilled in the cold night air, shivering with fear and hatred of those who had done this. And hatred of his brother Conrade. He tried to pray, but the words eluded him.

Christophe dug a hole in the soft ground with his sword. Tears streamed down his cheeks as he said a last farewell to his beloved brother. Then at dawn he covered him with the newly turned earth, blessed him, and left, an emptiness in his soul.

Chapter 3

Etienne rose early and went softly to the front door of the inn. His two sons had not returned, and he was anxious, more anxious than he would admit to their mother. "Where are they? Have they but delayed until daylight? What has happened to them? My sons, oh, my sons," he murmured to himself.

Conrade slept peacefully on the floor of the living room. Veronique had slept at last, in bed with Sidoine, her tear-stained cheeks rosy and flushed. Was she worth all this fuss? Etienne wondered grimly. He hoped that she was sturdy of nature, and a good kind soul, a good wife for Conrade, because if not, Conrade would be lost in America.

They had all risen and were breakfasting when Christophe finally returned. Etienne went out at once, saw the two horses—and Christophe alone. He did not need to meet the grim look of his youngest son to know the truth. The lad had grown up overnight.

"Grégoire?" he asked, his hand to his heart.

"I buried him where he fell. We spoke only a little— oh, papa," said Christophe, simply, and clasped his father in his arms. He did not weep, however, but only gazed with cold anger into the distance.

"How can I tell his mother?" whispered Etienne, wiping his face with his handkerchief. "Oh, my God, our Grégoire."

He did not need to tell her. She came from the inn, regal in her black dress, her white-haired head held high, looking at her husband and son and at the empty saddles. She bit her lips, and shuddered in the cool morning.

"Say nothing, I cannot bear it now," she said to Christophe, when he would speak. "We shall set out at once. None of us is safe."

"No, mother, one thing we will do," said Etienne, sadly, and he led them back inside. Conrade was at table with Veronique, teasing her. They were laughing as Christophe entered.

Christophe gave his eldest brother a hard look, and Etienne put his hand on the boy's arm.

"Allow me," Etienne said quietly. "Conrade, we have sad news."

Conrade jumped up, his handsome face turning anxious. "Grégoire, he is wounded? Where is he? I will go back and avenge him at once!"

"No vengeance, for vengeance is the Lord's," said Sidoine, in a murmur. She sank down into a chair, brushed her hand over her face, and was composed once more. She seemed older, thought Christophe, her face chalk-white and lined.

"You have done enough," said Christophe. "You have caused the death of—"

"Death? What do you say?" cried Conrade. Veronique shrieked and started from her chair.

Etienne said sternly, "I was afraid of this. Come, my sons, come to me." The three of them stood in a circle. Etienne held out his drawn sword, the hilt foremost. "This is the cross on which your dear brother died. Grégoire has sacrificed himself for us. Can we do less? I wish you to swear an oath on the memory of Grégoire."

Conrade was pale and shaking, longing to cry out and ask questions. Christophe was reluctant, his mouth tight, his eyes furious with hate and grief.

Etienne insisted. "My sons, place your hands on the hilt!"

Finally they obeyed. They joined hands, Christophe's slim and shapely, Conrade's large and strong, on the hilt of the sword. They bowed their heads as their father spoke.

"We will all swear, on the sword of Christ, and on the memory of our beloved Grégoire, always to be loyal to each other and to our family honor," said Etienne firmly. "*Together—Forever*. You will swear it now."

Conrade swallowed, and said, "I swear always to be loyal to our family, to our honor: Together—Forever. On the memory of our—Grégoire."

Christophe was more reluctant. He lifted his head and met his father's sharp gaze. The look was firm. He finally nodded. "I swear—on the memory of Grégoire—always to be loyal to our family, to our honor: *Together—Forever*."

It was done. Christophe turned away. He had longed to berate Conrade, to accuse him of responsibility for his brother's death by his foolish and hotheaded actions. But now the anger had drained from him. Nothing could bring back Grégoire. And he had his family to look after.

"Now, we must set out at once. They may follow us," he said briskly. "I will see to the carriages."

"You have not eaten, Christophe," said Sidoine gently, her look anxious. She knew his heart this day, and ached for him.

"I can eat on the road. Come, quickly, pack up and let us depart. I will pay the reckoning."

At Christophe's urging, they packed swiftly and loaded the carriages. Presently, Christophe had them on the road, Etienne and Sidoine in the first carriage, Conrade and Veronique in the second, while Christophe followed on the stallion. They rode all the day.

Christophe kept them at it, pausing only briefly for a drink of water and wine, a taste of bread and cheese. Still, it was late evening when they arrived in the port of Le Havre and sought beds for the night. They located an inn near the harbor, and went to bed thankfully.

Christophe was up early. Impatience rode him. They must get aboard ship soon, or Monsieur Le Clerc would find them, or an officer of the law, and all their haste would have been in vain. He ran down the steps of the inn and almost collided with a gentleman coming up.

"Gently there, young master," laughed the man, and stood back. "Are you in such haste, then?"

A man of some thirty-plus years, he had an open, frank face and long, curly brown hair. Christophe flushed, and apologized quickly. The man eyed him keenly, somewhat affected at the gravity of the lad's speech and his weary look.

"What do you here? Perhaps I can help you," he said.

"Why—I am going to see about ships—a passage to America, for myself and my family," said Christophe, deciding on boldness.

"Then I can help you," said the man, with a smile. "I take my own family aboard today, to sail to Boston. Perhaps you would go with us, eh?"

It was a stroke of great fortune, as Christophe was to think more than once in the years ahead. The man introduced himself as Monsieur François Portalis, and he was just leaving France with his family. He had gone to America once, liked it, bought a house and a small business in Boston, and was embarking with his wife and small children to return to Boston, now that he had a place for them.

Monsieur Portalis took Christophe down to the docks and introduced him to the captain of the American vessel which would sail the following morning at high tide for the port of Boston. Christophe agreed on terms of passage, knowing his father would agree, and went back to the inn to explain what he had done.

He found Conrade absorbed in Veronique and soothing her about the voyage. Etienne and Sidoine were beginning to realize that the death of Grégoire would leave them with only two sons, and the manner of his going was agony to them both, so useless, so crushing a blow. "He was ever a good, kind lad, why must the Lord have taken him?" moaned Etienne to Christophe.

"Not the Lord, but Monsieur Le Clerc," said Christophe, brutally. "And we must make ready to go aboard, father. There is no time for mourning. One day we must set aside some time to discuss this, but not now."

Etienne began to rebuke Christophe for his remark, but seeing the fierce light in Christophe's weary eyes, he stopped himself. He put his hand on Christophe's shoulder.

"You are right, lad. If his sacrifice is not to be in vain, we must be on our way. I will hurry Conrade and Veronique. Do you help your mother with her valises."

They boarded the vessel that afternoon, after paying what seemed an exorbitant amount of gold to the captain. But the two couples did have one huge cabin to themselves, with bunks for Conrade and Christophe in the long room below decks with about twenty other men.

Monsieur Portalis was kind enough to give Christophe much advice. Seeing Etienne's sad, vague eyes, and Conrade absorbed with his fiancée, he turned to Christophe. On the man's advice, Christophe went ashore that evening and purchased bags of grain and dried vegetables, some tea and sugar, and salt. They would need much food for the long voyage—and the ship's captain did not supply it for passengers. He also bought pillows to make the voyage easier for the women. Christophe arranged to sell the two carriages and five horses. There was no room to take them with him, and he patted the stallion for some minutes before giving him up. Monsieur Portalis had assured him there were fine animals in America. Even with these sales their gold supply was dwindling. Christophe counted it yet again, his young face troubled. Then he fastened it all into a money belt around his waist.

They sailed the next morning at dawn. Christophe had risen early. With Monsieur Portalis and his wife, he watched the sunrise and the buildings of the port fade away in the distance as they left France.

"I shall never see France again," thought Christophe. "Yet—yet I am not really sorry. France and her people have been cruel to us, the prison for papa—and oh, my God, how is Monsieur Lamartine now? Pray God he has not too difficult a death."

The journey was much longer than they had expected. A month went by, two months, and then it was January. Rough winds blew them off course, and it had to be patiently corrected again and again. The food threatened to give out; the passengers became restless, almost rebellious. Christophe stood guard some terrible days over the grain and other stuffs he had purchased, his pistol drawn and cocked, ready to fire if the others should try to take it from him. His parents' cabin was locked at all times. Sidoine was weak and pale from the long stormy voyage. Etienne was cheerful through it all, amazingly.

The older man would go on deck, converse long and earnestly with some new friend, and return glowing to the cabin to confide some new scheme.

"He told me that in America it is land that is valuable. We shall all lay claim to land in the West, and make a fortune on it!"

"But Etienne," said Sidoine gently, "I thought we would start a woolen mill."

"No, no, it is land, land that will make our fortunes."

Two days later it would be something else. Etienne returned, bright-eyed. "My friend says that he has a jewelry business in New York. It pays beyond all dreams. Conrade and Christophe and I can all learn the trade—"

Christophe learned not to argue with him. Conrade and Veronique did not even hear him. They lived in a world of their own, arms wrapped about each other to walk the stormy deck, or sitting starry-eyed on a rug in the sunlight on a good day, to talk of their future and plan their wedding day.

Christophe would turn his head away as they kissed or held hands tenderly. His rage had burned down, and he no longer hated them. He must not hate.

He remembered what Monsieur Lamartine had told him. "Hate, my dear Christophe, hurts the one who hates, more than any person whom he hates. It turns inward on oneself, like the acid with which we have worked, burning away sanity, reason, common sense. It is destructive to the one who hates. You must never hate. You must use reason, my lad. Think! Think! Understand yourself, and you will understand others."

In his idle time, Christophe strode the deck, thought of the old days, remembered the things he had discussed with his master, and recalled one by one the days and conversations with Grégoire. He would remember his brother always, and how he had died for them, and how he had said, "You must have a hard head for them all."

He had never realized so clearly how impractical Etienne was, or how much Conrade was like him. Grand schemes swam in their heads—how to accomplish them was vague. Christophe must plan for them all.

He thought again and again of what he must do when they arrived in America. Monsieur Portalis had offered to put them up in his home in Boston until they were settled. But they could not be settled until someone had work to do, and an income.

Christophe must find work. What could he do? He deliberated, and mentally drew up a list of his qualifications. He had worked with sheep, he had labored in a woolen mill and knew all the processes. He had run his father's estate, and the vineyards, along with his brothers. He had worked his father's printing press until Etienne was arrested and the press wrecked. Then there was the chemistry he had learned from Monsieur Lamartine. That might prove useful, he thought.

The days and weeks went on. They all grew tired of wheat porridge, but were grateful for that much. All were thinner, worn, anxious, as finally the ship sighted the port of Boston in early February. Christophe had stayed awake at nights to protect their stores of food, beside the locked cabin door, sitting up against a wooden chair to keep himself awake, and sleeping days, when Etienne would take his place.

He blinked at the port through weary eyes. He could

not believe it was really there. Small ships came out to greet them, and one brought food aboard. The passengers tore at it ravenously, and Christophe felt ashamed that he had had to fight them to keep his food from them. But his family must come first, always.

He finally stepped ashore with shaky legs, to gaze around in wonder. Sturdy earth beneath him! And great warehouses stuffed with goods, carriages rattling past with fine horses, and grand people dressed in silks and good woolens. He felt a very sloven, with his shabby clothing falling in pieces on his bones. But they had arrived—in America.

Monsieur Portalis was very kind to them. He ordered carriages, would not hear of payment, and took them to his small home, where he had expected to have his wife and children only. He gave up his own bedroom to Etienne and Sidoine Vallette, and the bedroom of one child to Veronique. The house was crowded.

Christophe went out at once to look for a job, any job. But he found himself embarrassed beyond words. No one spoke French in the warehouse, and he did not speak English!

He went to Monsieur Portalis's office and sat down in discouragement. Monsieur Portalis patted his shoulder and told him he knew of a Frenchman who would come daily to teach them all. When told of this later, Etienne was amazed that it was even necessary: surely all the civilized world knew French!

Weeks passed. Christophe tried to learn the new language quickly, but his tongue curled around the strange, hard words. There was no softness in them, he thought. And he yearned for the conversational nights at home in France, sitting about the fire, at ease, laughing and talking philosophy with Grégoire. Those days would never come again.

Conrade and Veronique longed to marry, but there was little money for a wedding. Even if they sold some of the silver, they could only afford a modest affair. Sidoine put her foot down, her economic soul horrified at the thought of selling the silver for frivolity. So Conrade

43

and Veronique were married in the front parlor of the home of Monsieur Portalis and spent their honeymoon in the child's bedroom.

Christophe had not missed the fact that a few of the guests were unkind enough to laugh at their poor English. He bit his lips. He was not accustomed to being laughed at. He had always been quick at his studies and proud of his intelligence. Monsieur Lamartine had often praised him—Monsieur Lamartine. And was he dead by now?

It was March, and still he did not have a job. He worked night and day at learning the language, but time and again he was turned away, humiliated, when applying for work.

He heard them speak before he was out of hearing. "Just another of them foreigners," a man would say, contemptuously. "Can't even talk English!"

One night he went home, discouraged. Monsieur Portalis was talking earnestly to Etienne. Over coffee, he spoke kindly but firmly of this situation. "You must buy some land, in Virginia," he told Etienne and the others. "It is one of the few states where an alien can buy land. I have been investigating for you."

"An alien!" protested Christophe. "But we have come to live always in America."

"I know, I know, but you must first obtain papers of citizenship. And before you can start a business, and achieve some status, and so on, you must have land. Only landowners are respected, and have little difficulty in borrowing money to start a business. You must get some land," he said firmly.

Etienne was thoughtful, and talked long to Conrade and Christophe that night. "He is right. We must own some land. My sons, you shall go to Virginia and look for a good parcel."

"In Virginia? It is a wilderness!" protested Conrade. "Veronique and I wish to purchase a house of our own in Boston. We try Monsieur Portalis's hospitality sorely, and besides—"

Besides, Veronique was going to have a child. The

couple knew it already and had confided in Sidoine. Conrade worried. He had sobered up somewhat on marrying; but his new responsibility fretted him. He had always been free to come and go, to court the ladies, to cut a fine figure at dances. Here people knew other dances, and laughed at his poor English, and turned the shoulder to him when he tried to compliment them or talk of politics. What did a Frenchman, new and raw to their country, know of anything at all?

"Yes, we must go to Virginia," said Christophe, after a long silence, as he stared soberly into the fire. Monsieur Portalis had been very good to them, but Madame was becoming irritable at their long stay—and no wonder. She had little room to move about, Sidoine wanted to take charge of the cooking constantly, and the young married couple irritated her with their demands.

"I see no reason to go to Virginia," said Conrade. "Why not buy land just outside of Boston?"

"Because it is all bought up," said Christophe, suppressing his irritation. "In Virginia there is land for homesteading, at cheap prices, and we could buy a large farm. We could set out our own vegetables, and with luck have some fruit trees. There we could support ourselves while we cast about for some better way to make our living." And Christophe went on to point out that a landowner in Virginia could become a citizen at once— that Virginia granted citizenship upon purchase of real estate, and was the only state that did so. "As citizens, we will have less trouble starting a business, whatever we decide upon eventually."

"Well, you can go about working a farm, if you please!" blazed Conrade. "I am not a farmer, and I like the life in Boston. I mean to go into society, and they will not laugh at me when I am in diplomatic circles. I met a man the other day—"

For once Etienne interrupted Conrade and rebuked him. "Conrade, you will run before you can walk. We cannot afford the social life until we are self-supporting. You know we owe much money to Monseiur Portalis for our room and food. You and your brother will go to

Virginia and see about finding a good farm for us at the best price we can manage. The gold we have saved from home, and perhaps some of your mother's jewelry, will pay for it; she has said so."

So it was settled, and none of Conrade's frowns could change Etienne's mind.

Chapter 4

Conrade grumbled much on the long ride down to Virginia. Christophe compressed his lips again and again in his anger, but finally his older brother, with mercurial change of mood, turned cheerful.

"Ah, but this is beautiful country," Conrade exclaimed in admiration as they rode through the wooded valley. "Look at the trees, how they glow in the sunlight. Spring in America—there is nothing like it, not even in France."

Christophe looked about, and his heart lightened for the first time in months. Yes, this valley was lovely. Green grass stretched out in long swaths from the river, which gleamed silver. The trees wore new, green tender leaves; some were pink with apple and peach blossoms. Wild flowers glowed pinkish white and purple in the shadows under the trees, and where they flung themselves to rest, the land was rich with dark brown earth.

They caught fish for their dinner, and built a fire that night to cook it. "This is a good life," said Conrade, contentedly. "Mayhap Virginia shall not be so bad."

Conrade felt even better a couple of days later. They fell in with two Frenchmen, Baptiste Clausel and his son Marc, who had become American citizens some ten years before.

They met at an inn, and the jovial older Frenchman invited them to come to his home. "There is much land about for sale, and some for homesteading. Ah, a mill? I know just such a place. There is a man, Swiss, who has a cotton mill on the stream not ten miles from me, and he is selling out and going further west."

Christophe was more suspicious of the man than Conrade, who took easily to a man who could tell jokes and dream big dreams like himself. Yet the man was kind, and the son was good at correcting their English politely, and giving advice to them on many matters.

Clausel showed them the land, the stream, and the mill. The Swiss was eager to sell, and the price was low. Christophe wished to go further, to ride on and explore the land. But Conrade was impatient to return home to his wife, to tell her all was settled, and that there would be friends nearby.

Christophe went out and walked up and down the stream. It was a merry, swift stream, and there were several small waterfalls which could be dammed for another waterwheel or two. He became more excited about the project. The land was fertile; some had never even been cultivated. Wheat grew like weeds, said the Swiss, and Marc had agreed. The grass was excellent for grazing; they could grow sheep with little trouble. The mill was already built, and men lived nearby who could work in the mill and give them a quick start.

It was agreed, and they paid a modest down payment. Then the two brothers returned to Boston, obtained a loan for the remainder of the money, rode back, and paid off the Swiss. He gave them good advice on the mill operations and then left at once, pleased to be going west.

Conrade soon became restless, however. He had heard of a small town house in New York City which he could purchase. The price of the mill on the stream, named Areuse for a river in Switzerland, had not been so high as they had feared. There would be money for a house for him. Civilization! New York was civilization, and Veronique wished it. Nothing was too good for Veronique.

The Swiss, before he left, confided to Christophe, "I had wanted to build a villa here one day, high on the bluff overlooking the Areuse. I was going to call it Neuchâtel, after my home in Switzerland. Ah, well, one day I shall do it—but further west."

Neuchâtel—that savored of France to Christophe, and he stored it in his mind for later.

Conrade returned to New York, bought the town house on more borrowed money, and moved into it with Veronique. The elder Vallettes remained with the Portalis family. Christophe set to work on the woolen mill; he bought wool at first from neighboring farmers, and began the process of spinning and weaving. He built a small log cabin for himself with two bedrooms, in case his parents came. He spent the long summer working, living outdoors, increasing in strength and tanning his cheeks. He lured six men from the nearby town to work in the mill.

It was a crude but vigorous life. The men who worked for him were German immigrants, hard-working, eager to please. They spoke English with Christophe, German among themselves. Back in Germany, some had relatives who were impressed into the Hessian armies, forced to serve where their lord sent them.

Some Irish also had moved into the town, which then had one dirt main street, a few wooden stores, a flour mill, and three dozen houses of stone and wood. A chapel had been erected for Protestant services of the Lutheran faith.

Christophe enjoyed his life. He felt at peace for the first time in years. Work with the wool was satisfying. He created some new patterns of tweed, and they sold well. He hired the wives of two of his workmen to knit in their homes.

On Sundays he attended the Lutheran services. How strange, to worship openly as a Protestant. He stood with the others for the hymn singing and knelt for the prayers, with a deep sense of gratitude for this simple, God-fearing, open society. How far were the secret police, the whispers of menace, the guillotine.

The town was raw, not aged with the patina of several hundred years. No vines grew over the stone wall.

The flower beds were fresh-planted with rose stock, small green bushes, peonies brought over lovingly in the ships, strange wild flowers from the swamps. The mill wheel turned and turned; even the clank of it sounded merry to Christophe.

He wrote enthusiastic letters to his parents. One day in late July, he was amazed to return to his small dark cabin to find it lit with candles, and inside—his parents.

Sidoine went to his arms eagerly and kissed his cheeks with unusual warmth for that reserved woman. She was pale, and slender. Etienne seemed frail.

They sat down to talk and dine together. Sidoine had laid out a fine lace tablecloth on his crude wooden table, and set the silver candlesticks with red candles on it. Christophe's gaze rested often on that sight. He had a home again.

"Ah, we wore out our welcome with Madame Portalis," said Etienne over his glass of brandy. "I am sorry for it. We should have left when Conrade did. But the money—ah, it is so expensive to rent. And Conrade and his wife did not wish us with them—" His shrug left the rest to Christophe's imagination.

"You are most welcome here," said Christophe warmly, hiding his rush of anger. How selfish Conrade was—why did he hurt them all so? "How lonely I have been. How good it was to come home and see the lights glowing, and to taste the good cooking of my mother."

She smiled, much pleased, and patted his hand. "Ah, we came as soon as we received your letter that the cabin was finished. I have been impatient to see you again, my son. And tell us of the mill—how does it go?"

They did not talk long that night, for his parents were weary. And Christophe had formed the habit of going to bed early and getting up at dawn.

The next morning, he rose at his usual time to find his mother up first, tending the fire in the hearth. He smiled, and gave her "Good morning" with a kiss. "How fine to see you today, maman. You are better this morning?"

"Ah, I am well again, now that we are in our own

home again," she said, with meaning. "How cosy this is. I do not regret anything, my son, except—Grégoire."

"We shall always remember him."

Conrade did not seem to, but the rest would. Christophe looked to the small desk in the corner, a crude affair he had bought to hold his papers. On it was the miniature of Grégoire, with calm eyes and a slight smile on his handsome face.

"And this is such a fine cabin," said Sidoine brightly, turning to the fire. "One large room for the drawing room and for dining, with the hearth at the end. It is all very comfortable."

She was being gallant and brave, thought her son. He knew the cabin was humble. But it held all the essentials. The fire drew well in the great hearth which filled one end of the room. The two bedrooms were behind the single long room, and there was a small privy behind the cabin. He drew water from the running stream when it was needed—it was pure and fresh.

Etienne rose late, but came out with a beaming smile. "I am so late. I shall not always be so. I mean to do my share of the work."

Yet he was frailer than Christophe remembered, thinner, with his handsome head light gray, and with lines in his thin face.

"You shall help me with the accounts, papa. I am poor at them," said Christophe quickly. "That will relieve me, if you will figure the payroll each week, and keep the books. Would you be willing to do that?"

"Of course, of course."

His father was pathetically eager to please. Christophe thought how humiliated they must have been under the tongue of Madame Portalis. How grateful he was to Monsieur Portalis. They would not have managed all this time without him. Christophe decided he would repay him in a material way as well as with words. One day, he would have money to repay him.

They settled into a routine. It was easier for Christophe now that his father was here. They went every day to the small one-room office near the mill and figured the accounts. Christophe would leave his father to the books, and go down to the mill to oversee the dyeing, spinning, and weaving. He would negotiate with men who wished to buy, and arrange payment to the farmers who brought wool to sell. The wool was very expensive, and he worried about that.

Etienne heard, through some French friends whom he quickly made in the neighborhood, that he could buy a ram—very expensive, but a fine breeder. He and Christophe decided to do this, and waited anxiously for offers after the ram was delivered and set in the pastures.

Marc Clausel came over often, and they made him welcome. He was more hearty than Christophe usually liked, but Christophe was grateful to the man and his father for their aid in buying the property. Their advice had been invaluable.

Marc introduced him to a Virginian, whom Christophe liked at once. Thomas Stratford was of English descent; his people had lived in America for more than a hundred years. He was in his thirties, married with two small children. Chistophe went to his house whenever he could, for they had much in common.

So the summer days ended, and autumn came, their first year in America—1796. Just a year ago, thought Christophe, they had been worrying what would become of them, whether Etienne would be sent to prison again. And now their fortunes had taken a strange turn, and they were in America, starting over.

Etienne talked to Christophe more freely now, treating him as a man. Christophe was only nineteen, but he had shouldered the task of building a home, buying a mill, and operating it, like a much older man.

On their way to the office one morning, as the sun gleamed on the waters of the Areuse and the yellow willow leaves fell gently into the murmuring waterfalls, Etienne began to speak seriously of their future.

"Christophe, much as I have figured, and been optimistic, I cannot see how we can make much of a living at the mill. The operators in New England have been at

52

it so much longer; they obtain orders as they please. And cotton is much more suited to this climate than wool can be. We can sell to the North—yet—there is not much future in it. Whatever can we do?"

Christophe frowned. He thought this fresh worry had something to do with Conrade. Conrade had written often, complaining of the lack of money, and asking when the mill would be operating at "full capacity."

"If Conrade would come and help, instead of living a gay life in New York—" he began bitterly.

Etienne held up a frail hand. "No, my son, that is not the answer," he said gravely. "Even if Conrade came and helped, the mill would not produce much more than it does. We should have to build a second mill, and a third, and the orders do not warrant this kind of expansion. We must think of something else, some other business to begin."

Christophe nodded, feeling guilty at his quick readiness to blame Conrade. "You are right, father, I have not thought far enough ahead. We shall put our brains together and come up with an answer, never fear," he added cheerfully.

Etienne smiled, and patted his arm. "Of course we will."

Christophe's one amusement these days was to go hunting. One Sunday afternoon, he went out with his friend Thomas Stratford. Thomas said he had seen some deer; if they could manage to bring one down, it would vary their diet this winter.

The October day was brisk and sweet. The wind was in their favor, rustling gently through the golden and red leaves. They walked slowly with Thomas Stratford's two pet hunting dogs at their heels, until the animals caught wind of something, and went to a point.

"A deer," breathed Thomas, his eyes sparkling. Christophe nodded, loaded his rifle, and aimed carefully. The gun misfired, and the deer bounded away.

"Damn it all!" exploded Christophe in fury. "This gunpowder is not worth the money to blow it up. I have

53

made worse in my first efforts in the laboratory of Monsieur Lamartine."

As he had raged in French, he had to repeat it in English once he had calmed himself. Thomas nodded ruefully. "The American black powder is poor, I admit it. I try to buy from a Pennsylvania firm that does some good work. But occasionally it will not fire at all. It is too damp, I think. And the rifle exploded once in my hands. I thought it was all over for me!"

They walked back to the Stratford home, a fine white-pillared house set on a hill about five miles from Christophe's log cabin. Christophe looked about whenever he entered, and vowed to have one even larger and grander one day.

Mrs. Stratford came out to greet them, giving them a sympathetic look. "You return early. No luck?"

"We saw a deer, but the powder misfired," explained Christophe, with a grimace.

"Too bad. But come, and I will introduce you to a dear—of another variety," she said demurely, and with a laugh caught hold of his hand and drew him into the fine parlor.

The dimness of the room did not permit him to see the occupants until his eyes adjusted from the bright sunlight outside. Then he made out the slim form of a girl just rising from a light green sofa near the hearth fire. He caught his breath.

Mrs. Stratford said in her soft drawling voice, so sweet and low and feminine, "Amelia, my dear, permit me to introduce you to Christophe Vallette, newly come from France. Christophe, this is our dear cousin, Amelia Stratford."

Christophe stammered something in French and took her slim white hand in his. He was overcome with the vision before him. She was of medium height, with brown curls covered with a little cap of yellow and white lace. Her dress was a simple muslin, with yellow ribbons at the high waist. How her merry brown eyes sparkled at him, how kind and sweet was her smile. She spoke in the same soft drawl of her cousin by marriage.

"How do you do, Mr. Vallette? I am so happy to meet you. Thomas has spoken much about you."

She spoke slowly and clearly, as though understanding he was not yet so familiar with English. He caught every word she said, and sat down beside her to listen and gaze, scarcely able to speak for the wonder of her.

She was lovely, but not vain. She was impulsive and feminine, catching up one of the small children to hug her and hold her on her lap for a time, playing with a toy to amuse her. Christophe watched the dimple play in the rosy cheek near his, and wondered for the first time in his life what it would be like to touch that cheek with his lips, to claim that form in his arms.

He learned that she was two years younger than he, a lovely maturing seventeen years of age. Her father owned a plantation in southern Virginia—she did not say where. Her smile and bright eyes bemused him; he scarcely knew what he said or did.

Presently Mrs. Stratford said to them, "Amelia, take Christophe to see the flowers. You were remarking just this morning how beautiful they are."

Her knowing smile made Christophe blush. Amelia jumped up, and made a little face at her cousin, but laughed, and held out her hand to Christophe. He stood, took the hand almost reverently, and went out the French windows with her to the autumn gardens. They walked the paths together. She seemed to know what he said, whether he blundered awkwardly in French or spoke haltingly in English.

They looked at the bright marigolds, the brilliant zinnias, the tall larkspur. The colors blurred in Christophe's gaze. He could see nothing clearly but the beautiful face and form of Amelia. Her soft laughter rang like bells, her mouth was pink and sweet.

They walked and talked for a time, and once her brown cloak slipped from her shoulders. He leaped to restore it, and touched her slim arm as he did so. How soft and silky was her flesh; he longed to clasp her arm in his. But there was something innocent and reserved about her, and he respected her.

When he left, he asked if he might come again the following Sunday, his look seeking hers eloquently. She smiled. Mrs. Stratford said brightly, "But you are always welcome, Christophe. Come as often as you choose."

Christophe went home in a daze. To cover his bemusement, he talked at some length to his father about the misfire of his rifle, and how poor the gunpowder was. Etienne listened thoughtfully.

"Well, you could make better black powder than that," he said, finally. "Monsieur Lamartine taught you well, did he not?"

"Yes, I know how it happens in the laboratory. Only the factory elements are new to me," said Christophe. "I looked about the factories, but do not know how they handle the black powder in quantity."

"Hmmmm," said Etienne, and was thoughtful throughout dinner.

The next week dragged for Christophe, who threw himself into his work and thought of little else. This week, hours were like days, days like weeks—until Sunday came.

He went over to Thomas Stratford's house promptly at three o'clock, anxious and pale. He wore a new suit of brown cloth, with a new light brown shirt. Would she notice he was better dressed than in his ragged hunting outfit?

Amelia came to the door to greet him, her smile shy this time. He gazed at her, his heart in his eyes. She wore a blue muslin dress, with deeper blue ribbons at her waist.

"Mary and Thomas wish to call upon your parents this afternoon. We thought of taking two carriages," she told him demurely.

Christophe thought of the poor small cabin, and hesitated. But she would know sooner or later how he lived, and he set his mouth and nodded. He was quiet on the journey, though Amelia chatted beside him and sent him gentle sidelong glances that comforted him.

She talked of the countryside and how she loved the

simple things, the changing of the seasons, the smell of newly turned earth and burning autumn leaves, the colors of the scarlet and yellow flowers. She asked him about his home in France, and for the first time in a year he found himself speaking freely about his home, and even briefly of Grégoire. Tears filled her gentle brown eyes; she put her hand impulsively on his arm.

"And so he died that all of you might be safe. How brave, how gallant! You must love him deeply."

He pressed her small fingers, feeling his throat too full for words. She understood.

At his log cabin, Etienne came out, and Sidoine was in a flutter. If only they had warned her. But no, and she must get out the lace tablecloth, the silver candlesticks, and serve a fine tea. Mary Stratford offered to help her while the older men talked.

"I should like to see the stream. I caught but a glimpse of it as our carriage came along," said Amelia. Mary gave her a teasing smile, but Amelia insisted. Christophe escorted her outdoors, and they walked slowly along the stream, in sight of the cabin where Thomas and Etienne strolled and smoked their pipes.

He pointed out the little waterfalls, and explained how the waterwheel worked, and how the cloth was spun and woven. She seemed quite fascinated with it all, and watched his face with her great eyes that seemed too large for her small face. Her hand rested lightly on his arm; her touch seemed to burn through the cloth. When she stumbled on a stone that turned under her thin slipper, he caught her quickly.

"Oh—I almost fell—thank you! Oh, dear—" She was a little breathless, recovering herself with a laugh. "How strong you are—like an oak."

"An oak?"

"Yes. It is the strongest thing I know," she said gravely, her eyes meeting his gaze. "You are—very strong, I think. Mary and Thomas admire you immensely. They have sung your praises since I arrived. You carry the burden of your whole family, they say, and have done so since you left France."

57

"They—they do me too much honor," he muttered, flushing, but pleased and proud that his friends felt this way about him. He wanted to look well in her eyes.

He never forgot that enchanted day. They strolled a short distance upstream, gazing at the brown rushing waters, admiring the charming waterfalls, watching the leaves rustle down from the willows and maples and oaks and join in the tumble of the winds. It was a scarlet and golden day, with the sky as blue as her dress. They paused, talked, strolled on, and finally returned reluctantly as Mary called to them.

They came in, flushed from the wind, Christophe's eyes as bright as Amelia's. Sidoine looked from one to the other. He was so young—yet—he had proved himself a man. Was he thinking of marriage already?

She watched Amelia, and approved of the girl. She laughed and told merry jokes, but she had her serious moments, and she had common sense. Sidoine also liked the Stratfords immensely, and thought them good-hearted and kind.

The Sunday was followed by others. Each time Christophe went to see Amelia, and sometimes the others drove back with them to visit and jest and plan through the long golden days. Thomas seemed interested in Etienne's schemes, and would listen patiently to one big idea and another, and make practical suggestions about them, every bit as though he believed in them. Christophe and Amelia would sit with the others for a time, or go out for a walk on the good days, and stroll along the Areuse, as the trees turned brown and were stripped of their bright leaves.

Christophe had never been so happy. All the evil times seemed to have passed like a bad dream. Here he strolled in freedom along the stream, beside his home, and thought of building a great house for himself and Amelia, up on the bluff. A house with white pillars, with every comfort for her, with every convenience. And one day, they would have children. A wife and children of his own! It was too great a happiness to be borne in silence, and on workdays, as he walked briskly along the river from the mill to the pastures, he sang the old French songs.

November rolled in and darkened the skies. Then it was December, and a rush of orders for woolens came in. The manufacturers were interested in the cloth of the Vallettes, and could they supply more of the colors of orange and brown stripes? They liked the reddish hues—could they send more?

Etienne and Christophe worked late at night, and so did the workers. The cloth poured out into beautiful piles, was bundled up, and sent off to meet the ships and be sent north.

Then a letter came from Conrade. The men came home one night and were met by a pale Sidoine. "Veronique is very ill, she expects her child in January, and there has been bleeding," she told them somberly.

They all read the letter. Conrade was distraught. Veronique was sure she would die. She begged to be taken home to France, and Conrade did not know how to handle her. He urged his mother to come and help him.

Etienne was too fragile to be driven north all that way. Christophe felt he could not leave the mill, yet he must. They debated into the late hours, and slept on it, and still did not know what to do.

Baptiste and Marc Clausel came the next day, and heard the story. They too had heard from Conrade. Baptiste looked grave.

"I fear the worst," he finally said reluctantly. "It is the way my wife died, in childbirth, after much bleeding. She needs comfort and a practical woman who knows how to aid her," he said to Sidoine. "If you will entrust yourself to the care of me and my son, we will take you to him."

"How good you are!" exclaimed Sidoine, and Christophe shook their hands silently. Etienne looked very relieved. It was all arranged, and within two days the Clausel men took Sidoine Vallette north to New York.

There was only a brief letter from her on her arrival.

59

Veronique was very ill; she would do her best, Conrade was distracted. Then silence.

Christophe had hoped for a happy Christmas and New Year. Always at home, until this past year, they had had a beautiful celebration, a time of peace and family. But Veronique's needs of course came first.

Mary extended an invitation, and so Etienne and Christophe spent Christmas with the Stratfords. There was feasting and merriment and toys for the children. Christophe had made some bullets of his own and managed to bring down a deer, and that formed part of the magnificent dinner.

Christophe also had the comfort of Amelia's bright presence that Christmas. Secretly he hoped that his work might continue to go as well as it had, and that this next summer he might build a home for her. Would she marry him in the autumn? Then next Christmas, they would celebrate in their own home. It was a great secret joy for him, and he looked longingly at her.

She seemed to share his thoughts, for over the bright golden head of the small girl on her lap she gave him a smile and blushed. "I love Christmas, don't you, Christophe? It is a time of peace and goodwill, and for families," she said earnestly. "I am the only child of my parents, and they have been ill. I always longed for a very large family."

"I also," he said. "I hope some day—we share the same hope, do we not?"

She let him take her hand in his and squeeze her fingers. He went home on a high tide of emotion and love. He adored her. She was so sweet, so good. What a wife she would make! When he thought of her as his wife, the mistress of his home, the mother of his children, his happiness seemed almost frightening. He found himself praying that nothing would happen to mar this hope for them.

New Year's came. Christophe and Etienne went to call on the Stratfords, bearing gifts for the ladies. It was the custom in France to pay New Year's calls on one's close friends, Christophe explained to Amelia. Christmas was for children, New Year's for adults.

She was interested, as were the others, and Christophe explained other French customs. He told of the crèche they always made, with the little figures of the Virgin Mary and baby Jesus. "Though we were not Catholic, it seemed a good custom to us. We were secretly Huguenot. How good it is to be outward in our religion," he said, with a grave smile. "For many generations, we had to hide our feelings."

Amelia was Protestant also, and told him some of the customs of her church. And in the afternoon, though it was cold, she donned her cloak, and they strolled out in the garden, and stood beside the sundial which counted the sunny hours. The garden was white with frost, the flowers wilted, but still hope sprang in his heart. She was so beautiful, in her blue velvet dress, with her hair tied back in a blue ribbon, and a cameo at her pulsing white throat.

Two weeks later, they received word that Veronique had died in childbirth as had the infant, and Sidoine was returning home with Conrade as soon as he had sold the town house. What she did not say they read between the lines, and Etienne passed a weary hand over his eyes. "Poor Conrade," he murmured. "My oldest son—what sorrow!"

"He loved Veronique very much. He will take this hard," said Christophe compassionately. Loving now—adoring Amelia—he understood for the first time how reckless a man could be in his emotions. If any danger had threatened Amelia, or tried to part them, he would be furious. He would kill anyone who tried to step between them.

Understanding this, when Conrade came home, he welcomed him with a strong handclasp and words of gentle sympathy. Sidoine was weary, but Conrade looked beaten, bitter, bewildered. Everything in his world had gone wrong.

They had not been received well in New York. "All they think of is money," he exclaimed. "Money is their god. Our birth, our breeding, our background in France—all is nothing. How much money do you have? How much land? How many jewels? How expensive a home? All that is what counts to them."

Christophe listened, and tried to help him by turning over to him some work in the mill. To his surprise and pleasure, Conrade caught on quickly and worked feverishly. Only this would help him sleep at nights, Conrade declared.

"He is a good man. This has sobered him and he is settling down," said Etienne with great satisfaction. He had never really admired Veronique, and secretly felt that her death was an act of God. She had drawn Conrade from them, had led him a merry dance in New York. Now she was gone, God keep her, and they had Conrade back with them again.

Conrade worked well that winter. He spared himself little. Only when Marc and Baptiste Clausel came over did he pause to drink and make merry. He held himself aloof from others, wearing black dress and a grim expression much of the time.

Chapter 5

The wool orders that came in that winter were many, yet the money went out swiftly in wages. The three Vallette men debated long and earnestly whether it was worthwhile to build a second mill. Etienne was turning something else over in his mind.

Conrade and Christophe shared a bedroom and a bed. Since Conrade was large and Christophe also a good size, it was uncomfortable for them both. The house seemed too small for four of them.

As spring came on, Etienne finally summoned Christophe, and in the green shadows of the trees along the Areuse they talked. "I have been in correspondence with several manufacturers of black powder, my son," said Etienne. "It has been on my mind that we could venture into this enterprise."

"I have thought so also, father," said Christophe, with a sigh. "The wool will not keep us all. If I should marry soon, and have a family, I should want more security for us all."

"Indeed," said Etienne, giving him a quick glance. "Well, there is a Mr. Ward in Pennsylvania, about a hundred miles from here. He sent a cordial welcome for one of you to come and work with him and learn the business. I told him of your experience with chemistry, and he was much impressed. I hear he is a hard man, but just. And he has the most modern equipment of them all."

Christophe hesitated. Ordinarily, he would have

leaped at the chance to go. But to leave Amelia? He did not want to leave her. He saw her every Sunday. Recently he had kissed her and she had responded with unexpected sweet passion. The memory of her lips and the softness of her silky body against his had kept him awake several nights. He longed to marry, to have a home with her.

But he must think of the future of his whole family, he thought, not just of himself and Amelia. Finally he consented to go.

Amelia and the Stratfords came over on Sunday before he was to leave. Conrade sat gloomily before the fire; little made him laugh. As the parents settled down, Mrs. Stratford gave Amelia a smile, and the girl went for her cloak. She and Christophe went out into the spring day, in the gentle April breeze, and walked under the budding trees.

"I shall miss you so much, Christophe," murmured Amelia wistfully. "How long will it be, do you think?"

"Father said a year or two," he said, reluctantly.

"So long? I had best return home then," she replied, with a sigh. "My parents have written again and again to beg me to return, but I did not wish to when—" she stopped modestly, blushing.

"Oh, Amelia, the thought of leaving you has left me desolate!" he burst out, turning to her. He put his hands on her waist under the cloak. She wore pale yellow today, with brighter yellow ribbons on the high waist of her dress and in her brown curls. "You look like spring itself. How can I leave you? I love you." She gazed up at him, and he looked down at her, and in the shadow of the dark stone mill he drew her to him.

"Oh, Christophe, I do love you," she whispered at last, her lips close to his.

Her body yielded to his, and she put her arms about him under his greatcoat. He held her fiercely tight, and pressed kisses on her cheeks, on her soft pink mouth.

"You are the loveliest, sweetest girl in the world. I will love you all my life," he whispered. "Oh, God, to leave you is like dying—"

They walked further along the river, pausing to kiss in the shadow of a tree, near a bush, in the shelter of one of the silent greystone mills where the wool was dyed. The river rushed sweetly over its little rippling waterfalls. The apple trees were turning pink with promise.

Christophe caressed her pink cheek, his dark eyes gentle. "Oh, Amelia. I loved you from the first. When I saw you in the firelight that day—"

"And I was drawn to you at once. Mary had spoken so of you, and Thomas—" They paused again, and he kissed her mouth, feeling the passion rising in him.

"If only I might claim you for my own before I go," he groaned.

"Oh, darling, darling Christophe—"

Their steps had blundered into a thick mass of bushes. With a sigh he drew her down, to sit on his greatcoat, while he clasped her in his arms. She put her silken arms about his neck, drawing him to her. They swayed, leaned back on his coat, and he bent over her, pressing himself urgently to her. A great swell of emotion overcame him, he pressed urgent kisses to her throat as she drew her fingers through his hair and teased at his neck.

"Amelia—darling—oh, my love—I cannot leave you—"

"It will be so long—" she sighed.

"You will write to me—"

"Oh, yes—and you will write—"

But writing would not be enough. Cold words on white parchment. They needed to clasp and cling, and sigh, two young lovers rent with passion beyond containing. He lay on her soft body, and wanted her, and her gentle brown eyes were dim with dizziness. She closed her eyes, her arms about him.

"Amelia—let me—" His hand fumbled with her dress, drawing up the hem. She did not protest, sighing as he caressed the slim, rounded thigh. He could not stop himself; he went on and on, passionately yet carefully, his young, virile body convulsed and terribly in need of burying itself in hers. He pressed closer, and the deed was done. "Oh, God—my God, you are so sweet—oh, my love—" He groaned against her soft breasts, and felt her move convulsively beneath him. She trembled in his arms, and they lay there in silence.

Later he tried to apologize. They sat up, he drew down her dress carefully with trembling hands, and pressed a kiss on her knee. "Oh, my darling, I should not have done this. You know I honor and respect and adore you. If only we could marry at once—"

"You will come back, Christophe—oh, soon?" she sighed, and held him again longingly.

"Yes, I will come soon. Oh, my love—"

But the time grew late. They stood up finally, he brushed down her dress, examined her to make sure the grass stains were brushed away as much as possible, and drew her cloak about her. She straightened her brown curls, and lovingly brushed his hair with her hands. He would never forget the gentle fingers on his cheeks, on his hair and neck.

They walked back to the cabin, slowly, earnestly talking. He must serve this apprenticeship, then he would return. They could marry soon, perhaps within a year or two. He would build a house on the bluff for them, so they could be alone. Amelia said she would not mind if his parents lived with them: she adored them already, for they were as sweet and kind as her own. He kissed her for this, his hands gentle on her arms.

Mary knowingly examined them when they returned. They had tea and talked, then Christophe drove Amelia home while the others rode horseback. He kissed her one last time at the door, and left, exultant and downcast all at once.

He left the next morning for Pennsylvania. It was a long ride—almost five days. When he arrived, he found Mr. Ward brusque and hard, as they had said.

Christophe was assigned a room in a boarding house in town, and drove out some two miles to work each day. He shared a room with two other young men, and had little privacy. All were working in the powder mills from seven in the morning until seven in the evening, with one pause for a little lunch of bread, cheese, and beer. The rest were all German or Irish, and they were inclined to laugh at his accent.

Mr. Ward drove them all hard, but he was fair and he paid well. He took Christophe into the laboratory and taught him what he knew. Christophe was not impressed with the quality of their black powder. They made only the sporting type, a powder which called for more care than they gave it. They did not give it long enough to dry, and he resolved to learn from their mistakes.

He did learn much in the mills. He studied how they weighed out the ingredients, after making the charcoal by distilling the willow woods. He learned the process of refining the saltpeter and ladling it out of the cauldron. It was hot work, and dangerous. Then he worked with the sulfur, and helped purify it—all the impurities had to be cleaned out of its cauldron before the next crude sulfur went in. And he learned how the liquid sulfur was tapped off into containers.

The most dangerous part of the operation was combining the saltpeter, charcoal, and sulfur. He learned that different proportions of each went into military powder, which was heavier and had to have more power behind it, than into the sporting powder. Still different proportions went into blasting powder, which yielded gases that burst apart rocks as in blasting out coal or earth for canals.

Mr. Ward stuck strictly with his sporting powders and worked on processes of making them better. Christophe privately thought there was a greater future in the blasting powder. As more canals were built, more coal mined, and other products of the earth moved from their depths, such powder would be needed. Surely this was a growing market.

If war came—God forbid it—they could turn to military powder easily enough. For now the sporting powders, better refined than before, and blasting powder could provide quite a living. He wrote this to his father, and warned him to tell no one about it, even Conrade, as they might wish to keep their operations a secret until they could get well started.

He worked in Pennsylvania all that spring and summer. It was much hotter than he was accustomed to, especially in the powder factory. Amelia wrote often at first. Conrade and Marc and Baptiste Clausel had escorted her home, and Conrade and Marc had lingered for a month for the hunts.

"Your dear brother," she wrote in a pretty hand, "is so sad that one trembles for him. I try to cheer him up, and Marc and I think of amusements to entertain him. I think he liked a third cousin of mine, who is most beautiful. She looks much like Veronique did, he confided in me."

Another time, later in the summer, she wrote, "Conrade and Marc have come down for another visit. I was so glad to see them. Father is quite fond of them both."

Christophe frowned over these letters. In between she vowed her constancy, and told him of her love—but shyly, and less frequently as the months wore on. He was weary from long hours of work, six days a week. On Sundays he went for a walk in town, or out along the river where the scenes reminded him of his own Areuse. He always thought of Amelia, as the trees bloomed with fruit and then turned scarlet and yellow in the autumn.

Sidoine wrote to him sometimes, and told him his father was working so hard it quite frightened her. "Conrade helps when he is here," she wrote.

Christophe sat in the crowded room he shared with the other two men and meditated. It does not sound good, he said to himself. Why is Conrade not there *often*? All the time, in fact?

His only comfort was the memory of how Amelia had yielded herself to him and vowed her love. She would never have done that had she not meant to accept him as her husband one day. She wrote affectionately, but less often now. Finally in October, she wrote again from Mary Stratford's home and said she had called on Sidoine and Etienne and found his father rather frail.

"Conrade is a great comfort to them, however. He

takes on much of the work of the mill, so your father can rest more. How splendidly he has risen above his great grief. No wonder your family seems so close and fond of each other. I always craved a large family; being an only child is quite lonely."

Amelia was back near his home. He longed for her, and thought of her at night, when his weary body craved sleep. He lay awake listening to the snoring and groaning of his roommates, and hungered for the day when he might be alone with Amelia in their bedroom.

He planned their home. He spent nights and Sundays drawing plans for it. It would have great white pillars and a splendid drawing room for guests. A great central hall leading to a fine staircase. On the other side of the hall, a small, cozy parlor just for the family, with a beautiful fireplace of blue and white tiles such as he had seen in Boston. And upstairs, many bedrooms for the large family they would have. A huge master bedroom for himself and Amelia, other rooms for their children. A wing for servants—yes, they would have servants, so that Amelia could take care of the children and not weary herself with housework.

He had already secretly drawn a plan for the new black-powder mills. He believed so in the future of the powder that he planned to change the woolen mill into a powder mill. Then he would build small mills along the river, and make a race along it to draw off water for the waterwheels. The mills would be built sturdily with three sides of native stone, and the roof and fourth side to the river with light wood, so that the force of an accidental explosion would be directed harmlessly toward the river.

The home would sit high on the bluff overlooking the mills, so he could see the work, yet be alone with his wife up there. They would have stables for their horses, a little vegetable plot, grounds for flowers—for he knew how much Amelia loved flowers. And the view from the windows would be glorious, extending out over the river valley.

He grew more and more restless as autumn dragged

on. He longed for Amelia, and for his family. He had learned all he could from Mr. Ward, he felt, though he had promised to remain at least a year.

At last he could endure it no longer. He went to Mr. Ward in November and told him simply that he was homesick for his family and must leave.

"Well, well," said gruff Mr. Ward. "I was afraid of this. Won't keep your word and stay with me a year, eh?"

Christophe bent his head. "I—if you insist, sir, I will stay the year."

"No, no, lad, I won't keep you." The man frowned and coughed. "You're a good, hard-working lad, saved all your money, never went wild with the women like some of the others. You go home and enjoy your family. Got a girl, huh?"

"Yes, sir, I hope to marry her soon," said Christophe, more lighthearted, smiling a little. His eyes had grown weary from some close figure-work in the laboratory; now he wore small spectacles to aid him in the work. He took them off and folded the steel frames nervously.

In a gesture that surprised Christophe, Mr. Ward patted the younger man's lean shoulder. "I expect you'll go out and start a powder mill of your own," he said sharply. "But I wish you luck, yes, I wish you luck. You're a fine lad, and you have a good business head, a good, hard head. Work hard, work hard, and you'll have your dreams."

"Thank you very much, sir. May I thank you—thank you for your great kindness to me—" Christophe stammered in surprise.

"Nonsense, pooh. You make your own luck, Mr. Vallette. You'll be famous one day if you keep on. And you will keep on—you're the kind who works hard, and you're smart. I'll tell the bookkeeper to make up your check. You'll be aching to get off, I expect."

Christophe had sold the rawboned horse he had ridden north on his arrival. He had missed riding, but had spent little for himself. Now he went out to the stables, where he had had an eye on a fine stallion only four years old, a fine chestnut with the nervous stride of a thoroughbred and the deep chest of endurance. He bought it after haggling only a bit.

He packed, and set off the next day. He would be home by Sunday! He had not written, he would surprise them all, he thought happily, as he rode along in his greatcoat, huddled against the wind and the raw November rain. He slept out at night, his horse picketed close beside him, living on bread and cheese and some sausage Mrs. Ward had given him. He paid little attention to the weather.

When he got home, he would kiss his mother, hug his father, change his clothes, and go to Amelia. He would ask her at once to marry him the following summer. Then through the winter he would build their new home. So he planned, a smile on his lips as he absently kept to the dusty roads and highways down to Virginia.

He arrived on Sunday afternoon, tired, chilled through, hungry, to find the log cabin alight with festivity. Candles burned in the windows, guests strolled outside smoking pipes, huddled in cloaks. He gave them a wondering look, recognized Baptiste Clausel, and waved to him. The man waved back, startled, and went into the cabin hastily.

Sidoine ran out as Christophe slid down wearily from the saddle. One of the men came up to take his horse and reins. "I'll take care of him for you, Christophe," he said quickly.

"Oh, my son." Sidoine ran into Christophe's arms. "You came home. You have our letter?"

"Letter? No, not for two weeks, maman. You look well, maman," and he kissed her tenderly. "What are these goings-on?"

She drew back and stared uneasily into his weary, lined face. "Oh, Christophe—we are celebrating—it is Conrade, you see."

"Conrade, what has he done now?" asked Christophe drily.

Conrade came out, a grin on his face. He wore a

71

scarlet velvet cloak over his fine blue suit, a lace tie at his throat. "Christophe. You are in time to be best man at my wedding. You have my letter about it?"

"Wedding! You are to marry?"

"In the spring, my brother." Conrade clapped him affectionately on the shoulder. Weary, Christophe shuddered from the hard blow. He felt a chill of apprehension course through him. "First I shall build a fine house for my bride. I thought on the hill across the river will be a fine spot, away from the noise of the mill."

Etienne had now come out.

"And who is your bride, Conrade?" asked Christophe drily.

Etienne came up to them quickly as Conrade said, "Why, who but Amelia! So beautiful, so kind and gentle—and an American."

"You—lie!" cried Christophe, and sprang at him fiercely, thinking his brother jested cruelly with him. Conrade sprang back, his hand instinctively at the side where no sword now hung. Christophe struck his face; Conrade blinked at him.

"No—no—no fighting!" cried Etienne.

"You lie. Tell me you lie."

"But no, it is the truth," said Conrade slowly. "I marry Amelia. I have been courting her all this summer and autumn. No one is so gentle, so sweet, so loving, as my beautiful Amelia. Her parents have come to celebrate our engagement."

"Oh—my—God," choked Christophe, and drew his sword. He felt such a blind hate and passion that he would have run his brother through. Three or four men cried out, and someone gripped his arm.

Conrade backed up. "You are mad."

Christophe spat out his anger, choking over the words, spilling them out in French as the men crowded about. Only the Clausels understood, beside the Vallette men, and they exchanged significant looks.

"Amelia belongs to me. She promised herself to me. She promised she would wait until I returned."

Conrade went pale under his hearty tan. White lines

were engraved beside his mouth as he snarled, *"You* lie. She is *mine.* She loves me—she has said it. She would not lie to me."

"My sons, my sons, do not quarrel." besought Etienne anxiously. "Remember your oath. You will not quarrel. Our family must stand together: *Together— Forever."*

"While he steals my intended from me?" cried Christophe.

Conrade, having no sword, kept an uneasy eye on Christophe's, held steady in that bronzed hand. "Ask Amelia," Conrade said abruptly. "Go on, ask her."

Conrade turned and beckoned to the pale girl who hovered in the doorway of the log cabin. She wore white today, but it was no whiter than her face. Christophe gazed at her hungrily, incredulously, as she came slowly forward and clasped Conrade's arm in her slim hands—the same hands which had caressed him. The same body he had known.

"What is your quarrel?" she asked, timidly, in English. Her brown eyes avoided the keen look of Christophe.

Christophe drew a deep, pained breath. Her manner told him all he needed to know. "You are engaged—to Conrade, my brother?" he asked her in a dull tone.

She nodded, her hands holding Conrade's arm so tightly that her knuckles shone white. A ring adorned her fourth finger, the sparkling diamond ring that Veronique had once worn.

Christophe looked at that ring. "I wish you joy," he said ironically, with a significance she did not understand until much later. He emphasized the word *wish* heavily.

"Thank you. Do—come inside, Christophe. You are weary with traveling," she said brightly, still avoiding his look.

The engaged couple turned and went inside. Christophe lingered, looking at his father. "You knew—my hopes?" he inquired in French, very politely.

"My son, it was fair. She made her own choice."

73

Etienne did not venture to embrace him. He felt uneasy, somehow, with his younger son, who now stood with head held so gallantly high—as those going to the guillotine had done.

"Her own choice. But none chose to warn me by letter."

"Did she write to you? No? Then it was her doing," said Etienne, with a Gallic shrug, conscious suddenly that the Clausels were listening avidly. "Come, son, it is not so great a matter," he urged. "Come inside, join in the festivities. Meet her parents—you have not met them? Come, have some food and drink." He urged Christophe inside the small cramped cabin room where Conrade and Amelia stood at one end to receive the guests.

Sullen and quiet, Christophe attended the engagement party of the girl he had planned to marry. Stunned by her fickleness, shocked at his own cold fury at his brother, he stood morosely, not able to eat or drink. He was in a daze, simply standing and listening to the laughter and chatter.

Finally the guests left. Conrade, weary, yawned and went to the bedroom he had shared with his brother. But Christophe felt he could not endure to sleep there with him. He went out into the cold night, found his cloak, rolled up in it, there along the river Areuse, and lay awake, thinking, burning with rage and incredulous dismay.

He loved her—but she did not love him. She had deceived him; she had been too frivolous to wait for him. All those letters, all those kisses and that embrace—for nothing. Sometime during the night, he felt his spirit harden, as he had the night of Grégoire's death. For him, nothing would ever be the same again.

Chapter 6

The winter passed rapidly. Time meant nothing to Christophe. He worked much, ate a little, slept some, and worked again. He had moved to the home of his foreman, who had compassionately given him a bedroom in his own crowded house near the mills.

Conrade and Amelia were married in the spring. Christophe refused to be best man; Marc Clausel fulfilled that duty. Christophe had worked all the winter building new powder mills and converting the large woolen mill to powder. He had watched the new house rising on the hill across the river. A huge home, much larger than the one he had planned. Conrade was hopeful and extravagant—and his bride was bringing him an enormous dowry.

Christophe lived in an emotional daze, tamping down his feelings as he did the violent powders with which he worked. He objected coldly only when Conrade "borrowed" the carpenters and stone men to build his home. "You will have to hire your own men. The mills must be built this winter," he told Conrade.

Conrade went to his father furiously, and Etienne supported him, as he usually did the elder son. Christophe bit his lips, went to town, hired more men for the mills, and had to build more houses for them in the midst of his mill building. His debts seemed enormous, and he was ashamed to face his creditors.

Conrad helped little with the mills, but Christophe was glad the man was away much of the time. The mills were built as Christophe had planned, with Etienne doing the paper work in the office. Christophe was out much of those short winter days, and into the night, by the light of torches, directing the building of the stone powder mills along the Areuse.

Whenever he looked up across the river, to the hill beyond, he could see the gracious stone pillars of the mansion Conrade was building for his bride.

But the mills were built, finished on time, and in the spring the first kegs of black powder went out hopefully into the markets. And the results were slow, but good. Whoever used the powder liked the results, and ordered more.

The marriage took place in early summer, the celebrations lasting a week. Then the young couple took off for two months to travel through the South. Christophe worked furiously all the long summer days, and into the autumn. The newlyweds returned. Conrade lived up on the hill now with Amelia, and Christophe had returned to the log cabin with his parents.

The winter snows were heavy that year of 1798, and on New Year's 1799 Etienne and Christophe went up the hill to pay a call on Amelia, while Conrade came down the hill to call upon Sidoine. It was the custom. Christophe sat awkwardly in the grand blue and gold parlor, and kept his gaze from the girl he had hoped to marry.

She seemed lovelier than ever to him, though more serious, her gentle brown eyes grave. She smiled over their gifts, and with more pleasure at the length of golden brown wool Christophe had saved for her than at Etienne's gift of chocolates.

"How kind you are. This will make a beautiful gown," she said, stroking the material in her hands. She wore a stunning dress of pale green silk with deeper green ribbons in her hair.

They sat and talked for a little time, and then she suggested that she return with them to visit with Sidoine. "I have not even seen her for conversation in quite two months," she said. Pink spots burned in her cheeks.

They had brought the carriage. Amelia had little to say during the drive down the slippery hill to the bridge that crossed the river. She glanced about wistfully at the bare branches of the trees, and Christophe noticed that she looked at the bushes where they had lain that spring day. That fateful day when he had possessed her—only to lose her.

Conrade had already left the cabin. Sidoine sat alone before the fire, musing, her head bent. She looked up in surprise as Christophe escorted Amelia into the cabin. "You here? Oh, happy New Year, my dearest daughter," and Sidoine kissed her gently, eyeing her keenly.

Amelia seemed to have little to say, despite her urgent wish to visit with Sidoine. The older woman finally suggested to the men, "Why don't you go outside and have a pipe or two while we talk? I have not talked alone with my daughter for too long."

Christophe took the hint, and drew his father with him. They strolled out of the cabin, pipes in hand.

Once alone, Sidoine turned to Amelia, "Well, Amelia? Conrade has spoken to me about his wish to go to New York City for several months."

"I know—I am worried," sighed Amelia, her pink mouth drooping.

"He should remain here and work in the mills," Sidoine said. "But there is still bad feeling between him and Christophe. Still—Etienne is working too hard and long at the accounts. He needs help."

"Conrade says if Christophe would only agree to take on Marc Clausel as a partner, there would be no problem. We could go away and enjoy ourselves."

Her tone was not wistful, thought Sidoine. It was more hopeless. She probed a little. "And you do not wish to go to New York."

"Oh—maman!" The words finally came out in a rush. "I have just told Conrade I am—I am—expecting a child—and he still wishes me to travel with him. And I feel so sick sometimes!"

"I thought so," said Sidoine, with gentle satisfaction, beaming at her. "When I saw you today, I said to myself, you are to become a grandmother at last, Sidoine Vallette."

Amelia knelt down on the rug beside Sidoine, putting her brown head in the lap of the older woman. In a muffled tone, she admitted, "I am afraid, maman. Afraid. I told Conrade about two weeks ago that I was expecting a child. He was excited, and became drunk—at least, he drank quite a bit that night. And he insisted—he would come to the bed—and—oh, maman, I am afraid he will hurt the child—and me—" she finished in a low tone, twisting her hands together.

Sidoine compressed her mouth. "So." Her hand stroked the brown curls. She was silent a moment, gazing at the orange fire blazing in the great hearth. "My dear one, you must be firm. And I myself will come with you today and speak to Conrade. He must take a separate bedroom while you are with child. He does not think. And he will go out and drink with that Marc Clausel."

"Do you—think he will agree to staying out of—oh, maman, I feel so terrible about it."

"It is only sensible, my child," said Sidoine quietly. "You are slim, like Veronique. You could lose your baby. I will warn Conrade seriously he is to take no chances with you, or he will risk losing both of you, as he did Veronique and the child. It must not happen a second time. It must not."

"Thank you, maman," whispered Amelia, and turned her head into the cotton-aproned lap. Tears made a little wet patch before she sat up and wiped her eyes with determination.

"You have a maid you brought with you, Amelia?"

"Yes, maman—Essie."

"I think it would be best if Essie slept on a divan in your bedroom," said Sidoine thoughtfully. "And her husband Kandy is the valet of Conrade? Confide in them at once, and enlist them. When Conrade has been—drinking—too much, he is not sensible and kind. They must see to it that you are protected."

Amelia stared at the blazing fire. "I thought I was being foolish and nervous. Conrade said—but I can see that you are right. I shall not go to New York and risk losing the child on the trip."

"That is right, child. And I will speak to Conrade myself, this day."

So it was settled, and Amelia returned home with a lighter heart. She noticed how carefully Christophe took care of his mother and herself, driving slowly so they would not be jarred. When he handed her down, his hand strongly held her arm so she could not slip. She looked at his serious face, the brown eyes so grave, as his strong arm supported her.

In her bedroom later, as she rested, she had the wicked, terrible thought, "I should have married Christophe. Oh, why, why did I listen to Conrade? He is vain, thoughtless, his ego is easily touched, and he becomes so angry. And he must be the master and make all the decisions, no matter how foolish."

But marriage was forever, until death parted them, as the minister had said. She laid her arm over her eyes, until she felt more calm. Sidoine was so good, so understanding.

Conrade came in presently, frowning. "What did you say to maman? She is jumping all over me."

"I merely told her about the child—she was so happy," said Amelia, fearfully.

"She says you must not think of going to New York with me. Well, I am going whether you go or not. If Marc could be taken in as a partner I would not be needed here so much. Etienne does not need to work so hard."

He kicked at the furniture like a child. Essie came in quietly and hung up Amelia's cloak. Then she brought a bowl of lilac-water and swabbed Amelia's forehead. Conrade paced about the room, fuming about the hard work he must do and how he had to get away or expire of sheer boredom.

79

"There, now, sir," said Essie, in her light, quick tones. "You could go on up to that there New York City by yourself, sir, couldn't you? Sure, you could have a great time there, and Miss Amelia could write to you and tell you she is fine. Your pa would keep an eye on the house for you. You need a vacation, that's sure."

Amelia removed the cloth from over her eyes and stared at her maid, who had only half-hidden her dislike of her new master. The girl looked so innocent—

"Well, dammit, you're right, Essie. I do need a vacation. I haven't had any time off since our honeymoon. I can't stick it out all the time, like Christophe, I'd get as dull as he is."

"Perhaps you *should* go," said Amelia, faintly, taking her cue. "I should miss you so much, but we could write—" Essie gave her a big wink behind Conrade's back.

Within a week Conrade and Marc Clausel were on their way to New York City. They remained for two months; after they gained entrance to respectable society, an evening seldom passed without their taking advantage of their great fortune. Amelia spent the time peacefully, sewing for the baby, visiting with Sidoine, who came almost daily, and attending to the wives of workers who had problems, organizing a little nursery for their children. She learned many of the problems of the mills, and talked earnestly to Sidoine of them.

Conrade returned in better spirits as spring came. Their child was born in July 1799. They named him Kendall, for a man Conrade had met and admired in New York. Etienne hid his disappointment: he had wanted a French name for the first grandchild.

Christophe continued to say no to the partnership of Marc Clausel. The more he saw of that young man, the less he thought of his business ability. He had the same nonchalance as Conrade, the same indifference as Conrade to hours of work, the same lack of faithfulness, duty, reliability.

The winter came slowly. The new century, 1800 began. Christmas meant a series of visits from Amelia's parents and friends, toys for small Kendall, drinking and more excuses from Conrade on why he could not work that week. Christophe worked all the harder; it was his whole life. He took only a little time now and then to go hunting with Thomas Stratford or spend a Sunday afternoon in the Stratford home.

It was bitter for Christophe to see the children of his friends growing up, to remain in their beautiful home and then return to his log cabin. His mother said it did not matter, but the contrast between the magnificence of Conrade's home and his own was another source of galling jealousy to Christophe. He wanted better for his parents. Yet their debts were still too great to consider this. It was not practical. He did not consider marriage any more for himself. The girl to whom he had given his heart had chosen someone else.

He went on lone hunting trips that winter, to the south and into the mountains. They were comforting trips. He would go for a week or two and return refreshed by the solitude he had found in the woods. He took his sketch pad and pencils with him and drew the wintry scenes; a deer with lifted head alert, an old mountaineer drawing on his pipe as he talked of the old days. He saw an occasional Indian, and sometimes paused to exchange wary conversation. He drew a portrait of one, and gave him the sketch; the Indian examined it solemnly and put it into his hunting shirt. It was a different life from the mills, and Christophe enjoyed it.

He felt no fear when he traveled alone. It seemed as though nothing mattered enough to be afraid about. When one had lost what was most dear, he thought grimly, then life itself seemed cheap, not worth a shrug.

He had grown tough; he was hard on his men, yet fair, as Mr. Ward had been. He demanded much from them, and paid them well for it. When a man was injured in an explosion, he set up an infirmary in a vacant house and hired a man to watch over him and a doctor to come frequently. He gave the women the kinds of houses they wished, with plenty of ground for vegetable patches. On his solitary trips, he found himself dreaming of further improvements to the mills and to the mill houses for his mill families.

He had hired many Irish and many Germans: they had come over on ships like himself, though with no money. They would work hard; they were intelligent, and not afraid of danger. His foreman, Sean O'Grady, was as smart as they came, with little education, yet he picked up everything Christophe taught him about powder making and safety in the mills.

Christophe did his best thinking on his hunting trips. The sharp, clean air seemed to clear his brain of the sulfur fumes and the money problems. In another couple of years they would be making twice as much money. He thought of improvements to the sporting powder, a way to make the balls so they would fit better into the rifles. He devised a new way to pack the powder in smaller kegs, which they would make themselves. He even thought up a distinctive trademark design—a golden peacock on green grass—so that even those hunters who could not read would recognize the products of "Vallette and Sons."

And he would have none of Marc Clausel in the firm.

Late in the summer of 1800 there was an unusually hot spell. The river Areuse ran low. And the heat made the workers careless, or perhaps the powder was not perfectly dried.

Christophe was in the laboratory and Etienne in the counting house when the explosion rocked the area. Christophe froze, then ran to the scene. It was the loudest explosion he had ever heard. When he reached the site of the explosion he was sickened to see a leg and an arm lying on the ground some fifty feet from the mill.

Men ran about, some carrying buckets of water, some crying, women screaming. O'Grady was yelling, "Form lines to the river, wet the roofs of the next mills. God's name, wet the roofs!"

"How many are still inside?" asked a voice sharply from behind Christophe.

He turned to see Conrade, who had run up behind him. "I don't know yet."

"I'll go inside." And before Christophe could stop him, Conrade ran into the burning mill, reappearing with the broken body of a man in his sturdy arms. He laid him down gently some distance from the mill. "Another man still in—" he panted, tending gently to the broken form. A leg was gone, an arm—

Christophe ran inside then, and found a worker staggering about blindly in the mill. He guided him out, for he had been blinded by the flying particles.

No one else was inside. He left the men to be tended by Conrade and some women who had come running. They wet down the roofs and spent the rest of the afternoon cleaning up the debris and tamping down small fires where they started in the grass and trees.

It took another week to clean all the blood and flesh from inside the mill. The broken man died—fortunately for him, for he was little but a stump of himself. The blinded man went to the hospital in a nearby city. Christophe called on him every week, and promised him a job when he returned.

"But Mr. Vallette, what ivir can I do now, with no eyes?" cried the man.

"You're still whole, you've got your body, your hands, and your bright mind," said Christophe briskly. "I'll think of a place where you fit in, don't you worry about that. And your wife and children will remain in the house, and they are fed and clothed always. That is my promise to you."

"You're a good decent man, Mr. Vallette, and that's the truth of it," said the man gratefully, his hand groping out in Christophe's direction. "Others would be a-throwing me out and my family with me."

Conrade said much the same, clapping Christophe on the shoulder when he returned to the mills. "We must take care of them," he said gravely. "This is a dangerous occupation. If we don't take care of our men, they'll be drifting away to easier work. And dammit, we owe it to them. They take a hundred chances a day."

"Yes, we must help. It has to make up for the dangerous conditions in which they live. We are a small community of our own," said Christophe thoughtfully. Strangely he had not now resented Conrade's friendly touch, though he had avoided him for a long time. The explosion and Conrade's prompt, brave response had touched something almost dead in Christophe. They were brothers, after all, and Grégoire had died for them both.

"What about the man who died?" asked Etienne. "Amelia was with the family this morning; Kendall is the age of their youngest. She asked what we were going to do. The woman thinks she will be thrown out—and they have four children."

"They must remain," said Christophe, with a sigh. "There will be work for the woman, if she wishes. The laundry, taking care of the children—we will find something. And the house will be rent-free. I can see to it that they have plenty of food from our own garden."

"We'll both see to it," said Conrade, with more warmth than usual. His eyes glowed. "This is a family business, isn't it? We are all responsible."

Christophe went home in a thoughtful but more hopeful mood that night. The wound between them was healing. He must reconcile himself to the marriage. Amelia was happy with her child, and she came often to talk to the women, to talk to them about their children and how to keep them healthy. She gave them small comforts for their homes from her own money. Her marriage was lasting, growing, and Conrade was not so restless now.

When Conrade came again to ask him to take on Marc Clausel as a partner, Christophe listened to the end. "Well, well, I don't think we should make him a partner all at once," he finally said, as Etienne listened to them both.

Etienne Vallette, now that he was growing older, his shoulders stooped, his hair quite white, left many such decisions to his sons.

"Both Baptiste and Marc have been very good to

us," said Etienne thoughtfully. "Remember all they have done for us."

Christophe finally nodded. "Well, let us take in Marc Clausel as a bookkeeper, if that is what he wishes," he said reluctantly. "We shall see how he works, and if all goes well, he will be considered for promotion, the same as any other worker."

"But I want him a full partner in the firm," protested Conrade. "I have practically promised him—"

"He must prove himself first," said Christophe. "Ask him to come in and try the work. It may not prove to be agreeable to him. He will not want to bind himself to it if he does not like it."

So it was arranged, and Marc Clausel came into the business as a bookkeeper. Christophe tried to keep an eye on him, but was very busy himself. He left it pretty much up to Etienne and Conrade to train him.

The business grew the rest of that year, and in 1801 as well. Conrade and Amelia had another child, a girl this time, named Deborah. She was a small, solemn edition of Amelia, and Christophe was reluctantly enchanted by her. If all he had planned had come true, the girl should have been his. It was a painful thought, when he held the baby, gazed into her brown eyes, and held her tiny hand.

Perhaps marriage was not for him. He had met no woman he even vaguely considered marrying since Amelia was lost to him. He must satisfy himself with the children of Conrade, and be happy that the Vallette line would continue, though Grégoire was dead and he, Christophe, would not marry. Conrade would carry on the line, the name, and eventually the black powder business.

So the mills grew, and the yards grew. Christophe bought more land, enlarged the village of the workers, and added several more mills up stream. Orders continued to pour in. The Vallette sporting powders were in heavy demand by this time, for they had proved far superior to the others being made. They fired most of the time, they were rarely damp, and they fit the new sturdy rifles made in Pennsylvania.

Then, as the mills enlarged, Christophe turned to making blasting powders. Huge powder kegs went out weekly on wagon trains bearing the distinctive trademark of the Vallette powders. The golden peacock seemed to swell with pride as long hitches of heavy horses drew the laden wagons along dusty roads, along Indian trails, even into the Far West, into the Ohio country.

The Vallettes made enough to pay back their orignal loans in full, plus interest, and that heavy load slid off Christophe's shoulders.

Chapter 7

By the summer of 1802, Christophe was feeling extremely tired. His eyes hurt him from long hours in the laboratory. He felt stale and too weary to go on. He had been working night and day for years, and largely as a result of his efforts the powder mills were going well.

Christophe had good foremen—he had trained them himself and worked side by side with them. Conrade and Etienne did the bookkeeping, paid the men, and kept track of the thousand and one details of the orders flowing in from their agents scattered from New York to New Orleans.

Christophe came home one day in August and announced abruptly that he was going on a hunting trip.

"You must go, my son," said Etienne, drawing slowly on his long pipe. He rocked back and forth. "You might go for a longer time, two weeks, three."

Sidoine looked troubled, but said little. She knew that Christophe felt the need to go away. His eyes were red-rimmed, he was so very thin, and his shoulders stooped sometimes like those of Etienne. And he was but twenty-five years of age.

"Will you take Thomas Stratford with you?" asked Etienne, as Christophe got out his hunting clothes, his sturdy knapsack, his rifle and powder and shot.

"No. I shall go far; his family would be troubled, and he would worry about the harvest should we be gone for months."

Months? Etienne looked at Sidoine, who shook her

head in silence. When Christophe got that thin line about his mouth, the parents knew it would do no good to protest. He was at the end of his tether.

Christophe talked to Conrade about the accounts the next day, then told him he was leaving for a time. "But I had planned to go to Europe this autumn," protested Conrade. "I have heard conditions are much changed; I wish to see the situation in France for myself. I told you of this."

"You must wait until I return," said Christophe. He had spoken to Amelia about it; she was deeply troubled. Evidently Conrade had somehow gotten the notion of returning to live in France. He had several friends who had written urging him to return and move into diplomatic circles with them. Napoleon's government needed men who spoke both French and English, who knew America and the Americans at first hand. He might rise quickly in power and rank, perhaps even acquire a villa and a town house in Paris. Times had changed, with Napoleon, said Conrade eagerly.

"Well, when are you coming back?" asked Conrade. "I can put off my departure until then. But I have no wish to travel in the winter; the storms on the Atlantic are fearsome."

"I am weary," said Christophe quietly. "If I do not get away for a time, I shall break, I think. Conrade, do this for me. Look after the mills—and father. I worry about his health. Visit maman frequently, and beg Amelia to care for her also. But I must get away."

He had never spoken so to Conrade. The older brother gazed at him in alarm, then put his big hand affectionately on his shoulder. "But you do look terrible, Christophe. Yes, of course, you must go, and have a good long rest for yourself. You should not drive yourself so hard. The work goes well—besides, we might all move back to France one day."

"Not I. My life is here," said Christophe. "And father and mother are too old and worn to pull up roots once more and make such a journey. I am thinking of building a house on the hill for them. They deserve better than a log cabin. Now that all the mill buildings are going well, I shall build a house—when I return."

"Splendid, splendid," said Conrade, giving him a long, puzzled look.

Christophe left on a bright August day, setting off on his beautiful, sturdy chestnut horse. He loved that horse, it had more speed and endurance than any he had ever owned or ridden. They had gone on many a hunting trip together. He packed his sketch pad in his saddlebags, several pencils, and a few clothes. He meant to rough it for a time, and regain his composure. He had felt so close to desperation this past year.

He had paid a call on Amelia the day before packing to go. Now in his mind as he rode was the picture of her with Kendall and tiny Deborah in her arms. Her grave brown eyes, so wistful, yet so sweet. The maturity of her lovely face. Her concern as she begged him to take care of himself.

Did she still have some feeling for him? It was bitter consolation to think that she might. He must—he really must put her out of his thinking. But seeing her frequently kept the thought of his lost love ever in his mind.

The first nights he felt very restless. He rode ever south and further west into the mountains. He found an old mountain man and stayed a couple of nights with him in his cabin, but enclosed spaces had no attraction for him now. He sketched the man—and rode on.

His mind gradually emptied of troubles, and he slept better. The crisp air of the mountains sang in his blood; he lifted his head and sang out loud, the old French songs, the chants, the carols he had sung so long ago. The chestnut pricked up its ears and trotted briskly along the dusty trails, the dim paths in the green and golden forests.

He saw mountain flowers he had never seen before, and sketched them where they grew, shyly in the long grasses, some blue as the sky, some brilliant orange, some a pale pink. He lay on the bank of a brown rushing stream and caught a fish with his hands—it came that close to nibble at his fingers. He cooked and ate the fish that night over a low fire on the coals.

He had little need for his rifle and shot, though he kept them ever ready. His eyes grew more alert as he traveled. He knew he had long since been traveling in Indian territory. Several times he caught a glimpse of a brown form slipping away into the deeper forests. Some knew him from previous journeys, but they were wary of all white men.

He caught rabbits in snares, and cooked them for his supper. He dug roots as the mountain man had taught him, and cooked them also. He grew brown and tanned, hard and more supple, throwing off the stoop of his laboratory work. His glasses lay neglected in the saddlebags.

He traveled slowly, paying no attention to the passing weeks. He thought he had probably been gone a month or more when he finally ventured deeper into the mountains and one afternoon, toward nightfall, came out into a clearing. He drew rein and stopped to gaze as half a dozen Indian women splashed and washed clothes in the cool stream. One caught sight of him and called out to the others, pointing.

He rode slowly forward, keeping his head up, his rifle held loosely in his hand. It pointed downward. As he came up, several Indian men appeared as if from nowhere and surrounded him warily, staring at him. He held up his hand steadily in the peace signal.

One spoke to him in English. "You British?"

"No—French, now American," he said, in the accent he had never lost.

The women gathered up their clothes and fled. The men relaxed slightly and beckoned him to their fire. He got down, took care of his horse, moving carefully so that they were always in his view and he in theirs. He wanted no one shooting him in the back with one of those swift arrows.

He came to the fire and crouched down with a grunt of satisfaction. "You—what nation?" he asked.

He puzzled out their answer. They were Cherokee,

they said. Several spoke English, in a sort of stiff, very correct grammar. They must have gone to a mission school, he decided. They spoke swiftly to each other in the Indian tongue; then they turned back to him and asked him to stay the night with them.

He nodded, and thanked them courteously for their hospitality. While a woman came to the fire and began to prepare the evening meal, Christophe took out his sketch pad and began to sketch the scene; the blazing fire, the Indians lounging there, the lone dog crouched near the horses.

When it was finished, an Indian took it from him gravely and studied it. "Uh—us—us here," he motioned to himself and to the others.

Christophe nodded. The sketch was passed from hand to hand. Even the woman stared at it, then grinned, showing broken teeth.

He made another sketch of one of them who wanted to pose for him. He was a splendid young man, tall and proud, but he was teased by the others as he sat there, head erect, holding his bow and arrows so that the Frenchman might draw him. He endured their jesting, then accepted the sketch proudly and passed it around.

They ate then—some rabbit stew cooked in a pot with some onions and other greens that Christophe did not recognize.

He rolled up in a blanket for the night, his rifle at his hand. He made no other gesture of caution. The next morning, he wakened early, tended to his horse, and came to the fire to accept their hot herb tea and meat.

"You go—with us today," said one of the men, gesturing to the horse.

Christophe nodded. "If you wish me to come, I come," he said, indifferently. He felt a little glow of excitement, though he knew it would be rather dangerous to go to their larger encampment. Someone might decide they wanted his horse and rifle enough to kill him for the booty.

They packed up carelessly, evidently not intending to go far. They rode out, with Christophe as a guest in their midst. The handsome one sometimes rode at his side and showed off his English, pointing to the mountains, a lake, a stream, and translating them into Cherokee.

By noon, they rode into a larger camp, set in a very pretty spot in a valley of the mountains. A stream ran through the center of the camp, and some log cabins were set about. This was evidently their permanent camp.

A man came out to greet them, a handsome man, taller than the others, his arms folded, a scowl on his face as he saw Christophe. The men greeted him with respect. The women walked off to their own tents or cabins.

Christophe was introduced. "Monsieur Vallette—our chief, who is named Red Hawk, because he pounces on his prey," explained the handsome one proudly.

Red Hawk stared steadily at Christophe with a hard, black gaze. Christophe gazed back respectfully, bent, touched his forehead with his hand, and then came erect again. The hard, black gaze did not soften. Red Hawk pointed at the rifle.

"Me—take," he said emphatically.

"No," said Christophe, politely, shaking his head. "This is very powerful rifle. It is my friend, and goes where I go."

"Uh. Powerful? My rifle no good, it does not hit the deer." This was evidently a point of chagrin with him. The other hunters were listening keenly to this dialogue. Christophe noted that they had come back empty-handed from the hunt—unusual for Indians.

"Maybe I can help you," said Christophe thoughtfully. "I know much about rifles and the powder that blows up in them."

Red Hawk was suspicious. "What can you do? We best hunters in land. Our fields are full of game, but our rifles do not hit them. Arrows best."

"Your powder may not be good," said Christophe. "Tomorrow, when the light is good, we try."

"Huh."

Christophe was invited to the fire and given food and a place to sleep. He kept his eye on his horse, staking him near to himself, a definite but polite sign to his hosts that he meant to keep his stallion. It was like a diplomatic game—just such as Conrade enjoyed playing, thought Christophe, with an inner chuckle.

During the afternoon, he lounged near the fire, sketched the Indians who would pose for him, and noted out of the corner of his eyes the women who came and went. They were shy and wary of him. And he was not supposed to look at them. But he saw them anyway.

Red Hawk was waited on at dinner that night by a comely young Indian girl, obviously his wife, for he patted her shoulder and gave her some of the better parts of meat from his dish. As the meal ended, he asked her a sharp question. She nodded to his cabin.

Red Hawk frowned and issued an order. The squaw padded away on her leather moccasins and presently returned with a younger girl. The men politely gazed away, but Christophe watched her from beneath the shadows of his lashes, while seeming not to look.

The girl had long, blue-black hair and kept her head down submissively. She wore her deerskin garment gracefully, but her walk was awkward, as though she were not accustomed to the thin moccasins. When she finally raised her head and accepted the plate the Indian chief insisted on handing to her, Christophe caught a glimpse of her face and her eyes.

He tried to stifle the gasp. Her eyes were bright blue, and her face, though tanned, was unmistakably that of a white woman. She had a clear complexion, pink and cream. Her features were different from those of the Indians, her forehead broad, her chin pointed, and her nose definitely a tilted snub.

A white girl! Here—and belonging to Red Hawk! She was not here willingly, that seemed clear. So she must have come as a prisoner.

Christophe lowered his gaze and accepted some tea, drinking it thoughtfully. Poor child. She had not a hope.

If she kept rebelling against that arrogant chief, she would get whipped—or worse. He was the kind that wanted his women bowing down to him.

Red Hawk snapped an order at the girl, and she bent her head, set down her plate, and took his plate from him. She brought his cup of hot tea to him, and held it as he took it slowly from her, his gaze keen on her face. She nodded submissively and went away. Red Hawk's gaze followed her, dwelling on the rounded form, the long, slim, tanned legs.

The next day Christophe took out his powder, shot, and rifle and explained in simple terms to the Indians why their powder did not fire. They could not understand. It looked much the same to them. Finally he challenged them.

"I will go on a hunt with you. Let me have the first shot at a deer, at a rabbit, at any target you will name. You will see how this gun fires."

That excited and pleased them. They set out that morning, and Christophe kept his rifle loaded and ready, his eyes keen for the first sight of a deer or smaller animal. Red Hawk took great delight in leading the way. His scarred face told of many battles he had enjoyed, and his manner left no doubt that he was always the winner.

Soon the laughter and bantering of the Indians ceased. This was serious business. If they did not get meat for the winter, they might starve. So they rode more slowly. Then someone in the lead shot out his arm. They halted and slipped down from their horses. Christophe let one of the younger boys hold the reins of his stallion along with his own and crept forward.

There in a sunny glade some hundred yards ahead of them browsed a fine buck and three does. Christophe caught his breath. The Indians were looking to him for a signal, fingering their rifles. He nodded, holding up his hand for caution.

He crept forward, on arms and knees, cautiously, until he was about fifty yards away. Still a distance, but

94

the deer might get wind of him any moment. If the wind changed—

He checked his load, steadying his sights on the buck. He held his breath. If he failed—

He fired. The buck sprang into the air, then dropped with a thud. The does raised their heads, stupidly gazing about, then bounded off on rubbery legs toward the underbrush. Christophe reloaded as rapidly as ever he could and fired again. One of the does went down.

A great cheer went up from the Indians as they ran forward. They called to each other, clapped Christophe on the shoulder, and examined the deer joyously. Red Hawk wanted to examine Christophe's rifle, but Christophe shook his head. If the Indian took it apart, he explained, he might damage it. Two men were detailed to take the deer back to camp at once and have the women skin and dry the meat. The men went on, hopefully. Perhaps the Frenchman had changed their luck.

And indeed, it seemed so. That afternoon, they sighted a large black bear, heavy with his own fat, seeking out a tree trunk in which to hibernate for the winter. Christophe brought him down with a single shot.

There was great joy in the camp that night. While one group of squaws, with the help of some men, busily skinned the animals, drying the meat for the winter, another group of squaws prepared a great feast. Soon everyone ate and drank until late into the night.

The next day they went out again. This time Christophe gave two of the Indians, Red Hawk and the handsome one who had befriended him, some of his own powder and bullets. Each brought down a deer and other, smaller game—a half-dozen turkeys, some possum and rabbits.

Now Red Hawk condescended to smile on the stranger. Christophe was permitted the freedom of the camp, and came and went as he pleased. He went on any hunt with them he wished to, for he was their "luck," they told him.

Christophe remained with them more than a month. He saw them ready for the winter, cabins snugly caulked against storms and rains, meat drying in the smoke house. October turned to November, and the skies darkened with the threat of storms to come, as well as the smoke from the great mountains about them. Dusty blue mists seemed to hang from the mountains. The rains and even snows would come soon.

"I must go home," he said to Red Hawk one evening, as they finished their dinner.

"Stay with us, brother, through the winter," beseeched Red Hawk. Their gazes met, and Christophe shook his head.

"My brothers, the Cherokee, have been good to me. I have shaken off the worries of my own life, and been revived again, here in the woods among the streams and mountains of my brothers," said Christophe, raising his voice so all might hear. "You have dealt kindly with me. I shall remember you always in my heart."

"Stay with us," they urged. "There is more merriment in the winter. We will find a squaw for you."

There was snickering and nudging among them. Christophe had already gently refused the offer of one man's sister, a rather comely girl.

"My mother will await me with grief in her heart if I do not return to her. My father grows aged and gray with the work. I must return and help him again," he told them in words they would understand.

That night, he lay awake thinking of the concerns that awaited his return. Conrade might be furious at his long absence. Would the orders be filled? There might have been a fire or explosion—what might have happened to them all?

A movement beside him, stealthy and soft, brought his hand to his rifle. Cool fingers rested on his hand, a whisper gentle as the wind in spring reached his ears.

"I beg you—when you go—take me with you."

It was the white squaw. He had never spoken to her. She was jealously guarded by Red Hawk. She kept her

96

sullen self to his cabin much of the time, though she helped in the work as told.

He had noticed her, though, with her sad blue eyes and bent head, her blue-black hair shining in the sunlight. Sometimes she was beaten on the shoulders by Red Hawk's other wife, who was jealous of her. But she never murmured or complained.

He stirred. It would make enemies of his "brothers." But he pitied her. Could he, a white man, leave her to her fate? It would be a sad one. She might be dead before long. She would never adjust to their life. And Red Hawk was a hard man, certainly cruel when crossed.

He recklessly decided, and whispered, "Yes. Be ready at dawn, just before dawn go to the woods behind us. Wait near my horse. Take nothing but your clothing, or they may suspect."

"Thank you—"

The words drifted away; she was gone.

Christophe slept some that night, but before dawn he rose, stretched, and ambled down to the stream. He drank, and then quietly filled a water bottle and tied it in his saddlebags along with his clothes, his sketch pad and pencils, his bullets and powder. He carried his rifle with him. Some Indians stirred; one sat up and watched him until he went back to his blankets and lay down again. His brain was busy with plans.

When the one who had sat up was lying down again and seemed asleep, Christophe crawled slowly to his horse. It was staked near the woods. He saddled it quietly. The girl appeared like a ghost beside him, her eyes wide and fearful.

He swung her up into the saddle, where she sat astride, the short deerskin garment showing her long legs and knees as she fumbled to take the reins. He pointed ahead; she nodded. He walked softly into the woods, to where the other horses were gathered in a crude rope corral.

He cut the rope with his knife and waved a blanket at them; they ran off into the woods, startled. Then he got on his stallion behind the girl, and they started off.

Behind them someone whooped. The Indians had wakened.

The girl shivered in the cold dawn. The November day was crimson in the east; it would soon be light. They crashed through the woods and out to the grassy plain beyond, where Christophe had often hunted with the Indians.

He let the chestnut out. Speed counted now, and the horse was fresh.

Behind them a rifle fired. The distance was too great, but the shot gave sufficient warning of the Indians' intentions. He set his mouth grimly, and they rode even faster. The girl was uncomfortable in the saddle, but she said not a word of complaint.

They stopped once, in the heart of another forest, and he gave her some water from the bottle and a hunk of dried deer meat to chew on. Talk could come later.

He had decided to head straight east. There, there would be settlements, while to the northeast there would be only more mountains and valleys and wild streams and rivers to cross. Fortunately, he knew this country now.

This time he got into the saddle and took the girl up on his knees. He was lean and hard, strong as a young oak, he thought. Amelia had said that once—that he was as strong as an oak.

The girl was of medium height, lean but rounded, tanned from months in the sun. Her long black hair streamed back. She gathered it up, for it bothered his vision, and tied it back with a string of rawhide from her hem. Then they rode on and on.

His great horse moved in giant strides across narrow streams, up onto the far banks, and on. Behind them, two or three Indians were now riding their recovered horses. Christophe caught a glimpse of them twice when he glanced back from a ridge. They pursued the pair grimly, probably driven on by the furious prodding of Red Hawk. And their horses were good—small, sturdy Indian ponies that could run all day.

He dared not sleep that night. He let the girl rest for

two hours, but he believed she did not sleep either. When he put a hand on her shoulder, she got up at once, stiff as she must have been.

They rode more cautiously through the rest of the night, the stars to the east guiding them. No settlements yet, but another day would bring a few scattered ones. If they lived.

He had no illusions about what would happen should they be caught. They coveted his horse, his rifle. Now he had done the unforgivable: stolen his host's wife. The fact that she was a white prisoner would mean nothing to them. She belonged to Red Hawk.

It was evening of the next day when they came to the first white settlement. The girl sagged against his knees. The horse plodded along, his head down. Christophe knew he presented quite a sight, dusty face and all. The girl wore his blanket around her shoulders; she still looked like an Indian till one saw her face.

The settlement was only three cabins. Men came hurrying out, rifles in hand. An older man made them welcome and gave them his cabin, probably concluding they were man and wife. They slept that night for the first time in what seemed like forever, rolled up in blankets before the fire. A woman made porridge for them in the morning, served with homemade sausage and never had it tasted so good.

Christophe picked out a gold coin from where he had hidden some in his hunting garments and bought a smaller horse from one of the settlers. A woman sold him a crude coat for the girl. Thus fortified, they went on. They had a long way to go yet.

Chapter 8

Christophe did not feel safe until four days later when they came to a larger settlement. He had seen no sign of the Indians. No doubt they had turned back by this time.

He took a room in a crude inn for himself and the girl—and only now did he learn that her name was Moira Denis. That night they had a fine dinner in the small dining room—beef and potatoes, greens, and even some pumpkin pie.

As they drank their coffee, he noted the curious looks given them. The men were polite, but they wondered about them.

"I noticed a store in the settlement," he told Moira quietly. "We'll go out first thing tomorrow and get you a dress and some shoes. I wish I had brought more money with me."

She gave him a frank smile and tossed back her blue-black hair. She was happy now, and the sullen look was gone. "I don't care. You have been so gentlemanly to me, Monsieur Vallette. I can make my way now, I'm free!"

He smiled also. "Freedom—it is everything, no?"

"Everything."

Her blue eyes sparkled, and she nodded her head firmly. She had a strong Irish accent. She had not complained one word on the dangerous and exhausting trip they had just completed.

He smoked his pipe outdoors on the little wooden

porch while the girl went up to their room, washed, and went to bed in the crude rush-mattress bed.

He was thoughtful, turning over matters in his mind. The next day, they bought a dress and shoes, and also a comb and mirror, and went on their way.

They stopped about noon to drink water from a fresh stream and to chew on the dried meat he had bought at the store. He lay on his elbow studying the stream, thinking some more as he smoked his pipe.

"Well, Moira Denis," he said lightly, after a time, "tell me of yourself. Will your family wait for you somewhere? Where do you wish to go?"

She sat cross-legged, her dress carefully drawn over her knees. She gazed out at the distant blue, smoky mountains behind them, as though remembering the long days of hopelessness as a prisoner of a haughty Indian chief.

"I got no family, Monsieur Vallette," she said finally. "I'm Irish, I come over here with my pa four years ago. He got the ship fever and died. They tossed him overboard after we said a few prayers." The blue eyes were sad, but she shed no tears. Her lips were set. "When I got in, I found me a job with a family; they had eight children, and was glad of some help. I likes children, and we got along fine."

Her grammar was poor but her voice was low and sweet. She had instinctive good manners, eating her food slowly and chewing politely, with her mouth closed. She washed when she could, and took care of herself, combing her hair with long strokes that made it shiny.

He listened intently as she talked. He had noticed something else about her, and wondered if she would speak of it. But he would let her do this.

"My boss decided to move further west, where he got him some land. Some Injuns come by, Red Hawk, he was with them. He looked at me, and I hid. He come again. Another time he come, they was all off to a barn dance for the day, with me left with the two youngest ones. My, they was sweet chillun, I hope they was all

101

right—after. He carried me off." She stopped with a sigh, her hands clenched at each other.

"We had a long ride back into the mountains. He treated me cruel at first, then when I didn't fight back no more, he was better to me. His first wife, though, she didn't like me one bit. She kept scolding him in Injun, then she'd hit my shoulders. But they fed me and give me clothes to wear."

She had spunk, he thought. She had spirit and gallantry. She did not complain of her lot.

"What will you do now, Moira?" he asked, drawing on his pipe.

"Well, I figure I can git me another job with a family," she said, drawing idly on the sandy ground. She drew a house, with a chimney, with smoke coming out, he noted, before smoothing her palm over the drawing. "I likes being in a family. I only has a few cousins back home in Ireland. And there ain't no point going back, they don't have enough to eat as it is. After ma died of having no food, and my brothers and sisters, they all went, pa and I decided we'd leave. Our landlord was cross 'cause we couldn't pay the rent money no more. But he said he'd pay our way if we'd leave and let him rent to someone who could pay."

It was the same story he had heard from some of his Irish workmen. The situation in Ireland was getting worse. Whenever a potato crop failed—and it seemed to do so more frequently now—they would starve to death or leave Ireland for the new land of America. In Ireland the land belonged to landlords, some of them in England where they cared nothing for the poor Irish, as one of his foremen had told him passionately.

"I've had an idea, Moira," he said casually. "I want you to think about it carefully."

"Yes, sir?"

He had never planned to marry, but this girl touched his heart. Besides, he had saved her, and he felt as though she belonged to him, like a lost puppy he had rescued. Yet she was no puppy, but a girl of sixteen, alone in a strange country.

"You don't want to go back to that other family, do you? The one you worked for?"

She shook her head so firmly that the blue-black hair spun around her slim shoulders. "No, *sir,* it's too close to them Cherokee. They'd find me again, they would."

"Well, Moira, I'd like to take you to my home with me. I have never married, though I am twenty-five. I'd like you to marry me, and help me make a home."

The blue eyes stared at him. "Ye're daft!" she gasped, finally.

He grinned. "I may be, Moira, though I'm not sure what that is. You mean, crazy?"

"I don't mean to be rude, Monsieur Vallette," she said swiftly. "But gentlemen like you, well, you don't marry the likes of me."

"I am a working man, Moira, I'll tell you about that later. For now," and he rose and knocked the ashes out of his pipe, "let's be on our way, and you think about what I asked you."

By her silence on the ride, she must have been thinking hard. She would give him a long, puzzled stare from time to time. They stopped for the night a little early, beside a swiftly running stream. He "tickled" some fish and got a fine catch for summer. Moira deftly slit and cleaned them, padded them with gray clay, and set them in the fire. Then she went out a little distance and returned with some greens for the pot. She had learned much from the Indians, he thought, or perhaps she knew already by experience what was edible and good.

After they had eaten and were lying back contentedly in the firelight, he said, "Have you been thinking over my proposal, Moira?"

"Yes, sir," she said, soberly, the brightness dying on her face. "Reckon I'll have to say no, thank ye kindly."

"Why, Moira?" he asked, placidly. He was used to waiting for what he wanted.

"Well—the truth is, Monsieur Vallette—I'm going to have a baby—he's Red Hawk's."

"Um. Seems to me you need a father for your child,

Moira," said Christophe. So she was honest as well as kind and generous.

"Ye knew?"

"I guessed. You see. I have a—a sister-in-law, and she has two children. If I had realized earlier, I'd never have had you ride so hard. I hope the baby wasn't damaged. You—you don't feel badly, do you?"

She stared at him. "Well, I never—in all my days—I never met anybody—" She choked a little over the words. "Never—did I meet anybody—who'd care that way, how I felt—"

He reached out and patted her slim hand. "Moira, I want to take care of you—and the child. Red Hawk was a fine man, though a tough Indian. His son or daughter will have good blood. And so do you. Let me take care of you both."

She hesitated, her head drooping. "It wouldn't be fair—to you," she whispered. "They—your family— they'd know—they would laugh at you—and me and the baby."

"I don't think so," he said, his mouth hard. "I'll look after that. But that reminds me, I haven't told you about myself. Moira, I'd like to tell you about my life. You called me a gentleman. Well, I'm from France, and I was a farmer—and a chemist, and a book printer, and many things."

She opened her eyes wide. Lounging there, on his elbow, he began to talk to her about his earlier life. She was the best listener he had ever had. Or perhaps he felt like pouring out to this gallant girl what he had never told anyone.

Christophe talked of the early life, of how his father had been imprisoned. How they had worked the printing press. He told about his fine, gentle master, Monsieur Lamartine, who he could only suppose had gone to the guillotine.

"All for being on the wrong side? It's just like Ireland," Moira blurted out fiercely. "Oh, Monsieur Vallette, is there any justice in this cruel world?" Her blue eyes fairly blazed.

"I do not look for justice, Moira," he said bluntly. "I look to myself and my own to protect us. One must fight all the time, be on guard, and pray to God to give us help."

"Oh, that's just the way I feel!" she cried, impulsively. She gave him a wide smile and a firm nod of her head.

He told her of the problems of the Huguenots all through the centuries of troubles in France. How the Vallettes had to pretend to be Catholic in order to remain alive. How the priests themselves had hunted down Huguenots and killed them on the sword or on the rack. Then he began to wonder if he had blundered.

"Are you Catholic, Moira?" he asked, interrupting his story. "I am sorry I offend—"

"No, no—no offense. I was Catholic in Ireland, sure, but much good it did me. The priest came only to bury us," she said bitterly. "It ain't God and Jesus and the Virgin Mary I feel against, but sure I don't feel much for any priests. They helped not a whit. There be some good ones, mayhap, there was one who met the boat, who helped me get a job. But over in Ireland, that did not put food in our mouths, or pay the rent. I watched me mother die, and me baby sisters and brothers—and my God, it was horrible."

He took her slim hand in his and held it gently. "I know, Moira, I know. It is hard to stand by and see one's own hurt and dying. I—I'll tell you about Grégoire."

And so he told her about the death of Grégoire, and tears came to her eyes as he told what he had never related to anyone. He told of his anger at Conrade, as Veronique rode with them, of how the two lost themselves in kisses and caresses, forgetting the recent death of Grégoire. He told how he dug a grave with his sword, and wound the body in the cloak and buried his beloved brother. He told of the long journey to America, and the trials of that journey. When he had finished that part, it was late, the sky was purple-black, and stars prickled the night sky.

105

"There, now, that's enough for tonight," he said. "We'll sleep, and go on tomorrow. I think we shall ride north now, and head for my home, Moira."

She would have protested, but he hushed her gently and rolled in his blanket to sleep. Moira rolled up in a blanket also, near the fire, and gazed at his placidly sleeping face.

This fine gentleman—to want to marry her! She had thought him crazy. Now, after the talk, she could see him more clearly. She had observed him in the camp. He had refused the Indian squaw, but not in a way to insult the girl or her brother. He had gone out hunting and brought home game. He had showed the Indians about powder and bullets, had talked to them as equals, but with any sneers. And he had rescued her, bravely and gallantly.

What kind of man was he? He seemed a knight of one's dreams, she thought, unable to sleep. She had told him about the baby, and he had just said he would take care of them both. Great God, thought Moira, what luck have I stumbled into, after the long years of woe?

She still thought she should go ahead and get a job with a family, bear her child alone, and care for it and herself. She was brave and young, and America held many jobs she could fill. She could manage. But, oh— what if she did not have to struggle by herself?

He was such a fine man, a brilliant man, a hard-working man, who loved his family. Why had he not married before? She puzzled about that. There was some mystery there.

The next day he talked cheerfully about the countryside as they rode north. It would be some days, even a couple of weeks, before they would come to his home. He told her about it, how it lay in a pretty valley in Virginia, along a stream called the Areuse. He told how he wanted to build a house on the hill for her and for his aging mother and father.

"You would not mind that, Moira? To have my parents with us? They are both so gentle and good, but they cannot manage by themselves much longer, and mother should have help. I thought to hire a cook and a maid and butler—"

"Good land," gasped Moira. "Why, I'd be willing to scrub and cook and do for your family meself. Ye'd not need to marry me for that, Monsieur Vallette."

"Don't sell yourself short," he advised her abruptly. "You have quality, Moira."

She chewed on that thought all the day, and liked it. It made her proud and happy that he said she had quality.

They talked more that night. He continued his story, which held her as fascinated as a child with a fairy story. He told her about their times in Boston, how he and Conrade had hunted for a place for a woolen mill. How he and his father had decided to turn to making black powder. As she listened, fascinated, he told her a little about the making of the powder, how he had improved it with chemical experiments.

Sometimes she thought he did not talk so much to her as to himself, explaining to himself what had happened. It seemed to give him a release.

Then finally, one night, he told her about Amelia, a little. He told how he had been practically engaged to her when he went off to study the black powder; and how he had returned to find her engaged to his brother Conrade, whose first wife had died.

And Moira, studying his face in the firelight, knew then why he had asked her to marry him. He still loved Amelia, and would always love her. It made her feel a little sick and lost.

She wrestled all that night and the next day about the problem. Christophe would never love another woman as he loved Amelia. If Moira married him, she would be cared for always, but he would not love her. He could not—he loved Amelia. His face had revealed that clearly. When he spoke her name, of how lovely and ladylike she was, Moira felt a pang of jealousy so deep inside her it hurt.

She still thought and thought. She could help Christophe. She could make a home for him and his parents, whom he obviously adored. She could make him comfortable, she thought. She could housekeep, she would slave and die for him, she thought fiercely. Anything, to help this man who had saved her and was so kind and good.

She finally said that night, "Monsieur Vallette, I have decided."

"Yes, Moira, you will marry me?" He gave her his gentle, understanding smile. "I thought you might, when you saw how I needed you."

She flushed and looked away, but he took her hand and clasped it firmly. "Yes, I will—marry you. And I'll work for you, Monsieur Vallette, and your family, until I die. I swear it."

He raised her tanned fist, and kissed it. She stared at him, amazed. "Thank you, Moira. And now will you please call me by my name, Christophe? I keep looking around for some gentleman named Monsieur when you speak."

They laughed together softly for the first time, and he squeezed her hand.

"I admire your courage and your honesty, Moira," he said, later. "I shall be proud to have you as my wife. I do not want you to think about working hard for me. Though I know you, now, and you will work hard. But be my wife, my companion. I can talk to you as I never talked to anyone in my life."

"Not to anyone?" she asked, thinking of Amelia.

"Not even to Grégoire," he said, his voice low and choked a little. "Perhaps later we could have talked, but we were both shy and young and awkward. But I need you, Moira, to be my friend and companion, as well as my wife. Will you be all this to me?"

"Yes—Christophe—I would be honored," she said, and it was a solemn pledge.

When they reached the next settlement, they found a preacher. Christophe at once asked the date, and was pleased to hear it was the sixth of December. "Hum, sixth," he mused.

Moira looked at him curiously. "What is so good about the sixth?" she asked.

He only laughed and shook his head. "We shall be married on the eighth," he said, with decision.

And so it happened. He arranged with the preacher, and a kind woman and her husband at the inn agreed to be witnesses. They had a small wedding ceremony, and the innkeeper prepared a wedding feast of turkey and ham, potatoes, greens, and a huge mince pie. There were red candles on the table in pewter candleholders, and Christophe seemed especially pleased with these.

Christophe later showed the marriage certificate to Moira. She studied it carefully, proudly. No one had said a word about her obvious pregnancy. "My, that looks nice," she said, of the small piece of parchment.

"You're not looking at the date, my dear," he said, and pointed at the figures: 8-12-1802.

"That's for December eighth," she said, looking up at him with her head to one side. "Isn't it?"

"Oh, yes, my dear. But to anyone else, it says August 12, 1802. Eh? And so your baby will be born legally, to us both. How is that?"

She gasped, and he chuckled with pleasure. She clasped his arm. "Oh, Christophe, how good you are. And how clever."

"Oh, I think I am most clever," he said, with a rueful grin. "I managed to rescue my bride from the Indians, and force her to marry me, and now I shall have a fine son. Eh? And we were married in August, right after I met you, Moira. That is our story," he said more seriously. "I want our son to have a good start in life. You see, I left home in early August. If I met and rescued you early, then we could have married at once. Then we decided to ride about, and enjoy our honeymoon for four months. That is our story, and the only lie in our married life, my dear. All else is true. I met you and wished at once to marry you."

And he dropped a gentle kiss on her forehead.

"Oh, Christophe!" She was overcome. He had managed it all, so she would not be ashamed before his family. "How can I ever repay you?"

"There'll be no talk again of repayment, my dear," he said. "You shall be my wife, and I your husband. We shall, moreover, be friends. I think I am a most fortunate fellow." And indeed he looked very pleased with himself.

"If only I was better educated, or from a good family," she said, in a low tone. "I wish I was better for a wife for you."

He gave her a grin, and there was a mischievous twinkle in his eyes that had not been there for several years, though she did not know it. "My dear, you shall be a very good wife to me. After the baby is born, I shall expect you to be a marvelous wife. Until then, *I* shall take very good care of *you*. But beware—after that. I told you I was hungry for a wife, didn't I?"

"Oh, Christophe!" And she turned a bright, vivid red. He laughed joyously at the bright blue eyes, caught her to him, and kissed her red mouth and her scarlet cheeks. "Oh—my—Christophe—"

Chapter 9

Christophe and Moira arrived home just a week before Christmas, stopping first in a small town some miles away for two days: Christophe was known there, and could obtain credit.

To Moira's amazement and delight, he bought many clothes for her, even a grand bonnet of green with light green ribbons. They hired a carriage and drove home in style, the stallion hitched behind them.

It was cold and chilly, but the sky was a vivid blue the day they came home to the Areuse. Before Christophe could pull up the carriage, his parents were running out, and men ran from the mills to greet them.

Moira felt overwhelmed. Christophe laughed, greeted them, and held his mother in his strong young arms and hugged her.

"Look what I have done, mother. Brought home a wife. You kept nagging at me until I have married a fine wife. Darling, this is my mother; mother, this is Moira."

Sidoine cried and hugged Moira, and Etienne hobbled up to her also. Someone went to fetch Conrade, and he and Amelia drove down at once to greet them.

The foremen from the works came up shyly to be introduced. When the Irishmen learned that the new young Mrs. Vallette was Irish, they were immensely pleased.

"Sure, and ye couldn't ha' chosen a better wife than

an Irish girl," one said impulsively, then looked embarrassed and anxious.

Christophe clapped him on the shoulder. "Sure, and ye're right, and all," he said, in his French accent in an atrocious imitation of the Irish, and they all laughed and were at ease together.

Oh, there had been problems at the mills, and Conrade was ready to pour all his grievances into Christophe's ear. But the first days were merry for all that, and Christophe's Christmas was as happy as he could wish.

Etienne and Sidoine held open house, and the tables were set with the silver candlesticks with red candles in them. Moira was lovely in her crimson dress with her blue eyes shining in the wonder of their welcome. Amelia was grand in her green silk, with the baby in her arms and her lovely face shining at Christophe. Moira looked at her, and then away, and smiled determinedly at Sidoine, who made her so welcome.

There was much talk about the new house. Christophe dug out his plans for the house, and he and his father talked until late at night over them. Moira looked at the plans in wonder. She could not understand the need for such a grand place. When she and Christophe went to pay a call on Amelia and Conrade on New Year's, she comprehended.

The big house was so grand, with white pillars looking over the Areuse shining from a distance. And inside, there was the huge drawing room, with a rosewood piano and a Persian rug on the parquet floor. Amelia showed Moira about very graciously. The children were adorable, coming down politely to greet them, with the maid holding the boy by the hand.

Conrade on that New Year's was full of his troubles, and he pouted like a child, thought Moira. He wanted to go to France this winter, he said over and over. And he had not been able to go more than twice to New York in the past year.

Amelia had not gone with him, evidently. Moira caught the quick understanding glances between Amelia and Christophe, and gazed down at the blue and white fragile china cup in her hand. They drank tea, but it was not like the strong, smoky tea she was used to. It was light and delicate, a green tea all the way from China.

Moira was silent much of the time. She held small Deborah on her lap, and thought of the time when she would have her child. Christophe was determined to have the new house built by then, and her baby would be born in the family bed in a master bedroom. She patted the small baby hands, and bent an attentive ear to the babble of baby talk from the tiny child she held.

"If you would only trust Marc to take care of all the books, I could go to France in the spring," Conrade blurted out angrily. "You have never believed him capable of doing all the work. Well, he is—"

"I will not discuss the matter until I have seen the books," said Christophe, firmly. "And certainly not on New Year's. Let us have a festive time, my brother, and forget our cares."

Amelia hastily changed the conversation, and spoke of a new family that had arrived in the mills, and of the new house they would build for Christophe. She turned to Moira with a gracious smile that yet managed to seem sad. "I hope you will let me help you plan for the house, Moira. I would dearly love to do that."

"Sure, and I'd be glad for any help," said Moira, with reserve.

"I have my ideas on the colors I should like. Moira has only to approve," said Christophe, easily. "Conrade, when you were in New York last, did you speak to the friends you have at the china import house? I should like some fine china like this for Moira. What colors should you like, my dear?"

Conrade brightened up and spoke quickly. "I went over to the warehouse, Christophe; they had a fine new shipment in. Why don't you write at once and ask them to send some samples? If you bespeak some, they will save them for you—use my name!" He forgot his fretfulness, and spoke of other suggestions for them.

Presently Christophe gave Amelia his New Year's gift, a huge box of imported chocolates. She smiled up at him.

"You always remember how fond of them I am, Christophe," she said.

Moira swallowed, and took herself to task for jealousy. Indeed, she was ashamed later, for Conrade came down the hill later in the afternoon and gave gifts to her and to Sidoine. Sidoine received a fine white shawl, which she declared she would wear only on grand occasions, it was so beautiful and delicate. To Moira, Conrade gave a lovely blue velvet cloak.

Moria was amazed, and kept stroking the velvet. "Amelia chose it," Conrade admitted. "She said it would match your eyes. Do you truly like it? She will be so pleased."

"Please thank her for me—she is far too kind—"

"You are our sister," he said, kindly. "The only quarrel we have with you is that you and Christophe denied us the pleasure of being at your wedding."

"Oh, I dared not bring her home unwed," said Christophe, with an edge of irony. "Someone else—such as Marc—might have snatched her from me."

There was an uneasy silence. Sidoine broke it by praising her shawl again, and Moira got up to serve the tea.

Later Sidoine brought up the subject again. "We were so—surprised," she said to Moira, "that you did not wait to come home and be wed. And you but sixteen."

"Christophe insisted," was all Moira could say. She had a feeling his family had been shocked by his haste. Let them think what they would, just so they did not find out the true reason.

Shortly after the new year was ushered in, Christophe had workmen break the hard ground for the new house up on a hill across the Areuse from Conrade's grand mansion. He paced it out himself, in the cold, brisk air, and the first spadeful was turned by Etienne. Tall, spare, his hair quite gray now, he seemed fragile to

114

Moira, and she tried to spare him and Sidoine work when she could.

But Etienne would go up daily to the new house to see how it was coming along. "It shall be as grand as our villa in France," he declared to the women. "We shall have velvet draperies once again, Sidoine, and the finest china. Our Christophe has planned it."

"It is the house of Moira," Sidoine reminded him gently, with a glance at the new bride. "It shall be her choice."

"Oh, maman," said Moira, "I shan't care where we live, so long as—I mean, wherever Christophe wishes," she said with a blush.

Her new parents were delighted with her. And so was Christophe. He had someone he could talk to freely, someone who listened for hours to the plans he poured out.

Only on the iciest, windswept days did Moira stay indoors. Every other day she liked to go for a long walk along the Areuse, usually visiting the new house and watching its progress. And Christophe would accompany her whenever he was not absorbed in his work in the laboratory.

They would talk—how they would talk. He would tell her about his latest project, an attempt to make finer sporting gunpowder. And she would listen. She began to understand as she listened and absorbed what went on. She talked to the Irish wives, and visited them, and asked Christophe what might be done to help when a woman had trouble with a baby or when a husband drank a bit too much on a Saturday night. Amelia came down often to help in the nursery, her own children left with the maid.

On long walks Moira had Christophe to herself, and he would talk on and on about the house, the colors for the rugs, the furnishing of the bedrooms and nursery in the house, of how they would entertain; whether to have a flower garden as well as a vegetable garden. He had hired servants before she knew what he was about. A black couple from town was anxious to start—also a gardener, a maid, and a man for the stables.

Christophe confided in Moira the problems about Marc Clausel. "He is not a hard worker," he said, frowning a little. "I should not hold this against him. However, I have discovered that when Conrade went off to New York, Marc went with him, leaving papa to the books for two weeks at a time. Papa is not strong."

"He is—jealous of you all," said Moira slowly. "Marc feels that you do not trust him, that he would be a full partner if Conrade had his way."

"If he pulled his own weight, I would consider it," said Christophe sharply. "But he does not. He is extravagant, a poor manager. He had four of the men idle for days because he had not ordered enough sulfur. And he will not visit their homes and see to their complaints about roofing. I must do it myself."

"Oh, Christophe, you do too much yourself," she burst out. "You find it hard to let things go and make Marc do things himself. He just waits for you to take on the job."

Christophe stopped and turned toward her, amazed. He asked angrily, "Are you saying that if I had waited—but it could not wait! If the roofs were not fixed, the children would be cold."

She flared up. Her Irish temper sometimes surfaced and she had trouble controlling it. "Christophe, you drive yourself too hard. If the children were cold, it is the fault of the workmen for not reporting the damage to you before winter set in. The roofs were leaking long before the winds and snows came. You take too much on yourself, and expect Marc to do the same. No wonder he is angry."

"That you should take his side!" said Christophe, furiously, and they marched on up the hill, silent.

Moira's will weakened first. As they approached the house, she whispered, "I am sorry, Christophe. You are right, I am wrong. Marc does too little. I am only angry because you wear yourself out trying to do it all."

He turned and put his arm about her. "Oh, Moira, it

is I who should apologize. I neglect you for the sake of my work. I was so late last night—the food was cold, and so you end up working even harder to take care of me."

She rubbed her cheek briefly against his shoulder, more shaken by his embrace than she wanted to admit, even to herself. "It was nothing. What good am I to you, if I don't see that you have hot food in you and take care of yourself?"

They laughed and went on to the house hand in hand, surveying the progress. The walls were up, the roof on. Now the carpenters were carving beautiful doors of native walnut and oak, laying parquet floors of several woods that contrasted beautifully, light and medium and dark. She sighed with delight and wonder at the lovely rosewood staircase rising from the wide front hallway.

"We shall move in within four weeks," declared Christophe that night. "Finished or not, we shall move in."

"But Moira will not want to move in," said Sidoine, "with the workmen under her feet."

"You mean, you don't want the workmen under *your* feet," retorted Christophe with a laugh. "But Moira shall move in. Her baby comes in May, and it shall be born in the house."

They said no more. Moira felt her heart swell with gratitude at her husband. He was so gentle, so considerate. They slept in the same bed, but he had made no gesture toward sex with her. He was sweet with his kisses, his arm about her, anxiously tender and caring. But he did not give in to overwhelming passion, for he felt that making love might damage the baby—he had said so frankly. She wondered how he had acquired this knowledge, then remembered Amelia and the sad look in her eyes when Conrade drank too much.

They did move into the house in April, when the apple and cherry trees were blossoming in pink and white. The willows along the river had fresh, tender, green leaves, and drooped into the blue waters of the Areuse.

The furniture, which had been arriving during the

winter months and which had been set in sheds to be sheltered, was already in place. The workmen set the bright new rugs into place, with the elegant Persian rug in the drawing room. Moira directed the placement of the blue silk sofa and matching armchairs, and of the delicate Queen Anne straight chairs and matching tables against the walls. On them she set the family silver bowl and the candlesticks brought from France.

Amelia came over unexpectedly the second day after they moved in. Carpenters still pounded at the doors, and the kitchens were shut off because the doors were often opened. The bedrooms still lacked curtains, though the draperies had been hung.

"I hope you will not mind, I was so eager to see your home," Amelia said charmingly to Moira. Christophe was down at the mills, as he usually was.

"Oh, I am longing to show you around," said Moira spontaneously. Even though she knew how Christophe felt about Amelia, and guessed that Amelia herself still had some tenderness for Christophe, she could not hate the older woman. She had been kind and gentle, welcoming Moira graciously. And that sad look in her lovely brown eyes would melt the heart of a stone, thought Moira.

Moira showed Amelia about, moving awkwardly with her weight. Amelia soon called a halt. "But I am not being considerate. You are surely expecting your baby soon?"

"Just a few weeks now," said Moira, with a grimace. "Lord, I feel so top-heavy I could fall down."

"Christophe would have my head," said Amelia simply. "He talks of nothing but the house, and of you and the baby. I have never seen him so happy. Nothing must happen." And she urged Moira to sit down in the drawing room and be waited upon.

When Amelia offered to come and help when the baby was born, Moira could not refuse. Amelia smiled at her and took her hand. "I am so sure everything will be right and good for you," she said softly. "You are such a happy creature, and you make Christophe smile

118

and laugh. He has not done so for years, believe me, for all the events of France—he has told you?—they almost broke his heart."

They were able to talk like sisters then, and when Amelia left that day, Moira felt much better about her. Christophe would always be loyal to his wife, and did make him happy—Amelia said so.

The baby was born on a stormy night in May. The days had been pretty and blue-skied, the flowers blooming in the gardens. The spring rain came up and turned into a thunderstorm. And on that night, baby Tristan was born, with no doctor available.

Amelia came over, arriving drenched in a cloak and bonnet. She and Sidoine helped with the birth, throughout the night and into the next day. Christophe paced up and down the lower hallway, gnawing on his lips, rudely refusing all food and drink, though Etienne urged him gently to take some and find some rest.

Frequently he went up the beautiful rosewood staircase without seeing it. All he could see was Moira's whitened, agonized face and the capable hands clenched on the flowered spread.

Finally Amelia called him and he came running up the stairs, two at a time, white and anxious.

Amelia held the baby in her arms, smooth and oiled, and wrapped in a white blanket. "A beautiful boy, just perfect," she said wearily, but with a smile for his anxiety. She opened the flap of the blanket and showed him the face.

Christophe stared down at the baby, not offering to take him. Amelia urged him gently, and finally he accepted the small bundle. The eyes opened and peered out, unseeing. Eyes of blue! The hair damp and glossily black, in tiny peaks. The face white and pink and smooth.

"He looks—just like Moira," he said with immense relief.

"Just like her—and you also," said Amelia gallantly. Christophe drew a deep breath, bent over, and

119

pressed his lips tenderly to the tiny forehead. The little fingers clenched the edge of the blanket, and he kissed those also. Amelia watched him, her brown eyes flickering.

She took back the baby, and he went in to see Moira. The girl was almost asleep, exhausted by her ordeal. She opened her eyes when he took her hand and raised it to his lips. "Oh, Christophe—did you—see him?"

"He is perfect, darling," said Christophe. "He looks just like you." He understood the relief in her eyes, and bent and kissed her cheek. "Go to sleep, love. We'll look after him—I'll take care of him for you, my dearest."

Sidoine was happy to care for the child also. The house began to be a home, lived in, with the demands of the baby its center. Moira recovered, and was soon up and about, directing the house with her usual cheerful composure. Her laughter was pretty to hear, as was her singing to the baby.

"Things go well now," said Sidoine contentedly to Etienne. They spoke in French, as they did to each other, never at ease in English. "Ah, yes, I was fearful about our Christophe, when he did not marry. But Moira—ah, she is the girl for him. So strong, so courageous, with such cheer, and a good housekeeper."

"Oui, she keeps everything in order," said Sidoine. As she was getting older it was pleasant to remain in her bedroom till later in the morning, knowing that Moira was up and about, directing the cook and the maid and the butler, the stable hands, and the gardener. "She has as keen an eye for everything as Christophe himself does."

"A good companion to our son," said Etienne as he puffed happily on his pipe. He too was relieved that Christophe had come home at last. The burden had been heavy on the aging father, for Conrade was more a worry at times than a help. Christophe kept all efficiently moving. The orders came in, the supplies were ready when needed, and the agents did not complain so much.

Christophe was thinking along similar lines, as the

days slipped past, spring turning to summer, then autumn. He came into the master bedroom one night as Moira was giving Tristan his night feeding. Moira gave Christophe a startled look, then a blush came up into her face.

Christophe smiled down at them and took the little fingers gently into his own long, thin fingers. The baby's strong grip closed over his. He never got over the thrill when that happened. This little life clinging to his. How clear and straight the blue gaze now. Tristan knew him, and moved impatiently, hungry as he was, to be done with eating and held in the strong, sure arms of this big man.

Christophe sat down opposite them in order to watch the pretty sight. Moira was sitting in a rocking chair in an orange robe, with her long, blue-black hair twisted into a braid down to her waist. The open robe revealed the breast at which her son fed so heartily, with sucking sounds that made them smile. Her breast was round and full of milk.

"He seems hungry as usual," remarked Christophe.

"I cannot feed him enough. I have started giving him porridge," Moira answered, her head bent over the child.

"He grows rapidly. And he is a healthy child—the doctor remarked on how strong and sturdy he is. Is it safe for you to go to the homes of the working wives as you did today?" he shot out unexpectedly.

"Safe? What do you mean?"

"Safe for yourself and the child," he answered. "Conrade said you were down there today. Did you know there has been illness? Fever?"

She compressed her mouth, and her eyes sparkled with anger. "And the poor Irish can't be clean and healthy?" she snapped.

"You know I don't mean—"

"They can be as clean as anyone—if they have plenty of soap and water. That doctor should be shot. He stayed outside and made the women come to him."

"I have spoken to him about it," Christophe said

121

gravely. "If he cannot treat them well, I shall have another doctor in."

"He sneers at them, he looks down on them," she said. "Well, they are as good workers as him any day, for all they can't read and write."

"Now, Moira, you know I am as concerned as you are. And I am concerned that you and the boy shall remain healthy. Do not, I beg you, go down again until the fevers are cleared up. I have hired two nurses to help, and they shall do all required. I will see to it myself."

Her anger died as quickly as it had risen. "I am sorry, Christophe," she said meekly. "You know best. I was angry at the reports. But I shouldn't kick you for it—"

He smiled at her, bent over, and kissed the white breast at which the boy fed more and more sleepily. She flushed at his touch.

Tristan yawned and let the nipple go. He closed his eyes, and the grip on his father's hand relaxed.

"I'll put him in the cradle," murmured Christophe, and reached over to take up the drowsy child. As tenderly as his mother could have done it, Christophe laid the child down, covered him, and caressed his cheek lightly with his fingers. He remained at the cradle for some minutes, thoughtfully.

Then he turned back to his wife. Fastening up the robe at her throat, she did not meet his look. He felt a greater desire for her than ever. He had sternly suppressed that desire since he had married her. She must be allowed to have the child in peace and recover from the ordeal of her capitvity and the birth of the child. But it had been more than four months since Tristan had been born.

He went over to her where she sat in the rocker. He had slept in the larger dressing room since they had moved in, for her greater comfort. But now he longed for his wife, and was not in a mood to wait much longer.

She rocked uneasily. He put his hand on her cheek. "Moira, are you content?"

"Aye," she said simply. "More than that, Christophe. You have been most generous to me.

"Are you happy, then?"

"Oh, aye, I am," she said.

He smiled slightly. "I am not, Moira."

Distressed, she looked up at him. "You are not?" She seemed to pale, and looked apprehensive. "Oh, Christophe, what is it?"

"I want you to be my wife—completely," he told her deliberately.

Her cheeks flushed, and her blue eyes widened, seeming to fill her face. Her hair curled about her face, the long braid tossed back from her shoulder. She seemed so young, yet so womanly, so lovely, yet shy. He held out his hands to her. She put her hands in his and let him draw her to her feet. He took her gently into his arms.

His kiss was gentle and tentative, full on her red mouth. Her hands closed over his hard, lean shoulders, as he kissed her again and again. She opened her mouth hungrily to his lips, and he ran his tongue over her lips, then put it softly into her mouth. She gasped, her eyes huge. His hand pressed down over her back to her rounded hips. She was softer and even more feminine since the birth of the child, rounded, smooth, desirable.

He drew her to the wide bed in which she had slept alone for months. He took off her robe, and she slipped under the covers, wearing only the plain white cotton nightdress with sleeves to her wrists. He leaned over, blew out the lamp, and slid into bed beside her, turning to her at once.

He had thought about this for a long time. He wanted her to forget the cruel, bitter experiences with the Indian who had taken her girlhood so cruelly from her. He wanted her to know what it was to be loved and adored.

He drew off the nightdress and flung it across the

123

bed. He took off his own robe, and together they lay under the covers, exploring each other tentatively with their hands. He was delighted to find that while she was shy, she was not coy with him. When he showed that a caress pleased him, she repeated it, and soon he flamed with desire for her. Still, he waited for her to be ready.

He kissed the smooth cheeks, the red, fragrant mouth, the blue-black hair he had unbound from its tight braiding. He moved his hands over her silken shoulders, down her arms, to her hands, and over to her waist. Then he touched her breasts, full and warm and lovely. He cupped them with his fingers and kissed them where the baby had drunk. She was even softer and sweeter than he had imagined in his dreaming.

He kissed her for a long time, down her slim, sleek rounded body, to the thighs, all over her, until he felt her with his hands and knew she was ready for him. Her fingers gripped his head, stroked over his sinewy shoulders, down to his back, and below. He moved over her, and very slowly, deliberately, he drew them together.

It was hard to keep his head, to remember her inexperience in the seductive art of love. He tried hard, but with her body under his, the thighs parted, her softness melting to him, he finally forgot to slow down. Faster and faster he moved, until he was sobbing for breath and found the release he had desired for so long.

Limp, he lay on her, then rolled off, still holding her to him. Drums pounded in his ears; he was drowsy with satisfaction. Yet he was anxious for her sake.

"Was I too hard on you, Moira? God, you are so sweet—"

"Oh, Christophe," her voice came so low, he could scarcely hear her. "Can it be—like that—then?"

"Better than that, love. Oh, much better," he assured her.

"Then I'll believe in heaven once again," she said, and her arms drew his head to her breast.

Chapter 10

Conrade determined to return to France. Amelia refused, at first gently, then more adamantly, to accompany him.

They quarreled over it openly, to the distress of Sidoine and the others. On an October evening, the family had gathered in the drawing room of Christophe's new home. Moira had served coffee in the beautiful new blue and white china with the gold rims.

Conrade turned to his wife and demanded that she come with him. He was due to sail in two weeks from New York. Pale and quiet, Amelia said gently, "No, Conrade, I shall not go."

"You are my wife! You shall go! I have heard from my friends that I shall have a grand welcome, and much work awaits me. How dare you refuse me?"

She looked at him with her sad brown eyes and twisted her hands in her lap, a nervous gesture unusual for the composed lady. Moira drew a deep breath and looked toward Christophe.

He was looking very thoughtful. Etienne finally said, "I do not see why you do not go, my daughter."

It was unusual for him to rebuke Amelia. He loved her deeply and respected her for her care of Conrade and the two children. She bent her glossy dark head, as though his words bit deeply.

Christophe was on the verge of saying something rash. Moira jumped in quickly, setting down her cup with a little bang.

"There now, I can see why not," she said firmly. "Why should she pick up and with the children and all, and set out, when it isn't sure what is there for her? No house to move into, not sure of her welcome there. Let Conrade go first, and find out the true situation."

Amelia looked at her gratefully. Christophe nodded at Moira, pleased.

"Moira is right," Christophe said as calmly as he could. "Conrade has only the word of some enthusiastic friends. The situation might be more dubious than they imagine. When we left, it was under a cloud. It would be best for him to venture alone, and see how matters lie."

"But I want my wife with me," pouted Conrade, tapping his big boot angrily on the blue Persian carpet.

"Sure, now, it's a job to move a wife and two children, the servants and all," said Moira, in her practical manner. "Why not wait a few months? If all goes well, you can send for her."

"I shall not leave America," whispered Amelia. Moira shot her a warning look as Conrade exploded.

"Not leave America? You shall go where your husband goes!" he raged. "If I go to Africa, you shall go there."

Amelia seemed on the verge of tears. So Moira got her off by herself in the bedroom upstairs.

"Now, Amelia," she said earnestly. "Don't say your shall-nots to Conrade, it makes him madder than a bull. You bide here, and let him find out the situation. I don't trust that Mr. Napoleon. He fair turns my blood cold, he does. But you just keep saying that Conrade shall go first and see what happens. Stick to your guns, girl. Christophe shall persuade him to go by himself, never you fear."

"Oh, Moira, you are so good to me. I am afraid to go—afraid—away off there in France, away from— from everyone—" Amelia put her thin hands to her face and stood quite still. Moira patted her shoulder awkwardly, and was stunned when Moira turned to her and held her tightly.

"There, now, don't you fret," Moira soothed, closing her sturdy arms about Amelia, shocked at the girl's frailty. "Christophe will take care of it all, you know he will. You stick to your story, let Conrade find out what is there, and prepare a house for you first. I warrant he'll be back by spring, full of some other big plan, with France forgotten entirely. Who wants to go back to France to live? Pooh, nothing is like America, it's a grand place, it is, and you don't have to grease nobody's palm to start a business and all."

Amelia laughed through her tears. Moira wiped the woman's eyes gently and urged her to see Tristan now, to see how he had grown since the last week.

Moira had a word for Sidoine's ear, and Sidoine spoke to Etienne. Then Christophe said some calm things to Conrade, and finally, grumbling, Conrade set off alone to France.

He wrote back enthusiastically. The sea voyage had been smooth, he had wished for Amelia more times than he could name. He had been greeted like a long-lost friend. The old times were done, everyone could see it. Madame Lamartine had received his call; she was old and frail, but everyone respected her, and her sitting room was full of callers.

Other news followed, some not so good. He had gone to the family villa. It had been burned down in their absence. Peasants tilled some of the fields with vegetables. The vines were trampled to dust. He was not welcome in that village. Monsieur Le Clerc had turned very peculiar—was ill in the head, everyone said. Conrade, seeing no point in settling there, had returned to Paris. He was staying in a town house with a friend and his wife. They had been most gracious.

A later letter spoke of his new acquaintances. He could start over as a diplomat. He was welcome in the highest political circles. He met Napoleon, and was impressed with him, "a brilliant mind, a commanding soul," wrote Conrade. He was looking for a town house for himself and Amelia, but the best ones were taken.

Meantime, in the little working village along the Areuse, things went along rather smoothly. Christophe worked long days and sometimes into the night in his study. But when he came out, there was Moira with hot coffee and food, and sympathy for him. There was young Tristan holding out his arms imperiously for the tall, gentle man to hold him. Etienne was not well—that was their one big worry. Sometimes he remained in bed in the mornings and went down to the office only in the afternoon.

Sidoine worried over him, and spent more of her time with her husband. They sat in their warmed bedroom, or in the beautiful drawing room overlooking the Areuse, and talked of the old days.

Amelia came over sometimes, bringing her children to play while she talked of practical matters with Moira. Together they would leave the children to Sidoine and the servants and go down to the village to see to the needs of the women and families there.

They had started a little hospital. A male nurse was installed, who seemed well trained and capable. He had served in the navy, and was aquainted with many types of injuries. When one man was hurt in an explosion and lost his eye, the man handled the situation well and saved his life.

Moira and Amelia found more and more in common. Moira's guess about Amelia proved true: she was expecting a child in May. It was one of the reasons she had not wished to travel.

"Of course not, we shall look out for you here. Imagine traipsing all over the world while you're expecting a baby," said Moira, vigorously. "Why don't you write of this to Conrade?"

Amelia was unexpectedly stubborn, her chin set. "I shan't draw him back. He would blame me, should he find good expectations in France for his career. No, let us wait and see how well matters thrive for him. Please, do not tell him of this."

Moira promised, and so did Christophe, looking

throughtfully and compassionately at Amelia. "If this is the way you wish it, Amelia," he said to her gently.

She nodded her smooth brown head. "Yes, Christophe, I shall not request him to come home. Pray, do not reveal my condition to him. Will you warn Mr. Clausel?"

"Oui, I shall do that." And Christophe frowned, thinking of the brash young man in his finance offices. He was keeping a close watch over Marc Clausel, and over the bookkeeping, sometimes returning to the office at night and going over the books.

He had always left the books to his father and Conrade. He was not well versed in accounting. Yet he was becoming suspicious of sums that had been disappearing. How could they? He went over and over the accounts, the sums paid out and sums received. Surely Marc Clausel was not double-dealing with them. He had seemed honest, though he was frivolous and given to drinking with lighthearted companions at nights and on Sundays.

Christmas was joyous, with three small children to care for; the children's eyes gazing at the lights on the tables, staring uncomprehendingly at the brightly wrapped presents, delighting in the little cakes and special puddings, made them all merry. When whole families from the working village came up to sing them Noel, Kendall and Deborah fairly danced at the windows.

The holiday weather was icy and cold. When Amelia first came over with the two children, Moira urged her to remain for the entire holiday. She finally consented when Christophe added his kindly urging.

"You don't want to go about in the carriage. The horses are slipping on the roads now, and what will it be like if all this freezes over?" he said gently to her.

"But your home will be so crowded—" she demurred.

"Nonsense," said Moira. "We are all family, and how nice it is to be with a big family again. In Ireland, we was all starving, and Christmas was nothing at all. This seems like heaven to me."

Amelia clasped Moira's hand and agreed to remain. And indeed, she was no trouble, nor were her children. She brought her maid over with her, and the maid helped out willingly in the house.

Moira spoke seriously to Christophe that week. "I think Amelia should remain with us until the baby comes, Christophe. She ain't well, I'm thinking. She mopes about and doesn't eat proper. I'll see to her quiet-like, not bothering her. And she can talk to me, I think."

Christophe took her in his arms and pressed his face to her thick, dark hair. "You are the best wife in the world, Moira, and the kindest soul."

"I want everybody to be happy," said Moira simply. "And she worries about the house and all. Sure, the servants can keep it up while she's gone, and we'll poke our heads in sometimes. No need for her to fret and fume, when she should be saving her strength."

That night, lying in Christophe's arms, and listening to his quiet breathing, she thought she was as happy as anyone could be. He did love her, though his first love had gone to Amelia. He held her strongly, and made love to her so sweetly it almost made her cry with joy. She wanted a baby for him, all his own, and one day she would have one for him, she vowed. He adored Tristan; no one could guess the child was not his own. He fussed over the boy, and held him, and kissed him.

How fortunate the child looked like Moira, and not like his Indian father. What nature would he have? Moira often wondered and worried. The Indian had been haughty and proud, arrogant and willful. His own men were afraid of his moods. Would Tristan grow up like that?

She forced her thoughts from that. She would think only of the present and the future, not the past. She lay under Christophe's arm, her hand on his shoulder, loving his gentle strength. He was so decent a man, she thought. She had helped wipe out the lines of strain

130

from his face; he laughed more often—even Sidoine said that. She would see that he ate properly and slept right and was relieved of all worries about the family. She was young and sturdy, she could take care of them all, and not feel it. How lucky she was to have such a husband.

Amelia came to her on New Year's. The presents and thank-yous had been exchanged, the hearty meal cooked and eaten—the turkey had disappeared, as well as the goose and mince and pumpkin pies.

"My dear Moira, Christophe has told me of your generous offer, to have me stay here until the baby—oh, I cannot do that, but you are so very good to offer." And Amelia kissed Moira on the cheek, her own face a little flushed.

"And why not? Why should you be over the river and up on the hill by yourself, when you could be here with us?"

"Oh, Moira," Amelia laughed a little, helplessly, her eyes wistful. "You are sorry for me because Conrade is away. But indeed, I can manage."

"Sure you can, you're good at housekeeping. But with the baby coming, you don't want to take chances. And I know you, you'll be after keeping the house scrubbed and the curtains washed and all. And putting yourself out to look out for the garden in the spring. No, you're better off with us, Amelia, and welcome you are."

"You are good to me, but I cannot accept. This is your house, and you have so much to do—"

Moira had been thinking much about this. Now she interrupted her sister-in-law brusquely. "And you could do me a big favor, if you've the time and are inclined."

"I could?" The listless eyes brightened. "What can I do? You're twice the housekeeper I am, and you manage the children with no trouble. What can I do?"

"Well, it's a problem to me—you know, I can't talk right. And I want Christophe to be proud of me. He invites these here big men on business, and I talk like

131

a—a stupid Irish girl. I want to learn to talk proper, like you do—though I'd never be the lady you are."

"Oh, Moira, don't say that. You are—you are just the right wife for Christophe, he says so." And now a light flashed in Amelia's brown eyes, and she turned slightly away.

Moira repressed her own feelings, and said lightly, "I would feel a heap better if I could talk right. Could you learn me what to say, Amelia? Maybe talk to me and correct my English?"

Amelia bit her lip. "I—could, Moira, if you're sure you want—"

"I am sure. I've tried to learn myself to read and write, but I can't much. Can't even read them papers Christophe brings home from the city. I see the headlines and don't know what they mean."

"If you really want to—I didn't realize you did not know how to read—oh, Moira, I'll be glad to do it!"

So it was settled. Each morning when the work was finished for a time, Moira and Amelia settled down in the drawing room with papers and books. Amelia was a gentle yet firm teacher, and soon Moira learned how to express herself. Reading was more difficult. She plugged away at it, however, determined to learn how to read and write. Christophe looked on gravely, but finally approved.

"Are you sure you want to work so hard, Moira?" Christophe said to her after a week of lessons. "Females don't have to learn how to read and write. And you work hard all the day."

"That ain't brain work," said Moira. "I mean—that—is—not—brain—work." She breathed heavily as she said it. "I don't want your sons to be ashamed of me, Christophe!"

He grinned, unexpectedly. "So—sons? You mean to give me another boy, do you? That is good news. How soon?"

"Oh—Christophe." And her face turned scarlet as he kissed and teased her gently.

The letters from Conrade now came less frequently. Amelia watched for the ship post, and was sad for days when nothing came. Christophe bit his lip in her presence, but exploded angrily to Moira.

"If I know Conrade, he is involved with another woman by this time. He has no conscience, no constancy. By God, wait until he comes, I shall give him the edge of my tongue."

"Do you think he would truly spend time with another—but yes, I suppose so. He does not have your compassion for women, Christophe. He thinks nothing of hurting a woman, so long as he is pleased himself. That is where you differ so much."

Conrade was having a rather cool time of it in France, though he would never write home about it. Christophe's surmise had been correct. Conrade had found himself in love with a beautiful, worldly Frenchwoman. However, she was as cold-blooded as she was lovely, and he found himself in debt over her. She asked for diamonds and gold as proof of his love.

He found himself longing more and more for gentle Amelia, who asked for so little and gave so much. He was homesick, he admitted to himself, as the winter wore on and promises of positions as a diplomat turned to ashes.

He was shrewd also, with Vallette intelligence, and saw that Napoleon was constant to no one but himself. His favorites changed with the wind. The court was expensive; appearances were dearly bought. The money Conrade had brought with him was practically gone. And when he tentatively asked some of his new friends for a loan, their excuses were matched only by their coolness to him.

Rumor came also to his ears that Napoleon was short of funds, and that was the reason he had sold a vast portion of land—the Louisiana territory—to America the previous year. In December 1803, the United States took formal possession of Louisiana at New Orleans.

Napoleon needed funds for war, to pay for troops.

133

And he had sold the land, which meant more land was open to settlement in America. More opportunities there. And France seemed old, tired, a former *grande dame* with lined, rouged cheeks, whereas America was as fresh, as young—as Amelia.

He decided to go home that summer. He was surprised at himself thinking of America as home. However, as soon as he announced his intentions, certain feelers were put out. Would Monsieur Conrade Vallette be interested in a position of high regard in the government? Would Monsieur Vallette come to see the Chief of Police? Would Monsieur Vallette be satisfied with a modest salary until he had proved himself by obtaining certain—ahem—information?

He took the next ship home, fuming to himself as he paced the deck. That they thought he would be interested in a position as a spy against his adopted country! He was sick about it, and the hot July days were spent in an agony of remorse that he had even considered living again in France. He had left his beloved Amelia— he had heard little from her, and her letters had been reserved and wounded.

He thought more and more longingly of his wife, his home, his children. As soon as he disembarked he eagerly purchased a new carriage and horses to take him home, and arrived unheralded in early August of 1804. He found an unlighted house, with the servants playing games in the back. He roused them angrily, and one told him that Madame now lived in the home of Christophe Vallette. Conrade was furious.

"Behind my back," he fumed, racing the tired horses back across the river. "She moved in with Christophe. How dare she. Has she no regard for me, for my reputation!"

The butler met him at the door. Conrade went into the warm, lighted rooms and found his wife with Moira in the drawing room. And Amelia held a small baby on her knee. At the sight, Conrade lost his anger.

"Amelia—my love—what is—what is this?" he stammered, overcome with emotion.

Amelia had tears in her eyes. Moira had flown to greet him, then dropped back. Amelia did not rise, burdened as she was by the small child. "Conrade—I can scarcely believe—it is you!" Amelia cried.

Tactfully, Moira left the room. Conrade dropped to his knees beside his wife. His strong emotional nature was rent.

"My love—you have had a child and told me nothing?" He drew back the light blanket about the baby, and stared down at the small handsome boy. "A boy—a son—and you said nothing. When was it?—When?"

"In April, Conrade. Oh, my dear, you look so weary!" Her gentle hands caressed his scratchy face. He kissed her palm, then laughed ruefully.

"And I have not shaved! What a fright I must appear. Did you know before I left—what this—"

"I was afraid to travel," she said simply. "I might have lost the child. But I did not want to hold you back."

He kissed her hands again and again, then rising he sat beside her to hold her and the child within his arms. He was overcome with feelings. She had endured all this, not sending for him.

"My dear, why did you not tell me? How wicked of you, my love—no, not wicked, but very very wrong. To spare me so—I should not have gone to France had I known."

He thought of the greedy woman he had lived with that winter and flinched at the memory. How different was his Amelia, and how beautiful she was in the lamplight, her face soft and welcoming, her brown eyes glowing with his unexpected coming. He kissed her cheek and her hands again.

"Never, never again, keep such a thing from me. That you endured the childbirth alone, without me—oh, my darling—"

"You must not blame yourself, Conrade. I wished you to find out what you could of the life in France. Did you—did you find it to your satisfaction?" Anxious eyes studied his face.

He shook his head decisively. "No, it is different—but still as corrupt as before," he said firmly. "I could not endure it. Would you believe—you must not repeat this—but they wished me to spy on our country. Our America! The brazen idiots."

"Oh, no!" She turned pale at the thought. "You would not—"

"Of course not. Never. This is my country, and yours. We have begun a fine life here, this is the place for us."

Christophe hesitated in the doorway. Conrade rose to greet him. The brothers clasped each other, arms hard, hands patting each other on the back. "My brother, how I longed to see you," sighed Conrade. "I have such stories for you."

Christophe's hand pushed up the spectacles over his eyes to his forehead, and he beamed wearily at Conrade. He had obviously been working in the study. Moira hovered behind them.

"I imagine that you have, brother. But first, have you admired your new son?"

"Yes, and scolded Amelia for not sending for me. And you, Christophe, I blame you—no, I will not blame you. You and Moira have obviously cared for my darling wife and children. How I thank you."

Sidoine came down the stairs, to be greeted and hugged and kissed. Moira went to see about dinner and to make sure the carriage was unpacked of Conrade's possessions.

Conrade reveled in their spoiling, in the close attention they paid to his stories of life in Paris. He enjoyed holding his new child in his arms, hugging the other two who had grown—he told them—quite beyond recognition.

He remained at Christophe's house for two days, resting, then moved himself and Amelia and the children back to their own home. There was no more talk of moving to France—that was finished, he told them. France was not for him—or for them. The people were corrupt, venal, always thinking of bribes and instant wealth and spying. He quite convinced himself as well as the others that he could never be happy in such a country.

He and Christophe finally had a long talk, walking beside the river on a warm August day, where they could be overheard by no one.

"I am unhappy to report the unsatisfactory behavior of Marc Clausel," Christophe told him formally. "I know you are fond of him. But he has left the work many times to go off about his travels. He drinks heavily, and gambles away the money he earns. His father is weary of him, and scolds him often, but he will not change. I wish to let him go."

Conrade thought about it. "But Marc Clausel and his father were immensely good to us," he said, without heat. "Remember how good they were to maman, driving her north, taking such care of her. I know that Marc does not have the best business head in the world, and he has his vices—who among us does not? But as the eldest son I will do everything in my power to prevent you from letting him go. Think of it—how papa would have to work."

Christophe finally decided to let the subject go. Instead, he finally tackled the problem by hiring another bookkeeper, a man he trusted, and set him under Marc Clausel, with the excuse that the business had grown so large that they needed two accountants. He told the new man, quietly, to take careful notice of what went on, and the man was in fact quite keen. He watched what Marc did, went over the accounts with him, and at nights and on weekends he and Christophe went over and over the books. Christophe felt they were being cheated, but he would have evidence in hand before acting.

And so the autumn came, the leaves drifting down to tumble over the little waterfalls of the Areuse, making crimson and yellow patterns in the water. Moira often walked along the Areuse with the children, striding along with her brisk walk.

Christophe would come out when he saw her walking

toward his office. Sometimes he frowned, unconsciously, as she paused to converse in Gaelic with a workman, or to laugh with one of the women. She was no lady, like Amelia, with her chin high and her grace so indescribable. Moira was an Irish woman, all cheerfulness and exuberance, all warmth and generoisty. She was a good wife.

Christophe would step out then, and take Moira by the arm, or pick up one of the children who had grown weary and carry him along. They would talk briskly about the mills and the families. Moira would make him laugh with her quick wit, or make him think more deeply with her compassion for them. She made the day light, he thought.

The Areuse flowed along, serenely, except for the little bubbling waterfalls which furnished the power for the powder mills. And the orders came in, more and more. There was talk of renewed war with Britain, but that seemed remote. Surely they would not go to war again—the Revolution had settled all that.

They made black powder for sporting rifles and guns, for blasting out the new canals and the coal mines of Pennsylvania. Business grew, and the wagon trains of black powder kegs went out from the small Areuse valley to the trails of Pennsylvania, down into Tennessee and Georgia, and to New Orleans. The country was growing fast, and the powder gouged out roads and turned the course of rivers, and aided in a thousand ways as the pioneers turned their faces to the West.

Chapter 11

Etienne Vallette said that that Christmas was the merriest and best he had ever enjoyed. He sat in a deep armchair, the new baby, Reginald, on his lap, and watched them all with a glow that brought red flushes to his thin cheeks.

Moira bustled about, busy as ever—plump as a pigeon, thought Etienne, bubbling with joy that she was to have another child. She wore her apricot chiffon dress proudly. Amelia had helped her choose it. Etienne's thoughtful look went to her other son, Tristan. Was it his imagination, or was there almost no Vallette in him at all?

The boy was sturdy and tall, given to frowning and imperious demands which only Moira's patience could meet. And he was as dark as an Indian, even long after playing outdoors all summer. There was a bronze cast to his face, and his high cheekbones—Etienne sighed. There was some mystery here. Conrade teased Tristan and called him "the wild one," to Christophe's strange fury.

The silver bowl sat in the center of the rosewood table, filled with beautiful roses that Christophe had sent for from the South. The silver candlesticks, polished to a high gloss, stood beside the bowl. Etienne's gaze lingered on them wistfully—all that remained of their previous life in France.

He and Conrade had talked long hours since the latter's return. Conrade had told him wild stories of the corruption in the government, of the bribes given and received, of the police and their methods, and of the political prisoners who disappeared and were never heard of again.

Yes, there was much to be said for America. Here, the Vallettes could be free to work and their families could grow in peace.

Thin sounds of children's singing rose on the air. Etienne stood up slowly, awkwardly, and carried Reginald to the window, to look out as the men and children sang their Noels on the veranda. The others gathered around, sturdy Kendall holding Deborah by the hand, Tristan jumping up and down in impatience to go outdoors also, Moira holding him back with a gentle word.

Christophe picked up Tristan so he too could see outside, patting him soothingly. Tristan put his head down on Christophe's shoulder, his sturdy arms about his father's neck. How weary Christophe seemed, he worked such long hours. But there was peace on his face, and a smile in his eyes for Moira as she gathered up the baskets of apples and oranges to give to the children.

Conrade and Amelia had come over for the day and evening with the children. Conrade had grown plumper, and now resembled a prosperous merchant, thought Etienne, dispassionately. He wore a gray silk suit, and the waistcoat scarely fastened over his plump belly. He drank too much, and his face was reddened by more than the cold winds.

Amelia was as slim as ever, beautiful and graceful, in a green and gold silk gown, a white lace bertha about her white neck. Was she more frail? Or did she just look so next to the stout Conrade? She took the sleepy Deborah in her arms, and rocked her, a smile on her soft red mouth.

Logs burned in the immense gray stone fireplace, and the fire crackled high. After the carolers had been thanked and had gone away singing, Moira had the thick, rich cake decorated with chocolate and nuts. Wine in bright crystal glasses was served by the butler. The children had their fruit juice and sweets. Tristan snatched a sweet from Deborah and was scolded firmly by Moira.

Tristan scowled at his mother and then looked at Deborah's puckered lips. His brow cleared, he marched over to the small girl and poured a handful of sweets into her blue starched lap. "There, Deborah, that's for you—from me," he said arrogantly.

She stared at him, then smiled, and began eating one of the strawberry-shaped candies daintily. "And you tan have one too, Trist," she lisped. He graciously accepted one. Moira shook her head and laughed.

Amelia sat down at the rosewood piano and played softly the carols the children had been singing. Kendall came over, knelt down at her knee, and attempted to sing the songs to her soft prompting.

Tristan was so big for his less than two years, and Deborah so small for three, that they were much of a size. She was so dainty, he so sturdy and Indian-dark; they made quite a contrast.

Etienne looked at them again and shook his head. He did not know what to think of it. And his old brain seemed to fail him at times. Sometimes he called Christophe "Grégoire" by mistake and was unaware of it. Sidoine sat down beside him and filled his glass of wine.

"What a beautiful Christmas, my dearest," she murmured happily.

"The loveliest in the world, with our family all about us." He patted her slender, blue-veined hand. "With the best wife in the world, the finest sons, and all our grandchildren. I have never been so happy."

"And I," she said, clasping his thin hand with her strong one.

"Shall we be so happy and contented when we are their age, Moira?" Christophe murmured teasingly to his wife.

"If God is willing," she said, drawing a deep breath of content. At least she was going to give Christophe a child of his own. God knew, he was good to Tristan, but between them lay the secret knowledge of his birth. They had already spoken tentatively to each other of

141

whether they would ever tell Tristan of it. Christophe was against it, Moira was not sure.

Tristan interrupted the happy mood by snatching a toy from the older and larger Kendall. Conrade grew angry. He bent down and snatched up Tristan, surprised and resentful, and thrust him at Christophe, who rose quickly to take the boy.

"Here, take your wild one. He's going to knock them all over. I dread to think what he will be like when he is older."

Amelia gazed in apprehension from the piano, her fingers poised on the keys. Moira had turned pale.

Christophe blazed at his brother. "Keep your tongue in your head. My son is strong and fine, generous and good. I will not have you speak of him like this. I have warned you."

"My sons, my sons!" warned Sidoine, her voice trembling. "I beg of you—do not quarrel on this holy day."

"The children are tired, and fussing," said Amelia, rising from the piano bench. "Let us take them up to bed, Moira. It is past eight o'clock."

Conrade scowled after them, not offering to help. As Christophe carried Tristan up, he heard the boy mutter into his neck as he held him close. "Why does Uncle Conrade call me wild, papa?"

Christophe tried to compose himself. His fury must be contained, he told himself. He said firmly, "He is wrong to say so, you are a good and fine boy, my own son. Come, let me undress you for bed. You must be tired. Did you not have a fine time today, Tristan?"

Christophe washed the boy's sticky fingers and face, undressed him, tucked him into his bed, kissed him tenderly, and blessed him. "Now, you will say your prayers."

"Don't want to go to sleep," said Tristan.

Moira rustled in. "Now, Tristan, don't be a naughty boy. Say your prayers, and thank God for your good father, and your wonderful granny and grandpa, and all your cousins."

Under her firm eye, Tristan mumbled a quick prayer and subsided. Christophe went on downstairs, thoughtfully, while Moira went to see that Amelia had her children settled. She helped with the little girl, like a small doll in her long white nightgown and blue eyes, and her fluffy hair about her delicate face.

"Do you wish for a girl, Moira?" smiled Amelia, as they went downstairs again.

"Laws, I don't know, Amelia. I want a boy for Christophe, but your Deborah is so sweet—maybe both," she said, with a laugh.

"Just so he is healthy and well," said Amelia. "That is what I pray for. You must let me help when the child comes. You have done so much for me."

"And you for me," smiled Moira, squeezing her arm. "I talk much better now!"

"You have always been so generous," murmured Amelia.

In their bedroom that night, Conrade frowned while undressing. "You know, Amelia, I think it is strange about the boy, Tristan. He doesn't act a bit like Christophe."

Amelia did not pause in brushing her long, brown hair with firm strokes. Her face was in shadow, and her lashes covered her sad brown eyes.

"He resembles Moira," she said. "I have always thought so. He has her eyes, and her ways."

"Wild ways," grumbled Conrade, fighting his stocking until he released it and drew a sigh of relief. "She is as tough as old boots, I think. That child doesn't look like a Vallette!"

"Conrade, it is wrong to speculate about your brother's family like this," said Amelia, a break in her voice. "He has been so good to us all, a strength to the family—"

"I am the eldest," cried Conrade, turning around in surprise. "I am amazed at you—I am the eldest, and the head of the mills. You know how much papa leans on me."

She sighed. "Yes, of course he does, dearest. But

143

Christophe does all his share. You—you have always said so—"

"You think more of him than of me," he accused, flushed with wine. "I wondered that you spent the winter with him while I was gone. Marc Clausel told me how people talked of that—"

Amelia went white. It was not the first time Conrade had said this. With quiet dignity, she reminded him, "I was with child, and not well. Moira took me in, and treated me like a sister. I am surprised you have listened to the gossip. It is not like your generous nature, Conrade."

Conrade scowled and grumbled, but was never immune to flattery, as Amelia had learned the hard way. He fell into bed, and was soon snoring, the quantities of wine and rich foods rumbling in his belly. Amelia lay beside him, awake for a long time, her fist to her mouth. She had succeeded in diverting him from the topic of Tristan—but at what a price.

She thought of the tall, straight child, Tristan, his proud, flashing eyes, the arrogant profile, his demanding ways. The high cheekbones, the bronze tint to his skin. Christophe had married away from his family, dearly as he loved them. And Moira was not one to marry so quickly, within a few days of meeting a man. She was deliberate, canny, shrewd. Yet they obviously adored each other. Moira had a soft look when she gazed at Christophe, for him her voice gentled; she would do anything he asked.

Yes, Tristan could be the child of another man. She had wondered herself, but had suppressed the thoughts as unworthy. Now Conrade had stirred it all up. If only he would keep his thoughts to himself. She did not want trouble again between Conrade and Christophe; too much had happened in the past. Let there by peace, she thought, in agony, let there be peace in the family.

She knew Christophe's pride, his spirit, for all his quietness. He would not endure having gossip about his son. She must try with all her intelligence and wit to keep the gossip down. It was the least she could do for him—and for Moira.

New Year's 1805 came, and the men paid their accustomed calls on the ladies. Christophe rode up the hill on horseback, carrying boxes of chocolates to Amelia and a lovely bonnet Moira had ordered for her sister-in-law. Conrade came down the hill and across the river in a carriage, and sat in the drawing room, joking with Moira and teasing his mother gently. He brought bottles of French wine and fine white scarves for them both.

Moira went about more and more heavily, the child moving within her. Christophe worked hard and talked earnestly to Moira about his business problems. After the child had been put to bed, and the elderly parents had retired, they would sit in the drawing room, Moira sewing for the new baby and Christophe with his papers strewn about him.

Christophe could talk to Moira about any subject on earth. She would listen keenly, put in a question or a word, and encourage him to go on. She did not always understand the new inventions he was working on, or why it was necessary to keep the gunpowder dry or to shape it better—but *he* knew, and that was enough for her.

He talked about the orders for the frontiersmen, and how difficult it was for the wagon trains to go so far. But they must follow the frontier. Black powder was needed to blow up tree stumps as they cleared the land. It was necessary for fighting the Indians, for the law men trying to keep some order among the brawling, belligerent men who tamed the frontier, but could not themselves be tamed.

He confided the problem about Marc Clausel. She listened in silence then, wishing he had fired the man long ago. The longer he remained, the more of a nuisance he was, and the more difficult to dislodge.

Some of the Irish foremen talked to her, respectfully but urgently in Gaelic, confiding in her as an Irish girl and the wife of the boss. Marc Clausel was disliked and distrusted. He saved their paychecks so skillfully that

145

they did not know how to protest. Etienne Vallette and even Conrade had always been rigidly careful, scrupulously fair, and the Irish and the German workers did not know what to do about this new development.

Maybe Marc was right, maybe the sums were withdrawn for the insurance and the charges for their houses. But if not—Moira hesitated, and did not tell Christophe for a time. She, too, wanted peace. And perhaps she was wrong. Perhaps the workers misunderstood.

The new child came, a son, born in April. He was small but sturdy, with eyes like his father's. He had the high Vallette forehead, and Moira adored him from the first. They named him Antoine.

Amelia came to help, and beamed over the mother and child. A doctor came also, shook his head over Moira, and talked quietly to Amelia. The young mother was not in good health. He talked to Christophe, who told Moira, and weeping a little, she agreed.

She had to have an operation, and it would mean no more children for her. Another child would kill her, said the doctor.

"I wanted—a daughter—for you, Christophe," she said after the weeks of recovery. She clasped his hand tightly, turning her face to the window. "I wanted a little girl—"

"We have been blessed with two sons, my dearest," comforted Christophe. "And I would take no chances with your life, Moira! How could I bear it if—" he choked over the words, and bent and kissed her hand humbly.

She stroked her hand on his head and neck. "Oh, Christophe. You would manage—if—"

"No, I would die, I think," he said quietly. "Do you know, that you uphold me, comfort me, sustain me? You are the best wife I could ever have—"

And she smiled at him, and he caressed her cheek, hating himself that mentally he had added the words—except Amelia. He set himself to soothing her, promising her a trip to New York one day, spinning images of their future.

He must not compare her with Amelia, he must not, and he never did—except when he was weary and heartsick.

And he was that way before the end of the summer. He finally discovered that Marc Clausel and his trickery had put them into debt with the agents. The new bookkeeper came to him in haste one June morning and told him.

"I finally figured it out, Mr. Vallette," he said, turning his hat round and round in his fingers, shuffling his feet. "I wrote to each agent, and asked what we owed him or he owed us. I said we was straightening out all the books."

"And what happened, Mr. Corey?" asked Christophe in an even voice, leaning back in his chair wearily and rubbing his eyes. He had a feeling he was about to discover a very unpleasant truth.

"The accounts don't agree, not at all, Mr. Vallette. I went over and over it meself. The agents say they paid, and it don't show on the books the way they say. Reckon the difference is about $100,000 now."

A silence fell between them. The man was miserably staring at the ground. It was what he had expected to find, but he knew how Christophe felt.

"And it was—Marc Clausel?"

"Yes, sir. In his handwriting. The accounts of money paid to the agents, which is about twice each time what they say he paid. And that ain't all." Corey nodded his head, and swallowed hard. "The men here—at the works—they been cheated, like they told me. They come to me time and time again, and I promised to find out. Their paychecks was shaved."

"Clausel?"

"Yes, sir."

"Where is he now?"

Corey looked at his employer uneasily. He respected the quiet-voiced man, but he saw a terrible rage rising in him.

147

"He's down at the office, sir, just come in. I said I had to report to you about some orders right off, and he let me come up the hill to the house."

Christophe said, "Pull up a chair. We'll go over the figures, just to make sure."

He went over the figures with Corey. The man was clever and thorough—and honest. He pointed out the places where the paychecks had been shaved, where agents had been debited more than they should have been, how the accounts had been made to balance. Christophe nodded. Ordinarily he would have gone to Etienne, but his father was ill. And Conrade was off in New York on another of his restless jaunts. He had heard of a scheme to start a textile mill from some friends, and was full of a plan to move to New York.

By noon, Christophe was sure. "All right, Corey. We'll go down and I'll speak to Clausel this afternoon. You keep out of the discussion. Clausel has a bad temper, and he'll blame me. I want you out of it."

Corey stirred and said respectfully, "Sir, I ain't afraid to stand up and speak my piece."

"I know you aren't. But I am the boss, and it's my job."

Christophe ate little that noon. He said nothing to Moira, who was clearly worried about him. He went down the hill to the main building and into the book-keeping office, a little distance from the mills. Corey was bent over his clerk's high desk, perched on a stool, his heels on the rungs. Christophe nodded to him. "Afternoon, Mr. Corey."

"Afternoon, Mr. Vallette."

Clausel heard them speak and came to the door. "Well, well, I am honored. Christophe Vallette come to see me," he said, mockingly, in his half-friendly, half-condescending manner, imitating Conrade unconsciously.

Christophe went in and shut the door. "I've been going over the books, Marc," he said somberly. "Much as I respect your father, I shall have to ask for your resignation."

The man went rather green, and sat down hard on his chair. "Wh—what d'ye say? What d'ye mean? You're out of your head!"

Christophe stared at him steadily. His temper was under control. "You have cheated the company for more than two years," he said slowly. "You have shaved the payroll and kept the money for yourself. And you have falsified the accounts of our agents. I figure it amounts to more than $100,000. I know you don't have the money to pay. What do you mean to do about it?"

Marc Clausel blustered, then raged. Christophe was implacable. He showed him entries in the books and demanded an explanation. Marc was fairly caught, and took refuge in anger and threats.

"I'll pay you back—for smearing my name!" he cried. "You can't prove nothing. And after all we did for you and your mother and father. Why, if it wasn't for me, your father would be dead and in his grave. I carried the burden—"

"And paid yourself too much for it," said Christophe sarcastically. "No, you're through here, I can't afford your high salary."

"You can't afford to let me go. Your father can't do it, and your lazy brother won't do the books. You *need* me."

Christophe told him, "I'll do the books myself rather than keep on a cheat and a scoundrel. Now get out, now—today. And if you're wise, you'll leave the state. I won't have you near."

Marc Clausel flung on his handsome bottle-green coat and left in a rage. Christophe called in Corey and turned over the work to him. Later in the week, Christophe found a promising, eager young apprentice to help Corey, and settled back down into his own laboratory work.

A few days later one of his Irish foremen told Christophe that Clausel had not left the state, nor gone home. He was staying in a rooming house in town, drinking heavily. Still, that did not alarm Christophe. But when the fire bell rang one clear summer afternoon, breaking the stillness with its alien clanging, he jumped from the laboratory and ran to the mills.

Smoke poured from the main powder mill. "Oh, dear God," he cried, and raced faster. Men squeezed out of the mills like seeds out of a lemon, running to the burning building, snatching up hoses and fire buckets. Some ran to the river, forming lines swiftly.

They flung water on the fire, and more water, bucket after bucket. The hoses were laid out, and some spurted water on the burning mill and adjoining mills. Christophe helped, with dread in his heart. If the fire spread to the saltpeter room, they would all be dead. The place would blast to the sky.

"No, no, Mr. Vallette, go away now—you must not do—" Christophe heard one of the German workmen cry out. Shocked, he saw his father in the bucket brigade, manfully lifting one heavy water bucket after another and passing it on. His gray hair stood up in the slight breeze, and his normally pale face was red with exertion.

Christophe sent a man over to make his father stop, but the man could not. Christophe was working hard, throwing buckets of water over the nearby buildings, soaking them well. He yelled to his father, "Father, please, give over. Go back and help in the office—I beg you."

"No, no, I shall help," his father called out in French, his brown eyes shining with excitement.

It took several hours to put out the blaze. Four men were badly burned and sent to the infirmary for treatment. Nine others were slightly burned, among them Christophe, whose arms were singed—yet he had not stopped to have them treated.

Finally the fire was out. Christophe gasped for breath. He could feel the burning in his very lungs, where the hot smoke had penetrated. He turned as someone touched his shoulder gently.

"Mr. Vallette? I'm sorry, sir, it's your father. He's fell down in a faint."

Christophe pushed his way through the crowd of women who had gathered at the sidelines. He found Moira bent over his father, kneeling on the grass beside him, supporting his gray head in her arm, while she soothed him in her Irish lilt.

"There now, there now, what for did you work yourself so hard, father? We'll have you back home in a jiffy, and won't maman be scolding you?"

Christophe knelt across from her. His father's eyes were closed. Stretchers were brought for the injured men, and one for Etienne Vallette.

He was carried back up the hill to the lovely house he had enjoyed so much. Sidoine sat with him all that night, and Moira with her. Christophe came in to them again and again, but there was little change.

Etienne lingered on for three days, and then quietly, one night, he left them. He had looked up into Sidoine's face, smiled at her lovingly, tried to speak, sighed, and was gone.

They buried Etienne Vallette in the new cemetery on the hill near Conrade's house. It was a beautiful spot overlooking the Areuse, with shade trees all about. Conrade returned hastily from New York and sobbed unashamedly over the grave.

Christophe did not weep. He stood silently, gazing out over the valley, filled with such hate that he could not even pray. He had heard that morning from one of his Irish workers.

"Mr. Vallette, sir, sure and I have to be telling ye. There's a man in town, sir, and he's a-bragging he got a hundred dollars from Marc Clausel for a-setting that there fire. I had to tell ye, sir, and would ye be letting me go with ye to beat him up when ye find him?"

When the funeral was over, and the respects paid, Christophe set out with the Irishman. They looked for a week, but Marc Clausel had turned tail at last and disappeared. His grief-stricken father wept, as he told Christophe he had had no word of him, and was ashamed bitterly of what his son had done.

"He was spoiled and weak, but I never thought he

would descend to this. My own son, my only son! To be the cause of the death of one of my best friends! I can never live it down."

Christophe thanked him and left. He rode hard and fast, the Irish worker with him, but they did not find Marc Clausel.

Christophe returned home exhausted, still coughing from the smoke in his lungs. Moira scolded him gently, and put him to bed. "How can you do this to yourself, Christophe? Don't you know how your mother and the children depend on you? Vengeance is mine, I shall repay, saith the Lord, and you cannot continue like this, my dear."

"I'll find him—I'll kill him with my bare hands—I'll kill the bastard—paying a man—" He was cut off with his own choking coughs, and Moira helped him sit up until the attack was over.

When he was more calm, Moira talked to him, coolly, practically. He must not waste his life seeking vengeance. Marc did not mean to be found. Besides, the damage was done. In her common sense way, she made him see the foolishness of trying to chase over the wilds of America with a gun, hunting Marc Clausel.

"Besides, his own guilt will be chasing after him always," said Moira thoughtfully. "Do you think he can live with himself after this? No, no, his guilt will always be riding on his back."

"I should have fired him long ago—"

"Forget the past. Live for the present—and the future. Little Tristan has been begging me to let him come to you. He cannot understand why he cannot see his papa," she coaxed.

So he finally let himself be persuaded to give up the chase. But he vowed never to forget, nor forgive—and the breach between him and Conrade deepened.

Within a year, Conrade moved his family to New York, where he joined the textile firm his friends had started. He was the "front man," showing patrons through the firm, charming them, complimenting the ladies on their good taste—and moving in gracious circles in New York society. The business did well; and Conrade and his family had a splendid house in town.

Christophe toiled in the powder mills, applying himself more than ever. Amelia sometimes wrote little reserved notes to Christophe, while to Moira she wrote often, at great length, and freely.

In the summers, Amelia and the children came to the Areuse, opened up the house, and the children played together. Amelia seemed wistful, thinner than ever, touching only lightly on the delights of New York. She always wore silk or satin, looking gracious and aloof. Conrade would come for them at the end of the summer, looking self-satisfied and plumper than ever.

And so the days went, and the months, and the years, and the Vallette family business prospered as the times prospered.

PART II

1860–1880

Chapter 12

Moira Vallette sat in her soft rocker and gazed out over the scenes she loved so much. Below her were the mills, and beyond them the Areuse, freeflowing green and white now in the sparkling June sunlight.

Up on the hill across from the Vallette house stood the gorgeous mansion of Antoine's widow and two children, John and Flora. Conrade had sold the mansion to Antoine when he'd finally decided, after the death of Amelia, never to return to live on the Areuse.

The families of Christophe and Conrade had grown apart. After their mother's death, the children of Amelia did not come to the Areuse for the summers. They went instead to Europe or to their summer cottage on the ocean. They lived in a world apart, in the world of New York society. Moira sometimes saw their names in the newspapers, and the marriage of her nephew Kendall had been an event of the season. Yet none of the Areuse Vallettes had attended. It had been a busy summer, and Brett had been born that autumn.

Dear Brett. Brett Christophe Antony Vallette. The image of his father Tristan. Thank God, thought Moira, that Tristan married the lovely and gentle Lavinia Townsend. She had been the saving of him. The wild one had always been so impetuous, so arrogant, and so difficult before Lavinia came into his life.

Moira looked out over the hills. She had sat here many a time, waiting until late in the evening, until Christophe finally trudged up the hill wearily from his laboratory. He would see her, pause, and wave his arm like a boy, grinning. Then he would come more swiftly up the hill, reach her and say, "Another day and much work done, my dear."

That day lived in her memory—the day that he had not walked back up the hill. He had fallen over in the laboratory—like a tired child, one of his assistants had said to her. They had thought him in a faint, until one felt his cooling hands and face. He died quietly, as he had lived. For many years he had fought the cough in his lungs and the growing frailty of his slim body.

Thank God for Tristan and Antoine, then. They had taken over the powder mills and the offices, and enlarged them and had gone on to build the business. Tristan married, settled down amazingly, and loyal Antoine followed where his beloved elder brother led. Except in his marriage.

Wild Tristan married such a gentle sweet girl; he had been tamed. Antoine married the following year, but he made the mistake of falling for a beautiful face, not realizing the selfish cold mind that lay behind it. Emilie Sturtevant Vallette lived in the mansion on the hill now, as she had desired, but she lived there a widow, with her two children. Antoine had not even lived to see the two children grow up. And Tristan had driven himself even harder—until the horrible day of the explosion in the powder mills. He went in to rescue some of the workers, and did not come out. There had been little enough of him to bury. They gathered up some fragments, sealed them in a small box, and buried him on the hill beside his father.

Brett then came home from the University of Pennsylvania and immediately took over the powder mills. And from that day he seemed hard and driving to everyone but his granny. Moira smiled wistfully. Only she remembered the young Brett, his blue eyes shining, urging her to tell him more stories of Irish folklore, and to tell of the days of her Indian captivity. Only Brett knew of his father's birth, for Tristan had told him, just as Moira had told Tristan when he was of age.

Always she told them how Christophe had rescued her, how good he was, how he had adored Tristan. However, she had felt that knowledge of their true heredity would help them curb their wild tendencies, their very natures which resembled that of the haughty Indian chief rather than that of the gentle, scholarly Christophe Vallette.

Someone tapped at the door. She started, and turned her faded gaze to the open door. "Come in—oh, Brett, I was just thinking of you, my dear."

He came over to her, tall and sturdy, straight and handsome, bent to her, and kissed her forehead. "Dreaming, granny?" he teased, in the gentle voice he reserved for her. She could smell the acrid odor of the chemicals on him.

"I was—of the days when your grandfather would come up the hill. And of your father, and the way he took over the mills, just like you did. I'm a lucky woman to have such fine sons and grandsons."

She looked at him keenly. He had closed the door after him, softly, so that they were alone in the small bedroom she had chosen for herself after the death of Christophe. She had her four-poster bed with its old-fashioned canopy, with the mosquito net over it in summer. She had her old rocker, in which she had fed her babies at her breast and rocked them to sleep. With them she was content.

"What bothers you, Brett?" she asked, gazing into the blue eyes so much like hers.

He smiled ruefully and sat down opposite her in the big armchair that had been Christophe's. He rubbed his hands over the chair's worn arms that his father and grandfather had touched. "I had a letter, granny. From Stephen Vallette. Kendall's son."

"Oh? And why would he be writing? Never a word have we had from them since last Christmas."

"I wanted to ask you, granny; what was Uncle Conrade like?"

She put her hand to her heart, to the lace bertha that matched the little white lace cap over her white hair.

"Oh, land, Brett, will you stir up the past?" she protested.

"The past governs our present," he said thoughtfully, his gaze turned to the scene beyond her window. He looked up at the hill across from the Vallette house. "You have told me of them. But it was long ago. And you were reserved when you spoke of Conrade and Kendall. Tell me about them."

Moira smoothed the mauve cotton dress with her thin hands. Vallette and Sons had grown beyond the wildest dreams of old Etienne. They had wealth to spare. She could have worn diamonds as Antoine's widow did or silks like Emilie's, she thought with contempt. But Moira stuck to her simple ways. She wanted it that way.

"Well, now, Conrade was always thinking of himself," she began cautiously.

"Selfish," said Brett bluntly, his eyes narrowing in the tanned, aristocratic face with the high, bronzed cheekbones.

"Well—yes. He was selfish. I told you the stories; you remember them, Brett. He moved them all off to New York, and worked in textiles. But he wasn't above taking the money for his share of the powder mills all those years. Christophe said he owned part of them, though he did nothing for it. It was Tristan and Antoine who bought him out finally, though it cost them dear."

"And lazy," said Brett, following his own thoughts.

"Well, he always thought a bit more of pleasure than of work."

"And Aunt Amelia?"

Moira's gaze softened. "Ah—Amelia, she was a good-hearted, generous woman. Intelligent, and so smart, and educated. And tactful. Lord, she learned to make her way around Conrade; she had to, to keep from getting crushed by him."

"Who did Kendall take after?"

"Um. Well. At first, I thought he would be like Conrade. But he came to visit summer after summer, and he was a good boy. Generous to his sister and to small Reggie. He would play with Tristan and Antoine, and I remember him saying to me, 'Aunt Moira, they're younger than me, but give them the best cake.' And he would let them play with his toys—though Tristan did break his wooden gun, I remember that."

Brett rubbed his chin thoughtfully as Moira rocked and reminisced. He was turning things over in his mind. He took out the letter and opened it again. "Let me read this to you, granny."

"Sure, lad."

He loved the Irish lilt of her voice, so like that of his workmen in the mills. Emilie said she was common, and had talked about her behind his back to the futile rage of Antoine. Brett had given her a dressing down about that just recently. She wouldn't say it again, not in his hearing. He still burned when he thought of her snobbish tone, her tilted nose. Moira was the best, finest granny a man could have, she had been a good mother and wife, she had sweetness to the core, and she was smart, even if she couldn't always understand the gazettes and books.

He read the letter to her, tactfully avoiding having her struggle to read it. Her eyesight had faded with her years.

"My dear cousin Brett,

You will be amazed to hear from me. The last time we met I believe I snatched my best boat out of your hands and boxed your ears for taking it. For which father duly spanked me. But do let us let bygones be bygones.

"I am planning a trip to the South on the behalf of our textile mills. As I am traveling about, I hope to pay a call on you and Aunt Moira and all the others on the Areuse. I want to make acquaintance again with all my cousins. Kendall Vallette sends his regards, and would have come, but for some stiffness of his legs.

"I do beg you to let me come and stay a few days with you. Father speaks of pleasant summers on the Areuse, and I vow he would come should he be able to make the journey.

"Looking forward to meeting you in a somewhat more sedate manner than we parted, I am,

> Most sincerely, your cousin,
> Stephen Vallette"

Brett folded the letter again and set it into its envelope after noting the bold, black flourish of the handwriting.

"Clever," said Moira absently. "Light humor. Wonder what he wants?"

Brett grinned. Just when he thought Granny Moira was going gentle and elderly, she came out with one of her devastatingly shrewd remarks. They sometimes made his sister Bridget wince, for she was gentle and devout, and thought the best of everyone. But his other sister, Rose Marie, would giggle and cap her if she could.

"So do I wonder. You know, if the elections go the way we think they will this November, the South may secede," he said, gravely. He never did granny the insult of talking down to her. "And we are in the South, in Virginia."

"You think Virginia will go with the South?"

"I fear so, from the talk I have heard. From my dear brother-in-law, for one. Rose Marie picked herself a fine one."

Moira touched his long, clever hand. "Ah, do not say so, my dear Brett, not in her hearing. Do you not think she grieves enough in her heart?"

"Aye, and I grieve with her. He is lazy, boorish—ah, enough of that. What shall I tell this Stephen, who may come to see which way the Vallette powder mills shall blow?"

"You believe he may come to spy."

"He has never expressed any interest in visiting us before," said Brett, gazing out the window again. "And I have been approached at great length in infinitely cunning ways, from many directions, by those who touch finger to lip and wink, to find out whether Vallette will continue to sell powder to the South should war come."

Moira's eyes grew wistful. They had lived through wars before, the war with England lasting from 1812 to

162

1815, and the one with Mexico, which had dragged on and on. Tristan and Brett had enlarged the mills to accommodate the powder needed for this latter war. And the canals had needed more powder, and the new railroads, blasting their way to the West Coast. Representatives of the railroads had come to the Vallettes, remaining for weeks, guests in their home, to arrange for more black powder.

Should it all come down now to a horrible war of brother against brother, father against son—cousin against cousin?

"Brett, would you sell—to the South?"

"The issue has not yet come up," he said, so shortly that she knew he was brooding about it. "When it does, I shall decide."

"And rightly, I am sure, Brett. Well, as to this Stephen, if he doesn't come, others will. And I am curious about Conrade's grandson. Yes, I should like to see the lad."

"The 'lad' is but two years younger than I," grinned Brett, rising. "And this time I might do more than snatch his boat from him!"

"He has not married, either?"

"No, granny, and this is not the time for a lecture from you on the virtues of holy matrimony. I like the ladies, but not for keeps." And Brett laughed and went out.

There was great curiosity in the Vallette family on the Areuse when news that their cousin Stephen from up North was coming for a visit.

Rose Marie had come for the summer. She had matured since her early marriage to a handsome plantation owner's son. Ingram Lombard was a younger son, and so his brother would inherit the plantation. Rose Marie, romantic and dreamy, had fancied herself on a plantation, away from the chatter and noise of the factory making black powder.

She had been quickly disillusioned. Ingram toiled not, neither did he spin—nor was he the more attractive for it. Instead, the long nights of dancing and drinking, the days spent sleeping off hangovers, his chasing of slave girls in the fields, had all contrived to give her a much truer picture of her husband than all the romantic courting they had done.

She came home summers, childless, brittle, thinner than ever, an overbright gleam in her eyes and a sarcastic touch to her quick tongue. Moira watched her moving about the house, and felt sadness. Rose Marie was turning sour, thought Moira, and she was only twenty-five.

Tristan's other daughter, Bridget, was younger by two years, but a modest, shy girl who liked nothing better than to work in the kitchen, or to sit and knit and crochet. She was plain, her hair drawn back from her broad forehead. She dreamed over books, blushed when she was spoken to, and was an awkward dancer. Brett had tried his best by her, introducing young men until Moira had taken pity on her and told him to cease. The girl was not made for marriage; she was afraid of men.

Stephen arrived on a summer evening, just as the Vallettes had gathered on the veranda. Moira was rocking in her favorite rocker; Bridget sat nearby with her crocheting. Rose Marie was talking with her usual vivacious gaiety, only covering the dissatisfaction of her life by amusing stories. Brett was sitting with his pipe, in a rare moment of idleness.

The handsome chestnut caught their eyes first. Rose Marie said, "Who's that? I don't recall a horse like that in the neighborhood."

Brett stood up and peered keenly through the dimness. The horse came on and a stablehand ran out to catch the reins as they were flung to him. The man got down, slowly, as though weary, and dragged off his thick saddlebags.

He came up to the veranda, lifted his head, and gave them a long, smiling stare. "The Vallettes, gathered, by all that's holy," said a crisp northern voice.

"Stephen Vallette, I believe?" Brett came down and offered his hand, which he then found in a strong, hard clasp. He stared sharply at the handsome, smiling man. Lines of weariness were graven beside the full, sensuous mouth, but the large brown eyes were sharp. "Welcome! We've been expecting you."

Stephen came up the steps with him, set down his heavy saddlebags on the veranda, and gallantly approached Moira first. "You must be Aunt Moira—father sends his best regards and a kiss." He bent over and pressed his lips to her soft pink cheek.

"Kendall's lad. How happy I am to meet you," said Moira. She pressed her slim hands over his strong, hard ones. She searched his face in the dim light for some resemblance, and found it. "You look like your grandmother Amelia—the same coloring. I grieved over her death. She was a sweet lady."

"Thank you, ma'am. She spoke often of you; so does my father still." He straightened and looked about.

"Brett Vallette," Brett introduced himself, then his sisters. "Your cousin Rose Marie—now Mrs. Lombard. And my sister, Bridget Vallette."

"Ma'am," he bowed to Rose Marie, glancing at her keenly. Then he smiled and bowed to Bridget, who ducked her head. "Well, well, this is a pleasure. I have more messages than I can tell in five hours, they can wait until tomorrow."

"You must be weary, and hungry. Bridget—" Brett began, but she had already scurried away to the kitchen. Stephen seated himself gracefully in a chair, sighed with exaggerated loudness, and grinned at them all.

Moira questioned him gently, placidly, in generalities. "Your sisters are well? And young Titus? He is in school? Your father is well? Your aunt Deborah? She was such a pretty little girl, so sweet and amiable."

"She still is, Aunt Moira. She has six children, and manages them without raising her voice. I'll name them all when my brain is cleared from this pesky journey." He thanked Bridget with a quick smile when she came out with a cool mint julep, followed by a maid with a tray of food. "You are too good. It is long past your dinner hour, I feel sure—"

"We have eaten, yes. Have you traveled far and fast?" asked Brett, as though idly.

"Made it in four days," said Stephen, then shot him a hard look. "I should have come by the new railroad, but I wanted to use my horse. He'll be useful in the backwoods going down to New Orleans, my final destination. I declare, father has told me a hundred places I must go on this journey."

He ate with gentlemanly good manners, but as though starved. Bridget refilled his coffee cup. Rose Marie was rocking back and forth, half-hidden in the shadows.

When he had eaten, Rose Marie stood up slowly. "I'll show you to your room, Cousin Stephen," she drawled. "Granny has had it ready this entire month, waiting for you. She could scarcely wait to meet you."

He grinned down at her, hoisting the saddlebags. "And you, my dear cousin?" he mocked lightly. "Could you scarcely wait also?"

"My patience is strong, dear cousin," she replied, as they went indoors and crossed to the rosewood staircase. "You see, what I remembered of you was when you pulled my hair."

He laughed aloud, the pleasant sound echoing through the large hall and up the stairs. "My dearest coz. I beg your forgiveness. I hope my manners have improved—I know that my taste has matured."

He looked down at her mockingly as they mounted the stairs together. He studied her blue-black hair, the vivid blue eyes, the handsome figure in the crinoline and low-cut blouse. "Mrs. Lombard? And where is your lucky husband?"

Her mouth tightened, the generous lines stiff. "At home," she said shortly. "At the plantation in South Carolina."

"He must miss you—immensely," said the soft, crisp voice.

166

She shrugged, and led the way to the room at the end of the hallway. She pushed open the door and glanced about. The large four-poster bed had its mosquito net in place; there was fresh hot water in the pitcher, and the lamp was lit. "I think all is in order, cousin. If you wish anything, please ring the bell rope. We retire early in the country, and granny's room is across from you. Please do not disturb her."

"I hardly ever carouse after midnight, dearest cousin." He laughed aloud, though softly. "Is your tongue always so pointed?"

The pale cheeks flushed; she gave him an angry glare and a false smile. "Always, sir," she said bluntly, and turning with a swirl of blue skirts, left him.

He closed the door, stretched his shoulders, and finally removed his handsome brown jacket. He rubbed his back and yawned. He was here, that was all that mattered for the moment. Tomorrow he would have a good long talk with Aunt Moira. Kendall had said she was the best bet for talking over matters.

Brett. A sharp fellow, with a shrewd look, for all his slow drawl. And much business sense. He had built up the mills since he had taken over, and they were worth millions. Tomorrow he must see about a casual tour of the place. He wondered if it could be true—that the Vallettes were capable of turning out a million pounds of black powder in a year.

The smile disappeared. He unpacked his saddlebags and thrust some papers deeply into a hidden pocket sewn into their sides, then made sure they were fastened shut. Then he threw the bags, casually, into the bottom of the handsome wardrobe chest.

He would sleep well—and be ready for tomorrow.

Rose Marie went to bed in her room, restless and aching somehow. She clasped her arms to herself, held them hard with her hands, and gazed out at the quiet night. This was home, and usually she felt more calm after a summer here. This summer might be different.

167

Stephen had a sharp tongue, and a glance that saw deep.

Brett, in the master bedroom, prepared for bed with his usual meticulous routine: long pocket watch and chain on the dresser; studs in their box; waistcoat and narrow collar on a chair. He paused, removed his boots, then sat with his arms on his strong, narrow thighs.

Something about Stephen disturbed Brett—there was caution under Stephen's careless air. And he had ridden hard to get here.

What did he want? War was in the air; maybe he was getting jittery. But Brett was not given to jitters. He dealt in facts, in solid orders, in chemical formulas that worked, in sales that must be contracted for.

Granny Moira had said that Conrade had charm, but was lazy. This man had charm—but he was not lazy. There was a lithe strength to that tall, slim body. He lifted the heavy bags with ease, even after a day's journey. He ate and drank with precision, as though to stoke his body with fuel for more work. Not a glutton, not a lazy hound like Ingram Lombard. (By God, I should have forbidden that marriage, thought Brett.)

He finished undressing, put on his long nightgown, and slid into the wide bed. He felt no need for a woman. If he wanted one, he went discreetly to another city, indulged in an expensive woman, paid her, and departed.

But the subject of marriage nagged at him. He dismissed the thought of Stephen against tomorrow. However, he thought about the Vallette company—and his heirs. If he did not have an heir, that cold-blooded John Vallette, Antoine's son, would inherit. And he was too much like his mother, Emilie.

Brett frowned into the darkness. He was thirty-two—time he was married. But dammit all, he didn't know a single woman he cared to marry. What the hell was a man to do—marry *anyone*?

When he thought of the good marriage of his parents, and of his grandparents, he rebelled against the thought of making a poor marriage of convenience. No, he

168

wanted to love and respect a woman before making her his wife and the mother of his children.

He punched his pillow and soon slipped into the deep sleep of a man who works hard and lives honestly, his life an open book, without secrets.

Chapter 13

Stephen was charming to all of them. He listened respectfully to Granny Moira, urging her with a laugh to tell him more stories of the old days. His brown eyes were warm and filled with humor.

"Now, that reminds me of the story father told, that Granny Amelia told him," he would say, lounging back in the long chair, a tall glass of whisky and water at his side. "Do go on, Aunt Moira. What happened to Christophe and Conrade after Grégoire died? Father said they had a difficult voyage—"

And so she would recite the old stories, her blue eyes sparkling with pleasure at having such a fine audience. Brett came sometimes and listened with them, stretching out wearily on a chair, in silence, a half-smile on his generous mouth.

Bridget would duck her head at any attention, so Stephen would content himself with a smile in her direction, or with a warm thanks for a fresh glass and a tray of cakes. Rose Marie he taunted lightly, with a grin and a sharp wit that matched her own. For each, he had attentions.

Emilie Vallette drove over with John and Flora and was immediately excited by the presence of this handsome Northerner. "But we must have a ball for you," she drawled, her face flushing with pleasure. "Brett, have you arranged a dance for our cousin? You have not? But he must remain longer. We shall have it in our home."

"You are very generous and kind, Cousin Emilie," said Stephen, gravely. "However, I do not mean to put you out. And if you mean to introduce me to any charming young ladies, I need no more than the three in my presence." And he bowed engagingly to Rose Marie, Flora, and Bridget.

Flora fluttered, giggling, for all her engagement to a local young man. John gave him a sober, thoughtful look, sitting solidly on a hard chair, his legs crossed to show his boots and thick shoes. Rose Marie darted a hard look at him, then looked to her brother Brett.

"I should like to hold a ball for Stephen, though he assured me he meant to go on within a few days. We have been urging him to remain longer," murmured Brett, his face showing nothing but courtesy.

Emilie insisted on having her way, and Stephen gave in gracefully. So preparations were begun for a ball to be held in the mansion on the hill. There was a ballroom there, unlike the Vallette house above the mills. Conrade had adored dancing and parties. Servants were put to work waxing and polishing, invitations were sent out, and refreshments were planned.

Meantime, Stephen finally had his tour of the powder mills. Brett had put him off with one excuse and another, until finally he gave way abruptly. "You are serious, not just idly curious, dear cousin," drawled Brett, with a smile at Stephen. "Well, I shall satisfy you. Today we shall tour the mills. First, we must find some shoes for you."

"Shoes?" Stephen hid his feelings by sticking out his handsome leg before him and making a face at his handsome brown leather boot. "I am not dressed properly?"

"You have nails in your boots," murmured Bridget, then blushed when he looked at her in comic amazement.

"Doesn't everyone?" he asked.

"Not in the mills," drawled Rose Marie, as though rather bored by it all. "One must wear leather shoes with wooden pegs. Otherwise a fire might start—the striking of nails on the floors where black powder might have dusted could set off a fire or an explosion. All the men change to leather aprons and leather shoes with wooden pegs."

"Ah—I see."

Brett added, "You should be careful to leave behind your watch and chain, and any metal or coins in your pockets. I'll see to your boots. We'll have a jacket for you to change to. Ah, I see you are wearing studs—if you would leave them off, please."

"Of course, Brett." Stephen was as serious as his host as he absorbed these instructions.

He was ready when Brett prepared to leave the house that morning. He expressed surprise that all rose so early and set about their duties, including their guest, Rose Marie. She rose as early as the rest, and took over the dusting of rooms, supervising the maids efficiently. Bridget saw to the kitchens and prepared the menus. Even Moira came down, fully dressed, to join them for their early breakfast.

"All work here," he said to Brett as they started down the hill, striding along. They were about the same height, both with wide shoulders, lean hips, and long legs. "And does John Vallette also?"

"Aye, he works in the office, writes to our agents, attends to that side of the business."

"And you?"

"I work in the laboratory much of the time. We are constantly experimenting with new methods," explained Brett. He was more cordial this morning, as though he had decided to trust Stephen.

They came to the great general factory area, and Brett chose shoes and a jacket for Stephen. A few latecomers were chatting, but they fell silent as the stranger came in, eyeing him curiously. Brett beckoned to one of the men.

"One of our foremen, John O'Grady. My cousin from New York City, Stephen Vallette."

Stephen shook the great hand and smiled. "How are you? You have been here many years?"

172

"Aye, I was born here, sor," said the man simply. "Me father, he come here when he was but a lad, he married here, and we all live here."

"You must feel great loyalty to the Vallettes," said Stephen.

Brett gave him a sharp, thoughtful glance, then indicated they were ready to proceed.

They went to the first building, where rough saltpeter was being refined by boiling in a huge kettle.

Stephen pointed to the tools with curiosity. Brett nodded. "Tools are only of wood or copper, so they won't give off sparks. No iron or steel tools permitted."

"Can a fire start so quickly?" asked Stephen gravely.

"In an instant," said Brett, his lean face hard. "It is our constant danger. Even as lads, playing here, when we saw a spark we would dive out the nearest window or into the stream. 'Fast as the divil!' as we said."

Barrels of water stood near the mill walls. Stephen pointed to them mutely.

"Always filled," said Brett.

Brett showed him how the saltpeter was cooled in a large vat, in constant motion, so it would crystallize. From there, it was conveyed to wooden washing chests, where water was poured over it to flush away any remaining impurities. Then it was dried and placed in bags, to await mixing with the sulfur and charcoal.

Crude sulfur was placed in closed iron cauldrons. Lead-off pipes fed the gas into cooler chambers to liquefy it.

The charcoal was usually made from slow-burning black or gray willow. Brett showed Stephen the by-products that had been found useful—the tar for patching work on buildings and for making creosote.

"We are learning not to let any part waste," said Brett. "In the lab, we constantly experiment to find new uses for the by-products. One day, their value may exceed that of the black powder itself."

Stephen was silent much of the time, but not from lack of interest. His brown eyes were intent on all that

173

Brett showed him, and he listened with feverish interest to what his cousin told him.

Brett briskly explained all the operations, telling Stephen how many days the charcoal must burn to be prepared for making gunpowder. Then they saw the sticks of charcoal and the lumps of sulfur pounded together and crushed. The dust from this was combined with the saltpeter, in amounts that depended on whether they were making sporting powder, blasting powder, or military powder.

Brett cautioned him as they approached the next mill. "We'll just glance inside. A man watches this constantly. He must add water from time to time, so that the powder does not become dry, or the dust from this might explode."

Stephen nodded respectfully, his brown eyes gleaming. "It is all much more complicated than I had expected," he said. "And you experiment constantly to make better powder?"

"Constantly," said Brett, "and my father before me."

"Father said you had a bad explosion in 1857," said Stephen.

"Aye, three men killed, four badly injured," said Brett. "We have fire drill; the men know what to do. But sometimes the explosion comes so rapidly, that one can do nothing but take out the bodies." His mouth had tightened.

"I beg your pardon. I had forgotten for the moment that your own father lost his life like that—"

"And I might myself," said Brett brusquely. They left the mill to stroll along the river. Brett's brow was furrowed. "Sometimes, I worry, Stephen. I have not married; I have no sons to carry on. Rose Marie is not happy in her marriage; she has no children. And John, I think, would coldly sell the lot if he found it a burden to carry on."

Stephen was surprised at this burst of confidence. He looked with sympathy at his cousin, striding along with his hands in his pockets, staring at the cool waters of the Areuse. "I say, that is hard. And you want the business carried on. It has been in the family for four generations, counting Etienne."

"Aye. And this place—" Brett raised his gaze to the gentle hills, the valley, the flowing river. "This place is our home, our heritage. Ah, well, I did not mean to burden you with this."

"Thank you for your confidence," said Stephen, simply, and put his hand on Brett's shoulder for a moment. "If—war should come, what would you do? Close the place? It is very vulnerable to attack."

Brett shrugged; a shutter seemed to come over his bright blue eyes. "I don't know. I'll wait and see what happens."

"On the other hand, the powder would be much needed—by both sides."

"I know that. I have been approached—by both sides," said Brett drily.

Stephen's brown eyes glittered a little; he turned from his cousin and gazed out over the Areuse. "And you are in the South," he said softly.

"We are on the border, Stephen. And always we have fought for the United States," said Brett. "Friends of ours were in the War of 1812, and many neighbors were in the navy in the battles then. Friends and neighbors—the Stratfords, the Bruces, others—have fought for our country. Shall we sit by and see the country rent in two?"

"So you have been considering what to do," said Stephen.

"Aye, and not deciding," said Brett. "Come, I have not shown you the final sheds where we keep the barrels of powder until they are loaded on wagons."

"I am surprised that you still use horses and wagons for transport," said Stephen, as they walked to the cooperage. "I would think the railroads—"

"Aye, we tried that. But workers found that black powder was on the train and refused to ride with it. The insurance went very high, and we returned to our wagons. There are still accidents, but few. Our drivers are trained to be extremely careful. They go slowly, but

175

they deliver the goods, all over the States, as far west as the Mississippi River," said Brett proudly.

They discussed the problems of transport, then Brett showed him his laboratory before they returned to the house for luncheon.

Brett seemed relaxed with Stephen. But the conversation did not return to the possibilities of war between the states. Stephen courteously did not press it, though he did return to the mills by himself that afternoon, walking about, reviewing silently to himself all that Brett had told him of the operations.

Yes, the mills are vulnerable, he thought. But the men were loyal—and tough. They knew how to use the guns that were stacked in a mill near the entrance to the grounds. And they knew their black powder and the deadly balls they made. They would defend the mills, should the need arise.

He returned to the house in mid-afternoon, climbing the hill slowly, with appreciation for the clusters of shady oak and hazel trees. He would turn from time to time, to gaze out over the valley to the hill opposite, where the great mansion with its white pillars gleamed in the afternoon sun. Hedges surrounded the houses of the workers, below in the valley, and plots of flowers were laid out around them: roses and peonies; zinnias flaming orange and red; pale, creamy rose magnolias; petunias of pink and violet and scarlet.

It was a beautiful place, and Brett obviously loved it. Stephen went into the dim, cool hallway and made his way up the rosewood staircase, his bronzed hand running lightly along the sleek railing.

He walked silently along the carpeted hallway to his bedroom. Nearing it, he stiffened, and his brown eyes glowed like dark coals. The door was slightly open, and he heard the rustle of papers.

He opened the door silently, saw the intruder, and stepped inside, quiet as a panther. He clicked the lock behind him, and stood still. The girl whirled around, her blue eyes wide with shock.

Rose Marie clutched his papers in her hands, with his

saddlebags flung open behind her on the bed—Rose Marie, in a white petticoat, a blue wrapper over it, her long blue-black hair cascading down her back.

"Not having a siesta, Rose Marie?" he whispered.

She opened her mouth for a pert reply, but could only swallow. He covered the few paces between them and took her long, white throat in his hands.

"I should kill you, you interfering little bitch!" he whispered. He glared savagely into her frightened white face. "Snooping about—what did you find?"

He shook her violently in his grip. "Let me go!" she cried.

"Softly, now. Tell me, what did you find?"

Her blue eyes were dazed but defiant. "Papers—with invisible ink to write on them. And maps—"

"God, you devil!" For one violent moment he thought he would kill her. Endangering his mission, the first week! And his own cousin!

His hands slowly tightened on her throat. She caught at his wrist strongly, but could not move it. Her blue eyes became glazed; she pulled back more weakly. He took a shaking breath and loosened his grip. But he still held her firmly.

He thought like fury. What could he do with her? He stared down at the beautiful face, the loosened black hair, the willful mouth, and the slim, rounded body outlined under her loose white robe. She had dropped the papers; he kicked them away from their feet. With one hand he flung the saddlebags onto the carpet.

He knocked her down onto the wide bed. She gasped, and he clasped his hand over her mouth. "Listen, Rose Marie," he said, in a harsh tone, but very quietly, aware of Moira sleeping just across the hall. "You listen to me, and listen well."

He pressed his lean body against hers and noted the weakening of her struggles. Yes, she was hungry for a man. Deliberately, he pressed himself to her, still holding her throat in one hand, his other hand over her mouth. He hissed at her, "You will not say one word to anyone about this. Not one word, understand? You will not speak to Brett, nor indicate in any way you know anything about me."

The blue eyes glared at him. He drew a deep breath. She wriggled under him; he felt the stirrings of desire. It would not be difficult to want her—God, she was beautiful—

Savagely, he pulled up the white robe. Her face changed, she looked shocked, wild. She began to fight him, but he ripped the robe up to her waist. He freed one hand to unfasten his trousers, then yanked off his jacket and shirt and underclothing. Naked, he sprawled over her, and began to kiss her mouth and throat.

She sputtered at him, and clawed at him with her free hands, until he took them in one of his and held them above her head. Deliberately he kissed her, down over her throat to her rounded white breasts. Her legs were held tightly together; she felt stiff under him. He guessed that her husband treated her brutally, took her and left her unsatisfied and in pain.

Deliberately, Stephen ran his hand down over her thighs. She shivered, and her blue eyes held fright. He ran his hand over and over her thighs, gently worked them open, then pressed his fingers to her. She was dry and hard.

He nuzzled at her throat, kissing her earlobes, kissing down over her shoulders and bared breasts, to her waist. She squirmed and struggled under him, glaring at him with hate in her eyes. He went on and on, remorselessly, with a sure touch. He could not afford to lose her now.

"You are adorable in your anger, little spitfire," he whispered in her ear. He felt her stiffen in surprise. He whispered endearments to her, stroking her breasts. "You are so soft, so smooth. God, you are beautiful."

He caressed a nipple with his mouth and worked gently upon it. She was shuddering, but finally he felt her relax. He pressed himself more firmly against her. His head was spinning; he must not lose control of himself. He whispered, "Rose Marie—God, let me do this—let me—"

178

Softly, he ran his hand over and over her thighs. Coaxingly, he pressed his fingers to her. (Hadn't her brutish husband ever made *love* to her, did he take her like a slave girl in the fields? He had heard about those southern "gentlemen" who raped more easily than they loved.)

She was very thin, but she had long beautiful legs, a long, smooth belly, a lovely pair of breasts. He propped himself up to enjoy the sight of her blue-black hair strewn over his pillow, her eyes closed tight, her red mouth scarlet from his kisses. Bruises showed on the white throat where his fingers had gripped her.

He moved to lie on top of her and make her feel the pressure of his lean thighs. She stiffened again; he soothed her with words and kisses, until finally he worked her legs apart and thrust himself between them. No need now to hold his hand over her mouth; she was moaning softly, and writhing under him. He thrust, and thrust, slowly, feeling her give way to him.

In silence he took her, and enjoyed her, and made her enjoy him, with subtle caresses and a slow, sure touch. When she shook and it seemed she would cry out, he bent over swiftly and pressed his open mouth to hers and thrust his tongue between her lips. Holding her thus, he shuddered to a finish in her.

She was trembling, and he held her in silence for a time. Then, when she had recovered, she tried to sit up, but he held her back. He bent over her, gazed into her unfocused blue eyes, and sighed, quietly, gently, "Rose Marie. You're going to promise me that you will say not one word to anyone about this. Not one word, not one hint, not one whisper."

The blue eyes slowly came into focus and her stare turned to a glare of hate. "You damned devil! I'll tell Brett, and he'll kill you."

"I think not, my dear." He held her firmly, so she would feel his strength and not try to get away. "Listen to me. I am on a mission more important than you, the family, Brett, anyone. And I will not be turned from it.

179

You will give me your promise before you leave this room, that you will never betray me."

"I'll see you in hell!"

He was amused in spite of his predicament. This girl was all fire and spirit—like the black powder, ready to go up in a flash from any spark.

"No, my dear, I think not. You are in a hell of your own making," he said deliberately. "Now, when you leave this room, this is forgotten, the maps, the papers, all. Or—"

"Or what?" She squirmed, but found she could not get away from his firm grip. "Afraid? My brother will murder you, you know."

"No, I shall have a very pleasant stay with my cousins, the Vallettes, attend their ball, and leave with great regret. When I return from New Orleans for a brief visit this autumn, to say farewell before I go north again, it will be to find all peaceful. You understand me?"

His grip tightened threateningly on her arms. She moved to sit up; he let her, still holding her. Their naked bodies were close together on the wide bed; she was gazing reluctantly at the fine-sprung brown hairs on his broad chest. "I understand," she finally said, sullenly.

"And I have your promise, the promise of a Vallette, never to betray me, even to your brother?"

Her eyes blazed.

He continued ruthlessly. "Or I shall call someone in—your granny, for example, to see you. I shall say you lay in wait for me—hungry for a man, no doubt, since you have been long absent from your husband. I shall suggest that since you are so—promiscuous—that you be returned to your husband—"

"You cold-blooded devil!"

"Your promise!"

She bit her full red mouth. He found himself staring at the lips, the white teeth, the soft whiteness of her shoulders and arms. "I promise," she finally agreed, sullenly. "Now let me go."

"You may go. However, I shall keep this—" He held the torn nightdress before her. It was trimmed in blue embroidery, with her initials on the round neck. "If you are tempted to betray me, remember I shall have your nightdress as a—tender—reminder of our afternoon together. You would find it hard to explain why it is in this condition—in my possession, eh?"

She slid from the bed, reached for the blue robe, and set it around herself. He gazed at her from head to foot before she swung the robe in place and fastened it with shaking hands. He went to the door.

"I'll hate you forever," she whispered viciously.

He smiled and bowed, then unlocked the door. He glanced down the long hallway quickly. "All clear," he motioned to her.

She fled. He watched her reach the safety of her own room, and the door swung shut after her. Then he closed and locked his own. He let out a long sigh. What a woman!

He wondered if she would keep her word. She had her reputation to consider, but what if she was so furious she went to Brett anyway? He would soon know.

He rested, after putting away the torn nightdress and the papers and maps. He would be on his way in three days. He lay, his hands behind his head, thinking, thinking.

He went down early for dinner. Rose Marie was already there, moving about the parlor, directing the setting of the table in the dining room. She sent a maid in with a tray of drinks for him and a pot of tea for her grandmother. He had a calm conversation with Moira, centering about the ball the next night, his visit to the powder mills, her memories of his grandmother.

At dinner, Brett was calm and rather weary. Rose Marie had red spots of color in her cheeks. She was dressed demurely in a high-necked blue and white swiss-dotted muslin, the ruffles falling over her long hands. She avoided Stephen's look, but he smoothly addressed her from time to time, watching her sharply.

The evening of the ball was warm and humid, with thundershowers threatening from the west. Stephen put

181

on his brown silk suit, the fine white lace shirt with the ruffles, and his signet ring. He came down early and had a drink and a chat with Brett, who was handsome in a blue silk suit.

"Well, we will miss you, Stephen. You have lightened our days," said Brett, raising his glass to him as they sat on the veranda, waiting for the ladies to appear.

"I cannot tell you how much I have enjoyed my stay here."

"You cannot stay over?"

"I wish I could, but I have all that business—many miles to cover. However, I shall return in the autumn, if I may, for a final visit before my return to New York. It may be late."

"You will always find a welcome here," said Brett courteously, with some warmth.

"Thank you, Brett. I confess I am happy to find some cousins much to my liking." They both rose as the girls came down, escorting Granny Moira carefully by the arms.

Moira wore her best ruby-red silk dress, old-fashioned, slim-waisted, which set off her white hair and white lace bonnet. She beamed at them with her faded blue eyes. "How handsome you look, my dears," she said fondly.

"Don't flatter them, granny, they are impossibly spoiled already," said Rose Marie quickly.

Brett laughed down at her; Stephen narrowed his eyes. She sounded almost her natural sarcastic self. Twin spots of color flared in her smooth cheeks; her blue-black hair was drawn back from her face into a smooth chignon, showing the high cheekbones and beautiful chin. Next to her Bridget seemed a small, scared mouse in brown.

Rose Marie had dressed defiantly that evening. She thought she hated her cousin more than she had hated anyone in the world. She had to wear an older dress, though the crinoline was still in fashion, being wide-hooped with four layers of flounce. The gown was of blue taffeta with a low, round neck. To hide the bruises on her throat, Rose Marie wore a lace bertha about her neck, fastened with a cameo of tortoise shell surrounded by tiny seed pearls. Eardrops to match dangled from her small ears. The gown was caught up with small silk roses over the entire skirt.

Stephen drove Moira and Bridget, while Brett drove Rose Marie in the carriage behind them. The trip was not long. Brett said once, "Do you like our cousin, Rose Marie? He seems a fine chap."

"Fine enough," she said carelessly. "Rather egoistic, I think, but charming enough."

He was silent for a minute. Then he said, gently, "Rose Marie, your granny and I have thought and worried about you. Should you like to remain here with us this winter? We could make the excuse that granny is not well—and truly she is not as well as she was."

Rose Marie leaned her cheek against his shoulder. "Brett, you are good," she said, a catch in her throat. "Ingram would be furious if I do not return, though."

"I can manage him," said Brett grimly. "I—had it in mind to obtain a divorce for you. He is—not what we want for you, my dear. Forgive my mentioning it. But you look so sad at times, our hearts ache for you."

"I—I will think about it," she whispered. The thought was so new, so overwhelming, that it caught her breath.

"We'll say no more of it now. But do not plan to return now."

"I had planned to stay the summer." Inwardly, she had thought she might stay until Stephen returned in the autumn—only to prove, she hastened to add to herself, that she had kept her word to him. She sensed that he did not trust her, and it made her furious. She hated him, but—but his embrace had been so devastatingly sweet and sensual. She had never felt what she felt in his arms that afternoon. He must be very clever with women, she thought bitterly.

The mansion on the hill was lighted from top to bottom. Servants darted out to take the horses and help the

183

ladies down. They all wore smart uniforms; tapers flared in the night at the spacious doorway.

Emilie stood in the hallway to greet the guests, John beside her. She beamed at them all. She adored parties, especially when she could show off the beautiful home of which she was mistress. Tonight she wore a favorite green silk and lace gown, low-necked, with a strand of pearls about her fine throat. John was handsome and stodgy and rather plump, stuffed into a bottle-green suit. Flora was already dancing with her fiancé, gazing up radiantly into his face.

The music was coming from a five-piece orchestra half-concealed in a bow window. Emilie greeted the new arrivals with a little cry. "Oh, you are practically late, my dears. How charming you all look. Grandmother Moira, should you be out in the night air?"

Moira bore her concern with composure. Nothing could have kept her from the ball, and Brett knew it. When he had seen his sisters settled, he asked her for the first dance, and she smiled up at him and took his arm. They floated about the room, the tall handsome man and the small, fragile, white-haired woman.

"The best dancer here," he whispered in her ear. She chuckled with pleasure, and tapped him with her fan when the dance ended.

"Now find yourself a pretty partner. I long to see you with a lovely girl on your arm," she said. Presently, she saw him with Julia Vining, and nodded wisely.

Julia was a beautiful southern girl on a visit to the Stratfords. She was a close relative of theirs, and she and her small plump sister Cecilia were already favorites. Julia was tall, slim, with long dark-blond curls and blue-gray eyes, altogether beautiful and rather spoiled. But Brett could tame her, thought Moira, looking her over critically. She longed to become better acquainted with the girl, for Brett had been with her much of this summer.

Stephen was dancing with Bridget. My, he was a nice young man, and so courteous, thought Moira. He even made shy Bridget feel a little at ease. When the dance finished, he escorted her to a table and gave her a glass of punch before leaving her to another young man.

Rose Marie danced one after another with young men she scarcely remembered. She laughed and made witty remarks, all the time burning inside that Stephen was ignoring her. If he had come up, she had vowed, she would have cut him dead, no matter what it cost. But he gave her no chance—and that made her even more furious.

Stephen was devilishly handsome, throwing back his head to roar with laughter at some remark of the men he stood with. Rose Marie looked away, her heart pounding, her fan fluttering. Could she ever forget that afternoon, that hateful, shameful afternoon? She still felt the hard muscles of his arms under her, the skillful caress of his hands, his senuous mouth against her flesh.

She was gazing thoughtfully at Brett dancing with Julia, his dark head bent intently to her lifted face, as she spoke with animation, when a touch made her jump. Stephen held her hand and drew her to her feet.

"My dance, beautiful one," he said smoothly, and laughed down at her tension as she tried to pull away. "No, no, don't make a scene."

She was swept into his arms and into the music of the waltz before she could utter a word of protest. He did dance divinely, she thought, and she surrendered herself to the music and his strong arms, whirling her around and around, until her blue skirts flew about her little blue slippers.

"You dance as well as you love," he whispered.

She gasped, outraged, and pulled back. He pulled her closer, and whirled her around again.

"You can go to the devil!" she whispered when he bent his head near hers.

"Oh, I plan to, my dear, I plan to, very shortly," and he flung back his head and laughed aloud.

She felt cold through. He was going into terrible danger, spying and riding and traveling about the South, when everyone was on edge about the elections this autumn and the terrible prospect of war. She felt a shiver wrench her.

"I am sorry that it was necessary for you to cover that beautiful throat tonight," he whispered before releasing her.

"*You* know why," she said tautly, and blushed furiously as he slowly gazed down her length.

"Yes. Rose Marie—I shall return this autumn. Shall you be here?"

Someone was coming toward them, a husky young son of the region. She nodded quickly. "I—shall remain here," she said swiftly before turning to her new partner with a smile. Stephen's hand pressed hers hard before releasing it.

She was tingling all through when she smiled and danced with the husky man, who tossed her about like a bale of hay. She did not even notice when he kept stepping on her toes. Stephen wanted to see her again. Why? Because he did not trust her? Or because he simply wanted—to see her again?

She tried vainly to fire the hate in her heart, but could not. She felt hot, and fanned herself vigorously when the dance was over, accepting a glass of cool punch with gratitude. Still she felt warm and trembling, quite unlike her cool, sarcastic, controlled self.

Chapter 14

Brett stood in one of the doorways to the open veranda, watching the dancers while he chatted idly with several of his neighbors. Stout Frederick Stratford was talking earnestly about the possibility of war should South Carolina secede.

"Nonsense, it will never come to that," said another man firmly. "Just a fuss in the family, that's what I say. It'll all come right after harvest. They need our crops, just as much as we need their manufactured products."

Brett's mouth twisted. He hoped they were right, but all his instincts told him otherwise. He had gone to Washington in the spring and talked with some men who were quietly stockpiling arms and ammunition, and who asked about his stores of black powder. Still, they had placed no orders. A man from Virginia, he felt they doubted his loyalty. He himself felt terribly torn.

He loved Virginia; it had nurtured him and his family for four generations. But if the southern states seceded, what would he do? Could he sell the black powder and shot to blow up his friends and neighbors? On the other hand, should he sell to the South, when he felt they were wrong to pull away from the Union? Or should he attempt to remain neutral and sell only sporting powder, or turn to woolen textiles, as he was tempted to do?

He knew Stephen had come to sound him out. But he could give his cousin no answer. Perhaps by the time the man returned in the autumn, he would know.

Julia Vining danced by with Stephen, flirting with him

with her long, dark lashes, her mouth quirked in the adorable way she had. Brett's heart quickened. She attracted him sensuously; he saw that there was fire in her. She stopped in a corner with Stephen and said something that made Stephen smile and bend to her, taking her fan and flirting it gently at her shoulders.

Damn the girl, she must be always after some man or other. Then when she had one in her palm, she tired of him. It had made Brett cautious. He would give no woman such power over him that she tied him in knots.

He strolled over to them. "Julia, may I have this dance?" he asked, holding out his hand to her.

The blue-gray eyes flickered at him; she turned from him and back to Stephen. Her soft drawl came. "Why, Brett honey, I promised this dance to your handsome cousin, Stephen. Why, I do think he is just the most handsome man—"

Stephen raised his eyebrows, slipped his arm about her waist, and led her away to the dance. Julia smiled sweetly around his shoulder at Brett, and there was something in the glitter of her eyes that repelled him.

Brett turned from the sight. Savagery in his heart, he went toward the table of drinks. On the way, he saw gentle Cecilia, Julia's sister, her rose dress settled about her, sitting on a settee beside his sister Bridget. Both looked so withdrawn, so anxious and serious, that he was drawn to them.

They were much alike, though Bridget was even more shy then Cecilia. He paused before them, smiled, and bowed to Cecilia.

"Bridget, you will not mind if I take away your companion? And you will save a dance for me?"

His sister blushed, lowered her glance to her hand, and said something in a muffled tone. Brett looked about as he drew Cecilia up with a gallant hand. John was nearby; he came at once and bowed to Bridget.

"Oh, I'm glad," whispered Cecilia. "She has not danced much all evening except with your cousin Stephen. He is so gallant; he dances with us all!"

"He pleases himself," said Brett with a smile. "Who could resist so many lovely girls?"

The earnest gray eyes met his for a moment, then she looked shyly past him to the throng. "You know what I mean," she said, in a low tone. "Some men hover only about the most beautiful girls, like Julia and your sister Rose Marie. But you—and—and Stephen—you are both so kind to us all."

Brett changed the topic, which made him feel uncomfortable. He, too, had hovered about Julia. He had seriously considered proposing to her. But she left him uncertain with her flirtatious ways. If she did marry him, would she be constant, would she become the good wife and mother of his children that he desired? Would she nag him to attend parties when he was worn out and weary? Would she listen to him patiently, as Granny Moira did, when he had troubles, or would she turn an impatient shoulder to him when he tried to talk to her?

At the end of the dance, as he drew Cecilia out to the veranda he noted that she felt as warm as he did. "It is not too cold for you out here, Cecilia?" he asked, his hand on her bare arm.

"Oh, no, doesn't the breeze feel good? And I love the view from here of the river and the mills. What is that light going back and forth?" She pointed with her round, plump arm and small fingers.

"That is the night watchman. He watches for possible fires" he said. He did not add—and for possible damage to the mills by men paid to cause trouble. The men in Washington had warned him that there might be people about trying to do just this. All the powder mills were adding watchmen and checking identity passes at the gates.

The veranda grew crowded. Brett put his hand under Cecilia's arm and drew her silently with him down to the smooth lawn. They walked slowly from the lighted area and paused in the paths about the flower beds.

"How good it smells here," said Cecilia, drawing breaths. "Roses? Yes, and phlox."

"You enjoy flowers as I do," he said, turning his attention fully to the girl. She was quiet, but poised, more than he had thought. She did not flutter, nor blink at him, nor stutter. She had a round, sweet face, brown curls that bobbed about her cheeks, fine gray eyes that saw much more than one believed at first. She was small, coming only to his heart, about five-feet-two, much shorter than her tall, more handsome sister Julia. But she was a nice girl, he decided.

Her silence was not sulking; she was restful. She gazed into the night, up at the stars, as though she really saw them and enjoyed the night sky.

"You will stay all summer?" he finally asked, putting his hand again under her round, plump arm and drawing her along the garden path.

"Yes, Mrs. Stratford has been most kind. She urges us to remain longer, but I know she has guests coming in September."

So they would leave by September. Brett was thoughtful. If Julia left this autumn, she might not return. She might marry soon; she was too attractive and too sensuous of nature to remain unmarried much longer. He had kissed her, and he knew the passion of her slim rounded body. But—did he want to marry her, to take the risk?

He found himself rebelling against marriage. Look how unhappy Rose Marie was; his heart ached for his lovely sister. She was sarcastic at times, but there was no meanness in her. She was bitterly hurt and sad.

He remembered all too vividly how Antoine had been hurt again and again by Emilie. Could he endure a hellish marriage like that? No, a thousand times no. Better never to marry at all than to be ground in humiliation into the dust, to grow to hate one's partner for insensitivity and meanness. But would Julia be like that? Or was she but restless until she married and found her mate?

They turned and walked back slowly to the veranda. Julia was there among a small group of admirers. She saw them approach as they came into the flaring lights.

Cecilia? I am shocked at you," she said with her light

laugh. "I had not thought to find a chaperon for you. I trusted to your discretion."

Cecilia came to a halt and tore her arm from Brett's light grasp. "I—I am sorry—" she mumbled. "I—I—"

Brett said smoothly, "We were admiring the gardens and the coolness, Julia. I recommend them to you, and to any one, or all, of your beaux." He took Cecilia's arm very strongly in his and escorted her up the steps, past the grinning men, and into the ballroom.

In the ballroom, he looked with pity at Cecilia's red-flushed face and tearful gray eyes. "Do not mind her," he recommended gently, and put his arm about her to draw her into the waltz.

He was shocked when she said, "Oh, she is so angry with me. She will be cross with me tomorrow—She counts you one of her best beaux."

"She has no hard claim on me," said Brett, as calmly as he could, but anger raged in him. Cecilia's look was fearful; she genuinely dreaded her sister's anger. "If she says anything, tell her she is free to choose her beaux—and so are you."

"Oh, I could never say that—not to Julia," she gasped.

He moved her around and around in the waltz, said something lightly to her, but could not bring a smile to her soft, quivering mouth. Finally he brought her to Rose Marie and whispered, "Be nice to the child—her sister is being nasty."

Rose Marie nodded quickly, her glance compassionate, and soon turned the conversation lightly to some amusing story. She kept Cecilia with her and Bridget, in another circle of men, and finally the girl regained her composure. Stephen joined them soon, and asked Cecilia to dance, then Bridget, then Rose Marie, so no one could accuse him of partiality. Brett noticed that he did not approach Julia again, nor did Brett. He had had enough of that spoiled beauty for the evening.

The next day was Sunday. A gentle rain was falling. After the rain cleared in the afternoon, Brett decided to take a long walk. He had much to think about. He strode along, not paying attention to the direction of his walk. But he was annoyed a little when he found that he was heading for the Stratford home down the hill and his thoughts were of Julia.

He was about to turn and start back when he saw a pretty picture. Two children ran in circles about a laughing figure of a woman. Cecilia, bundled in a gray cloak, held out her hands to them.

"Come now, do not tease me, you are too fast for me," she cried out, her rosy cheeks testifying to the exercise she had been indulging in with them. Brett strode on toward them, and was spotted by one of the children.

"Uncle Brett!" cried the little boy, and ran to him, holding up his arms.

"Well, Jerry, what are you doing here?" Brett leaned down, and swung him up in his arms, smiling into the dirty, eager face. "Playing in the mud, eh? And having a grand time, I warrant." He felt the small wriggling body against his own, and felt a pang for the fact that he had no children.

He carried the boy back to Cecilia and the little girl, and bent down to receive the enthusiastic wet kiss of the little child. "How are you, Miss Cecilia?" he said, straightening, with Jerry's hand firmly in his own.

"Oh, quite well, thank you, Brett. And you?" Her cheeks were flushed, her gray eyes shy and uneasy.

"I shall turn and walk with you a space," he said cheerfully. "Or why not come with me back home? Is it too long a walk? The children seem full of energy."

"Oh, yes, and they are under everyone's feet, so I brought them out."

"You have company today?"

She grimaced and nodded, brushing back some curls that had tumbled across her cheeks. The children dashed ahead of them, enjoying the unexpected outing. "Yes, a house full of gentlemen, and some ladies, too, have come visiting. The are all discussing the ball with great energy, and tearing apart anyone who is not there today."

Brett laughed, and she smiled with him. "I dread to think what is being said about me, but I shall not be concerned about that," he declared. "Did you enjoy yourself?"

"Oh, yes, very much. You are so kind, and your cousin, and your sisters."

He noticed that she did not mention her sister Julia. Had she come out to escape the crossness of that sister? Cecilia stumbled a little on some rocks, her small, booted feet wavering. He put his arm protectively under her elbow and held her upright.

"The footing is unsure there. Hey there, Jerry, do not get too far ahead of us, and bring your sister back." At the sharp authority of his tone, the children turned back and scampered about them. They walked slowly in the watery sunshine, enjoying the fragrance of the meadow, and the gurgling of the liltle stream that flowed into the Areuse. A small white rabbit darted across their path, and the children cried out in pleasure. Cecilia smiled fondly down at them.

"What pleasure they have in small things," she murmured. "I had almost forgotten what it was like to be a child."

"You are not so far from childhood yourself, my dear," he teased her.

"Oh, I am, I am. I am nineteen years old."

"A truly great age," he said solemnly. She gazed up into his sparkling blue eyes and began to laugh, her cheeks pink.

"Oh, I sound like a fool," she said.

"Never, just—very young and sweet," he said.

They walked in silence across the meadows; he helped her and the children over a stile, then on. It took almost an hour to get to the Vallette home, and he promised to send them back in a carriage after they had had some tea.

Rose Marie and Bridget were serving tea in the drawing room, for themselves, Stephen, and Moira. It seemed very serene and peaceful for Cecilia and the children. Rose Marie took the children, washed their faces and hands, and brought them back, chatting nineteen to the dozen, as Stephen teased them.

Cecilia set off her cloak; a maid took it away and showed her a room where she might brush her hair and wash her hands. She returned to find Stephen and Brett chaffing Moira, who was relating some story with great gusto. She paused in the doorway to enjoy the scene. They teased her, but they adored her, one could tell. Cecilia hated to think how Julie spoke of Mrs. Vallette, calling her Irish-poor and married far above herself. "She'll never be anything but a poor Irish working girl," she had said often and contemptuously.

Cecilia thrust the thought of Julia from her. She had endured a painful tongue-lashing that morning on the subject of stealing a sister's beaux from her, and some cruel remarks about how pitiful it had looked, her hanging on Brett's arm. "If you were pretty, I should not wonder. But he can only pity you," said Julia, with her usual cold cruelty.

"I know that," said Cecilia quietly, but that did not turn away the anger. She had escaped only when the luncheon bell rang. She had volunteered eagerly to take the children out that afternoon—anything to get away from Julia's smile and cold, warning, blue-gray eyes if Cecilia attempted even to speak to a young gentleman. Julia considered every eligible man within range to be her own property.

The young men jumped up when they observed Cecilia in the doorway. Brett came forward to greet her. Stephen held a comfortable chair for her, and patted a cushion into it.

"You must be very weary, entertaining those two lively young ones all afternoon," said Stephen warmly.

"Oh, no, I enjoyed it," she said, exchanging a smile with Moira. "How are you, Mrs. Vallette? Did you enjoy the ball?"

"Immensely," said Moira with great satisfaction. "I danced with my grandson, and several other gentlemen, who do not consider me past the age of dancing. I shocked my daughter-in-law, and that always gives me great pleasure."

Brett flung back his head and laughed heartily; so did Stephen. Rose Marie came in with the children, smiling. "I heard that, granny. You are being naughty," she said brightly.

"You take after your granny," said Stephen, getting up again to give her a chair. "Hey, there, Jerry, do you remember the game I taught you?"

"Yes, let's play." To Cecilia's surprise, the handsome young man got down on the floor and played a game of spillikins with Jerry—and let him win. Rose Marie held the sleepy girl on her lap, and Bridget brought in the tea with one of the maids.

It was a warm, cozy afternoon, with no nastiness, and Cecilia enjoyed it immensely. After tea, Brett asked her to play the piano for them, and she got up at once. She did not feel awkward with them.

She did not have the large, long hands that Julia had to play the flashing, sparkling, difficult numbers. But Cecilia had a nice touch at the piano. She played some popular songs, and some of the old ones, and drifted from them into a composition of her own. Finally she stopped.

"Very pretty, my dear, very pretty," said Moira Vallette. "It reminds me of when Amelia used to play. So soft and soothing."

"I can just remember my mother telling how Amelia would play," said Stephen. "Let me see, I was going to try to figure out what relation we are, Cecilia. You are third cousins to the Stratfords, and Amelia, my grandmother, was a second cousin—"

"On the other side," said Cecilia, with a mischievous grin. "And we are third cousins, twice removed."

Stephen groaned; Brett laughed.

"Oh, we must be going home," cried Cecilia presently. "It is past six o'clock. Their mother will be wondering if I have lost the children."

"I'll get the carriage," said Brett at once. "We must

not have you in trouble. Stephen, did you say we would call on them before you leave?"

"As I plan to leave tomorrow or the next day, it might as well be this evening," said Stephen, slowly. "Aunt Moira, would you excuse us for a couple of hours?"

"Of course, dear boy, though it troubles me to hear you speak of leaving us," said Moira, warmly.

Rose Marie looked down at the little girl in her lap. "I'll get their coats," she said briskly.

Soon Brett brought the carriage around. He drove; Stephen held the small, sleepy Jerry, and Cecilia the little girl. It was a silent drive to the Stratfords. The children were half asleep.

Cecilia wondered what Julia would say to her this time. She would pay dearly for that happy afternoon.

Brett was thinking deeply. And so was Stephen.

They went on to the Stratfords, and a boy came running out to hold the horses. "We will be a couple of hours," Brett told the boy, as Mr. Stratford came out to greet them.

"You have missed the greatest part of the company," he said, scolding them. Stephen gave Brett a wink missed by their host. Cecilia caught the look, and felt happier inside. The men had deliberately held back from being caught in that "great company." Brett could have accompanied them to the Stratfords, instead of taking them to his home. And he had not; he had not gone directly to Julia.

Julia was sitting in a great blue armchair, which set off the gold of her hair and the regal pale blue silk of her dress with insets of French lace. "My word, Cecilia, you look a dowd," she said, when they came in. Her bright eyes missed nothing. "Don't tell me you went visiting looking like that. Do go and change your dress."

Cecilia felt the crimson come up in her cheeks. "I was out walking the children and—and—"

"And I insisted on bringing them all home with me, for a visit with us," said Brett, smiling charmingly on them all. "Forgive me for spiriting her away, Julia. We

196

have seen little of Cecilia on this visit, and Rose Marie and Bridget longed for a chat with her."

Cecilia made to slip away; Brett caught at her hand, right in front of Julia.

"No, do not leave us, you look lovely with the color in your cheeks. Everyone here would benefit by going outdoors into the fresh air," he said casually, sitting down on the sofa and drawing Cecilia down with him. "Look how fresh and clear is Cecilia's complexion. Females do not exercise enough."

Julia's eyes glittered; she leaned forward and gave him a battle over his words. "Exercise, indeed! And who danced every dance last night? While others dawdled out in the moonight? I have every bit as much energy as—as anyone."

Stephen let his laugh break the uneasy brittleness of the conversation. "You must not quarrel tonight. I have come to make my graceful leave-taking of you. I wish to retain a fond memory of gentle southern conversation—no fire-eating, or I shall not have the courage to continue my journey."

"Ah, where do you go from here, Mr. Vallette?" asked Mrs. Stratford, promptly taking his cue.

Brett let the talk flow on without him. He felt the coolness and the quiver of Cecilia's hand in his, and he finally let it go reluctantly, as Julia was glaring at them both. He felt some wonder at himself. He felt oddly protective toward Cecilia, fond of her, as he was of Bridget when she was being tormented.

What was the matter with him? Didn't he love Julia? He desired Julia; because she was beautiful and sensuous and appealing; she was his type, he thought. Tall, stunning, regal. But there was something lacking, some softness and warmth.

Cecilia was all softness, all gentleness, toward the children, toward her friends. She had played beautifully for them that afternoon, in such a soothing way that he had felt quieted and comforted. He had looked at her brown curls, her earnest, round face as she played, and thought it would be easy to love her. She would make a fine wife and mother. She liked flowers and stars, dancing and laughter, gentleness and comfortable talk. She was uneasy with malice and sarcasm; she did not say spiteful things about others. But a wife—for him?

Stephen took his departure within two hours, and with many promises to see the Stratfords on his return, they finally left. Brett drove briskly, staring straight ahead.

Stephen glanced often at him. He finally said, "I do not envy Miss Cecilia tonight. Did you see the way her sister glared at her? I should not like to receive the edge of that tongue."

Brett sighed and moved his stiff shoulders. He had been sitting erect for hours, and anger burned in him. "I feel the same way. Yet Cecilia has as much right to entertain herself as Julia. Why should her sister feel she can rule the girl?"

"She is a beautiful woman, Julia Vining," said Stephen thoughtfully. "But there is a strong streak of cruelty in her. She must hit out at the weak. Perhaps she longs for someone strong to rule her. That might make her more womanly. On the other hand, I should not like to attempt it, not that task. For me, marriage should be a sanctuary, a holy place, where I might find love and peace. Not a battleground, Lord, no."

"I think she is much like Rose Marie, strong and spirited."

"Rose Marie is strong, yes, but she is sarcastic because she is sad and sees no way out of her situation. She has spirit. But Julia—no, she is mean, and cruel, and could be petty in her revenge. I beg your pardon, Brett." He turned quickly to the other man. "I did not mean to malign her, I believe you like her very much."

"I like her, but sometimes—love can be blind. I do not mean to be blind, when I love," said Brett.

"Nor I. Good luck to us both." And Stephen laughed, a rollicking, defiant laugh at the skies.

Chapter 15

Stephen left two mornings later. As Moira went back to her chair, after kissing him a fond farewell, she sighed regretfully.

"Ah, he is such a fine young man. Would that he lived closer to us, that we might see him more. If only Conrade had not moved his family to New York—"

"If only the moon was not made of green cheese," said Brett, gravely, with mischief in his blue eyes, and she laughed up at him, shaking her fan at him.

"Oh, you tease. But you shall miss him also, Brett. I noticed that you were able to talk freely to him, and he has good ideas and common sense. He is not frivolous, and full of grand, useless plans as Conrade was—oh, dear, I did not mean to say that." She frowned, scolding herself in a soft mutter of Gaelic, which she still used from time to time.

Rose Marie was restless that summer. The flowers had bloomed early, and some were fading by late August. She took long walks in the woods, sometimes with Bridget, sometimes with Brett on a Sunday afternoon.

She finally wrote to Ingram and told her husband she would not be returning home this autumn. "Granny Moira is not well, and the household is too much for Bridget," she wrote, her tongue in her cheek. "I know you have much work to do on the plantation, and you had not planned to be home for Christmas. You shall not mind if I remain here a few more months."

Ingram Lombard wrote back at once, in his imma-

199

ture scrawl. "You must come home, I look a fool with my wife with her relations miles away. Don't be an idiot. I know we quarreled, but it shall all be mended—"

She waited a time to answer that, then wrote discreetly, not to rouse his ire, that she hoped to remain longer. Fortunately for her, she had her own income, safely invested in the Vallette mills, and Brett saw to it that no one touched it but her. She was immensely grateful to her brother. Most women faced the indignity of having their husbands immediately take over their inheritance and spend it as they pleased.

She strode along the Areuse in her soft boots, talked to Bridget idly, sometimes met Cecilia with the children and brought them all home for a visit. She never met Julia in the woods; Julia did not care for nature. The older girl often went visiting, or gallivanted in a small company of young men and ladies into town.

Rose Marie noted that Cecilia came willingly, and blushed when Brett came near, her gray eyes soft and gentle when she gazed at him. And Brett bothered to come home early when she was there, lingered to talk, and smiled at her. And he relaxed when she played the piano.

He did not seek out Julia much that summer. He danced with her at neighborhood dances, and conversed politely with her, but there was a coolness now not of Julia's making. Julia would flutter near him, place her long, slim hand on his arm, and gaze up meltingly. Brett would answer courteously, smile down at her, and presently move away. He did not act like a man courting a maid.

Rose Marie finally ventured to speak to Bridget, as safe a confidant as one could imagine. "Do you think that Brett no longer cares for Julia Vining?" she asked one afternoon as they strolled along beside the river.

"I hope not, Rose Marie. Oh, I hope he is no longer interested," said Bridget, with unexpected fervor. "I dreaded so much that one day Brett would come home and say they were to marry. How could I live with them? I should wither under her tongue."

Rose Marie's hand squeezed that of her small sister. "I know how you feel," she said gently. "She makes me feel—inadequate. She will speak of children, and look at me, as though to say, 'Why are you not having children?' And she will gaze at my dress, and at once I wonder if there is a tear in the hem."

"Really? Do you feel like that with Julia?" asked Bridget, wondering at her cool, composed sister. "I thought it was only me—and Cecilia."

"And speaking of Cecilia, here she comes," and Rose Marie waved at the gray-cloaked figure and the two children scampering about her. "She is good to those children; they have been neglected otherwise this summer."

"I think she is also glad to get away from—you know."

Bridget always saw more than Rose Marie expected. They walked to greet Cecilia and saw that her face was pale and wan.

Rose Marie asked what was wrong. Cecilia gave a vague smile. "Oh, one of the children was sick this past week. The elder boy. I volunteered to stay up with him, and I am a bit weary from it."

Rose Marie bit her lip to keep back a sharply angry remark. Mrs. Stratford, good as she was, could not refrain from making use of her gentle young guest.

"Come back with us now," she urged, and they turned back to the Vallette home. Rose Marie took over the two younger children, and when they arrived at the house Cecilia lay back wearily in a chair, as though she could not move again. Brett came home about five and sat down to talk with them.

He took Cecilia and the children home and returned with a grim mouth. "They use her like a servant," he said angrily to his sisters. "I wonder how she is used at home."

"Her older brother is married, with three children and a nature like that of Julia," said Rose Marie bitterly. "I would imagine she is treated much like this."

"And they go home—when?"

"They had thought to go in September. Now Julia speaks of sending Cecilia home while she remains." Rose Marie gave Brett a look from under her lashes. "For some reason, Julia wishes to remain. And Mrs. Stratford's guests who were to have come are not coming. They are in Louisiana, and they said if war comes they wish to be in their own home, safely away from the border."

Brett frowned, and said nothing the rest of the evening.

To Rose Marie's fury and amazement, her husband arrived a few days later. Ingram Lombard was so lazy she had thought he would not make the trip. But there he came, with a carriage and two of his coachmen, all of them tired.

She went out to meet him and received his kiss on her cheek with coldness. "Well, Ingram, I am amazed at you. You have come for a visit, I suppose?" And she gave him a cross look.

"To bring you home, where you belong," he said, in front of the servants.

She took him into the house, indicating to the servants where his luggage was to go. "I am in a small room—the bed is not large," she said, indifferent to his scowl. "This will be a more comfortable room for you, Ingram."

"There is plenty of room for you here with me," he said. "Move your things to my room. We shall depart as soon as I have rested."

There was an obstinate look to his large jaw, and his cheeks were flushed with more than liquor. She went to see Brett as soon as he came from the mills.

As a result, a maid slept in her room with her, on the long day bed beside the window. Ingram was wined and dined until he could scarcely stagger up to his bedroom every night, and he slept like a log by himself.

He still insisted that she must remember her wifely duties and return home with him. They fought it out finally, on a stroll in the gardens beside the house on a warm September morning.

He kept looking at Rose Marie, smart and pretty in a violet muslin dress, with a lace bertha and her bonnet with violet ribbons tied under her chin. She was staring straight ahead.

"You keep asking me to return," she said finally. "But you have not said what you mean to do."

"I shall not obey my wife," he sneered. "No woman tells me what I shall do. I shall visit the slave quarters as often as I choose, and have a nice, warm, brown girl in my bed whenever my wife turns cold."

"The boy Ben, what have you done about him?" She said it coldly, ignoring his other remarks.

"Oh, I have taken him into the house; he is training to be a footman." And Ingram laughed. "My eldest son! He looks much like me, everyone says."

Rose Marie's face remained cool and remote, hiding the seething fury behind it. Ingram had fathered half a dozen children on his father's servants, and was proud of it. He bragged that his children were smarter and more handsome than any others, and something was wrong with Rose Marie that she did not produce sons and daughters for him. He did not understand the revulsion she felt for him, how she could not bear his touch. And it had been that way for five years.

"You seem to have your needs well cared for, Ingram," she said slowly. "I for my part do not wish to return to such a degrading situation. I am not accustomed to sharing a man with slaves. I think you have married the wrong woman."

"Now, now, Rose Marie," he said anxiously, turning back to her. His pudgy hands were on her waist. "Listen, I love you, I adore you, you little devil, you! I want you. Come on back, and we'll make a good marriage of it. We'll take another honeymoon, go anywhere you want. Want to go to New Orleans? We'll have a fine time there."

"No, Ingram. I am thinking of obtaining a divorce," she said quietly.

He stared at her, his sensuous, full mouth agape and ugly, his face flushing hotly. "A divorce? Never in this world! You have no grounds. I never looked at another white woman. I could do it—you give me no children. But you come on back, and we'll soon start a young 'un, you better understand that. I ain't letting you go."

She could not bear even to look at him, his gross body stuffed into his dandified yellow coat and trousers, the lace neck-cloth soiled where he had spilled coffee on it. She thought of Stephen, so neat and handsome, so cool and contained, with the smile behind his brown eyes. And she remembered the touch of his gentle hands on her, even when he forced her to his bed. He had not been cruel, not the way Ingram had been every night of their married life.

Ingram would not agree to a divorce, and finally left in a terrible fury. Brett sent him on his way, with cold courtesy. "No, I shall not force my sister to return to you. She always has a home with me," said Brett.

"I'll come back in a couple months. She'll cool off and come on back, or I'll lay a whip on her back," Ingram threatened. Brett just looked at him.

"You'll never touch her with a whip," he said in a soft voice. "Or by God, I'll kill you myself!"

So Ingram left, grumbling and stumbling with all the liquor he had drunk to see him on his way. Rose Marie took a deep breath of relief and ordered the guest bedroom thoroughly aired out.

September drew into October, and Stephen did not return. They did not hear from him, either, which worried Rose Marie. She began to wonder if he was in trouble, or even—wounded? He might have gotten into a quarrel with one of those quick-tempered Southerners.

With Rose Marie's encouragement, Cecilia decided to remain as well. Mrs. Stratford was more than glad to have her; she helped so much with the children, even teaching reading and writing to the boy. When Julia complained, Mrs. Stratford rebuked her sharply.

"Cecilia is a lovely guest, I shall not send her away." Privately Mrs. Stratford wondered, for Brett Vallette came over often and gave Cecilia as much attention as

Julia. She wondered—would he see gentle Cecilia for the lovely girl she was? Could he resist the power of the imperious Julia, her beauty and charms, her sensuous appeal? She hoped so. Living with Julia, she had come to know the girl thoroughly, and found her full of conceit and very spoiled.

Cecilia would crunch through the woods full of autumn leaves with the children, and laugh with them, and wonder if that day she would see Brett. She seemed to live from one day to the next for this purpose alone. A day in which she saw Brett was touched with golden wonder. A day without him ended in disappointment, a sigh, a hope for the next encounter. He had such blue, blue eyes, she thought, lying awake in the small bedroom at the back of the house. Julia had the grand front bedroom opposite her host and hostess. But Cecilia could see from her window up the hills toward the Vallette mills, and at night the glow warmed her heart.

Brett told Cecilia one day she must not walk about in the woods for a time. He warned his sisters also. "My watchmen have spotted a man in ragged clothing. He might be just a poor man out of luck, or he might be one of the incendiaries."

At their wondering looks, he explained brusquely, with an anxious frown, "Men who go about setting fire to mills, and such."

"But the powder mills, Brett," gasped Rose Marie. She had a drawn look to her, thought Cecilia, as though she waited and worried. Was she upset about her husband? She never spoke of him.

"I know. We have to be very careful. We are vulnerable. A touch of fire—and it all could explode."

Rose Marie was thinking of that when she spotted the man two days later. He lingered near the stables, and the stablehands stopped to glare at him.

She picked up her skirts and went down. She faced the man and saw a tired, drawn look in his eyes. "Sir, what are you doing here? I shall inform my brother—"

"Is he Stephen Vallette?" the man asked in a low tone.

205

Rose Marie felt a chill down her back. She stared at the man. Behind the heavy grain of stubbled beard, behind the weariness and dirt, she saw intelligence—and a gleam.

"No, Stephen Vallette is my cousin," she said quietly, so the stablehands would not hear. "What do you want with him?"

"When's he coming?"

"I do not know. We—we expect him any time. What do you want with him?"

"I been waiting for a long time. Can't wait longer," he said, in a sort of crisp voice. "You—his cousin?"

"Yes, I am Rose Marie Vallette."

He seemed to hesitate, searching her gravely, but not rudely. He was not a crude man. "Guess I got to trust you. Would you give him a message when he comes? I can't stay on."

She drew a deep breath. Intrigue—violence—danger? But Stephen had drawn her promise not to betray him.

"You can trust me. I will give him the message when he comes."

The man looked about. She began to walk toward the kitchen door. "Come, and I'll give you a plate of food and some hot coffee," she said, in a louder voice.

He followed her toward the kitchens. At the edge of the house, a furtive, dirty hand went to his pocket and he drew out a brown object about three inches long, a capsule with something white in it.

He shoved it quickly into her hand. "Mighty good of you, ma'am. I'd like to wash up at the pump, then eat a bite. I'll be right on my way."

She nodded; her hand went to her pocket and returned empty. Inside, she told the cook to give the man some hot food and coffee, then a bundle of food to take with him. "Down on his luck," she said. "He's going on as soon as he is fed."

Brett was down at the mills. Bridget was sitting with Moira, who had not slept well the night before. Rose Marie went quietly up to her bedroom, searched out some gold coins and some paper money, and wrapped them in a blank sheet of white paper. She went down again to the kitchen.

She found the man sitting on the back steps, eating hungrily, but neatly. He glanced up at her warily, his dark eyes glazed with weariness.

She worked about in the kitchen, helped make up a packet of meat, bread, and cheese, added a jar of peaches, and set all in a checked cloth. She brought it to the man as he finished.

"Good luck, then, and may you have a safe journey," she said, cheerfully.

"God bless you, ma'am. I surely thank you for your goodness." He wiped his mouth, got up, and accepted the packet. Silently, her back to the cooks, she indicated the small twist of paper she set in the corner of the knapsack. He nodded; his eyes gleamed with gratitude.

"Goodbye, then," she said, and went back into the house. From the upstairs window she watched him trudge away. Was Stephen seeking shelter in some house in the South? Would some kind woman not question him, but give him food and drink and a cheery word?

Oh, but Stephen was different. He had a horse, saddlebags, money, and infinite resources. Still—she would be happier when he returned to the Vallette mills and she could see him for herself.

It was a chill October day when Stephen returned, just a week later. Rose Marie saw him coming and ran to meet him. She could scarcely hold back a cry when she saw his face clearly.

He was so thin his cheekbones stood out sharply against the dark flesh of his tanned face. He got down slowly from the saddle, and a stablehand ran up to take the horse.

"Well, Rose Marie—" he said slowly, and flashed a smile, with a faint question behind it.

"You're late," she said, as sharply as an anxious wife.

"Got held up. I mean, by business," he added as she gasped. "Can't stay long. Where's Brett?"

"I'll send down to the mill for him."

She called a servant, who ran down the hill to the powder mills. Bridget came out and exclaimed kindly, "Oh, cousin Stephen, you need feeding up."

"I've been looking forward to coming," he said, with a sigh. "Seems a long journey. Feels like I've traveled over every inch of the South."

He wanted a bath and a change of clothes. Rose Marie gathered up his torn, dirty things and took them down herself, leaving a suit of Brett's and some shirts and underthings for him. It gave her a curious feeling to be handling Stephen's clothes, dirty and worn though they were. She turned them over to a maid reluctantly.

By the time Stephen had bathed, changed, and come down again, Brett had arrived from the mill. The two men clasped hands. Brett eyed his cousin in silence.

"I look a sight," said Stephen, with his usual gay laugh, though his brown eyes did not echo the laughter. "Been traveling a long time."

"We'll hear your news soon enough. Relax, and make yourself at home." Brett pushed him gently into a comfortable chair. Moira took his hand and patted it with her frail hand.

They talked lightly, had a drink, and toasted Stephen's safe return. Then they dined, and he went to bed early, exhausted.

Brett stayed around the next morning. Stephen went to him, and sitting in Brett's office they talked a long time.

"There's going to be war, Brett," said Stephen, with somber emphasis. "I want to be back in New York by the elections. But I think Mr. Lincoln will win, and if so, the Southerners will be bitterly angry. They hate him; many talk of secession."

Brett nodded, rocking back in his chair thoughtfully. He rubbed his chin. "I'm going to open the woolen mills again," he said, as though changing the subject. "May close down some of the powder mills, but I have to have work for my men."

Brett said no more of that, but asked about some of

his agents whom Stephen had seen. Stephen gave him a dozen messages, and they talked of where he had been.

"They won't buy textiles from us in the North," Stephen said, with a flash of bitterness. "Some firms have dealt with us for twenty years. Now they won't place a single order. They'll buy cotton from the South. By God, it's hard lines. Father will be terribly disappointed. I expected some resistance, but not this. Not a fresh order did I get, and some hinted when the present contracts run out they'll buy no more—not until they see which way the wind blows."

"It blows war, I think, cousin."

"I fear so. You here in the valley—are you protected enough? Is there a militia close by?"

Brett sighed. "There is talk of forming one. I shall have to decide what to do. The mills and the family must be protected. That is my first consideration."

"Rose Marie is still here. Is she staying?" Stephen was looking down at the glowing tip of his cigar.

"Yes, she is staying," said Brett definitely. "I won't have her going back to South Carolina. That may blow up first. And her husband—damn his hide, I cannot endure him. I hope to get a divorce for her—you will not repeat this, cousin."

"Of course not," said Stephen quietly. "I—traveled near there. I understand his nature is not good. He brags of his many by-blows."

"Yes, she finally told me. It was the last straw." They smoked in silence, in comfort, for a time before rejoining the ladies.

Stephen spoke reluctantly of going on within a couple days. "I am grateful for your hospitality, Aunt Moira. But my family will need me. Father must hear my news."

"You'll surely come again soon, now that we know you?" Moira begged him, patting his arm with the tiny reassuring pats of a woman who longs to help a dear one.

He smiled down at her, his sensuous lips gentle and

compassionate. "I wish I could promise, Aunt Moira. You may be sure I shall try."

Rose Marie waited to see him alone. The capsule seemed to burn a hole in her capacious pocket. Finally she saw him in the upstairs hallway.

"Cousin?" She hesitated, and he returned from the door to his room. They met about halfway down the hall. "I have a message for you," she said in a low tone.

He looked at her shrewdly. "Come—" He went into her bedroom, leaving the door open. "What is it?"

She took out the capsule and handed it to him, touching his strong brown fingers as she did so. She saw him turn greenish-pale under his tan, and the fingers closed convulsively on the capsule and her hand.

"In God's name—where did you get this?" He was crushing her hand.

She told him, in a low tone, about the ragged man and his message.

"And you have told Brett?"

She flung back her head proudly, the blue-black hair streaming down her back, tied only loosely with the broad amber ribbon. "No, I told no one. I promised."

"Thank you, from the bottom of my heart," he whispered. He put the capsule in his pocket, but retained her hand. "Tell me of him, how he looked, what he said."

She told him. He questioned her sharply again and again, about how long the man had lingered, about what he had said, about his appearance, about where he was going.

Then he asked, "Why did you do this, Rose Marie? You are a Southerner."

"I am against the war," she said defiantly. "The South is foolish, damn foolish to bring this on. They must not succeed in pulling away."

He looked at her keenly. How trustworthy was she?

"I thank you again," he said, and raised her hand to his lips. His lips on her fingers reminded her of the day he had taken her, and a hot flush came to her cheeks.

Stephen left two days later, and she had no further

private conversation with him. When he left, he kissed Moira, then turned to Bridget and kissed her cheek.

Rose Marie gazed at him, her blue eyes unconsciously wistful. Stephen, taking her hand, drew her gently to him. She felt herself against the strength of his lean body for a moment; he kissed her cheek slowly.

Brett came to him then, and the men hugged each other. "You will have a care," said Brett, a choke in his voice. "Remember that we value you."

"And you—you will all have a care. Let me know how you do—you will write?"

"We will all write," promised Brett. They watched him on his way.

Rose Marie began to write to him soon. She felt a terrible need to have contact with him, even if only by letter. She told him the gossip of the neighborhood, the news of their family, how the people had reacted at the news of the election of Abraham Lincoln. "You would think a demon was approaching the White House," she wrote, in scorn. "Even babies will not be safe. Did you ever hear such nonsense?"

Later, she had important news for him. She thought a long time, then defiantly recorded it in the letter, phrasing it carefully.

"An agent of Vallette's in South Carolina wrote for a large order of black powder. Brett refused him, and also the rifles he requested. He fears if war comes it would be used against the Union. He has also begun to turn down requests from other agents in the South. Some black powder was seized in New Orleans. Brett was very angry about that."

She made it sound gossipy and trivial, but hoped it would be of use to him. Stephen, receiving the letter, was troubled. He finally went to his superior officer and showed it to him.

"We must check our sources and see if this is correct," said the man, an Army intelligence officer, after making a copy of the important paragraph. "This cousin of yours, Rose Marie, can you trust her? What do you know of her?"

"She is spirited, a good woman," said Stephen slowly. "She is bored with her marriage; she detests her husband and returned to live with her brother. I shall want to know if the information is correct."

It proved out, and Stephen drew a deep sigh of relief. He had wanted to believe her. The information was valuable to him. Perhaps she would write more often and tell him more.

Chapter 16

Though they lived a quiet life, full of work, on the Areuse, the winter seemed to speed past. Rose Marie studied the gazettes intensely and talked to Brett in the evenings. Cecilia and Julia came sometimes with the Stratfords; they all spoke of war approaching.

Just before Christmas, 1860, South Carolina voted to secede from the Union. In January, 1861, Mississippi followed, then Florida and Alabama. News item followed news item, each more dreadful. Troops in the southern states seized federal arsenals, taking over rifles and gunpowder from the federal troops. In Florida, Fort Marion was captured with no opposition. More forts were taken in Louisiana.

Brett refused to send powder to the South, though his southern agents begged and sent representatives to him. Then the threats began to come in.

Some southern officials called on him and said that if he did not supply them, they would force the closing of his mills. Reluctantly, Brett sent a small supply, but he slowed down production. He opened the woolen mills and transferred many of his men to work on the wool. He bought up supplies of wool from many farmers in the area, and started a new mill. He came home late at nights, tired and grim and silent.

He organized a local militia. Many of his own Irishmen were quick with guns, and they were drilled into a fighting force. He put many on night duty to watch for incendiaries. They patrolled the mills, kept the gates locked day and night, and walked the fences which surrounded Vallette and Sons.

"This is all so dull, not a ball in a month," complained Julia in late March.

They all looked at her in silence.

In the middle of April news came from South Carolina that Fort Sumter had been fired upon. The fort surrendered to Confederate troops. War officially began, the dreaded War Between The States.

"How silly they all are! Oh, do you think they will come this far north?" cried Julia, fear in her beautiful face.

"I fear they will," said Brett grimly.

Julia's brother sent four of his men north to bring Julia and Cecilia home. He planned to send Julia on to Florida.

"We will be safer there, in Florida," said Julia, with relief. "Lord, Lord, who would think this could happen? I do hope there are some nice soldiers at the forts in Florida, and we can have some gay times." She flirted with Brett from under her long lashes, but her mouth tightened as she saw him turn to Cecilia.

"May I inquire what you plan to do, Miss Cecilia?" he asked her formally.

"My sister-in-law has written. She has had a fourth child and will need my assistance." Cecilia spoke gravely, but there was a weariness in her eyes, a droop to her shoulders.

Brett left, but paced the woods impatiently on his return home. He was not ready to make this decision, yet events forced him to it. He went to Rose Marie.

"Rose Marie, I am asking you and Bridget to beg of Cecilia to come and remain with us. I wish her to pay us a long visit, but I do not wish the request to come from me."

Rose Marie patted his arm. "I understand, brother. Bridget and I shall make a strong request. She shall be safe here—at least as safe as in South Carolina, slaving over those children."

"She is weary to the bone," he said bitterly. "Julia

214

will always be safe and protected. But who will look after Cecilia?"

"We shall, be sure of it," said Rose Marie, and took her cloak and carriage and collected her younger sister. They were driven over by one of the coachmen, and at the Stratford house found all in confusion.

Cecilia was busily packing for herself and Julia, going from room to hallway where the trunks were opened. Julia was entertaining in the drawing room, laughing and fanning herself at the many compliments from her beaux.

Rose Marie did not pause in the drawing room. She went directly upstairs to Cecilia before anger could cause her to make a rash remark. She and Bridget found the girl bending over, flushed of face, packing some of her sister's gowns, assisted by one of the Stratford maids.

Cecilia straightened up. "Rose Marie! How splendid to see you." Her smile was wistful. "I did not think I would see you again before—before we left."

"Let me help you," said Bridget, and took over the deft folding of garments while Rose Marie drew Cecilia into the quiet back bedroom.

"This is yours?" asked Rose Marie, casually, looking about the neat plain room.

"Yes. They have been most kind to me."

Rose Marie stifled the words that wanted to rise. "You have been good to them," she said pointedly. "Now I wish you to be good to us. Bridget and I shall be lonely and quiet, I fear, with the war here upon us. Brett does not mean to send us north. Will you come and remain with us?"

Cecilia started, then gasped a little. "Me? You mean Julia?"

"No, my dear," said Rose Marie, in a low but sharp voice. "Not Julia. We wish *you* to come. I understand Julia will be safe enough in Florida, having her balls."

"Oh, I should dearly love to come. But my sister-in-law needs me—"

"There are servants there to care for the children,"

said Rose Marie bluntly. "They are not your concern."

"But Julia will be furious," whispered Cecilia, twisting her hands together nervously. Now that her flush had faded, her cheeks were wan and pale.

Rose Marie put her warm hands on the small ones of Cecilia. In a murmur, she said, "Brett wishes you to come. Do say you will, and I shall have your trunks moved out with us today, at once. We can move quickly, and Julia will not have a word to say. She will not wish to spoil any illusions of her beaux."

Rose Marie's blue eyes sparkled with mischief. At last, some action had come along to still the restlessness of her heart. Cecilia looked at her, her gray eyes wide.

"You—you truly want me—to come and remain? It may be quite a long time."

"Quite long," said Rose Marie serenely, with a smile. She squeezed the small hands encouragingly. "Come now, say the word, we shall pack your trunks and have them downstairs in a trice!"

"Oh, yes—yes—yes—thank you!" Cecilia gave a little laugh. "I cannot believe it. Oh, yes, I will come. And I am all packed but for my valise."

"Good." Rose Marie called to Bridget to come. The girl came willingly and helped Cecilia pack the last items into her valise. Rose Marie, meantime, slipped down the back stairs and begged two of the stalwart footmen, with a charming smile, to carry Cecilia's two small trunks down to their carriage out the back way, unseen.

While they did this, she went to seek out the hostess. Mrs. Stratford, her mouth open in surprise, finally managed to stammer, "But what in the world will Brett Vallette say?"

"Oh, he wishes her to remain," said Rose Marie, and gave Mrs. Stratford a small wink, wickedly. "We shall say nothing, eh, so that Julia's temper will not be roused? But it was Brett's idea. The wind blows that way, my dear."

The two women chuckled mischievously together. Mrs. Stratford waited at the stairs. Rose Marie and

Bridget brought Cecilia down, dressed in her cloak and traveling bonnet, with her valise safely in Rose Marie's grip.

Julia looked up casually; the blue-gray eyes widened as she saw them all. Rose Marie said cheerfully, "We shall say goodbye, and farewell, and good times to you, Julia. I know you shall enjoy Florida. Cecilia is coming with us for a visit."

"She—what?" said Julia sharply, rising. All her young men rose with her, looking curiously from one to the other.

A carriage pulled up at the doorway, and soon Brett Vallette came in, neat in his gray suit and short boots. "Ah, there you are, Cecilia. Have the girls persuaded you to visit with us? Good, we shall be on our way."

Julia flung on him. "Brett, honey, you are all turned mad," she pouted charmingly. "Have you forgotten Cecilia is needed at home? We leave tomorrow."

"Oh, I think she must pay us a good, long visit; we have seen little of her this winter," said Brett firmly. "Do enjoy Florida, Julia."

Her face paled; her blue-gray eyes sparkled with fury. She tried to contain her temper. "You are being utterly foolish. Just because I would not remain with you—" She said it clearly, so all would hear her.

Brett smiled. "Did someone beg you to stay? I did not hear it, but of course, you are most popular."

"Too popular for your liking. Any woman of yours must shut herself up in a harem," she snapped. One man laughed aloud.

"I didn't know you were an authority on that matter, Julia," said Brett, coolly. He turned to Mrs. Stratford. "Thank you for your hospitality to Miss Cecilia. Say goodbye to her, Cecilia—though we shall have the Stratfords over often."

Before the women could speak, Julia cut in again, her voice high and shrill: "What are you doing, Brett? Do you think to spite me? I told you I didn't care whether or not you enlisted."

His mouth went thin, as he stared at her. The young

men, some in uniform, stiffened, and there was a murmur of anger.

"I am not enlisting because I must remain at the mills, Julia. I told you this," he said evenly. "What I do is not your concern."

She flung back her head and laughed, and the sound splintered in the silent room. "Tell that to these young men, who have gallantly enlisted and are off to fight for the cause."

"Yes, why have you not enlisted? Others can manage the mills," said one young man, belligerently. He stepped to Julia's side and tucked her hand into his arm. His gray uniform gleamed with newness; he was very conscious of the gold on his sleeve.

"I am the manager of Vallette and Sons," said Brett. "And I do not discuss my business with strangers." He turned deliberately from them.

"You do not need to explain yourself to anyone," said Cecilia, unexpectedly, her cheeks poppy-red, her gray eyes angry. "Julia, this was too bad of you, to speak so to Brett. He has been kind and good to us."

"Kind? Does that excuse a coward?" flashed Julia. "All these men have enlisted—only Brett Vallette—of the great Vallette family—who brag about their fighting past—"

Mrs. Strafford and her husband stepped forward hurriedly. Cecilia said gently, "Oh, Julia, you know better than that. How poor are your manners today."

The gentle rebuke seemed to cool her. Brett bowed stiffly to the company, offered his arm to Cecilia, and escorted her to the waiting carriage.

Rose Marie and Bridget were helped into the carriage loaded with Cecilia's trunks and hat boxes. Brett helped Cecilia into his carriage. His mouth was tight.

Once they were on their way, Cecilia said quietly, "I beg your pardon most humbly for that scene, Brett. When she has time to think, she will be sorry for it."

He managed a shrug. "I think not. Has Julia ever been sorry for anyone but herself?"

"She was speaking in the heat of passion," said Cecilia. "But I am forgetting myself. I wished to thank you very much for your kind invitation to remain at the Vallettes' for a time."

He relaxed a little. "I do not wish you to return to the South. It will soon be torn with war. Perhaps we will be safe in Virginia. If not, I shall send you all north."

"You are too good to me," sighed Cecilia, looking about with pleasure as the horses stepped briskly up the hill toward the Vallette home. The very pillars and windows seemed to gleam a welcome to her.

"And you, Cecilia, you cannot defend yourself, but you make quite a spirited defense of me!"

She glanced up at him, but he was smiling down into her eyes, and she smiled in return. "Oh, Brett, no one needs to defend you. You are strong, and you know what you will do. I am sure you have thought carefully about your duty, and where it lies. Your conscience is much stronger than those of young men, who are thrilled by the thought of battle, and do not know what horror war is."

He patted her small, gloved hand, and thought again what a quiet little soul she was, with a mind of her own.

Cecilia found life vastly different at the Vallettes'. Her life began to revolve around Brett. She could sleep as late as she chose, but she had always risen early. She did so now, to find the entire family downstairs at eight o'clock, ready to breakfast together.

The charming first hour of the day set the tone. They would talk, sometimes seriously of the war news, then more lightly of the weather, the work in the mills, the drilling of the militia. All the girls had piles of wool they were knitting into sweaters and blankets. Even Moira with her dim eyes was working away.

Brett went down to his laboratory and the office at the mills six days a week, from nine o'clock until six or later. When he finally came back up the hill, he was silent with weariness.

Rose Marie or Cecilia would fix a drink for him; he would sit down and relax with them. Sometimes one would play the piano, and he would sit with his eyes closed, the lines slowly smoothing from his hard face.

John Vallette came sometimes and they talked for hours in the study. They agreed most of the time on policy, though John was all for doing things as they had always been done, and Brett often wished to do something new. Still they got along well, and both were partners in the operations.

There was little entertaining that spring and summer. At any party, gaiety seemed quenched by the talk of war. More and more of the young men appeared in gray uniforms, stiff and starched, with gold braid on their sleeves. And presently they would disappear.

Sundays were peaceful. Brett often walked in the woods, and asked Cecilia to come with him. She went willingly, her small hand in his arm, her gray eyes unconsciously adoring as she looked up at him.

Brett found he could talk about his problems, and she would listen and encourage him. She did not always understand about the mills, or the chemical processes he was trying, but in explaining them to her, they became clearer to him.

"You are an excellent listener, my dear," he said one summer afternoon as they strolled in the green dimness of the woods near the river. The Areuse flowed swiftly these days, full of waters from the north, sparkling over the little waterfalls, green and gray in the shadows.

"Thank you. I feared you might find me foolish. I have had little education," she said in a low voice.

"You learn quickly. I notice that you are reading some of the books in the library. May I recommend others to you?"

"Oh, I wish that you would. If only I had had more education, as Rose Marie has had."

"She will be happy to teach you what she knows. And Bridget is excellent with mathematics and spelling."

"If they have time—"

"They will be glad to make time. They love you—as I do. No—not as I do, for I love you as a man does the woman he wishes to make his wife."

220

Cecilia stopped quite still, gazing up at him. His blue eyes were grave, not teasing. He touched her pink cheek with his tanned fingers.

"Oh—Brett—" she managed to whisper.

"And you, Cecilia, how do you feel?"

"But I thought you—you and Juila—or someone grand—"

"Just tell me how you feel," he said impatiently.

"Oh—I—love—you—" she murmured, so that he had to tilt his head to hear her. Their first kiss was tentative and sweet. Then he gathered her up in his arms, and she felt the first kiss of love and passion that she had ever known. Her bones felt as though they melted in his strength. Her lips burned under his; she moved them and answered him eagerly.

She was very pink, her gray eyes shining, as he finally let her down.

"You are such a tiny creature, I must be careful not to hurt you," he said tenderly, loosening his arms and smiling down at her. He looked somehow much younger today, and eager. "I thought when we danced that you were but as high as my heart, yet you float in my arms like a soft, pink cloud."

"Oh, Brett," she said breathlessly. She could not believe it. "When—when did you first—"

"Last winter," he said promptly. "At the ball for Stephen, you remember? We went outdoors and looked at the stars, and I saw them reflected in your eyes—"

"Oh, and you thought then—" She was radiantly happy. She had felt such love for him stirring in her heart, and yet she had thought him in love with Julia. She had seen him look at her tall, elegant, laughing sister, and had seen the dark fire in his eyes. Now she could forget that—all that misery—

"Yes, and now, tell me, when did *you* first know?" he asked impatiently in his turn.

"Oh, I think when I first set eyes on you," she blushed. "I thought you were the handsomest, best, finest man I ever met. And you spoke so well, and were so—so commanding—and fine—"

"That pleases me well," he teased. You must think up more compliments for me, for I like them. Now kiss me."

He did not think then of Julia, except with anger when he thought of her taunts, her meanness to her sister. He brushed from his mind the way he had kissed her, held her tightly, longed to possess her sensuous body and perfumed mouth. What he felt for her was an animal desire, he decided later. That could be forgotten.

Cecilia's brother wrote, soon, crossly, that she must be prepared to come home at once. They needed her. Julia was in Florida, and not able to come.

Brett said, "I shall answer this letter for you, my dear. I think it is my right."

Rose Marie said, "He will wonder that she stays on, Brett," warningly.

"Now, I can manage it," laughed Brett. The lines seemed to have disappeared from his forehead and cheeks. "Cecilia and I shall be married shortly. If he wishes to give his sister away, he must come soon. Otherwise the honor shall go to Frederick Stratford."

And so it was. Her brother was furious, but wrote reluctantly and gave his permission, as she was but twenty and he her guardian. They did not hear from Julia, and learned later that she was not informed for a time about the marriage, for fear of her anger, which even her brother dreaded.

Frederick Strafford gave her away. The mill foremen and their wives attended, and the Vallettes turned out together. It was a small, quiet, wartime wedding, in the church they attended every Sunday morning.

Cecilia wore a delicate gown of white lace which Rose Marie had helped her choose. Blue ribbons were drawn through the lace in the bodice and the full skirt, and the same shade of blue trimmed her white full bonnet.

Brett wore a brown silk suit. Cecilia gazed up at him, thinking how very very blue were his eyes today, how shining and clear. How handsome he was, how tall and fine. She was the most fortunate woman in the world!

Even the whispers at the reception did not trouble her, for did not Brett, her husband, stand at her side? "I thought he would marry the *sister*," whispered one woman, a friend of Mrs. Stratford. "She is so beautiful and tall, they made a fine couple, I thought."

"Julia Vining? Is she here? Did she come? What did she think of this? He was her constant escort . . . Spite? Did she mock him about his slowness in enlisting? What? He has not enlisted yet?"

Cecilia curved a protective hand into her new husband's arm, and smiled and smiled. She was so happy today, nothing must mar the occasion.

And she was accustomed to spiteful tongues. Julia had taught her well. Only now she did not think of Julia anymore. Julia was in the past. Brett was her present, her future, her beloved. She belonged to him, and he to her, forever.

Chapter 17

They had no honeymoon. Brett said, "I promise you a sweet one later, dearest, but now I cannot go away. It is too dangerous for us, and for those at home. Do you mind very much?" He gazed down anxiously at her radiant face.

She smiled serenely. "I don't care about anything, Brett, but being with you always."

"My darling!" He kissed her gently, with a sort of awe. What had he done to deserve such generous, overflowing love? She gave with both hands, completely, holding nothing back.

He was amazed at her on their wedding night. She was innocent, untaught. But she was so sweet and loving that he could have believed her a wife for years.

He tried to be very careful with her. He had been anxious, especially, since she was so small. But she was so relaxed with him, so eager to meet his every caress, that they came together without much trouble at all. He buried his face in her throat, pressed his lips to her rounded breasts, caressed her round hips with his hands.

"I cannot believe how lovely you are," he whispered, after the first embrace. "I should have insisted on marrying you months ago. If I had known what I was missing—" He propped himself up and smiled down at her teasingly.

"Are you as happy as I am?" she murmured against

his throat, as she drew herself against him. "No, you cannot possibly be as happy."

"Do you challenge me?" and he mock-growled against her hair.

She giggled, and the sound made him feel young and carefree. She was soft as a young child in his arms, but mature and giving in her caresses. Her soft hands moved over his chest, his shoulders. "Kisses, at half a pace," she whispered, and he met the challenge, stifling the laugh on her lips.

They lay long that night in the master bedroom in the Vallette house. He thought of the many nights since his father had died, when he had lain there alone, wrestling sleeplessly with the multitude of problems of the work he had inherited so young. He had grown hard in his dealings with people, seeing the way women—like Julia—were attracted to him for his money, his appearance. He had struggled to make the right decisions for the mills, the family, and the workmen who depended so completely on him.

And now here was someone to share the burden with him. A woman who listened sympathetically, who spoke thoughtfully, who believed in him, who trusted him to do the right thing. A woman who adored him, and gazed at him with shining gray eyes and did whatever he asked. It made him feel humble, yet very proud.

They slept for a time, Brett relaxed and warm as he had not been for many years. When he wakened, he saw the morning light through the long, white draperies at the windows, the mosquito netting over the old canopied bed. He looked at the face of the sleeping girl at his side.

How lovely she was, now, with the soft roundness of her face, the pink of her cheeks, the mussed brown curls about her shoulders. His hand softly smoothed her rounded shoulder and touched the pink nipple of her breast. The dark lashes moved, the white eyelids opened, gray eyes looked up into his with a sort of dazed dreaminess.

225

He smiled down. "Remember? We are married," he whispered.

"Brett—Brett—" she sighed, and lifted her arms to him. Her hands stroked slowly over his strong arms and shoulders; he bent closer to touch her mouth with his. Then passion went through him like a warm knife, and he needed her urgently. He kissed the rounded breasts, lower to the waist, and thighs, knowing she welcomed him and would never resist. She wanted him also; she loved him.

He felt her hands ruffling his hair, then her kisses on his neck as he drew over her. She was adorable, so pliant to his wishes, so eager to respond, as hungry as he was for the loving.

They came together again, smoothly, easily, as though married for a long time. It amazed him again, how she wanted him, how her young body moved with his.

He did not know until much later that Cecilia, anxious about pleasing her new husband, had gone to Rose Marie, who, a little embarrassed, but anxiously willing to help, had told her as much as possible. Then Moira had told her more, as Cecilia sat on a footstool at her feet and listened intently.

Moira knew, and remembered well, how her husband had been with her, what she had learned in the many years of her happy marriage. She told her, warned her, advised her, and Cecilia listened well.

Now, when Cecilia lay back, she whispered, "Brett, are you happy with me?"

"So happy, darling. I cannot believe this, you are so small, yet we fit together so well."

She buried her burning face against his chest, well satisfied. It was worth the flinging away of her natural modesty to make Brett happy. And she felt so—so very good. She could run her hand over his strong chest, twine her fingers in the thick, curly hair that matted it down to his waist. She could kiss his shoulder, run her fingers over him, and he would lie back and his blue eyes would half-close in lazy satisfaction.

Presently, they must rise, and wash and dress. Only now it was all new and deliriously sweet, for as she moved about the room, he would look at her and smile, in that new intimate way of his. And she could see the way he tugged on his trousers, or talked as he fastened his shirt buttons, or frowned over his neckcloth.

They went downstairs to breakfast, and to church together. She tucked her mitted hand in his arm, with a new strange pride of possession. She was Mrs. Brett Vallette, and no one would—no one could—take that title from her, nor the sweetness that went with it.

She wondered a little, during the sermon as her thoughts flitted, what Julia was thinking. They had not heard from her. Was she furiously angry? She probably had a dozen new beaux by this time.

Then her thoughts turned to Rose Marie and to the request Rose Marie had made a few days ago. Rose Marie had asked Cecilia, in a casual manner hiding anxiety, if she minded if Rose Marie and Bridget stayed.

"Mind? Oh, Rose Marie, this is your home."

"Not quite. I am here because of Brett—oh, well, someday I'll tell you about Ingram and myself," said Rose Marie, flipping her hand. But she looked sad and somber.

Cecilia hastened to reassure both of her new sisters-in-law that she was more than pleased to have them stay. And Bridget must have a home always with them, she told the girl. "If you do not wish to marry, Bridget, I want you to stay with us forever. However," she added, thinking of the days when she had struggled with the children of relatives, having no authority, but having their care and welfare anxiously on her hands and mind, "I don't want you to do anything but what you please. If—when—we have children—"

"Oh, I shall love to help you take care of children," said Bridget simply, finding it easy to be frank with Cecilia, as shy as she was. "You see, I don't feel—able to be around men, just Brett—and cousin Stephen. But other men—I cannot endure it. I do like children,

227

though. And I love to cook, and plan meals. If you allow me to remain, I shall be grateful always."

Brett was the happiest of them all. He worked hard, but there was always Cecilia to come home to. She helped with Moira, for his granny was older and more frail, yet unwilling to admit her weakness. Cecilia could persuade her to sit with her feet on a stool and rest her eyes with little pads of cologne-water over them. Cecilia could persuade her to eat light custards and poached eggs. Cecilia could coax her to sleep a bit in the afternoon. She never pushed, she just took it for granted that Moira would wish to do this and so—and Moira did, like a child.

Ingram Lombard came north with a double mission. He swelled with his own importance. He closeted himself in Brett's office for four hours, drinking and smoking Brett's fine Cuban cigars, telling him what he must do.

"You must increase the production of the powder mills, Brett! The South needs gunpowder. And yours is the best. I told them I could persuade you, and they sent me here to demand that you improve the mills. They cannot pay anything to help you build, but you can manage with increased orders."

Brett listened in increasing anger, and put him off. Afterward he went for a long walk. Ingram kept up the pressure, and told Rose Marie also that he meant for her to return with him this time.

"And no nonsense," he said. "My brother has left it to me to run the plantation, and his children are all young. You are needed there."

"Aren't your colored girls enough? Or have you freed all the slaves?" she snapped. "What shall you do if all the slaves are free? None will run to your calling."

He was furious, and they quarreled bitterly. She refused bluntly to sleep with him, and Brett quietly abetted her. Cecilia kept quiet, troubled, but fully on the side of Rose Marie. Ingram Lombard was such a bully.

Brett talked with Cecilia at length. "If I close down

the powder mills, no one in the North or South can say I play favorites. Besides, it will mean greater safety for us here, as no one could blow up the mills and cause damage and injury."

He paused, and pulled on his cigar. "On the other hand, the men need the work. The younger ones have enlisted, or been drafted, but the older ones must continue to work for their families. I have not enough work in the woolen mills to keep them all busy. Besides, some are not suited to the work. Powder work is all they know. And the coopers who make the kegs will be out of work also."

He finally decided to close the powder mills temporarily. He would put the men who could not be used in the woolen mills to work at other jobs.

The carpenters at the cooperage could build more houses and fences and mend his house and the Vallette mansion on the hill across the river. Powder men could be trained for woolen mill work, or work in the vegetable gardens. They would support themselves, and close out the world of war.

He told Ingram his decision, after he had worked it out with Cecilia and Rose Marie and Bridget. John Vallette protested, but not vigorously. He just hated all change.

Ingram Lonbard exploded. "You are a fool and a coward," he yelled at Brett in the study. "I would never have expected it of you. But yes, I might have. You are selfish. You will never think of the South, your own country—"

"My country is the United States of America," said Brett, a white line about his mouth.

"Then you are a traitor to the South. The Confederacy shall hear of this. And all your neighbors also. They will revile you as I do."

Lombard departed, and at once sent word that he had enlisted. He was a captain, and sent a picture of himself in full dress uniform to Rose Marie. She flicked her long fingers at it contemptuously.

"He would rather be a captain in the army than have

to run the plantation," she said angrily. "He knew that his brother depended on him for the work there, but he would not work. He may be in for a surprise in the army. They might expect him to fight. What a jolt for poor Ingram."

Cecilia took the picture Rose Marie threw on the floor and looked thoughtfully at it. Ingram was rather like an overstuffed rooster, strutting in the uniform which did not conceal his plump belly and double chin. She set it on the table, and later Bridget discreetly put it in Rose Marie's room. Rose Marie promptly stuffed it under some bedding, where it was not found again for years.

Brett's decision to close the powder mills was not popular with many of his neighbors. Their sons and husbands had gone off to fight, most of them for the South. A few had gone to the northern armies, but these kept still, for they were not liked in Virginia. Some accused Brett outright of cowardice.

He took the jibes with straight lips and burning eyes. He refused the factory orders, sending letters to all his agents that the Vallette mills were closed indefinitely.

Some ostracized the Vallettes. Even Emilie did not complain—unusual for her. "No, Brett," said his frivolous aunt seriously. "I feel you are right. War is horrible. You cannot make gunpowder that might one day blow up our northern cousins. I have thought often of dear Stephen, and wondered where he was. And my John says you are right."

Brett, amazed, patted Aunt Emilie's plump fingers and said, "You are a good sort, auntie. I shall try to see that you do not suffer financially. After the war, we shall start up again, and all will be well."

"Oh, well, I don't need any new dresses," she said bravely. "And your uncle left me enough jewelry to last a lifetime. Dear Antoine. I cannot help but be glad he is not alive to see this terrible time. I feel so for Flora, and her dear man."

Flora's dear man was Donald Gregory, who had gone to enlist for the North.

Cecilia said later, "I think that must have influenced your aunt, and I'm so glad, Brett. It would be terrible for her to be bitter about your decision. And John has been splendid about it."

"Yes, he has turned to work in the woolen mills, and gotten us about a dozen new orders. He is a good soul."

They worked hard, and stayed much to themselves that autumn—the first year of the war. If they had known how long it would last, they might not have felt so cheerful, in their quiet solitude, with the family gathered about.

Their mill workers were loyal. No grumbling was heard. The foremen reported that they felt the workers understood the situation and would say nothing to hurt Mr. Vallette. They had their gardens, and worked diligently in them, putting up fruit and many cans of vegetables for the winter. Brett bought some sheep, tried some for the wool, killed several of the lambs for meat, and had three men buy some pigs and keep them for fattening. They would need them this winter.

It was a lonely life, there on the Areuse. Brett did not want Cecilia and the others to go out, even together, to face possible hostility in the countryside and town. Battles were coming dangerously close. A stray unit of Northern or Southern infantry might come near, and Brett kept watchmen at the place night and day.

Shortly thereafter, following much thought and serious discussion, in conference with the entire family, Brett and John Vallette freed all their slaves. They felt it only right and proper. Then they had the task of explaining to the two dozen former slaves what freedom meant. "Does it mean we has to go to war for the South?" one man asked fearfully.

"Or for the North?" asked another.

"No, no, you are free to make your own choices." Brett looked at the puzzled, anxious faces. He felt great compassion for them. They were like children, his children. He had known them all their lives, and some of their fathers and mothers had worked for his parents.

Cecilia said, "Ask them to stay on for us, and work

231

for wages, Brett. If they do not know how to keep the money, you could hold it for them, as you do for the mill workers, and let them shop in the company store."

He suggested this, and they agreed, in relief. He had the carpenters help them build better houses on Slave Row and clean up the place. He quietly arranged for some of those who had lived together for years to be married by his own pastor. The children were baptized, given first and last names, and duly registered in the church records.

A battle took place nearby and two days later a train came through their small town with a load of wounded on the way to hospitals in the South.

Cecilia, Rose Marie, Bridget, and Brett loaded up four carriages and drove with the coachmen into town. They were met with some curious stares and some jeering words. However, most of the neighbors were willing for the day to forget their hostility.

"A sad event, a sad event," said one man to Brett, his gray whiskers quivering. "I cannot remember when an event has so torn us apart. Brother against brother, neighbor against neighbor."

"War is never anything but horror," whispered Cecilia, as the train stopped on the tracks and the townspeople came forward. It remained there for two hours, and the women went up and down the packed cars.

The walking wounded came outside and sat down in the sunshine, dazed, heads in dirty white bandages, or arms in slings, or limping as they hung on the shoulder of a buddy. Some of the women changed the bandages and applied ointment. Others brought drinks of cool water and cups of hot coffee. All brought food and distributed it to the men in the crowded railroad cars. Brett went in with basket after basket, coming out with a grim hard face, his blue eyes glittering.

"Some of the Northern wounded are in chains," he said to Cecilia, curtly.

"Oh—no, Brett—no."

"Like animals," he muttered. But he continued to

take water and food to the Northern and Southern soldiers alike, officers and enlisted and drafted.

Some of the men were mere boys, children. Cecilia knelt beside one boy and gently asked his name and age. "Fred Mason, ma'am, aged sixteen. I'm a bugler," he said proudly. His right arm had been blown off; he was pallid and weak, but his eyes shone.

Cecilia was sick to her stomach when they got home. They were all quiet and weary. Brett wanted to burst out about the horrors, but it would do no good. His women were looking like death.

They spared Moira the talk of it, and turned to speaking of a recent cheerful letter from Stephen and one from his sister Lucy. Lucy and the others would be happy if any or all of them would come north to stay with them during the "unpleasantness," as Lucy said.

Brett spoke to Rose Marie about it later. "Should you like to go, sister? Cecilia will not leave me, nor will I let her go, unless it becomes too dangerous here."

She thought about it, her head bent. Brett thought compassionately how the gay spirit seemed dashed from her, his buoyant, lively sister. Finally she shook her head.

"No, Brett, not now. I couldn't leave now. Perhaps— if it becomes dangerous, later—"

"All right. But let me know if you change your mind."

She nodded soberly and went on with her knitting, the white needles clicking quickly.

In early November 1861, Brett had visitors. They had not written first. His only warning was a messenger coming up from the gates.

"There be three grand officers in blue uniform, Mr. Vallette, and they will see you now!"

"Officers? In blue?"

He was stunned. This was Southern territory. Had Northern officers come brazenly through the lines to him?

He told the man to bring them to his office, which he still kept in the midst of the empty powder mills, and then he went out in the wintry sunlight to greet them.

They rode up, cloaks blowing in the wind, keen eyes weary, but looking all about them—three officers of the Union Army, looking smart in blue uniforms and gold braid.

They got down and introduced themselves. Brett sent the horses off with two of his men and their orderly, and then sent word up to the house to prepare rooms for them.

"You are kind, Mr. Vallette. Probably you understand why we have come to you," said the senior officer, Colonel Molloy.

"As a scientist and businessman, I deal with facts, not guesses," said Brett Vallette drily, and ushered them into his small office. He found chairs for them all, and seated himself at the scratched desk that had belonged to his father, and to his grandfather before him. He took comfort at times at the thought of Tristan Vallette, and Christophe Vallette, sitting here, leaning back in the chair, gazing out the window at the Areuse, meditating on the problems of their times.

Colonel Molloy was the spokesman for the group. All three officers watched him sharply during the conversation. They were tentative at first.

Colonel Molloy then spoke: "Word came to us that you are not selling black powder to the South, though you have been urged, even threatened, to do so."

"That is true," said Brett, cautiously. "My decision was to close the powder mills. We now operate two woolen mills, and are considering a third, to keep the men employed."

"Your agents are all over the States, Mr. Vallette. You have agents in New Orleans, St. Louis, New York, the capital—"

"Correct—as far as you go. They will no longer be my agents as soon as their present stock is sold."

"Hm. You sold briefly to the South, but seemed reluctant to do so?"

Brett felt a little tingling along his spine. "I am reluctant to make black powder for war purposes, gentlemen," he said. "I am in the business, which has been run by my family for four generations, to make sporting powder and blasting powder for canals and railroads—but not military powders. We have not made military powders since the war with England in 1812 to 1815."

"With the exception of the war with Mexico," said a younger officer quickly.

"Quite right. I forgot that." Brett frowned to himself. "At that time, I gave orders to make certain sporting powders for military use. We also manufactured a small amount of cannon powders."

"And you are capable of expanding the mills a great deal, should you choose to do so."

Brett shrugged. "We could. But the mills are closed down. Many of my powder workers have enlisted—some on the side of the North, some on the side of the Confederate States."

There was a little silence in the office. A late fly buzzed drowsily near the opened window. The November chill came in, and Brett rose to close the window.

"We have been sent by the Department of War, and by Mr. William H. Seward, the Secretary of State, to request your assistance, Mr. Vallette," said the Colonel finally, tugging at his trousers and easing his legs. "As you may know, black powder is being made by several large companies, and a number of smaller ones, for the use of our military forces. Hazard Powder Company of Connecticut, Smith and Rand Company in New York State, and the Du Pont Company of Delaware have answered our call for more and better powder. We now turn to you."

"You do not have sufficient supplies?" asked Brett slowly. He was frowning slightly, though aware that they watched his every expression.

"What is sufficient, in time of war?" shrugged the Colonel. "Before you closed your mills, your black powder was some of the best in the world. I understand you personally supervised the experimentation in the laboratory."

"That is correct. I have a degree in chemistry, from

235

the University of Pennsylvania. And my father taught me much."

"We have had trouble with wet powders and insufficient rounds of ammunition for our armies in the West," said the Colonel, cautiously. "What we are sent to ask is this: Will you reopen the mills here, the black powder mills, and sign a contract with the Department of War to supply as much as 100,000 pounds within two months?"

There was a long silence. They looked at him. Brett had taken up a thick black pencil and scrawled some figures on the paper before him. He was thinking furiously. That would be 1000 barrels—could he do it? The mills had to be started up, they must make more charcoal, they had to train more workers.

He finally began asking questions. They were cautious in their answers, and he said, "I must consult with my cousin, John Vallette, my partner in this enterprise. May I take you up to the house for refreshment, then send for my cousin? How long can you stay?"

Another shrug, a grimace. "We must return as soon as our mission is complete."

"Very well. I shall try to have an answer for you within two or three days. I must talk to my cousin, my workers—"

Brett also consulted Cecilia, and found her sympathetic, and worried. She suggested several points. "Do you really want to begin with the dangerous business again? Can you get enough good powder men? Will the Southern agents retaliate against you? What did John say? Is he with you in this? Will this prolong the war?"

To the last question, he could only shrug, like Colonel Molloy. "Who knows! I only know now that my sympathies are with the North. I want them to win this terrible struggle. I am sorry for the South, but they have brought this calamity down upon themselves, with their pride and stubbornness—yes, and gallantry."

John talked thoughtfully to him, but soon turned from the question of whether they would do the job to how could they do it: the men, the expansion of the

236

mills, the problems of keeping the mills safe from Confederate raiders and the transportation of the black powder.

Brett did not get much sleep those nights. He lay awake, wrestling with his conscience and thinking of every angle. Finally he realized he too was thinking of *how* to do the job, rather than *whether* to do it, and he nodded to himself in the darkness. He turned over, laid his arm lightly over Cecilia, a small plump figure beside him, sleeping deeply.

She stirred. "Brett?" came her sleepy voice. "Are you not asleep yet?"

"I have been thinking. We shall do it, Cecilia."

"Oh. I am glad, I think," she said, stirring herself awake. "It is something that must be done, and the Vallettes can do it."

"Yes, I feel that way."

The contracts were signed the next morning, and the army men departed. Brett got busy at once, closing the woolen mills for a time, to put all men on the work of opening the powder mills. Starting the chopping down of the willow wood, burning charcoal. He had to send for more saltpeter, for supplies were low. The Department of War speeded up shipments of saltpeter via England from India, and he was able to get them within a month. The mills glowed with fires night and day as the war work began.

Brett posted more watchmen, and every visitor was scanned. No one must get in to damage the valuable works. They could blow everyone to kingdom come.

Chapter 18

Rose Marie spent a strange winter of 1861–62. She despised Ingram Lombard, yet when he wrote to her pathetically from an army camp, begging her to write, she could not refuse to respond. She sent him warm clothing, and wrote little gossipy letters which might amuse him.

Poor Ingram, he had at last gotten in over his head. Brett asked if Rose Marie wished to pursue a divorce.

Rose Marie sighed deeply. "Oh, Brett, I cannot do that to him now. He is so weak, it might finish him. I want the divorce. Yet—how can I?"

"I understand." Brett kissed her cheek. He was so happy himself, and he longed for his sister to be happy. "Perhaps the war will end soon—"

But he did not really believe it would. The Department of War obviously anticipated a long war in view of the supplies they were requesting. He had even heard that the building of railroads to the Pacific was being speeded up in case the war spread in that direction.

Rose Marie continued to write to Stephen. She wrote also to cousins Lucy and Elizabeth, both married and in their own homes, and they wrote cordially in reply. The letters sometimes were delayed, but were welcome when they came. They confined themselves to family news.

Stephen wrote cautiously, but begged Rose Marie for "more news of yourself and of Brett and work."

Rose Marie understood. In town she listened to news of troop movements. Twice she went to Richmond and returned with fragments of information. She wrote boldly to Stephen, hoping that the letters would not be intercepted.

She reported that Brett was now making black powder for the Union Army. "The mills glow night and day," she wrote. "Sometimes I lie awake, and watch from the window as the glow mounts in the sky. We had an explosion last week. One man was injured badly and lost his eyesight. We have all grieved for him, yet the work must go on. Thank God the main walls held and the explosion was directed toward the river."

At Christmas, she sent good wishes to them all, and added, "Brett goes to Washington this week for consultation. They trust him, I believe. We all miss him in this holiday season. We did manage to have a pleasant gathering at Aunt Emilie's, and all sang Christmas songs and drank hot punch."

She slipped tidbits of information between paragraphs of family news.

In January, 1862, she wrote, "We have all been upset and horrified. A man slipped into the grounds here, in spite of all our watchmen, and Brett believes he was sent to blow up the works. Fortunately, our good workman Mr. O'Grady spotted him and was on him in a trice, beating him up. He will not confess to doing anything wrong, and Brett turned him over to the authorities in town. Aunt Emilie sends her best regards, and wishes you might come to visit us again. We so enjoyed the ball on your previous visit."

In March, she had more news. "There was a bad explosion at the mills this past week. The grinding mill blew, and four men were badly hurt. One died the following day. We are much grieved. We are so proud of our men. They assured Brett they would not quit, and would continue to work for Vallette's. Such danger, such gallantry. Our Irish and Germans are truly Americans with us."

In April, she told Stephen, "Brett has been able to meet his commitments to the government, and to exceed them. He works six days a week, and his men with him.

239

Mrs. O'Connell is most disturbed; her son was involved in some action in southern Kentucky, and sent word his favorite horse was killed. She fears for his life with the raiders."

Three days after she had mailed this letter, the Vallettes had unwelcome visitors. Four officers in the gray uniform of the Confederacy came to call. The mill guards at the gates sent word to Brett, and he ordered them admitted.

The footman showed them into the drawing room, then went with gloomy face to call Rose Marie. The soldiers wished to speak to her, he said.

Rose Marie had seen them come up the hill. "Mr. Vallette will come. Delay a little, take coffee to the men, and inform them I shall come down as soon as I am dressed."

Cecilia came up to her. Rose Marie continued to knit quickly, thinking even more furiously. "Oh, darling, why did they ask for you?" whispered Cecilia, as though the men could hear them. "I have had coffee sent to them. They scarcely speak at all, they are all stiffness and gloom."

Rose Marie covered the small hands with her own and smiled reassuringly. "Do not trouble yourself with it, Cecilia. In your condition, it is not good for you or your baby to be worried. Do go lie down, or talk to Granny Moira. Please, do not come downstairs."

Cecilia swallowed, nodded, and went to Granny Moira, and read to her for a time, tense, nervous, but confident in Brett. She was expecting his child this autumn, and she wanted nothing to happen to the baby. Brett was so tender with her, so happy. Her soft mouth smiled as she thought of his gentle anxiety over her. How good he was, how kind, how loving.

Brett left the laboratory hastily, pulling on his jacket as he came. Tender green leaves graced the willows over the Areuse, drooping into the waters. Small waterfalls plunged with little splashing sounds; the grinding of the mills overlaid all, with the smell of the sulfur and saltpeter. He strode quickly up the hill, his face stern.

Why had they come? To arrest him for making powder for the Union? He had a right to make powder for whom he pleased. Yet they could make trouble. He was near the border of Pennsylvania. Should he move the mills north? That would take time and trouble and expense.

He went into the house and saw Rose Marie coming down the stairs, her face white as paper under the defiant rouge she had put on her cheeks. He stared up at her; she came to him and put her hand on his arm.

"They asked for me, Brett," she said in a low tone.

"My God, why?"

"I don't know yet."

They went in together. The four officers sprang to their feet, the coffee cups clattering in their saucers. Their gaze went from brother to sister and back again.

They introduced themselves, politely but brusquely. The man in charge produced a letter, folded and sealed, but broken open. "This is your letter, Mrs. Lombard?" He showed it to Rose Marie.

She took it; Brett looked over her shoulder as she glanced down the contents—the letter about Mrs. O'Connell's son in southern Kentucky.

"Yes, this is my letter. How did it come into your possession?" she asked, with cool composure.

"It was intercepted. Why have you written about secret matters to a man in the North?"

There was a brief silence. Rose Marie finally answered. "I write to my cousin. I often write to my cousins in the North. Have you intercepted all those letters?"

"No," said the officer grimly. "Don't you know you are sending important military information? You have seen the instructions to all Southerners: no information of military maneuvers is to be sent to the North."

She managed a shrug in her dark blue gown. "I merely write the news. If it disturbs you, I shall confine myself to gossip of the family and friends. In fact, that is what I have done. Stephen knows the boy."

"You are very casual with our lives, madam!" The

241

officer was becoming heated, a white line about his lips, his beard quivering. "This information is not to be sent. Do you understand?"

"Yes, sir."

Brett interposed smoothly. "My sister knows little of military matters, sir. She does the letter writing for the family, keeping in touch with our far-flung cousins. I am too busy for it, but I enjoy hearing from them."

"And are you very close to your *Northern* cousins?" the man asked.

Brett raised his eyebrows. "We are close to all our relatives, sir. My cousin John and I run the Vallette business."

"Ah, yes, and sell to the Union."

"I sell woolens where I can, the same with black powder. We have been in the business more than sixty years."

There was a brief silence. One man motioned to the officer, as though to caution himself against speaking of some matters.

The man collected himself. "Ah, yes. Where you sell is not *our* concern—*at present*. I have used Vallette and Sons powder, by the way. Excellent stuff. Good shooting."

Brett bowed, his blue eyes shining, his mouth compressed. "You are most kind, sir."

"About the letters, Mrs. Lombard—" the officer went on.

Brett interrupted quietly. "Mrs. Lombard, my sister, is married to Captain Ingram Lombard of the Confederate army, now stationed in Georgia. She writes to him frequently. Are her letters to him also to be stopped? He will be most upset."

The officers looked at each other in dismay, and began whispering to each other. Rose Marie tightened her hand about Brett's arm.

"I beg your pardon, ma'am. I did not know—I was not informed that your husband was in our service," the chief officer finally stammered. His face was red with annoyance. "I shall investigate and let you know about this. In the meantime, please be guarded in your letters to your—cousins—in the North. You must realize how dangerous this can be."

"I shall be more careful, sir, I promise you," said Rose Marie, pallid but quite composed.

The officers departed, refusing dinner. Brett closed the door on them, then saw them ride down the slope to the guarded gates.

Then he turned to Rose Marie and took her back to his small office at the back of the house.

"Now, Rose Marie, have you been writing long to Stephen, and sending him information?"

She nodded, twisting her long white fingers, her look frank but guilty. "Yes, Brett. I—I wanted to. He did not suggest it."

"But he encouraged you?"

"Yes, he is—"

He raised his large hand. "Don't tell me. I don't want to know. The fewer that know, the better."

He sat back in his chair, and stared out at the view without seeing it, the mills, the serene, smooth-flowing river.

"Rose Marie, I think you had best go north to your cousins," he said finally. "They may come back to hound you. You must leave, for your safety and ours."

She jerked in her seat, her blue eyes very bright. "Go—north?" she whispered. "But Brett—the trip—"

"I will go with you. We had best start now, tonight. By railroad, I think." He stood up.

She stood, too. "But Brett, Cecilia is expecting a child—"

"Yes, yes—and she must not be upset. Tell her little, except that I wish you to go north. And I shall return quickly. Let me send for John. Go upstairs and begin to pack. Lightly now. Two valises, and a hatbox. You can buy more in New York City."

She nodded and sped upstairs. Cecilia and Bridget came in as she began to fling things on the bed.

"I must go north," she said, quietly, but her hands fluttered in agitation. "Brett says so. He will take me.

243

No one is to know but you and John for the time."

Bridget stared at her, eyes wide, then automatically took over the packing of the valises, which her older sister was bundling about in agitation.

Cecilia said, quietly, "Is it your letters to Stephen?"

Rose Marie glanced up sharply. "You know?"

"I guessed. Let me think."

Rose Marie was pulling out a blue silk gown which Stephen had admired. She started to bundle it up to put in the valise. Cecilia had seated herself in a rocking chair, her plump form lowered carefully into it.

"No, not that one, Rose Marie," said Cecilia. Her sister-in-law stared at her absently.

"Why not?"

"I was thinking. Why would a lovely southern woman be traveling north in wartime? She would be troubled by the soldiers, asked questions. No. You must have a reason for traveling." Both the Vallettes gazed at her in surprise. Cecilia occasionally came up with something so sharp and amazing that she would astound them. "What do you mean, a reason?" asked Rose Marie.

"A reason they will recognize at once, and respect. Yes, I have it. A death in the family, some loved one, someone close." Cecilia put her finger to her lips, thinking, frowning. "Yes, a dear aunt, a beloved aunt. Stephen's mother."

"But she died years ago!" gasped Rose Marie.

"Who will stay to check that?" asked Cecilia. "You will dress in black, with a gray bonnet—that one—and black ribbons. Both you and Brett in black; look grieved and somber. He is escorting you north to the funeral, and you hope you will be in time to comfort the sorrowing."

"Good heavens, Cecilia," said Bridget soberly.

"I would never have thought—Cecilia, you have been reading too many novels." But Rose Marie's blue eyes sparkled; she began to giggle.

Brett came in. "What is going on? Are you hysterical?" he asked sharply. "I asked you not to trouble Cecilia."

"Nonsense. She is as calm as any of us. She has had such a bright idea, Brett. We must have a reason for going north in such haste. I am to wear black, and so are you, and we are grief-stricken over the death of a beloved aunt, Stephen's mother."

"You have all run mad. She died years ago—"

It was all explained to Brett, and finally he nodded and bent to kiss the top of Cecilia's head.

"Of course," he said with satisfaction. "It will provide us a reason. And few will trouble us in our grief. Very good."

And so they did it. Brett dressed all in black, even to his boots and gloves. Rose Marie looked somber in the black gown with full crinoline skirts, black and gray cloak and gray bonnet with wide black ribbons hastily sewn on by Bridget. They left that night, driven by John to the railroad station, and took the first train north.

It was a nightmare journey. The train was slow and crowded, with three cars of wounded soldiers going to a hospital. The moans of the wounded, along with the sighs of the women and the crying of children in the rest of the train, were sobering.

They had not gone a dozen miles when the train was stopped by Confederate officers. They dismounted, came into the train, and questioned everyone there.

They especially were suspicious of Brett and Rose Marie. Rose Marie took out a black-bordered handkerchief and buried her face in it, as Brett quietly explained their mission.

"Vallette? Of Vallette and Sons Powder Mills? And you are going north for a funeral?" The man was very grave and abrupt.

"Yes, sir. It is not forbidden to travel, is it? Our aunt was so dear to us." The fiction was becoming almost real to Brett as he went on and on, about how a friend had brought word his aunt was dying, then someone had telegraphed that she had died. Her children were grief-stricken.

"As you can see, we packed in haste. We take only a few things, for we mean to come back shortly. But we must pay our respects, and attempt to ease their grief. Our families have always been close."

A doctor traveling with the wounded soldiers came back impatiently to ask the officers why there was such a long delay. They argued in low tones. Finally the officers left the train, and it was permitted to continue.

The cars stopped and started fitfully throughout the night. Rose Marie could not sleep. The sleeping cars were all for the wounded. She and Brett sat on hard wooden benches. Bridget had thoughtfully packed some food: bread, cheese, meat, bottles of tea and water. They drank cold tea in the chill light of dawn as the train sat on a siding and the wounded were removed. They dared not leave the train for fear it would continue without them, or they would be detained.

They crawled on, and on. Then at one station, all were ordered off for inspection. Soldiers of the Confederacy went up and down the lines; officers snapped questions. Brett went over and over his story, and finally convinced his interrogators.

Another train came down from the North, arriving in the afternoon. After more official movements, the passengers were allowed to board, and they sat exhausted as the train went back up North along the clattering track.

They changed trains again in Philadelphia, and again had to meet inspection, this time by officers of the Union Army. Brett had to show identification; they were very suspicious of a Southerner in the North.

Brett had thought he might change his story there and tell them the truth. But a little thought persuaded him to stick to the original story. There might be spies about, traveling just as he and Rose Marie were doing.

So he stuck to the story of the dear aunt and her funeral, and the grieving family that awaited them. It was midnight when the train was allowed to proceed, after they had removed several men for further questioning.

Rose Marie leaned on Brett's arm as they began to pull out of the station. "Oh, Brett," she said, breathlessly.

"Courage, my dear. It is almost over."

"But you have to go back again."

"I shall manage."

At four in the morning, they pulled into New York City. They got off, looked about in a daze, and found a carriage to take them to the home of Stephen Vallette, where he lived with his father and youngest brother. Even at that hour, the streets were busy, noisy, and filthy with dirt and grime.

Brett knocked and knocked at the door, and finally roused a sleepy footman. As they came in, Stephen came down the stairs, pulling on a dark robe. "My God, Brett—and Rose Marie!" He hastened to them.

He greeted Brett, shaking his hand, and then turned to Rose Marie. She had flung back the dark veil. Her face was white, her eyes dark blue, her chin quivering.

"Oh, my dear," he said, breathlessly, and carried her tired hands up to his lips. She felt the strong, hard kisses on her hands, his strong grip.

They were given rooms; hot water was brought. In the pale gray dawn, Stephen sat up to hear their story. His face was grim; he nodded at Brett's crisp questions.

"Yes, we used the information; it was valuable," he admitted. "I can say no more. But my God, I would not have drawn Rose Marie into this trouble."

"I think she jumped in with her own stubborn will," said Brett with a ghost of a tired smile. "Well, what now? I must remain for the funeral—"

"Funeral!" Stephen stared at Brett as though he had gone mad.

"Cecilia's idea. A reason for our hasty trip north. I regret we had to say our beloved aunt, your mother, has just died, and we have come to comfort you in your grief."

Stephen's face was a study. He finally shook his head and took his leave, so that they might get some sleep.

The next day Stephen and Brett had a long talk before Brett departed again. Brett told him frankly some news of the South and told him his intentions. "I mean to enlarge the powder mills and to sell only to the North. There may be much pressure on me to sell to the South. I shall resist it. Tell the Federal Government I am loyal to the United States of America. Tell them I shall not give in, no matter what the cost."

In the stillness of the study, Brett told him of the conditions in Virginia, and Stephen took notes. He told of shortages, and of the fury of people who were drafted and saw others paying someone else to serve. He told of events in the towns and countryside nearby, of what he knew about troop movements.

"There, I can say no more, and do not expect me to write any news of this," said Brett, lying back in the great armchair. "I cannot risk the lives of my family. I could get news to you—but I shall not even try. My first duty is to my family, and the mills. You may be sure the mills will continue to operate."

"Be very wary of Southern operatives trying to blow up the mills," said Stephen gravely. "We have had news several times. The explosion in March is very suspect. We have reason to believe one man was able to get through."

"I wondered about that. We have been trying to be very careful."

"I would send word if I could—but often I do not hear of it until too late.

Brett gave him a tired smile. "Thank you, cousin. But we must depend on ourselves and our own militia and watchmen. We will increase the guard."

Rose Marie came down in the late afternoon, pallid and composed. She kissed Brett goodbye and clung to him. "You will write? I shall long to be with Cecilia on the birth of her child. I hope to return by that time."

Stephen interposed. "The war will not be over, not then. No, you must remain with us here. Lucy's husband is being transferred; she is desolate. I plan to move her and her children back home to this house, and you two shall be great friends."

"You are very good," said Brett. He clasped hands with Stephen; then the two men hugged each other.

"Take care of yourself and your good family," said Stephen. "We shall take very good care of Rose Marie."

"I trust her to you," said Brett, and kissed Rose Marie tenderly one last time. "Be good, my dear, and do not cause your cousins any anxiety. We shall await your letters eagerly."

He left, and though he never told them, he had a harrowing journey home. He was stopped every few miles on the railroad, first by Union officers, and later by Confederate. He had some gold coins with him and these he used to buy cold food and hot coffee. But he spent nearly three days and nights journeying homeward. He was weary to the bone, caught little sleep, was haggard and unshaven and dirty when he finally hired a carriage at the railroad station to take him to the house on the hill.

Cecilia greeted him calmly but her gray eyes were anxious. She sent for hot water and a tub, took all his clothes from him, and had them scoured in the sunshine. She let him sleep for an inordinately long time.

Moira wanted to hear all about the journey when he recovered. But he told her little, and warned Cecilia to say nothing. Moira grew more frail by the day; her wrists were thin as a bird's and her eyes dimmed. She was nervous and slept little. The sounds of the mills going all night distressed her. They wanted to change her bedroom to the other side of the house, but she refused.

"I keep thinking Christophe will come home from the mills," she said, rocking in her chair, looking out over the mills and the Areuse. "I must wait for him."

So her mind was slipping a bit also. Brett felt deeply about this.

Moira had lived a rich and full life, giving comfort and support to many members of the Vallette family, encouraging her children and grandchildren in every way she could. It was sad to see her ill, to see her frailty, to see her slip into the feebleness of old age.

But Brett knew, also, that she longed to join Christophe in death, in the heaven she believed in so passionately. She had told Brett many times, with simple confidence, "I know Christophe is up there waiting for me. I have to go to him one day. We aren't complete without each other."

In New York City, Rose Marie came slowly out of her terror and fright. Stephen had his sister Lucy and family move in, and Rose Marie became friends with them. But it was to his father she turned now.

Kendall was ill much of the time. Rose Marie read his letters to him and wrote for him at his dictation. As he spent more and more time in his office at home, she became his confidante. He told her about the textile business, how it operated, rambling on as his memory turned further backward in time. Stephen came and went, sometimes in the middle of the night, sometimes for weeks at a time, and no one questioned where he had been or why he went. His brother Titus had helped take over at the textile mills, but he was still young and inexperienced.

Lucy was three years older then Rose Marie, a charming, sophisticated, and cultured woman. When the two did go out, it was fequently to the opera, to a concert, or to a charitable event to aid the war effort.

Lucy confided innocently in Rose Marie. "We long for Stephen to marry. Is he not charming?"

"Yes, very. But I think he will not marry while the war lasts," said Rose Marie, with reserve. Lucy had helped her choose new, smart clothes, and today she wore a vivid green gown in the latest fashion, with a stunning bonnet of aquamarine. "Do—do you think he is interested in someone special? Forgive me if I pry." She could not resist the question.

"Oh, yes, he is much interested in a lovely girl in Boston," said Lucy, unaware of hurting. "Elaine will come to us at Christmas, I feel sure. She adores Stephen, but she is so much younger than he, I fear he sees her only as a child. But she is grown now, quite twenty-two, and so adorable."

Rose Marie felt a terrible pang. Elaine did come at Christmas, and she was gentle, sweet, pretty, and obviously adored Stephen. But Stephen told Rose Marie, "I shall not marry—until you are free, my dear. How I wish you could have gone through with your divorce."

"I could not," she said in a low tone. Her heart beat so hard it frightened her. Stephen was not being charming now; he looked at her so intensely she felt a burning inside her.

"I understand. You are—good and honorable. But after the war—" He took her hands, raised them to his lips. "Rose Marie, I have loved you since the first time, when I shamed you—and began to adore you. I have loved you since that moment."

She dared to look into his eyes and found the brown gaze intent and serious. "You—love—"

"Yes, I love you, so deeply. If only you were free. But I shall wait. Oh, my darling, if only I might love you as I wish. I know there is in you an answering hunger, I have seen it in your face."

"Stephen—we cannot—and you should marry—"

"When you are ready to marry me, my darling," he said quietly, with some of Brett's hardness.

When the war is over—
When the war is ended—
They said it hopefully, prayerfully, wistfully, despairingly, wonderingly. Said it again and again. When the war is ended—

Then she could go through with her plans, thought Rose Marie, lying awake, hungering for Stephen, her body wakened and wanting, as she had never wished for her husband. Surely Ingram would return to his plantation and his old ways. He had not changed his nature, he would never change. And she would be free.

If Stephen still wanted her then—
If—when—perhaps—maybe—

251

Their lives were built on such fragile premises, as the War Between The States dragged on and on.

New York City was loud, busy, bustling. Rose Marie wondered if she would ever become accustomed to crossing one of the wide streets. Carriages drove this way and that; the new horse cars carried large crowds from one end of the city to the other.

In the morning, droves of carriages went wildly downtown, causing traffic congestion beyond belief. At the docks, at the stock exchanges, at the shops and stores, business went on at a fierce pace all day. Then in the evening, the carriages all drove north again, uptown, to the new, elaborate mansions of the wealthy, to the sober brownstones of the middle class. Beggars crowded the alleys. Irish mobs roamed at nights, from pub to political gathering. Tammany Hall collected the ward politicians, Stephen explained to Rose Marie. "The Irish vote together. They want jobs, influence, a lift out of the slums. And who can blame them? They work hard for so little—when they can get work."

She had noticed the signs in some shop windows, "No Irish need apply." Appalled, she thought of Granny Moira, and of the thousands like her who had come to America from famine-stricken Ireland in search of a new life.

Chapter 19

At home in Virginia along the Areuse Brett had taken precautionary measures. He'd had a wall built around the Vallette compound; it enclosed the mills, the workers' homes, the mansion on the hill where Emilie lived with John and Flora, and Brett's own home. And there was constant vigilance. Watchmen paced up and down at all hours; the militia drilled regularly; and there was a home guard, made up of the workmen, several of whom had been invalidated out of the Union Army.

The Vallettes did little visiting; only old friends came infrequently. They tried to make their own cheer. John would bring over his mother and Flora occasionally. Or Flora would come alone and talk wistfully to her beau, Donald Gregory. Flora hoped to marry Donald the next time he came home on leave. Emilie wanted her daughter to wait until the war was over so they could have a grand wedding. But Flora was impatient and told Brett, "I don't want to wait. The war might not be over for years."

"You may depend on me for assistance, my dear, whenever he does come home," Brett replied and smiled gently at his cousin. He was fond of the girl, who was so like her father, Antoine. And, indeed, Flora married Donald that summer.

Cecilia had her child in the autumn, a son whom they named for Cecilia's father, Arthur. He was a husky, placid child—good as gold, as Cecilia said proudly. She had borne him easily, and had been bright-eyed and happy when he was brought to her after bathing.

Brett hovered over the crib, fascinated by the tiny hands, the wee fingers waving in the air, the bland stare of his son. His son! He could scarce believe it. And the child seemed to grow so fast, attempting to sit up before he was many months old.

They had a quiet Christmas in 1862. Emilie came, with John and Flora. The Stratfords came for dinner, and they celebrated with a Yule log and some hoarded wine. The silver bowl was polished brightly, as were the silver candlesticks which had been in the family for more than one hundred years. With red candles, they made a brave show.

Winter set in, and the battles were desperate: Fredericksburg, Charleston, Vicksburg, Gettysburg. They read the gazettes anxiously. A few letters arrived from Rose Marie. From what she said, they knew others had been lost or intercepted. However, she was well, and treated so warmly that the Vallettes in Virginia were reassured.

Another spring came, and a summer. Sometimes trains rolled into the small town, and the whole population turned out to help with the wounded. Brett sent carriages of food, bandages, and ointment to them by the foremen and men of his mills. He forbade the women to go in. It was a Southern town, and some neighbors still did not speak to them. He wanted no unpleasantness for Bridget and Cecilia.

There were several fires in the mills, but they did not have any proof that they were set by infiltrators. They could have started from a spark on dry timbers.

Word of horrible draft riots in New York City reached them that July, just after news of Gettysburg and Vicksburg. Frantically Brett wired Stephen to be reassured all the Vallettes, including Rose Marie, were safe. Hundreds had been killed; Meade's troops from Gettysburg were brought in to quell the riots.

Out in Ohio and Kentucky, Confederate General John Hunt Morgan made a spectacular raid behind Union lines. He was captured after twenty-five days of terror. Then in November he escaped.

Quantrill led a Confederate guerrilla force into Lawrence, Kansas, in August of 1863, looting, burning, and killing. Brett hid the gazettes from his family; he did not want them reading of such violence.

Confederate troops broke through at Chickamauga. General Lee's Army of Northern Virginia gained against General Meade's Army of the Potomac.

"What if the Confederates win?" Brett thought. He made emergency plans to move his family and workmen north into Pennsylvania should such an event occur. His name would be hated here—it was somewhat already—and vengeance would be taken on his helpless ones. He bent over little Arthur's crib broodingly.

In 1864, three major events occurred in the lives of the Vallettes. A great explosion rent the pressing mill, sending the roof and all four walls flying. Five men were killed, nineteen injured. They shut down the mills completely for a week to make sure all the fires were out, then gravely began to rebuild.

It had been horrible. John and Brett had just left the office and gone home. Fifteen minutes earlier, they both would have been caught in the explosion, perhaps killed. Parts of the mills and parts of bodies were found as far as two hundred yards away. They gathered up what they found of the men and buried them, with weeping and mourning that would last longer than the war.

Brett took part in the funeral, which was in the chapel on the mill grounds. A minister came, but Brett delivered the funeral oration. He praised the devotion and hard work of the men, their loyalty, their intelligence. He promised that the women and children they left behind would be cared for always. The widows would have their homes for their lifetimes, the children would be educated for whatever work they wished.

"It was all I could do," he later told Cecilia, wearily. "I cannot bring them back to life. Oh, God, the men we

255

lost. Mr. O'Connel, with us forty years. Pete Grady, Hans Bulow, Henry Muller—"

"And dear young Frederick Maurer," said Cecilia. She knew many of the workers; she had visited in their homes and knew their troubles as her own. She and Bridget visited the sick, made sure the school operated well, and employed the girls whenever they needed a new maid or two. They saw to the welfare of the workers in every way possible. She had just returned from their infirmary, where eight of the injured had been taken. The others were in the hospital in town until they recovered.

"Yes, yes, all the men, all the men." Brett shoved back his long, blue-black hair and rested his head on his hand. "Is it worth it, Cecilia? Must we be in such a dangerous business?"

He rarely spoke like this. Alarmed, she soothed him like a mother would her troubled child. "Oh, Brett, you know we must. Someone must, and Vallette powders are respected and used the world over. Our men know their work. Just think how few accidents there have been. And they take such pride in their work." She drew his head back to her breasts and stroked his shoulders gently. He felt so stiff and tensed.

"You are a good woman, Cecilia. What should I have done without you? Granny going so ill, and Rose Marie—" He bit his lip.

They received a long letter from Rose Marie, and it was the second major event of their lives that year. She had heard from a doctor in a hospital in New Orleans. Ingram had been brought in, gravely injured, following a battle some hundred miles away.

"You would be proud of him, ma'am," wrote the medical officer to Mrs. Ingram Lombard. "Your husband, Captain Lombard, conducted himself with gallantry and saved a unit of his men. However, I regret to inform you that he has suffered a serious injury of the head, which has affected his spine—"

It had also affected his memory. Sometimes he was in possession of his senses, sometimes not. Rose Marie wrote to Brett, "I would go to him, but cannot. I am refused permission to travel. Would you send him help? Gold would smooth his path, and obtain a private room and nurse for him. I am deeply troubled by the report. It seems also that the family plantation has been burned. My sister-in-law has taken refuge with her family in Louisiana, but she does not answer any letters of mine. I fear the letters did not get through."

Brett wrote to one of his former agents in New Orleans, a personal friend, and besought him to aid Lombard as well as he could and also to trace the sister-in-law. Brett was able to inform Rose Marie that the agent had found Ingram in an army hospital, and that he was well enough to be transferred into the care of an older sister of the agent, who had been a nurse and now was taking several private patients into her home.

Ingram's sister was not so easy to trace. Her family's plantation was deserted. She was finally located in a town in Mississippi, living with several relatives. Her children were well; the eldest boy was enlisting in the Confederate Army. She thought her husband was well; but she had not heard from him for three months.

The third event was entirely happy. Cecilia's second son was born, again in the autumn, and named Henry. He was a sweet-natured, contented child.

Brett lifted up two-year-old Arthur to see his small brother. Arthur gravely and critically regarded the baby, and demanded, "When is he going to play with me?"

Cecilia had promised him a baby brother who would play with him. Brett had some time and patience to inform Arthur that it would be a time before the baby was big enough. Meantime, he brought joy and pleasure to all of them.

Brett adored Cecilia, so placid and calm in the midst of turmoil. She always waited for him in the hallway as he came up the hill, then greeted him with a smile and a kiss and a keen look for his weariness. She would bring his slippers, put a tall, cool glass of rum and lime in his hand, and sit down with her knitting to hear his news, comments, problems, sighs of dismay, or weary pleasures in the day.

He could talk to her about his experiments in the chemical lab, his attempts to improve the quality of the gunpowder. He was working also with the by-products; it worried him that so much was wasted. Surely some use could be found for the wastes.

Bridget was in her element with the babies. They adored her. She told them stories, knitted for them, and took them out when Cecilia was engaged in other tasks. Her plain face glowed with delight in the two boys. And she was even happier the next year, when Cecilia gave birth to a girl.

"Oh, I was afraid you would have only boys!" said Bridget innocently.

Roseann was a little doll of a baby. She had blue-black hair, bright blue eyes, and a pretty round face so sweet and lively. She was the favorite of everyone at once, and in danger of being spoiled.

Cecilia had grown more plump with the babies. She was motherly, trotting about to see to everyone's comfort, worried about Brett, encouraging him to rest and go for walks with her. And she took the comfort of the mill workers very seriously, going two days each week to visit them.

Then suddenly, the war ended. They had become almost accustomed to the horrors in the newspapers and the endless railroad trains of wounded pausing briefly in town. Then the men began to come home.

Some had lost an arm, some a leg, the empty sleeves or pants leg folded neatly back and pinned. Their faces were lined; they looked aged—the hair of some had turned gray.

Officious-looking men came from the North, carrying carpetbags and looking grave and deliberate—and greedy. They took over the offices of the town and poked about finding out who owned what land and what slaves had not been freed. They tried to come onto the Vallettes' grounds, but Brett and John stood firm and sent them packing.

Flora's husband, Donald Gregory, returned home and entered the mill. He was a quiet, efficient lad, quick to learn and easy to be with. Brett was relieved to have him, and took to him at once. Flora expected a child, and her relief at having her husband home was touching.

Rose Marie came home, and soon she had Ingram brought up by two men from the New Orleans hospital. Rose Marie looked older, very fashionable; but her face was lined. She had helped nurse in a New York hospital, and she seemed thin and rather frail. Stephen had brought her home, lingered to talk a bit, then left, looking stern and rather exasperated.

Ingram came—and could recognize no one at first. His head was injured, and there was a great gash at one side near his left ear. He limped heavily when he could walk. He sat much of the time in a wheelchair, demanding his drink in the morning—and during the rest of the day as well.

Rose Marie told them, "The plantation was burned to the ground. Squatters have taken over, my sister-in-law writes. She does not mean to return to it. Her husband—died—in battle. She plans to remarry—a man in Mississippi."

When matters had calmed down somewhat, Brett took two of his men who had experience in surveying and went to see the plantation. He found squatters firmly in possession, upheld by some carpetbaggers who flourished papers before Brett showing that they had taken over the land for non-payment of taxes. Brett returned home.

"It will mean years of fighting in the courts, Rose Marie, and I don't think the land is worth it. We looked it over and the land has been overworked. Even if we get it back for you and your sister-in-law, it would take a vast outlay of money to get it back in shape."

"Let it go, Brett. Ingram would never work it anyway," she said with a sigh. Brett wrote a report to the sister-in-law, and had a courteous reply from her new husband, saying he had reached the same conclusion.

Brett found new orders for the powder mills. The railroads moving west would need vast amounts of powder to blast the earth and rocks out of their paths. Coal mines in Pennsylvania and Ohio needed black powder to blast out the precious heating fuel. He turned from military powder to blasting powder.

He gathered his old workers back once more, as they returned from war. Several of his powdermen returned without a limb, and he put them to work anyway. "You have not forgotten your skills; I hope your brains are not in your legs," he told them brusquely.

Because of the sluggish post-war economy, it was difficult at first to obtain orders for the Vallette mills. One reason for this was that the railroads placed only small orders. Yet Brett was patient and fulfilled what small orders he received either on time or ahead of time in order to gain a good reputation for Vallette and Sons.

He also experimented at this time with new sources of saltpeter. During the war it had been necessary but difficult to get the potassium nitrate from India. But now Brett had heard of Chilean saltpeter, which was composed of sodium nitrate rather than potassium nitrate. Vast supplies of Chilean saltpeter were available, but would it work?

In seeking the answer to this problem Brett spent long hours experimenting in the laboratory. The problem was that Chilean saltpeter absorbed moisture from the air and kept the powder too damp to use. He kept changing the proportions of the ingredients, glazing the powder for a long time, trying to keep it dry. If he could do this, he could cut his manufacturing costs since the Chilean saltpeter was cheaper and more easily available. He labored for several years before finding the solution to the problem that allowed Chilean saltpeter to be used.

Ingram Lombard was a problem. Rose Marie had set up a bedroom for him on the ground floor of the house, away from the others. She arranged a bedroom for herself next door, and saw to his nursing herself. He kept wanting her to go to bed with him, especially when he was a little drunk and not much out of his mind.

Brett worried about her. Rose Marie only shook her beautiful, glossy head. "He is impotent. He cannot rape me, nor will I let him come near enough to strike at me when he is in one of his moods. I can handle him."

"I could arrange for him to be put into one of the veterans' hospitals, and you could get a divorce."

Rose Marie and he could always speak straightforwardly to each other.

"No, Brett, I could not do that and live with myself. I must look after him."

"And Stephen?" Brett dared to say, gently.

She turned her head away. "I told him—to marry. There's a girl in Boston—"

He hated to see the bitter twist of her generous mouth. He hated it when Ingram was petulant and demanding, and she must wait on him and bathe him, shave him, nurse him night and day. But she was stubborn, and she would do it, as though having been unfaithful to him mentally, she must be faithful physically. She was beating herself with mental whips, thought Brett, but he could not change her.

Christmas was quiet, but they were at peace, and they counted their blessings again and again that winter. At least the war had ended—it had finally ended.

Granny Moira rarely left her bedroom. Bridget fussed over her, waited on her, and took Arthur in to see her. She would hold him on her lap and tell him stories of the old days, and it seemed to comfort her.

Then toward spring, she could no longer get out of bed. The doctor came, and shook his head. "She is strong of body, but she is wearing out," he said. "The end could come any time."

Still it was unexpected. Brett went up to see her one evening and found her sitting up against the pillows gazing out at the mills. The fires burned; her eyes sparkled at the sight.

261

She turned as he entered the room. "Oh, there you are, Tristan. Your father is coming up the hill," she said, and smiled sweetly at him, and fell over on the bed, a thin little bundle.

They buried her up on the hill, beside Christophe. Old Etienne Vallette was in the center of the burial ground. At his side was Sidoine, and to their right Conrade. To the left lay Christophe, Tristan, and Antoine. Lavinia lay next to her Tristan, and there was a vacant place beside Antoine.

Emilie wept silently, gazing at the empty plot. "I shall be there soon," she promised.

"Now, mother," John soothed her anxiously. "Don't talk so, don't, your thoughts are morbid." She seemed visibly older, clad in black, with a black bonnet shielding her face.

They all missed Moira, remembering her vigorous ways, the sparkle of her blue eyes, her vast fund of stories. Cecilia found Arthur in her old room one day, as she went up to clean there.

"Where's granny?" he demanded, his lower lip stuck out. "I want granny!"

"She went to be in heaven," Cecilia told him firmly. "We'll see her again one day. She went to be with grandfather."

Life went on. They gathered together the threads of their life before the war, but with a difference. Grim reminders were all about them. A mill worker awkward with a crutch under his arm, swinging about on one leg. Another worker, one arm doing the work of two, his empty sleeve pinned to his shoulder. Another, with half his face scarred. Great blackened ruins of mills that had exploded.

They rebuilt, but remembered. And the Areuse flowed as smooth as before. They cut down the willow twigs and branches, and the smell of the charcoal burned for days across the river, sending up its thin smoke on the summer air.

One day, Julia came. She had a wealthy beau in tow, but such an unusual one, they were amazed. She stayed at the Stratfords, but soon came driving up in her beau's carriage. Julia Vining still, she had not married.

She was tall as always, with dark, blonde curls piled high on her beautiful head. She was rounded, a little more full of breast and thigh, more sensuously attractive than ever.

She teased them all, laughing gently at them, not so cruel as before, as though softened by her experiences. She had not gone just to balls in Florida, she told them. She had nursed in a hospital there.

Her gowns were of silk and satin and taffeta and velvet. She wore that day a gown of azure blue, and a matching bonnet with plumes of the same blue. It made her eyes more vividly blue, and the gracious curves of her face were unlined. Next to her younger sister Cecilia, she looked ten years younger.

Frederick Keane, her beau, sat awkwardly in the drawing room, scarcely able to take his gaze from her for long. He was big and bluff, graying, with long sideburns and a long, drooping mustache. He was heavy; his small eyes crinkled in shrewd lines of flesh. Anyone more unlike Julia's usual flashingly handsome young beaux would be hard to find, thought Cecilia, with some amusement.

Brett leaned back in his big chair, laughing at some quip Julia had made. Cecilia looked at him fondly. He looked younger today; the work was letting up a bit, she thought. Darling Donald, he was such a big help in the mills. She excused herself to see to the tea tray and plan a big dinner for them all.

"How long do you stay, Julia?" asked Brett, in one interval.

Her blue-gray eyes flashed at him. "Oh, as long as Frederick can stay away from his horrid business," she drawled, her accent stronger than ever. She had such a soft sensual tone; her glance at Frederick was intimate.

Brett looked at her thoughtfully. She was traveling alone with Frederick Keane, though she stayed with relatives everywhere. She wore silks and velvets. Her gown was in a late style. Rose Marie next to her looked almost a dowd, while Cecilia—but Brett refused to admit that thought into his mind. Cecilia was like a small, brown wren, comfortable and fussing about her children anxiously.

Julia wore a diamond bracelet on one wrist, a gold and diamond watch on the other. More diamonds flashed from the brooch which fastened her elegant lace neckscarf. Her throat was long and smooth and unlined. When she removed her bonnet, her golden hair was bright as a gold coin, in beautiful waves and curls. Was she Frederick's mistress? Brett wondered why she did not marry him.

From Frederick's talk of his ironworks, Brett concluded he was a wealthy man. He had no southern accent; his talk was brisk and sharply to the point. A northern businessman and southern Julia. They were an incongruous pair, but he was obviously fond of her and proud of her. His carriage was the best and latest; his matched black horses were splendid.

"Julia helps me choose my clothes," he said proudly that evening, holding out his tweed-covered arm. "From Scotland. Ain't it splendid cloth? Strong as iron."

"Frederick judges everything by its length of service," said Julia, gently jibing. She did not have the cruel tone she used to have, and her smile at him was sweet. Perhaps she would marry him.

Julia lingered on for weeks. She seemed to enjoy visiting her relatives. She cooed over the children, and seemed genuinely fond of Henry, who most resembled Brett, and of Arthur who was stolid, standing beside his mother's knee and eyeing anyone else suspiciously. And she seemed to have changed her ways.

Bretty found her striding along in the woods as he took a solitary walk one late summer evening. He paused to see her coming, and she smiled and waved at him gaily.

"Isn't the air splendid?" she greeted him. She wore a more practical tan muslin gown covered with a dark brown cloak. "I have missed this scenery, I never knew how much. You did not write me during the war,

264

Brett," she reproached him, sliding her hand into his arm.

"Cecilia did the letter writing, and I enjoyed reading what you wrote," he said, calmly, trying not to show how aware he was of the beautiful slim body next to his. She matched his stride with her own, her beautiful long legs moving slowly.

"You have grown into an old sobersides. I wonder if you even know how to dance anymore," she reproached him again.

He looked down into her laughing eyes. "Dance? We have not had a dance since—since the war began."

"Foolish. Dancing helps one forget one's cares. And you have cares, Brett, they are all engraved here," and she daringly traced the lines down his cheeks and around his eyes.

"Don't, Julia," he said sharply.

"Why? Do I trouble you?" she murmured, and stood before him, refusing to let him go on. "Oh, Brett, we have not talked for so long. You have never told me why you married Cecilia so abruptly, and refused to let me know. I did not hear of it for almost a year."

"I love her. She is sweet and good—"

"And so motherly," said Julia with a grimace. "Does she think of nothing but the children?"

He frowned; she shook her head quickly.

"Forgive me, I shall not criticize her. She is sweet and good, as you said. But, Brett, there was something between us, something strong. I know it. Why—why did you turn from me?"

She faced him honestly, her hands on his lapels. He could breathe in her perfume, that blend of flowers and musk that was her own. He put his hands on her wrists and tried to push her further back. She leaned against him, laughing, her blonde hair blowing in the slight wind.

"Do I bother you still?" she teased, her eyes half-closed, her gaze on his sensuous, full mouth.

"No, of course not—do not do this, Julia."

"If I don't trouble you, you could kiss me—like a

sister," she taunted, and raised her beautiful oval face to his, her mouth pursed, tempting.

He looked down, bent over and pressed his mouth to hers. It had started as a light brush of the mouth, but at her touch it grew into something sensuous, hard, hurting, demanding. She gasped, as he drew back, and she put her long, slim arms about his neck. Her eyes were brooding.

"Brett—I love you. I have loved you, for a long time. Oh, God, you hurt me—how could you—how could you—"

Something like triumph filled him. She had loved him—she wanted him now. He kissed her again, her cheeks, her eyes, her brow, then down over the lobe of her ear, to her throat. She had her head flung back, accepting his kisses, her body pressed to his. He felt the heat rising in him.

Because Cecilia was expecting again, placid and plump, he had not slept with her for a time—he always moved to another bedroom while she was pregnant, so that he would not hurt her. He was hungry for a woman; his strong masculine nature wanted to possess and hurt and take and triumph. And Julia was here, pressing against him, urging her soft curves to his hard body—

Her arms pulled him down with her. They fell together onto the soft, summery grass. He pulled aside the blue cloak and fumbled for her dress. With a shock he felt her hand on his trousers, urgent, the long, slim fingers sliding inside, finding him. No decent woman did this, no one would know how—

But she did. And he wanted her desperately, the tormented desire rising furiously in him. Her dress was pulled up; he yanked at the fragile underclothing. He heard lace tear, felt the soft flesh under his fingers, as she held him, and urged him.

"Oh, Brett, darling, I want you—I have wanted you—there is no one in the world like you—God, darling—"

He lay on her, crushing her under his weight, and she only moved and sighed, and parted her legs. He pressed his mouth to her full lips, and felt her bite his lips savagely in a love-bite. She nibbled at his lips and tongue, and her own tongue darted into his mouth like a little red snake.

His mind emptied of all thought. He felt only strong desire, a hunger that could only be assuaged by the curved body under his. He struck deeply into the long thighs, and she cried out softly and yielded to him. He lay panting, then began to struggle for his satisfaction. Her hands helped him, her amazing, sensuous, long hands, stroking over his back and thighs. And he came in her, felt her shuddering into satisfaction with him, in a threshing, rapturous struggle.

It was such a wild experience—one that he had never felt before—that he quite blanked out for minutes. He came to, lying roughly on her, the soft body still holding him, and heard her laugh softly against his hair.

"Oh, Brett, I have longed for this—you love me—you love me also."

Love? He fumbled for his common sense. Oh, God, what had he done? He tried to pull away from her; yet her fingers teased him until he had to kiss her again and again.

Finally he pulled up from her, and, shaking, set his clothes in order. She only lay there, her blue-gray eyes half-closed and sensuously blazing, her lips crimson against the mussed tan gown pulled up to her chin.

"Get up," he said, hoarsely. "Get up, you little devil. You did this deliberately."

"I wanted you. I still want you."

"Get up. Or, by God, I'll go off and leave you like that." He indicated her brazen naked body with his hand, then could not help lingering as he looked down over her. What a beautiful woman—long, slim, sleek, creamy white, against the dark brown of her cloak.

"Stay for a while," she tempted him.

He cursed, brushed back his hair, and turned and ran from her. Her mellow, taunting laugh rang after him. He had to walk for a long time, cursing himself silently, and her also, before he could return home.

He went into the house the back way, up the back stairs, to his bedroom. He stripped, washed, and changed his clothes, scowling over the grass stains.

He had acted like a bull rutting blindly, senselessly!

How could he have forgotten his manhood? His responsibilities to himself, his wife, his children?

Dear Cecilia, so good and decent. How shocked she would be at him! Would Julia revert to her old ways and taunt her sister with his unfaithfulness? His mouth set grimly, he looked his old hard self. If Julia dared do so, he would also proclaim her acts. Her rich beau might desert her—no, he had best go to Julia himself, threaten her. If she told about him to Cecilia, he would tell Frederick, and she would not wish her diamonds to disappear from her wrist and throat.

But he was ashamed of himself, his passion that had betrayed him. He was ashamed that he had forgotten his wife, dear Cecilia, who had upheld him and supported him, and borne his three children. She was pregnant with his fourth child, and he had done this!

But God, he thought, his hands still for a moment, as he brushed his hair back severely. "How glorious she was," he muttered. "How glorious, and passionate—like a flame—like a shooting star—"

Chapter 20

Ingram Lombard grew worse, and presently he recognized no one at all. He lay in a heavy heap in his bed, soiling himself, and it was horrible to be in the same room with him.

Brett took over, for Cecilia was expecting her child soon, their fourth. And Rose Marie was driving herself to exhaustion. So Brett went out and hired a sturdy black man to come and live with them and take care of Ingram full time.

They all blessed the man again and again. He had nursed his former master in the army, and had experience with wounds and with men whose minds had collapsed. He was tall and strong, yet gentle.

Ingram went down and down, unconscious much of the time. Soon after Cecilia's child Marcus was born, Ingram died in his sleep.

It was 1867. Brett had been quietly keeping in touch with Stephen, telling him it would not be long now. "Do not pay attention to what Rose Marie writes to you," urged Brett. "She has a strong sense of duty, and her conscience torments her. I know why. For God's sake, be patient. I will keep you informed."

So a few days after Ingram was buried, up on the hill, Stephen arrived. Brett had written to him at once.

Rose Marie had practically collapsed after the funeral. She was thin, her face sunken, her blue-black hair streaked with gray along the temples.

Stephen came in from his carriage, fresh and strong,

vigorous and handsome in his blue silk suit and white linen shirt. Brett met him at the door with a sigh of relief.

"I started as soon as I had your telegram," he said quietly. Brett wrung his hand.

"Thank God; I think Rose Marie would not have sent for you," said Brett. "But I am not so prudish." He gave Stephen a grin. "You feel the same? She will not think so, she has lost her looks, she says."

"Women," said Stephen, with a grin. "Where is she?"

"In the drawing room, and I'll get Cecilia out of there," Brett promised, and went to call his wife.

She came at once. Brett pushed Stephen into the room, drawing Cecilia out with him. "Why—Stephen—" whispered Cecilia, in shock.

He gave her an absent nod, and went in and closed the door after after him. Rose Marie was huddled near the fire, her long slim hands held out to it, as though she had frozen on that September day.

"Rose Marie," said Stephen quietly. She started, then turned about, her eyes glazed with her thoughts.

He came and knelt at her feet, taking her hands in his, and warming them with his strong ones. "Rose Marie. My darling," he whispered, as she stared down at him.

She finally seemed to come out of her daze. "Stephen?"

"Yes, my love."

"I cannot believe it—I was thinking of you—"

"I should hope so. I have been thinking of nothing but you, for most of seven years," he said grimly. He touched his lips to the thin fingers tenderly.

The fingers trembled in his. "Oh, Stephen, why did you come?"

"To take you back with me," he said. "Married or unmarried, it makes no difference. I am not going to live without you any longer."

She drew back. "Have—have you looked at me? I think not. Stephen, I am old—gray—finished. I am thirty-two. Look at my face."

He would not let go of her hands. He gazed up into her oval face, at the brimming blue eyes, the streak of gray at her temples. "You have not been eating properly," he said with a quiet smile, teasing her. "From now on, you shall do as I say, and I shall look after you. How soon can you be ready to travel?"

She shook her head. "I am old—old—oh, Stephen, it is too late."

He stood up and drew her up with him, pulling her body close to his, feeling the trembling of her limbs against his strength. His arms closed about her, and he pushed her head down firmly onto his shoulder.

Against her ear, he murmured, "I have waited seven years. I am thirty-seven years of age, my darling. How long do I have to wait to have you again? I warn you, I shall not be patient!"

"You should have married that girl—"

He pressed his lips against her mouth, tenderly at first, then harder, catching fire from the touch for which he had hungered so long. He kissed the soft lips, until her mouth moved against his, and she clasped him with desperate arms and answered his every kiss, a lovely flush rising into her pale cheeks.

"Oh, Stephen—oh, Stephen—"

They were married two days later in the family chapel. Brett gave her away. She wore a pale yellow traveling gown and looked radiant. One could scarely recognize her as the same woman who had crouched before the fire that day. Stephen was laughing, and teasing, and tender.

He would not wait. They left that very day, to travel north by easy stages, stopping at inns. They went by way of the capital, making it a honeymoon, taking three weeks to get to New York City. Rose Marie wrote after they had arrived, "I am so happy, so very happy. It may be wicked to have married so quickly—I blame Stephen entirely—"

Cecilia, nursing baby Marcus, read the letter again, and smiled at Stephen's scrawled postscript, "I am the happiest man in the world. Thank you, Brett. I could not have endured the waiting without your encouragement."

"Oh, I do hope she has a baby before long," said Cecilia. "She longs for his children, I know it. And how lovely a mother she will be."

And within a year her prediction and hope came true. Stephen wrote at once, when Rose Marie was delivered of a child. "The girl is named Anna Moira, and you must come soon to see her. She is the most beautiful child in the world."

A son Darcy arrived the next year, and two years later came Matthew. Rose Marie had not been too old after all, thought Cecilia with delight. Rose Marie came each summer for a visit with Stephen and the children. How delightful it was to have a good long visit. Arthur lorded it over all the children, belligerently bossing the smaller ones.

Meantime, they had all been amazed and delighted when John Vallette married. John, forty, had chosen twenty-year-old Ellen Prentice, the daughter of a wealthy lawyer in Washington. John was proud as a peacock, and Emilie, his mother, was at first shocked, then happy, as he brought his bride home. Ellen was too gentle in nature to take over, so Emilie was able to continue her rule of the Vallette mansion across the river.

Julia wrote at irregular intervals; she was having a gay time with her new husband. She had finally married Frederick Keane, for he had insisted, she said, bubbling over about her jewels, her new gowns, a trip to Europe on her honeymoon.

Brett, reading this letter, felt his mouth go tight and his body warm at the thought of the delicious bride she would make. No virgin, but a sensuous, experienced woman. He hoped she would be loyal to Frederick, and not make the kind, crude man miserable. Brett found it hard to forget that day in the woods when he had lain with Juila and found such wild, stolen pleasure with her.

Frederick built a new home for Juila in Philadelphia.

It had eighteen bedrooms, and three formal parlors, and they gave balls at any excuse, she wrote. He was from an enormous family. One of his unmarried sisters kept house for her, leaving her free to enjoy herself. The iron business was doing very well, Frederick had given her sapphires on her birthday, and some stock in the company. Frederick was an angel. He allowed her to go to New York with one of her sisters-in-law, and spend a month enjoying herself, with no murmur of protest.

"Oh, dear," murmured Cecilia, to herself. Frederick was not wise to let Julia take the helm. Julia was not a good seaman, and as captain of their marriage she might wreck the ship. Cecilia read the letter again, reading between the lines. The handsome beaux who escorted Julia about New York, the flirtatious ways of the men there, the splendid parties she had attended, the opera, and the plays.

By 1871, Brett and his family were wealthy. The orders for blasting powder poured in with the increased work on railroads, which now stretched east and west, north and south. He worked six days a week, and into the night. He had two shifts of workmen, who worked all but Sundays.

Donald Gregory was promoted to assistant manager under John Vallette. Brett had charge of the laboratory. He had made the Chilean saltpeter work, and they switched to that almost entirely, with increased sales and profit, as the source was so much closer.

Stephen and Rose Marie came with Anna Moira, Darcy, and baby Matthew. Rose Marie bubbled over with happiness; her blue eyes sparkled as she talked with them all, gay and witty as ever. Stephen was handsome, older, with some gray speckled into his brown curly hair.

He was tender with the children, holding baby Matthew patiently while Rose Marie bustled about with the others. "You behold in me a domestic man," he said, with a smile, when Brett teased him.

Julia and Frederick Keane turned up abruptly, with

no warning. Because Brett's house was full to bursting, Emilie took them in. Julia came over often, and Frederick patiently followed her about, a wistful look in his bulldog face.

Only Rose Marie could match Julia's smart clothes, and Rose Marie did not have such expensive silks and taffetas with the new look of the bustle in back and the trim line down her front. Trains swirled behind her, catching up the children's toys.

Cecilia was pregnant with another child. "My God, Cecilia," said Julia to her bluntly, the first afternoon of her visit. She rocked lazily in the blue chair, her golden hair set without a hair out of place, her jewels sparkling on her hands and at her throat. "You work so hard. Four children, and another on the way. Stop it. You will make Brett poor."

Cecilia flushed a dull red, and Rose Marie sparkled blue fires at Julia. "We love the children," said Cecilia quietly. "Little Arthur already goes with Brett to the laboratory as a special treat. He is quick in school, and looks forward to university. And Henry is much like his father."

Julia smiled down at Roseann, staring at her from wide, fascinated blue eyes. "And this is a little doll; come here, darling," she coaxed. Roseann went to her, and played with the slim wrist and the diamond and gold bangles on it. Cecilia watched, and fought down a fierce demon of jealousy. Julia was so beautiful, and she felt such a dowd.

The men came in, Brett and Stephen and Frederick. Cecilia rushed about to order tea and to pour brandy for them. Julia watched, her eyebrows lifted in amusement.

"There you go again, Cecilia," she drawled in the old cruel tone, malice in her eyes. "Rushing about, getting red as a turkey-cock. Let them wait on themselves. You are really too plump for all that. You should watch your weight, even if you are increasing once more."

Frederick murmured, "Really, Julia," in a pleading tone.

Rose Marie exhanged an angry look with Stephen.

But it was Brett who turned on her, with the brandy bottle in one hand, the beautiful bulbous glass in the other.

"You go too far, Julia," he said, in a hard tone. He was cold with fury. "Cecilia is a fine wife, an excellent mother. You would do well to provide Frederick with an heir, instead of mocking your sister for making me such a happy father."

Julia flung back her beautiful head and laughed aloud, her smooth throat with no lines arched graceful as a swan's. "Poor Brett. So terribly domestic. Four children tangling your footsteps. And Cecilia getting heavier by the month—"

"Enough. I am fed up with your mocking of Cecilia. She has made us all comfortable and happy all these years. Granny Moira said over and over she was the best wife I could have had, and she was right. How dare you speak so of your sister. Never do so again."

Julia patted her hand over her mouth, as though to stifle the laughter. "Really, Brett, you are very cross with me," she said, mockingly. "Very well, I shall be silent." But her blue eyes did not promise any more than that.

Roseann had slid away from Julia and gone to her mother, sliding her small hand into Cecilia's. Cecilia clutched it, as though for her life and reason, and muttered, "I'll go for tea."

There was a small unpleasant silence; then Frederick sighed. "Ah—Brett, I was much interested in the operations of the powder mill. You could use some help here, couldn't you? Thought I might want to widen my investments—"

They began to speak, politely, of investments and the future of the iron business. Later in their bedroom, Rose Marie said to Stephen, "That bitch. She hasn't changed a bit. I could have struck her. Making fun of Cecilia—"

"Jealous of her," said Stephen, taking off his high

stiff choker collar and knotted tie. "God, that's a relief. Wonder why it's fashionable to choke oneself?"

"Jealous," mused Rose Marie. "Wonder why she didn't turn on me, then? I am married, plump with a new child. I haven't got my figure back."

Stephen came over to her and ran his hands tantalizingly down her beautiful curves. "I'm not complaining, my dear. And Julia doesn't attack you because you can fight back. Cecilia never could fight Julia; she was conditioned early to give in to her sister."

"Poor, dear Cecilia," murmured Rose Marie, then forgot her, as Stephen pressed a kiss on her throat, then took her completely into his arms. They could never accustom themselves to the delight of being able to kiss, embrace, and make love as much as they liked. They were married, it was proper, Stephen assured Rose Marie, with a devilish twinkle in his eyes. Sometimes, he reminded her of their first stolen embrace.

"You were so fighting-angry, a young tigress, but so very sweet and fragrant in my arms. I could not forget you, could not forget the feel of your young limbs with mine. I thought of you all that long journey. I had to see you again, I wanted you when I came back, did you know that? I wanted to steal to your room, and take again—"

"And those long years in New York," she would murmur in reply. "I didn't think you should even kiss me—"

"You could not stop me, my darling."

"But you wanted more than that—"

"And took it when I could—" he laughed at her flush.

"We were wrong—"

"But it kept me sane, until I could claim you—my darling, we were meant for each other, from the first. No power on earth could keep us apart."

"I think your father knew—"

"But did not blame me," said Stephen, gently, and hushed her with kisses.

Brett was still coldly furious with Julia when he met her near the river two days later. He stopped and stared at her as she came nearer to him, laughing.

"Oh, how angry you look," she said, with a pout of her red lips. She wore her favorite pale blue today, with a cloak of deeper blue. Her golden hair shone in the sunlight; she had taken off her bonnet and it swung from its ribbons. The new straight lines of her dress showed off the rounded curves of her breasts and thighs. The provocative bustle swayed when she walked.

"I am angry with you, Julia. How dare you speak so to Cecilia? She has been good to me, like an angel—"

"How boring, to live with an angel," sighed Julia, her blue-gray eyes sparkling devilishly in the sunlight. She tucked her hand into his arm. "Go ahead, I adore you even when you scold me. Come and tell me all the news."

He wanted to pull away from her. But the old attractive feel of her pulled at him. The slant of her eyes, the glint of them, the sway of her shapely body—

He turned and walked with her, away from the river. She asked about the powder works, and seemed amazingly well informed. She had taken lessons about business from Frederick, she said, with a shrug. "Nothing matters to him so much as business."

"Except you, Julia."

"Nonsense," she said sharply, a frown between her shapely eyebrows. "I am a pretty toy he shows off. He buys me these—" she held out her arm, and the diamonds glinted like fire in the sunlight. "To show he owns me. That he can afford me. He likes me to dress in the latest fashion. I take him to the opera, he goes to sleep. But he wakes up for intermission, in time to stroll the hallway with me, and show me off. Like a painted doll."

She had never sounded so fierce, so hurt. Brett said gently, "He does love you, Julia. His eyes are ever on you. He admires you. Why do you hurt him so?"

"Because he does not love me," she said curtly.

"He does."

"He does not." Then she burst out laughing, like a child, only her eyes were not like a child's. "There, how silly we are. Quarreling like fury. Never mind, forget him. Tell me what you do for amusement."

"Nothing much," he said. "I still go hunting with the Stratfords, or we go visiting."

"Dull, dull, dull," she said gaily. "You must come up to New York sometime, and I shall show you amusement. You will not believe your eyes."

Somehow they had reached a shady part of the woods. He stopped, uneasy. She had lured him before, and he had hated himself afterwards. He had no wish for more wakeful nights.

"We must go back. I had not meant to walk so far with you—"

He turned; she stood in his path, bonnet dropped to the ground. "Brett, I want you, I need you."

He felt the blood drain from his head, then come rushing back. "You are mad, Julia. We must not be together—"

"I love you, I always loved you. We should have married—"

"You are not the kind of woman a man marries," he said, cruelly, his mouth hard. "You are wanton, frivolous, always restless for new amusements. You would have driven me from my mind."

Her face showed hurt; she flinched, and her eyelids drooped.

"God, I'm sorry, Julia," he said, on a breath. "I should not have said that—"

"You meant it, didn't you? You deliberately, coldly, chose Cecilia because she was gentle, motherly. You make me sick, Brett Vallette." Her head flung back, she flashed at him, "I hate you, even when I love you. You refused to pay court to me, you refused to consider me for your wife—because you were afraid of me. Afraid! I might distract you from your precious work."

Because she was too close to the truth, he caught at her arms, shook her, and found himself with his arms about her. Her slim arms went up about his neck.

"Oh, Brett, Brett, I have wanted you, longed for you—" Her mouth whispered in his ear, kissed his earlobe, bit it. He groaned, flung her to the ground and followed her down.

What happened was inevitable. She had a strange hypnotic attraction for him. He went to her like a piece of iron to a magnet. He lay on her, kissing her wildly, her breasts, the bare shoulder, her white thighs where he had pulled back her lace underclothing. He bit and kissed, savagely, wanting to hurt her, wanting to take her so she would cry out and hate him.

But she was sweet and fragrant, and her long, slim body followed his movement. She wound herself around him, held to him with wet hands, panted, kissed his chin and throat frantically as he took her. And she cried out, softly, when he thrust into her wildly, and made her his for a long moment.

When it was over, he got up, his hands shaking as he fastened his clothes. "God, I hate you, Julia. Get up, I shall not see you again."

She sat up, smoothing down her dress. Her face was flushed and rosy; she looked young and sweet. "Yes, you will, Brett. You'll meet me again."

"Damned if I will!"

Her legs were long and white, her thighs—

He jerked his gaze away. Julia went on, "Yes. We go away again in two weeks. I want to see you again, alone —again and again. Brett. For God's sake—I love you, don't you understand? It has been hell for me these years—" She stopped and put her hands over her face.

He knelt beside her and took her into his arms. She sobbed silently against his shoulder, then pulled away, and wiped her face with her skirt. "No, I won't cry. I won't," she told herself aloud.

"Julia, don't go on like this—"

"I have to see you again. I have to know your arms about me, I have to have your kisses—please, Brett, I am begging you—"

His insides seemed turned out, he was wrenched from

head to foot. Julia, pleading, Julia soft and warm and begging—"

"Day after tomorrow, here," she whispered. "Oh, Brett, please. Just once more—"

He met her again, and then again and again, in the few days before they left. He hated himself, but he could not stay away from her. And their embraces were sweeter, deeper, longer, as they came together again and again. She was a fire in his loins, a blazing desire in his heart. He could not think of her without feeling the need for her. And she pressed her hands over him, learning of him again and again. "I shall have this to remember, darling," she whispered in his ear. "I shall have this—oh, Brett, I must have this—"

Chapter 21

Frederick Keane wrote from Philadelphia two months later.

"Dear Brett, I am the happiest man in the world. Julia is with child. She has become the most docile, sweet girl in the world. We are both so happy. You must come and visit with us. Julia is writing to Cecilia for advice."

He went on to ask about business, offering again to buy shares in the company, as he had some money to invest.

Brett read the letter over and over and laid it down on his study table. He was worried sick. Was the child his? Had Julia deceived them both? Why was she doing this? Was Keane incapable of giving her a child? Had she taken this road to give him an heir? Or had she meant it, that she loved him—

Grimly, he decided to go visit them, with business as an excuse. Cecilia thought about accompanying him, but he did not encourage her to do so. "You will want to be with the children," he said gently. "Marcus cannot be left, as he has been sick and the journey would not be good for him."

"You are right, Brett," she said, submissively, her eyes troubled. "Julia writes that the doctor has warned her to be very careful, to lie down frequently. Will you inquire of Frederick if I should come later? Will the birth be difficult? You will ask if she wishes aid?"

Brett bent over and kissed her forehead. "You are good, Cecilia, after all your sister has said to you."

"She hurts only when she is angry and hurt herself,"

said Cecilia gently. "And I have so much, I can well afford to be generous." She smiled shyly at Brett. "I still do not believe I was so fortunate that you chose me as your wife. I loved you so much, but I could not believe—"

"You had best believe, my darling, after ten years of marriage and four children," Brett said with a laugh. "What more must I do to convince you that I love you?"

He stopped her answer with his lips, feeling tender and gentle with her. She had been sitting up with Marcus, as he had been ill. And she expected another child early in 1872, only a few months before Julia's baby was due. He would not allow her to help Julia. It was too much to expect. She could endanger herself and their new child.

Brett left for Philadelphia soon after that conversation. He was amazed and thoughtful at the grandeur of the Keane home. Keane came from a large family, and all of them were engaged in the ironworks. His father seemed hard and tough, even in his seventies, and the other brothers talked business much of the time. The sister who had charge of Julia's household was severe and no-nonsense, and seemed quite capable.

Julia rested in her room all morning, then came trailing down in a long, cream-colored morning robe to lie in the drawing room and hold court. She had guests for every luncheon, and her laughter rose in musical belltones much of the time. Her eyes were bright, her cheeks rosy with color; she seemed happy.

Brett remained for a week, and finally managed to see Julia alone. They sat in her drawing room, waiting for Frederick to come home from work. Julia lay back languidly in her lilac dress, with the striped silk flounced overskirt. The lace-frilled sleeves were puffed and short, revealing her round, creamy arms. Her hair was piled high, frizzed in short blonde curls, and a black velvet ribbon circled her bare throat, a cameo fastening the ribbon. The off-the-shoulder bodice revealed her creamy shoulders and the tops of her full breasts.

She was an entrancing picture as she lay back on the chaise longue, her lilac slippers just revealed by her skirts.

Brett came over to her, stood over her, and spoke sternly. "You know I have been trying to have a word with you alone, Julia."

"My dearest Brett. It would not be proper," she said, with a taunting smile and a wave of her Japanese fan.

"Since when have you thought of proper ways?"

"Oh, I am about to become a mother. I have settled down and become proper."

The doors to the hallway were closed. He said, in a low husky tone, "Is the child mine, Julia?"

Her eyebrows raised, only a slight flush betraying her emotion. "Yours? Brett, how scandalous."

"I mean it. Are you deceiving Keane?"

"Nonsense, Brett. Do you think I would *tell* you if I were? Now, do go and pour yourself a glass of brandy. I think your nerves are shattered."

His mouth tightened. "I am quite serious, Julia. I came to find out—"

She shrugged lightly. "Would I tell you if I knew? I sleep with Keane, or did until my pregnancy. Now we occupy separate rooms. Is that what you wanted to know?"

He went over to the mahogany bar which Frederick Keane used for his guests and poured a glass of brandy for himself. He sipped slowly, inhaling the fragrance. Keane always kept the best. Her gaze followed him, studying the lean hips, the lithe movement of his body. As he turned about, she looked at the high cheekbones, the heavy reddish tan of his face.

"You know, Brett," she said idly, "I always wondered if there was some Indian blood in you. You are very dark."

He began to laugh. He laughed, and laughed, until he choked on the brandy. She rose up, frowning, as his laughter did not cease.

"What is so damned funny? Tell me. I demand it."

He managed to say, around the laugh, "You keep

283

your secrets, Julia, I'll keep mine! Oh, God, that is funny." He drank deeply of the brandy, and grinned wickedly at her. Oh, God, he thought. That was so funny. If Julia was having his child, it would be part Cherokee Indian. If she only knew—!

Frederick Keane soon came in, shoulders sagging with weariness, but his eyes brightening when he saw Julia lounging in the lilac silk. He went over to her at once and bent over to kiss her forehead.

"My darling, how do you feel?"

"Splendid," she said, with a pout. "I think the doctor is mad, keeping me quiet. I feel quite fine."

"But you will obey him, darling. For the sake of the child?" He was flushed, eager, awkwardly radiant.

"Of course, darling. I don't want anything to happen to the child. We must have a son, I am determined on it," she added, with a softening smile up at him.

She reached up and patted his cheek, as though he were but a child himself. She did have fondness for him; she never said nasty things to him, thought Brett, in relief. He finally decided to take his leave. Julia probably knew just exactly what she was doing. And so long as they both were happy, perhaps it was for the best.

Cecilia had her child, a girl named Caroline, in March of 1872. In June Frederick sent word that Julia had given birth to a boy, whom they had named James for Frederick's father. The whole family was excited, and Julia was radiant.

"But she had a difficult time of it, my poor brave girl. More than fifty hours in labor, as her body is narrow. The doctor almost despaired. She is very weak, and the baby is given to a wet nurse until she recovers. I do not know if we can risk having another child. But I am not alarmed, for we have James, and he is the sturdiest child imaginable. Julia sends her best regards to all, and particularly her admiration to Cecilia for daring to have five children. Seriously, we are all happy here at your good news. Forgive us for not writing sooner."

Frederick could be quite eloquent on paper; it was in

person that he was gauche. Brett folded the letter thoughtfully and put it away to be answered later. He still wondered if the boy was his. A son by Julia. He could not help feeling exultant. She had been determined to have the child. Was it his?

Frederick wrote again later, his letter full of the wonders of his son. "James is sturdy; he grows rapidly. He resembles Julia amazingly, the same tufts of blonde hair, the same blue eyes. She is now able to be up some hours of the day, and has entertained twice for dinner."

The following summer, in 1873, Julia came with her husband and son for a visit. She seemed restless, quick of speech, impatient with her small son. She confided in them, before Frederick:

"I am so tired of being tied down to the child. I must get away for a time, or go mad. I wonder if Rose Marie would take James for the summer and let me go to Europe."

Cecilia said at once, gravely, "But you must leave James with us, Julia. I shall be happy to have him. He is so good, no trouble at all."

"Oh, would you, darling? I long to go. Frederick wants to remain and talk business with Brett, but I want to go to Europe. I promise to return in the fall."

And off went Julia, accompanied by one of her best women friends and an older couple. Without a backward glance, she left James with them. It was but the first of several such jaunts.

The boy resembled Julia—but also Brett. Cecilia caught the resemblance at once, those startling blue eyes which Frederick Keane said were like Julia's. Those high cheekbones, which he thought resembled those of his grandfather. No, they were Brett's; he was the son of Brett, Cecilia felt sure. And the time was right. Julia had been here about the time of the conception of the child.

When the children played together, she could see how much James resembled Henry. She waited for Brett to say something, or Rose Marie, who came each summer for a visit. But neither said anything, and finally she no longer expected it.

She was hurt and angry at first, then resigned. After all, Brett had married Cecilia, not Julia. If he was drawn to her, like a moth to flame, who could blame him? But it did sting deeply; it hurt that he had betrayed her with her own sister. And Julia, gaily talking of how James was coming to resemble Frederick more and more. Cecilia felt cool to Brett, sometimes, not like her old confiding, happy self.

Brett worried about her a little, when the business permitted. He was working harder than ever.

"But we must get away for a vacation together, darling," he told Cecilia. "We must have a trip to Europe."

She only smiled and shook her head, afraid that if she accepted he might wish to join Julia and her troupe. And that Cecilia could not endure. "Not now, while the works are so busy," she would murmur, and change the subject.

Frederick Keane came down to visit often and stayed quite a time. He seemed to enjoy the family warmth, and they always made him welcome, although Brett had guilty feelings.

Frederick still wanted to invest in the powder mills, but Brett continued to refuse. It was still a family business. Now that he had sons, and John Vallette had a son, and Flora and her husband were having children, the business could continue with their sons. He did not want to risk having outsiders taking over.

Frederick Keane did not take offense. "Well, well, you know best," he said. "But have you thought of the work in South America? I think there is a market there for you. Let me investigate for you when I go down this fall."

Brett agreed, and was pleasantly surprised by the shrewd report Frederick sent back. He and John discussed it, and decided to sell some powder in Brazil and Argentina. The orders increased; they had to enlarge the mills again and again. Business boomed.

Within a few years, the Vallettes were so wealthy that

they could not believe it. Brett bought jewels for Cecilia; she said with a choked laugh that she felt like a prize cow with a blue ribbon on her. And indeed, a choker of diamonds did not suit her plump neck. Rose Marie gently suggested other gems, and brought from New York a fine pendant of gold with a large fine opal for her. Cecilia did enjoy wearing that, with the matching earrings.

Brett was becoming weary. The mill was in good hands. John was aging, but the foremen and Donald Gregory kept things moving well even when John was ill.

Rose Marie and Stephen were shocked at Brett's weariness when they came in the summer of 1879. "But Brett, you cannot go on like this. Working night and day. Surely you should take a vacation," Stephen told him sternly.

"I cannot get away." Brett pressed his hand over his eyes. "Frederick is coming to talk business, he will bring James—"

"And Cecilia needs to get away. Take her on a second honeymoon," Rose Marie urged him. "Have you seen how tired she looks lately?"

He did look up at that. "Cecilia? Oh, of course she must get away. Five children, and all the company we have had—I had to invite some men from New York and Washington to discuss the reports from South America—"

He looked haggard. Stephen worked on him, Rose Marie on Cecilia, each suggesting that the other should get away. And they succeeded. When Frederick came down with James, Rose Marie said briskly that they planned to remain and take care of all the children so that Brett and Cecilia could go away by themselves.

"Good idea, oh, splendid," beamed Frederick. "I had hoped to suggest something of the sort. We impose on them too much. But they are like my own family—"

He willingly agreed to stay on and help in any way he could, content to help audit the books that Brett had planned to work on that summer.

Brett and Cecilia set off in something of a daze. They had not gone on a journey together for so long they scarcely knew how to plan.

Once on the ship, Cecilia was almost appalled by its luxury. She gazed about their expensive suite and felt like whispering, "Can this be me?"

But the trip did Brett good; he looked better already for sleeping hard at nights and snoozing in the sunlight on deck. Brett finally said contentedly, "This is like a second honeymoon, darling." They were lounging in chairs on the deck, enjoying the sun's warmth.

At the silence, he glanced over at Cecilia, surprised at the expression on her face, half-exasperation, half-amusement. Then he began to chuckle.

"Oh, what an ass I am. My darling, forgive me! We never had that first honeymoon, did we? Married eighteen years, with five children, and never had a honeymoon!"

He reached out, took her small, plump hand, and kissed the finger with his rings on it.

"Forgive me, darling. I have treated you so shabbily. Any other woman would have complained long and bitterly."

"I have no complaints, Brett," she said very quietly, holding his hand tightly in hers.

"No, you never have, have you? Through the terrible war, all that work, caring for our mill people, the children—no man could have had a better helpmeet than I have had. How fortunate I have been," he said, and closed his eyes to rest again.

Eyes shut, he thought over those years. He was fifty-one, now, and able to look back with some satisfaction. He had kept the mills going through good times and bad. He had worked well with John, though their natures were much different. He had managed well—in all except that affair with Julia. No, he must not think of Julia. That shooting star, that maddening lovely, adorable wretch. He must forget her completely.

Cecilia gazed out over the swell of the ocean, her thoughts musing somewhat along the same lines. They had dealt well together. She thought he had been unfaithful to her with Julia, but he had never turned from Cecilia, nor mentioned the word "divorce," though she had seen his face sometimes when he looked at James.

Pray God they could continue to make a good thing of their marriage. It was all she had to hold onto. Without Brett, she would collapse. She was nothing without him. He was the light of her life, the center of her universe.

They went first to England, roamed about in wonder at the places they had read about, gazed at the Tower of London, gaped at the crown jewels. They went further afield, to Canterbury, to look with awe at the stained-glass windows and gather in the reverent atmosphere of the place. To Stratford, to walk where Shakespeare had walked. To Oxford, to smaller towns, thinking of their favorite books of Charles Dickens, Thomas Hardy, Jane Austen, Sir Walter Scott.

Brett insisted they see Paris, and they remained there a week. Cecilia was not comfortable in that fashionable city—she felt more a dowd than ever, even in a Worth gown and a tiara which Brett bought for her. She was glad to go on to the Riviera, then to Italy. There they roamed about Milan, then on to Florence, Pisa, and Siena, to see the places "just like in the paintings," as Cecilia said in rapture. She felt comfortable in Florence; they could walk about, between the narrow-walled buildings, along the cobblestoned streets, and imagine how it had been five hundred years ago.

They went back up then to Switzerland, to settle themselves in a chalet high up in the Alps, to wrap themselves in sweaters and coats and caps, and stare out in amazement at the sight of snow in summer. The icy stream slid past their windows; the melodious sounds of bells at dawn and dusk entranced them. There they relaxed, slept, ate, rested, and got back their strength, as though they gained it from the giant mountains.

Cecilia and Brett never forgot that summer in the mountains. They walked for miles, breathing the dry, crisp air, swinging their hands like children, laughing, or silent, communing with nature at its most beautiful. They did not pick the wildflowers, content to see them growing in fragile beauty in the shadows of great upheavals of rock and stone. They heard of the River Areuse and made a pilgrimage to it—that river for which their own Areuse had been named by the Swiss owner of the mills so many years ago.

"I feel like a little speck of history," mused Cecilia one night as they toasted their feet before the open fire in their chalet. "I gaze at the mountains. They were here a thousand years ago, they will be here a thousand years from now. We shall come and go, and make little mark; but they are here always."

"That is a fearful thought," said Brett, lazily smoking his pipe. "Our problems do seem to diminish, don't they? Things seem more clear in the mountains, somehow."

"Yes. That's what I mean. I get them straight in my mind—what is important and what is not," said Cecilia gravely.

"I think you always knew that, Cecilia," he commented, closing his eyes and leaning back his head.

"Not always, Brett. I just kept trying," she murmured in a subdued tone.

"That's all we can do. Say, did we get a letter from Frederick today, and Rose Marie? I want to hear about the children." He yawned and stretched as Cecilia reached for the letter to read it to him. She had scanned it hastily when it arrived, always anxious to make sure the children were well.

They finally went home in late August, rested and fit for another twenty years, as Brett said with a laugh. He drew her against his shoulder as the ocean wind whipped into their faces. "It's been good, Cecilia. We must do this again, and not wait too long."

"It has been so lovely, so like a dream," she whispered against his tweed coat.

"I adore you, have I told you lately?"

She smiled, and he pressed his lips to her cheek lovingly. Such a good wife, such a very good wife.

They arrived home and found the children grown beyond belief, Frederick happy to see them, Rose Marie and Stephen brushing off their thanks. "We were happy to do it. How well you both look. Now you must promise to come up to New York on a visit soon. No hiding away down here."

They were but settled into the work again when they received a wire from Frederick in New York City. "Julia seriously hurt. Can Brett come at once."

Brett went white. "What could it be? Hurt? One of those railroad accidents?"

"Oh, you must go. He must need you desperately, Brett." Cecilia stifled her jealousy, helped him pack, and saw him down to the railroad station in the carriage. She had been ill, and knew why. She dared not risk the rough journey.

The train seemed so slow, though it made good time that day. Brett arrived in New York in the mid-morning of the next day and went to the hotel Frederick had indicated. A pallid, stern-faced man met him. Frederick seemed to have grown old overnight.

"What is it? How is she?" asked Brett, gripping his hands, to give comfort and reassurance.

Frederick drew him into the luxurious suite. "Julia is in there," he nodded toward the bedroom beyond, the door slightly ajar. "I must speak to you first."

Brett took off his suitcoat and hat and sank down into a chair and refused the drink automatically offered. Frederick did not seem to know it was early morning, and Brett was parched for coffee.

"Julia—Julia has been here much of the summer," Frederick finally choked out. "She made some— undesirable friends. She has taken to drinking much—I did not tell you, it grieved me so. She scarcely comes home, takes no interest in the family, and all that. Even James—she hugs him, and forgets him."

Brett listened patiently, then noticed that a white-clad nurse was moving about in the bedroom.

Frederick poured himself a drink and drank down

half of the golden liquid. "She was in a bar," he said, finally. "There was a fight. Oh, she wasn't involved, but she shouldn't ha' been there, not with those men. There was a fight, they had guns. She was shot, twice, in the chest."

"My God," whispered Brett, sitting up straight. "Julia shot—in a bar?"

It was appalling, horrible. Frederick nodded. "They don't—expect her—to live. Doctor said—" he paused, his speech jerky, his eyes unfocused. "Said she just—hung on. Doesn't want to live, he says. Why, I ask you? Why doesn't Julia want to live? She has everything in the world; I give her anything she wants. She only has to ask, I get it for her."

The nurse came to the door as Brett stared at Frederick. It must be a nightmare; he could not be here in this plush, velvet-hung suite of the best New York hotel, listening to what Frederick was saying.

"Are you Mr. Brett Vallette? Mrs. Keane wishes to speak to you," said the woman, in a low, brisk voice.

Frederick started forward eagerly. But the nurse said, "Just Mr. Vallette, for a few minutes. She must not be wearied."

Brett felt like apologizing as Frederick dropped back, his bulldog face drooping dejectedly.

"I'll only be a few minutes. She will want you," said Brett, putting his hand on Frederick's shoulder.

He shook his head. "She never wants me," said Frederick, and he went over to the bar and reached for another bottle.

The nurse remained outside the door. "Keep her quiet, Mr. Vallette," she whispered. "She has something she must say. But don't let her get upset over it."

He nodded, and went in. The nurse closed the door softly after him.

Julia lay in a slim line in the bed, all straight lines, no curves. Her arms had been placed beside her body; her beautiful hair was braided tightly to keep it out of her way. Bandages showed just above the line of the sheet, and blood stained them.

Her eyes were open, though, those beautiful, wide, blue-gray eyes that could mock, or melt, or flash. They were dulled with pain and with the drugs they had given her.

"Brett," she breathed faintly, and her right hand stirred. He took the long fingers very carefully in his and pressed them. They were cold and stiff.

"I am here, Julia. What can I do for you?" he murmured.

"I am . . . dying. Listen."

"Save your strength. My dear, save your strength . . ."

"No." The eyes flashed with a slight anger. "Listen. James . . . is . . . yours. Frederick cannot . . . take care of . . . him. All to pieces. Will you . . . take James . . . take care . . . he is . . . yours."

His mouth tightened. "Frederick will want his son," he said deliberately.

The eyes flickered. "No. You must . . . promise."

"Oh, Julia," he groaned. "Why didn't you take better care of yourself?"

"No . . . wish . . . to live . . ." she muttered, and turned her head away. The fingers clung to his feverishly. "You promise?"

"If Frederick wishes it. Cecilia and I will take the boy and raise him as our own."

"You . . . promise?"

"I promise."

"Good. Brett . . . I love . . . you . . ." The murmur died away; she closed her eyes, and seemed to sleep. He waited; she did not rouse, and he went out softly and shut the door.

Julia died that afternoon, as the setting sun streaked with crimson the white lace curtains in the elegant hotel room.

Stephen came and helped with the funeral arrangements. They sent for several of Frederick's brothers, who came and upheld the man. He seemed broken.

Frederick begged Brett to take James home with him for a time. Brett agreed, and after the funeral he took the small boy to the house on the hill above the powder

293

mills. He told Cecilia that Julia had wished them to care for James, and that Frederick seemed unable to make plans for him.

"Of course, we will take him. What's one more in this big house? There is plenty of love to go around," said Cecilia, holding James to her plump breast.

Frederick came down later; he seemed broken and much subdued. He had flung himself into his work; he would never marry again, he said. The house was sold, he could not endure to live in it.

It was no place for a boy, anyway. He looked about their lively household and sighed, and asked them to keep James for him. "I cannot give him a mother's love, and you know much more about children. I'll pay for his keep, and gladly. If you will—"

"No talk of pay," Cecilia scolded him gently. "We are glad to have Julia's boy. And you must come often and see him. You won't be a stranger to your son."

He thanked them. He came down often, visibly aging. He took some interest in the powder mills, and could always talk business briskly, but the sight of James seemed to pain him more than please him.

Cecilia had become pregnant on their honeymoon. She bore a sixth child, Luke, in 1880, and he was a bright-eyed, healthy, husky boy from the first. He and James and Caroline often played together, the best of friends, though Luke was much the younger.

"He's a leader, Luke is," Brett said to Cecilia, one summer evening as they watched the children running down the slope and screaming with laughter. "Something of me in him, much of me, and much of you. He has a strong will, and much intelligence. And he's a fighter. You would think, as the youngest, he would give in much of the time—"

"Not Luke!" Cecilia shook her head. "It makes me laugh sometimes. He sticks out that lip of his, and won't give into any of them, not even to Arthur. Yes, a little fighter, Luke is."

PART III

1909–1919

Chapter 22

Luke Tristan Vallette sat in the back row of the small board room, writing out figures on a pad. His mouth was compressed, with his lower lip stuck out.

His oldest brother Arthur, near the chair of the board chairman, old John Vallette, glanced at him, then away. If Luke got difficult again, old John would forbid the younger members to attend the sessions at all. Luke was only twenty-nine; he was a chemist. Just because he had attended Massachusetts Institute of Technology was no sign he knew everything in the world.

Old John Vallette quavered on. In spite of his trembling hands and weak voice, he was in firm comtrol of Vallette and Sons. Ever since Brett had died of a heart attack eight years ago, in 1901, John had taken firm charge again, though he was now seventy-nine years of age. Here it was 1909, Luke thought angrily, and one would think it was 1800! Vallette and Sons would never change. John would not even allow a typewriter in his own office; everything must be written down by pen, as it had been always.

Luke scrawled "$240,000" on the pad—then the figure "1909." James Keane glanced over his shoulder, and grinned discreetly at the figures. He knew what was in Luke's mind: the cost of expanding the firm to make more smokeless powder. John was against it, firmly. No war was in sight, he said, and that was that.

Luke and James thought otherwise, but they were young men, said old John, and they should keep silent before their elders. They might sit on the board because of their large holdings of stock. However, he would not listen to them, nor would Arthur Vallette, Brett's eldest son. Donald Gregory was old and tired and would have liked to retire. Blinking behind his glasses, Uncle Donald half-dozed in the sunlight that streamed into the room.

Rory Vallette, John's son, had left the firm. Trained in business, he had become infuriated at the old-fashioned methods of Vallette and Sons. After fuming for a few years, he marched out and took a position in New York City, then out in Kentucky, with a new railroad holding company. He was going up rapidly; they had missed out on a good bet with Rory. John missed him, but would not admit he had been responsible for the departure of his only son.

James tapped on Brett's old pad, the one Luke held. Luke's mind went off on another tangent. Before Brett died, he had called his youngest son to him, who was the only one still living at home.

"You're the one most like me," muttered Brett, as he lay on his bed, his hand rubbing his chest uneasily. He had scarcely been sick a day in his life; the heart attack had caught him unawares. "I must tell you . . . something. You have a quick temper . . . like mine. Must tell you . . ."

"Be calm, father," said Luke, worriedly. Only twenty-one, he had hastened home from college on hearing of his father's illness. He and his father were very close, even more so since the death of his mother in 1895. They often went hunting together, talking intimately. Brett had told him dreamily about the old days, about how he had built up Vallette and Sons. He had left more stock to Luke than to the others, and the other boys had resented it, especially Arthur.

"Arthur . . . is . . . a stuffed shirt," said Brett, with an attempt at a grin. He shifted in bed, wearily. "He would hate . . . to hear this. Besides . . . doesn't need to know. Use your discretion about whom you tell, Luke. I leave it to you. You have good judgment . . . when you don't fly off the handle."

Then he told Luke about Moira and the Indian chief who had abducted her, about their heritage of Cherokee blood. "I am like him," whispered Brett. "I get wild ideas, get stubborn, the way he was. And Rose Marie, your aunt. Not Bridget, bless her good heart. Arthur takes after his mother, and so does Henry. Roseann . . . well, she is sweet, like her mother, and Caroline is a gentle girl. But you . . . and James . . ."

"James?" asked Luke sharply.

"Yes. He is . . . your . . . half-brother," whispered Brett, who had then told him simply of that story. "Never tell him unless you must. He has great pride in the Keane family. We never changed his name. And Frederick . . . well, he would have been crushed. I think he did suspect, but he put the thought out of his mind. Can't have the Keane family cutting off James either. You look after him, Luke."

And then he had died. They buried him beside Cecilia, up on the hill, and young Marcus, who had lived only to the age of nineteen, when he had died of some strange malady.

Luke was thinking about all that in the brightly sunlit board room when John Vallette addressed him sharply.

"Luke? I want you and the younger ones to leave the room. We'll be discussing finances and future plans now."

The underlip jutted out. Luke said, angrily, "What about my shares? Do you intend to vote them also, uncle?"

John's old cheeks flushed with rage; his veined hands clenched hard on his scarred desk. "Will you obey me? Leave at once, you and James."

"I think you are going to vote down the new powder mill I think we should have, uncle," said Luke, rigidly. His blue eyes blazed with anger. "I have a right to say what I believe about that. I am the one who made a study of the matter, I have talked with the army officials in Washington—"

"Without my permission," blazed John right back at him. "I warned you again and again about going behind my back—"

"They say there is danger of war in Europe. Our country must be prepared. Remember what happened in the Spanish-American War—when we were not prepared, and had to convert so quickly that—"

"Enough. You were only a child then. Now, leave before I have you thrown out."

Donald Gregory gasped at the words and flung out a placating hand. "John, John. Don't be so tough on the lads. They are interested in the matter. Let them remain and listen."

"They will only quarrel with me," said John gruffly, glaring at Luke.

Luke got up. "Don't bother, Uncle Donald. Uncle John is as stubborn as an old goat. Go ahead with your plans, but don't be surprised if I take my shares and sell them to Linvill-Ross. I'm in a mood to let them cut in on the action, and see how you like that."

And he stormed out of the room, leaving John to yell after him. James raced after Luke and caught up with him out in the powder yards.

"My God, Luke, what possesses you? You want to give the old boy a fit?"

"Yes, I'd like to," said Luke shortly. "And Arthur, too. My big brother, with his condescending look over his glasses. I could belt him one."

"Like the old days, huh?" chuckled James.

Luke grinned reluctantly without breaking his stride. He left the mills, James panting after him, and strode up the hill to the old homestead where he still had a room. Arthur had taken over the house, announcing in his pompous manner after Brett had died, "I am the eldest, it is up to me to keep up the place."

Saved him building a new house, grumbled Luke to himself, looking up fondly at the old-fashioned home.

"Remember how you took a running jump at him when he came home with his new girl and butted him in the stomach and knocked him into the pigpond?"

chuckled James, catching his arm. "Say, now, hold on, Luke. I can't keep up with your pace!"

"Come on then," said Luke, but he slowed down. James was getting plump; he was thirty-seven, and a little paunchy in the belly, as Luke told him sternly from time to time. "Get some exercise, it's good for you!"

"No, I was born this way; dad was plump," James always sighed.

Luke thought again of the secret about James' paternity. Should he tell James one day? No need for it, he thought.

"I'll ask Uncle Donald what went on in the board meeting. He'll tell me, if I beg enough," said Luke thoughtfully.

"Beg? Or twist his arm?" grinned James placidly. "What do we care anyway? The stocks continue to pay well."

"We aren't expanding as we should," said Luke, and let it go at that. There was plenty he didn't tell James, or anyone, keeping it tightly to his chest. He had gone over the books many a time without anyone's knowing it. He had let himself into the office at night, warned the night watchman, and read over the diminishing orders, the weakening fiscal picture of Vallette and Sons.

One day, Vallette and Sons might close suddenly, unable to continue. John was incapable of looking far enough ahead. Brett was the one who had stressed progress, using new methods, new machinery, new inventions to keep them ahead of the competition. After he died, John remained content to do what they had always done.

But that was not enough, thought Luke, churned up inside. He had gone around each summer for the past four years, visiting plants like theirs, talking to businessmen. He had gone to see Rory Vallette, and had talked at length with him. They had ideas they wanted to try, though Rory declared he would never return so long as his father exercised dictatorial control of the company and the family.

In time Luke did hear what had happened at the

board meeting. Donald Gregory reluctantly admitted that old John had decided not to enlarge the mills. "In fact, he is thinking of selling out to Linvill-Ross," he said quietly. "Your parting shot shook him; he thought you had heard a rumor."

"Sell out—Vallette and Sons?" Luke stared incredulously at his uncle, at the stooped, weary shoulders. He was a good sort, the kind who was the bookkeeper of every company, the old faithful whom everyone liked and overlooked. "He can't do that, not without our votes. Who does he think he is, God?"

"Yes, of course," said Donald wryly, with a grin. "He always did think so. Brett was the only one who could chop him down to size."

"How far has it gone?"

"Just talk, a few tentative offers. But Luke, if we don't get more orders from the railroads, we are going to sink. The more aggressive powder companies are taking the business away from us. We must produce faster and try out more of your inventions," said Donald earnestly, peering at Luke over his glasses. "You are young, yes, but you have excellent research methods. And John just sets aside your reports."

"I know that. He hasn't taken a look yet at the report on the possible new products from chemicals," said Luke grimly. "Two years of research, and he won't look at them!"

Luke's inventions were ignored, shunted aside; even the new tar for wagon wheels. The ideas for motorcars were snorted at—the motorcar would never catch on, it was a toy for rich playboys! So Luke's rubberized tires, his fabric covers for seats, even the gasoline fuels were filed in reports and put away.

Donald sighed. "Your Uncle John antagonizes everyone. You know, Barbara refuses to come home. She graduated from Oberlin College, out in Ohio, and has all those new ideas about women getting the vote and wearing pants, and all that, and she won't come home. She got herself an apartment in Washington with a couple of girl friends. John is having a fit."

Luke could not repress a grin. "How is young Freckles?" he asked.

Donald gave him a wise look. "You should drop in on Barbara. If you still call her Freckles after your visit, I'll give you a new rifle for your birthday."

"Huh? Has she changed that much? Gotten pretty?" Luke asked, rather idly, his thoughts more on the changes in Vallette and Sons than on his second cousin. "She always was a tomboy. I rescued her from more than one tree."

"More like a young wildcat now," muttered Donald.

Luke was paying no attention to him, pacing the room, his hands behind his back. He had an idea, and came to a pause. "Thanks very much, uncle. I appreciate your confidence."

"Not at all, not at all, Luke. Only don't tell old John," sighed Donald. "I'm getting old and can't stand his tempers much longer." He pulled himself out of the easy chair and stumped to the door with Luke. "Think I'll retire one of these days and just go hunting. And sit on the porch and rock the rest of the time."

"Tell that to your grandchildren," said Luke, with a grin and a pat on Donald's shoulder.

But out in his carriage, Luke began to think seriously. No one at Vallette and Sons even had a motor car, when they were all the rage. No, old John had decreed that motorcars gave off sparks, and sparks would set off explosions, and explosions would blow up the mills. So even though Donald lived a mile away and Luke liked to live in his apartment in the nearby town of Montgomery, they drove back and forth in carriages and kept stables of horses. Luke enjoyed horseback riding. But he secretly kept a motorcar in town. When John learned of it, *that* would be an explosion, thought Luke.

John was years behind the times, decades behind. And that was dangerous for Vallette and Sons. If he didn't keep up, Linvill-Rose would not even bother to buy them out; they would just let Vallette and Sons die of rottenness from within.

He sent a wire to Rory Vallette and within a week

Rory came from Kentucky to visit him. Luke arrived at the apartment to find his cousin coolly helping himself at the mahogany bar in the corner of the living room. Rory lifted the glass to Luke as he came in.

"I heard your horses neighing when I came," said Rory. "So Vallette and Sons has not changed at all, right?"

"Good to see you," said Luke, with unusual amiability. Rory eyed him over the glass. He enjoyed his young cousin, but he thought of him as a "young firebrand."

"Oh, I just dropped everything and came," said Rory, sipping the bourbon with appreciation. "This is almost as good as we get in Kentucky."

"Nice of you to say so." Luke poured a glass for himself, opened the box of Havana cigars, and offered them. When both had lit up and were sitting comfortably in the great overstuffed chairs before the fire, he began. "You are probably wondering why the haste."

"Right. I thought rot takes place slowly."

"The rot is going deep. Uncle John is against the expansion that we must make to keep the sporting powder going. And he closes his ears when I mention military powder. We are going to have war in Europe, I am sure of it," said Luke more seriously. "We have to be prepared this time. Not like the Cuban disaster. I remember all too well dad fighting to get the powder to the ships in time to do any good. I really think he wore himself out and that brought on the heart attack. He worked himself to a frenzy."

Rory nodded, his laughing face gloomy for once. "Yes, I recall. And old John sat by, rocking. God, it made me angry."

Luke mused for a moment, then went on, "I have heard that John is considering selling out to Linvill-Ross. Without our consent. We all have stock in the company. But as you know, he makes the decisions and tells the other stockholders later. He thinks because we are all family that we won't fight him."

"Most of them won't. You know how your sister Caroline is. But my sister Barbara thinks it is indecent that women aren't allowed to vote in *public elections!* She would fire up like fury if she knew what her old dad was up to. Have you heard her on the subject of women's suffrage?"

Luke waved away that change of subject. "No, no, don't start now on suffrage. I am serious."

"So is Barbara," said Rory, with a grin.

"To get back to the company," said Luke, his underlip out, "we are going to have to find a way to take over control. John won't change, and Donald is too tired to fight. Arthur—well, that boy was born stuck in the mud. I think he cares more for his flower gardens than Vallette and Sons, anyway."

"Could be."

"So I'm asking you to come back to Vallette and Sons," said Luke. "You have experience with modern companies. Help me figure out a way to take control of Vallette and Sons and modernize it. We have to make improvements, enlargements. We ought to be building a mill in Ohio so that the railroads can get powder conveniently nearby. And in Missouri—we could use a mill there."

"Treason, heresy," said Rory, in mock horror. "What would father say?"

Luke scowled. "What he has always said; Vallette and Sons has no need to enlarge. Quality, not quantity. No need to change with the times. Good management is the same as it always was."

"I can just hear him talking," chuckled Rory, his handsome face crinkling with humor. His flashing dark brown eyes glanced thoughtfully at Luke, who was getting all worked up about this. Rory at thirty-four found it hard to get worked up about anything. He had been born of an elderly father and a timid mother. He found his simplest solution was to leave home and make his own way. Now he kept on doing it, and enjoyed wine, women, and song equally and impartially. Many a girl had set her bonnet for Rory Vallette, his handsome good looks and his wealth equally attractive. He was weary of their obvious ploys and wary of their attentions. He wondered if Luke felt the same way.

It would be a pity if Vallette and Sons went eventually to the children of Arthur, Henry, Caroline, and Roseann. They were not dynamic the way Luke was. Luke could take hold of a subject and make it as explosive as the black powder for which Vallette and Sons had been famous for more than one hundred years. He could make the old company prosper once more.

But, thought Rory, I am no one to preach marriage to Luke. He would turn it back on me, and God's sake, I'm not about to marry. "Well, what did you have in mind when you sent for me?" he asked aloud.

Luke swirled the brandy around in the glass. They had finished dinner, talking like old friends, sometimes serious, sometimes laughing. He felt good, and warm, and relaxed.

"Talk, I guess. Advice. Sounding you out. If I should decide to fight the oldsters for control of the company, can I count on you?"

Luke looked directly across at his cousin, his eyes narrowed.

Rory gazed back at him thoughtfully, laughter dashed from him now. "I don't know, Luke. I'm in a good position where I am. However, the old ties pull. I am a Vallette."

"Good enough. Let's let it ride. You came here, I asked you for advice about selling more powder for the railroad, and I'll put it to Uncle John that we are missing more opportunities than he knows. You'll meet him anyway?"

"Sure. What excuse do I give for coming?"

Luke grinned a little twisted smile and said, "For the family reunion this summer, Rory."

"God, no. What family reunion?"

"Stephen and Rose Marie, the cousins and their children, all descending next week. Didn't you know?"

Rory groaned. "No, I wouldn't have come—yes, I would. I like old Stephen. He's a good sort. Wonder how little Angela turned out? She was all curves and a button nose, last I saw her."

"She's a young lady, I hear. Haven't seen her for years myself. I understand she is a dress and fabric designer for some New York firm. Anna Moira had a fit about her chick going into business, but Rose Marie was all for it. Rose Marie is all guts."

"She sure is. Ever hear about her adventures in the Civil War? She told me a little about it when I lived up there. Uncle Stephen looked mysterious, but he ain't talking."

"I think he could tell plenty, if he wanted." They dropped the subject. Rory noticed that Luke kept looking at his watch, a large gold one on the end of a long gold chain, stuck into his fob pocket.

"Going somewhere?" Rory asked.

"Date with Jessie Randolph."

"Do I know her?"

"Tall, blonde; you know the family."

"Oh, that one! Does she ever unbend?" kidded Rory. Luke grinned, a deep slash in each cheek. "Sorry. Didn't mean to tread on your toes."

"You won't. Shall I call it off so we can keep on talking? Or shall I ask her to bring her kid sister along?"

"Kid sister?" Rory grimaced.

"Twenty-two, blonde, long legs, drawl like honey, dances like a dream," enlarged Luke.

"I'm all for it."

Jessie was willing, though irritated that Luke had waited until so late to telephone her. On their way out to the motorcar, Rory asked, "About the family reunion. Where are they stashing everyone?"

"Uncle John is taking in about half of them, Arthur the other half."

"Then I'll go over and ask father for lodging," Rory grinned. "Maybe this won't be a dull trip at all."

"I hate to keep you talking business so long," said Luke, with exaggerated politeness.

Rory laughed. "Just keep me informed, Luke. I shall enjoy the fireworks when you get going. And by that time I might be tired of Kentucky and ready to move back to the Areuse. I have missed it," he said with a slight sigh.

"I would hate to leave it," Luke admitted. "I get furious at Uncle John, and mad as hell at Arthur. But I can't bring myself to walk out. It's in my blood."

Chapter 23

The family gathered together was a formidable lot. Angela Parrish stood back in a corner and watched fascinated and rather overwhelmed.

Her grandfather was the most distinguished of the Vallettes, she thought proudly. Old Stephen Vallette, gray-haired, still tall and straight, at seventy-nine, lean as a young man, his laughing eyes crinkled around the edges, his full mouth quirked at the corners. And her grandmother, Rose Marie Vallette, how lovely she looked in the soft old blue lace, the color of her vivid eyes. Anna Moira, Angela's mother, resembled her, with impatient gestures of her hands, the same daring laughter, the same zing to her life.

Angela looked about at the others, some new to her. Luke Vallette scared her. He was tall, lean, impatient, a scowl now on his dark face. He had high cheekbones, a heavy, ruddy tan, and blue eyes that looked right through you. Even Uncle Arthur was scared of Luke, thought Angela, though he tried to patronize him. She decided that nobody patronized Luke; he would just walk right over them—and give them a swift kick on the way. He had someting about him, some scarcely hidden violence, that made him seem volcanic.

"Looking us all over, darling?" murmured a seductive voice in her ear. She whirled around, almost dropping her full glass. A lean, dark hand rescued it for her, and brown eyes laughed down into hers.

"Oh—Rory," she said weakly. She had had a crush

309

on him years ago, when he lived briefly in New York. He would come into the room, and her heart would bound up lightly like a balloon. "I—didn't see you—"

"I saw you right off. You turned out beautifully, Angela." His eyes went over her so thoroughly that she felt all one blush. She was but five-feet-three, short beside his muscular height. He somehow made her feel weak, feminine, helpless. She straightened her spine. She was a working girl, a college graduate. She had made her own living for three years. And she would let no mere male look down on her. "Still the snub nose, but it is adorable on that beautiful pink and white face. Is it as soft as it looks?" And his hand briefly caressed her cheek.

She jerked back, feeling like a fool as he laughed softly. "Really, Rory, don't tease me," she pleaded.

"Why not? We're cousins, aren't we?"

"Third cousins, once removed," she said solemnly. "Granny explained on the way down on the train."

"My God," he muttered, and shook his head. "Don't you dare call me Uncle Rory, though, as you did when you were a bratty child."

She grinned a little, impishly. That is what had made him sit up and notice her that fateful evening in New York.

"Granny said we should treat everyone with respect," she said, feeling suddenly gay and happy. Rory made her feel that way; there was a sort of bubbling happiness about him.

"Of course you should, child. And I expect when I ask you to dance that you will always agree with your third cousin, once removed. Come along, you don't want that drink, it's too strong for children." His hand firmly removed the glass from hers and his arm went about her waist, as he swept her away to the polished ballroom.

In his arms, she felt light as air. He had such a strong, hard arm, like steel about her, drawing her closer as they moved in the old-fashioned waltz. Rory glanced about the room, a meditative smile on his full, sensuous mouth.

"Hasn't changed a bit. I can still see grandmother standing at the entrance to the room, receiving guests in her stiff black taffeta, with a flat, black bonnet on her snow-white hair. And her hands stiff with diamonds."

"You lived here all your life, Rory?" She could picture him growing up here in this beautiful mansion. He was like a southern gentleman of Civil War times and before; he needed only a sword at his side, a gray uniform, gold on his shoulders and cuffs, and he would be perfect. That glint in his eye, that proud tilt of his head, just like the portraits of their ancestors.

"Right. I used to roll down that hill out there, just after the gardeners had finished making it perfect," he grinned down at her. "And into the flower beds to pick some pretties for mother. Did I get cussed out for that!"

"She is so beautiful." Angela glanced at the scene near the entrance to the ballroom. Ellen Vallette stood with her hand laid gently on the arm of John Vallette, smiling up at him, her sweet face serene. She has the brown hair and hazel eyes of a Madonna, thought Angela. In that rose dress, with flowers in her hair, she seemed timeless, in spite of her graying hair and the little wrinkles about her cheeks.

"She is beautiful. Father adores her. In spite of the difference in their ages, she is the only person he ever listens to. And that isn't often!" Rory grimaced.

Angela did not try to reply to that. She had heard about old John Vallette and his tyrannical ways.

"So what are you doing now, Angel?" he asked.

"My name is Angela."

"But you look like an angel in that blue gown," he said gently. "I just can't picture you in the turmoil of business. Don't you hate the business world, and the rushing about?"

"Oh, no, I love it," she protested quickly. "They accept my designs, and want more. I have a whole line in the autumn show."

311

He groaned a little. "Oh, my dear, don't go all un-feminine and suffragette, please!"

"I don't see what is wrong with asking for the vote," she said, stiffly. "Mother is furious, so is granny, that Uncle John can make all the decisions about their stock."

Rory was silent for a minute, dancing with his cheek on the soft hair of his partner. She was pretty, and shy, but sweet, and she had a brain. Quite an unexpected little cousin—though he found it hard to think of her as just a cousin. And Luke was right. The others did resent John's control of Vallette and Sons. He would pass along this word when he could.

He glanced about for Luke and found him dancing sedately with Rose Marie Vallette. Luke was fond of his New York cousins. Rory gave him a wink as they went past.

"Are you angry with me, Rory?" came Angela's small voice at his ear.

He looked down into the anxious face raised to his. She had a sweet, round face, like a child's for all her vaunted business skill. And that cute button nose—he wanted to kiss it.

"I am," he said solemnly. "You have hurt me deeply."

"Hurt you?" She looked shocked and stunned, very vulnerable. "What did I say?"

"Come out into the garden, this is a private matter." He swept her deftly out to the veranda. She clung to a post, laughing a little.

"You're teasing me, Rory. I'm not going out into the garden with you."

"Yes, you are. Afraid?" he taunted, and swept her up into his arms and carried her out into the darkness. Before he set her down beside the rose hedge, he gave her little nose a quick kiss. "There, now we'll have a serious talk."

"Honestly, you're as much a tease as you ever were!" she scolded with a laugh in her voice. She straightened her skirts and looked about. "I'm not staying out here with you—"

"Yes, you are. I've been wanting to ask you about some textiles—"

"You're spoofing me."

"No, really." He tucked his hand into her arm, felt the rounded softness of her breasts under the fabric, and felt a little dizzy. What was the matter with him— too much spiked punch? "Now, Angela, does your company ever consider using artificial fabrics?"

She seemed to collect her thoughts with a great effort. "Artificial fabrics? Why—I think they are considering them. But they don't seem useful to us at present. We use satin in our evening frocks, and we are considering making bird feathers—imitation ones—to replace the real ones in hats. They are killing too many birds, you know."

"Yes, I know." They strolled on into the darkness and onto the smooth lawns. He felt curiously pleased with himself. He was back home, maybe that was it. Or the light feel of her silk dress brushing against his hand, the vibrant sound of her voice just below his ear, the confiding way she went with him across the dimly lit gardens. "Luke has been coming up with some new inventions in the laboratory. You'll keep this quiet, of course. But some day, Vallette and Sons may want to branch out into artificial textiles."

She digested that thought in silence. Rory gazed down at the sweet profile, the small button nose, the defined lips, and felt strangely protective. Imagine her walking about the streets of New York! He had ridden the horse cars and seen the bully boys at work. And she dared it all every day, to go to and from work. She still lived at home—Anna Moira insisted on that. But she worked, and designed her beautiful dresses, and planned the textiles, just like a man would do. No, more creatively than most men could.

"Will they turn, then, from manufacturing explosives to the textiles?" she asked.

"Do both, probably. Luke thinks there may be another war, in Europe this time. He has talked to army men in Washington."

He felt her shudder in the warm June air. He closed his hand over her arm and drew her gently against him.

"Does that upset you?" he asked.

"Oh, Rory, it is a horrible thought. Some of my friends in New York speak of it, as though it might be a great adventure. And they talk of flying airplanes, and dropping explosives down from them."

"I learned to fly in Ohio, under Wilbur Wright, one of the men who learned to fly first," he told her proudly. "It was a tremendous thrill. Up there in the air, turning about, and diving down toward the earth, then pulling it up again. Right up in the sky, like a bird."

She turned about abruptly, so quickly that they were face to face, her body against his, as his arm cradled her. "Rory. You didn't! Not up in one of those horrible airplanes."

"I did, honey. And I bought one of those horrible new motorcars, also, and I drive it everywhere in Kentucky. John would have a fit," and he laughed at the thought of his father's possible reaction.

She shook her head at him. "Father wants one also, but mother says she prefers the carriages—you know where you are with a horse. Oh, Rory, do you really *enjoy* driving a motorcar? With all the gases and smoke?"

"I really do. One day I'll give you a ride in my car."

She seemed to realize she was half-leaning against his body, and drew back. He tightened his grip, then let her go abruptly. He must be insane. This was his little cousin, Angela, ten years younger than he.

"I don't mind motorcars," she said, with a sigh. "But, if we have another war, I know it will be a disaster. Just dreadful. I have seen pictures the artists made of the war in Cuba. Bombs blowing up, ships blasted into the air, and the men—oh, the poor men, with their injuries. There is a man at work whose brother had both legs taken off—"

"This is a somber subject for a pretty night like this,"

he said, and changed the topic deftly. They came back from the garden to speak to several young people standing on the veranda.

Rory peered at one girl, in a pale rose gown of net and silk. "You can't be Sophia," he exclaimed pleasantly. "You're all grown up also."

"You did turn your back," said the young man beside her.

"Lionel?"

The man laughed softly. "Yes, I have just graduated from MIT. I'm coming into the works this summer."

"I would say welcome, but I'm not there anymore," said Rory, drily, as he gripped his young cousin's hand anyway. "Hope you last longer than I did."

After Rory and Angela had gone inside, Sophia turned to Lionel. "Do you think it will work, Lionel?"

He shrugged a little and put his hand lightly into her arm. "Let's walk." They went down into the garden, further than Angela and Rory had gone, until they could see the smoky lights from the powder mills across the river. The mansion was lit up with candles and flickering gaslights, for there was no electricity yet except in the kitchen. "I don't know, darling," he finally said. "I think John is too absorbed in the books and orders to bother me. But your father and mine—"

"They can be so stuffy and behind the times," whispered Sophia. It was heresy, but she had always been able to talk to Lionel. They trusted each other. "Uncle Henry is just as bad, echoing my dad. And they mock at Rory and Luke. I think they were glad when Rory stamped out and left them."

"Where are the older men now?"

"In the upstairs drawing room, talking business. Mother is furious."

"Let them stay there. They miss most of life," said Lionel, with a quiet passion. He drew Sophia into his arms. His lips lightly brushed against hers, then as he felt her response, he pressed his mouth more deeply against hers. "Oh, my darling, my darling—"

"I love you—so much," breathed Sophia.

"I'm going to speak to them soon."

Her slim hands clutched at his velvet lapels. "They cannot object. You have finished college; they don't want me to go away to school—mother hints of my marriage. Surely they don't think we are too young."

"No, but they may—raise other objections," he said, his voice stiffled. He held her closely to him. "Oh, love, if they part us, what shall I do?" It was a cry from his soul. He had adored her silently since childhood. Now she was nineteen, he was twenty-one, and they loved each other deeply. She was so sweet, so gentle. He would tremble when she touched his cheek with her slim fingers. And when they kissed, he wanted to die of pleasure. He had written to her from school, stiff letters, with a message beneath, in their own private code. She had read them, interpreted them, and written in return, innocently quoting poets from books they both owned. He would go to the book she mentioned, and the page, and read of the longing in her own heart.

"I think mother guesses. She was very suspicious when we danced so often tonight."

"I'd best speak soon. They will become accustomed to the idea. We must marry. I love you so deeply."

He pressed his mouth to hers, and felt her deep response. Her slim body pressed closely to his, they stood together in the darkness near the willow trees, and the branches drooped about them hiding them from everyone.

They often walked together in the daytime, going out to look at the flowers. They enjoyed nature, walking silently in the brisk air of early spring to look at wildflowers and enjoy the first primroses and the first shy violets. In the summers, they rode across the countryside, hand in hand, until they came to any farmhouse or open fields. In the autumn, they trudged even in the rain, shuffling through thick piles of red and yellow dying leaves, content to be with each other.

He would take his sketch pad with him and draw flowers. Sometimes he drew Sophia's face in the flower, as in a pansy. Or sometimes it was Sophia with a lapful of summer flowers, or a kitten in her hands. Or it was a landscape of Vallette and Sons, with the mills in the distance, and a smooth green lawn—and Sophia walking like a spring dryad across the grass.

Strangely, they were not forbidden to see each other. Sophia's mother thought of her as a child. Arthur thought of them as first cousins, raised together like brother and sister. Rory had looked at them oddly tonight. And later Rory remembered seeing them on the veranda, close together, not touching, but somehow "together," as though one could not see either one without the other. The faces, so serene and smiling gently, the heads half-turned to each other, the bodies so relaxed, as though nothing could come between them.

Rory went over to Luke during a brief intermission. Luke was at the long buffet table, moodily raising a glass to his lips. He had been drinking quite a bit, but drink did not confuse his thought. It only made him more dangerous.

"How's it going, Luke?" asked Rory, chattily, helping himself to a plate. He eyed the table critically, and chose a leg of fried chicken, some carrot sticks, and a helping of fruit salad.

"The old ones are in the drawing room, talking business," said Luke, his speech only a little slurred. "I'm going down to Washington next week. Got a couple buddies to talk to."

Rory looked him over thoughtfully. "Army buddies?"

"Right you are. And Uncle John has thoughtfully given me the assignment to tell the trustbusters to go to hell for him. Thinks they can be shut up or bribed to forget all about Vallette and Sons."

The leg of chicken did not reach Rory's lips. He set it down carefully. "Trustbusters?" he echoed in a low tone, sharply. "They are after Vallette and Sons?"

"Too right. Remember the Supreme Court's ruling last February in *Loewe versus Lawlor* about the conspiracy in restraint of trade? I hear they are going after Standard Oil Company of New Jersey. We're going to

317

get swept in, with all the powder mills we own and have shares in."

Rory stared at him. "Trusts," he echoed, and shook his head. "I didn't think they were serious."

"Oh, they are serious," said Luke bitterly. "Only Uncle John, in his good, old-fashioned way, thinks that Supreme Court justices can be bought as he has bought senators and congressmen. So—" He shrugged. "Luke is going to be sent to Washington, gotten out of Uncle John's hair for a time, and put to work buying his way about Washington. Makes me ill."

"You surely aren't going to try to buy—"

Luke scowled at him and shook his head, as a young cousin came up shyly to them. "Hello, Uncle Luke," chirped the young sprig, hopefully.

"Hi, there, Foster, remember your Uncle Rory?" Luke turned on the charm as one turns up a lamp, thought Rory. Rory shook hands with Caroline's young lad, calculated he must be about fifteen, and shook his head.

Foster was blushing. "Mother said if one of you doesn't dance with her, she is going to feel passé, whatever that is," he added doubtfully. "I don't think it's good."

"Caroline will never be passé, and you can tell her that, Foster," Luke said. "Okay, Rory, come and do your duty." He set down his half-full glass with a decisive gesture and pulled Rory with him.

For the next hours, they danced and made light conversation, teased their young relatives, marveled at how everyone had grown, danced with young Elizabeth and gentle Angela, quiet Sophia, and lively Anna Moira. Luke found he had forgotten half the names of his New York cousins, but they soon came back, and he identified them readily, Darcy's children, and Matthew's, and Chloe's, and a grandson of Lucy and a granddaughter of Titus. It was quite a big crowd when they all got together.

And some were missing. Freckles was missing, mused Luke, as he thought of his young tomboy cousin Bar-

318

bara, Rory's young sister. Knowing John, he was not surprised that Barbara had rebelled and left early.

Before the night was over, he remembered to get Barbara's address from her mother, Ellen. Luke decided he might as well have a little fun along with the gloom in Washington. He would look up Barbara, and she might get a surprise—so might he. Firebrand of a young career girl, Rory had said.

Rory was often with Angela. She could talk intelligently, once past her shyness, about her work in New York, the textile business, a buying trip to Paris, the coming styles and what they meant to their concern. Remembering the flighty young thing he had squired about, Jessie Randolph's younger sister, whose brains were in her feet, as Luke had said, Rory found Sophia and Angela refreshing changes. Or was he just prejudiced because they were his relatives?

At all events, he enjoyed himself. He and Luke drove back to Montgomery in the carriage at four in the morning, singing college songs at the top of their lungs and laughing like fools, as Luke admitted the next day.

"You're better than a mineral spring, Rory," he told his cousin over luncheon. "I haven't felt so happy in years."

"I think that is a compliment, for which I thank you, dear Luke," said Rory, pouring more hot coffee for them both. "A mineral spring. I have been called many names, poetic and otherwise, and I never recall that particular epithet. Since when have you taken to going to spas?"

"Never. Flora went to Saratoga one year and tried to drag John and Ellen with her. You should have heard what dear John said."

"He hates riding on the railroads anyway," said Rory.

"He doesn't hate their stock," said Luke.

"Oh, that way, is it? Hum. Is that why you are going to have trouble with the trustbusters?"

Rory was too keen. Luke had to remind himself that

319

the man's mind was much sharper than his handsome face and lazy manner would indicate. "Right. John has invested in many fields, and tries to control them from a distance. Vallette and Sons he keeps in his vest pocket, of course. And he thinks I can call off the dogs!"

"Good luck, my lad." And Rory raised his coffee cup to Luke.

Chapter 24

Vallette and Sons kept a suite of rooms on the top floor of a Washington, D.C., hotel near the Capitol building. Luke had checked in there as soon as he arrived and taken possession of his favorite bedroom with a view overlooking the Potomac.

The suite had half a dozen bedrooms with baths, three dining rooms of assorted sizes, and a permanent small staff of butler, cook, and maid. These in addition to three drawing rooms for formal parties, informal discussions, or business meetings made the place a logical headquarters for any member of Vallette and Sons.

Luke phoned his favorite army friend and made a date for the next evening. Then he began checking in with lawyers connected with the government.

One of them made an appointment with an influential Senator for him. They met the next day at the Senator's apartment for luncheon. It was an inauspicious occasion. The Senator, a jovial man, was unusually gloomy. "I can't do anything about it, Mr. Vallette," he said, flushed and uncomfortable, hemming and hawing because of his unease. "These young crusaders are out for blood. It's fashionable to go after the huge corporations."

Luke eyed the flushed face ironically. The man could be bought, discreetly, in ordinary times. However, the voters had seized on the issue of trusts, and the fervor for "busting the trusts" was sweeping from Washington, D.C. to the Far West. All of society's ills were the fault of the giant corporations who owned too much, some said. It was not right for an oil company to own the land, the mineral rights, the railroads that carried the tank cars to the processing plants, and the plants themselves.

Vallette and Sons owned more than the powder mills on the Areuse. Brett had bought land in Illinois and erected powder mills there. John had bought stock in the railroads that carried powder to various parts of the country. Arthur and Henry had purchased warehouses and land in New York City, New Orleans, and Charleston. Vallette and Sons even owned saltpeter mines in Chile and Brazil. Now the government was saying it was illegal to own the mines, the materials from which powder was made, the mills, the railroads that carried black powder, and the warehouses that held it. It was probably immoral, as well, to make so much money, Luke decided with a weary sigh.

With the newspapers after them with an almost religious fervor, and voters suspicious when Congress did nothing, the courts were beginning to act. Slowly, yes, yet cases were grinding out of lawyers' briefs into the juries' hands.

Luke looked out absently at the bustle of Washington. Horse-drawn trolleys vied with carriages, filling the dusty streets. An occasional motorcar streaked past, a blaze of red paint and chrome. People seemed possessed of a need to hurry, to rush from one place to another. A group of six suffragettes in navy blue and white stood at a nearby corner, placards in hand, talking earnestly to whomever would listen about the right of women to vote.

Luke returned his attention to the Senator. They talked at some length about the problem. Luke used all his powers of persuasion. He could talk intelligently to lawyers and senators and representatives. They understood business. But this was troublesome, and John Vallette's attitude did not help.

"The company must divest," the Senator kept insisting. "They cannot own a monopoly of black powder mills. They must sell off some of them, or permit other companies to grow."

"There are other companies; they can grow as they please," countered Luke, moving his finger impatiently over the linen tablecloth. He found it hard to keep his temper today. "Hazard is growing rapidly—"

"And John Vallette has already offered to buy it," said the Senator sharply. "We have had word that Vallette and Sons will pay high for the major stocks in Hazard."

"I guess he wants to expand into the Far West," said Luke, wearily. "I wish he would listen to me and let us build our own mills out there."

The Senator's ears perked up. "You're thinking of expanding? Mr. Vallette, I strongly advise against that. You will be in more trouble if your holdings grow. Let others build mills out West."

"And what if war comes, and we are not prepared—again?" asked Luke. "Remember the situation at the time of Cuba—"

The Senator looked pensive. "But you expanded fast enough then, Mr. Vallette. You could do it again."

"At the cost of my father's life," Luke told him grimly. "Yes, we expanded, and we were able to supply black powder in time to win that *little* war. What if a huge explosion comes, blowing Europe apart? Can we supply black powder and military powder to take care of England, France, Italy, and all of the Balkans?"

"We are preparing to investigate the situation, but I cannot believe—"

The Senator left soon after for another appointment. The lawyer said quietly, "They will investigate again and again, but they'll believe nothing until war comes. And then it will be too late. I am sorry, Mr. Vallette. I hoped he would see reason. He is on one of the most powerful committees—"

"You did your best. Well, I'll keep trying. What about some of the Representatives? Whom can I contact?"

They talked until past four, then Luke took a carriage

back to the hotel, his shoulders sagging with weariness. He could take a long hunting trip and be up at five the next day, springing with life. He could take fifteen hours in the laboratory and be ready for more. But these goddam meetings. They made him weary to death.

He took a long shower and let the needle-sharp spray run over his lean, tanned body. He lay down for an hour, then dressed for the evening in gray, striped trousers and a long frock coat with satin lapels. Washington could be very formal. He added a scarlet carnation to his buttonhole and flicked a speck of dust from his shoulder.

"Very smart, if I may say so, Mr. Luke," said the butler, who doubled as valet.

"Thank you, glad I meet with your approval." Luke exchanged grins with him. "Don't wait up for me; I have my key, and I may be out late, getting drunk, if the evening goes like the luncheon."

"Now, sir, you wouldn't do that."

"Oh, yes, I would."

He took his walking cane and started out. It was a stout stick, and if he should be attacked he was ready for anyone. The capital was crime-ridden, and Luke kept his eyes open for trouble. He took a hired carriage to the home of his army friend and arranged to be picked up again at midnight.

The evening started out very pleasantly. Colonel Mark Trent and his wife Lucille were comfortable hosts, and they had invited several couples and a smattering of pretty girls to entertain Luke. Mrs. Trent teased Luke privately.

"It's a crying shame, Luke, that you aren't married. You're too handsome and charming to be unmarried. Suppose I really set to work and find you a beautiful girl?"

"Too late, ma'am," Luke said solemnly, as Mark came up to them. "Mark found you first, and I'm left to weep."

"Oh, pooh." She tapped his arm with her fan sharply. "I'm serious, Luke. You ought to marry. Think of that huge firm. You need a son or two to follow in your footsteps."

"Is she after you again?" Mark Trent grinned at Luke, clapping him on the shoulder. "Tell her about that tall beauty with the golden hair."

Lucille perked up. "Who is she? Tell me?"

Luke laughed. "An old friend of the family, Jessie Randolph. But I'm not engaged, not at all, so don't get that look in your eyes, Lucille."

"I'll put a bug in her ear. There has to be some way to capture a man like you." She pouted, them drifted away to her other guests.

Mark indicated his study; Luke nodded and went with him. Colonel Trent poured brandy. Luke helped himself to the box of Havanas, and they lit up.

"The big, bad trustbusters are after us, Mark," said Luke, when he had leaned back and relaxed, cigar in hand. "I had a long talk with a Senator today; he says he can't help."

"Not Vallette and Sons! We need them," said Mark sharply.

They discussed the situation quietly for a time. Trent told him frankly that war in Europe could break out anytime.

"The Germans are messing around down in Mexico. We may be drawn into the situation in Europe, in spite of those who cry that we have nothing to do with England and the rest of them. And then if war does begin in Europe—" Colonel Trent shook his head. "It will make the Spanish-American affair look like pretty small goods, I tell you, Luke. It could go on for years."

"Our agents in Argentina and Brazil are troubled, and have asked for a large amount of powder to be sent to them," Luke told him bluntly. "And Mexico—John Vallette is still debating whether to fulfill their orders."

"Depends on who gets into control, and stays there. They are ripe for revolution. Should Díaz die—"

They discussed it back and forth. Porfirio Díaz, President of Mexico, might be deposed violently. A civil war had started in Honduras. Austria had taken Bosnia and Herzegovina last year, and further protests were expected. King Carlos I of Portugal and the Crown Prince had been assassinated in Lisbon. There was revolution in Turkey, and there could be trouble in the Middle East as a result.

"Do you think President Taft understands the problems?"

Trent shrugged. "I think Theodore Roosevelt is disappointed in William Howard Taft. He appears more conservative than we realized. He may pull in and have nothing much to do with the outside world."

They discussed politics and business until Lucille put her head in the door and scolded them. "It is past midnight, and half the guests have departed. This is too bad of you, Mark, and Luke also."

Luke took his departure and promised to call Mark Trent again soon. He thought he would have the Colonel's promise to interest the War Department in Vallette and Sons' problems with trustbusters. The army would not want to interfere with the making of munitions should war be coming.

It was a discouraging week, however. Luke saw other senators, some Representatives, and several lawyers employed by Vallette and Sons. He had a long, quiet, luncheon with Mark Trent, and heard the reactions of the army.

"They will do everything possible to head off interference with the making of black powder and military powder. They asked about the production of guncotton and smokeless powder. Can you come to report to them this week?"

Luke seized that opportunity thankfully and spent two entire days at the army's headquarters. With a blackboard and chalk, he demonstrated the progress of their experiments with guncotton, smokeless powder, and the deadly TNT, trinitrotoluene.

"We would like our observers to come and actually see your tests. Would you permit that?" asked one General tersely.

"Of course, sir. We should be glad to have you send

some of your men. We experiment daily with the powder on our firing range. Suppose you appoint some men for the laboratory, and some for the firing of rifles and cannon."

This was arranged, and the army men seemed very pleased with the cooperation of Vallette and Sons. Luke felt much more hopeful. Word would leak to Congress that the army was involved with experiments at Vallette and Sons, and that might dampen talk of trustbusting.

He returned to the suite rather wearily to find James Keane there, about to go out.

"Well, James. What brings you to Washington?" Luke paused in the door of the smaller drawing room to see his cousin redden, looking uncomfortable.

"Oh, just for a change. John Vallette was asking about you, so I volunteered to come to see what you were up to."

Luke's dark eyebrows shot up, he leaned in the doorway, hands in his pockets, and studied James. "So why didn't you come earlier, and help me explain to the army why Vallette and Sons is important to them?" he asked pleasantly.

"God, Luke, I ain't about to get involved with that." At his look of horror, Luke burst out laughing.

"So all you want is a vacation from Uncle John?"

"Can you blame me? He treats me like a child."

James had a sulky mouth, thought Luke. "Never mind, John can't last forever. One day, we'll have to run the company, and we'll wish him back, eh?"

"Never! Not I."

Luke laughed.

James added hurriedly, "You won't repeat that, will you? I mean, I wouldn't want to make trouble in the company."

James was indeed acting strangely. He had on a new brown, pinstriped suit, sapphire cufflinks, and a new pomade that smelled to high heaven. Luke eyed him narrowly. "Going courting, James?" he murmured.

James had a very deep blush around his chubby face.

327

"Oh, come on, Luke, I'm only going to see Barbara. Uncle John wants me to keep an eye on her."

"Barbara. Young Freckles," murmured Luke thoughtfully. "We're keeping you busy, James. One eye on me, one eye on Barbara. Wait up, I'll change and come along."

"Oh, no, no, I can't wait. I'm late already. Sorry about that, but I promised—dinner, and all that—party for me—" James exited in confusion; the door slammed after him.

"Hummm," said Luke, and went to his room to change. He showered, relaxed, and took dinner alone in the suite's small dining room. Then he began to think seriously.

James—and young Freckles? Might pay to call on that young Barbara, and see how she had turned out. He had intended to see her anyway.

He dressed again, in gray, with his short jacket, and went out in a carriage. He had the address. He looked with some disapproval as they arrived in the right street. It wasn't good for young girls to live alone. Barbara should be staying in the Vallette suite—it was large enough.

Light and music streamed from the opened windows of the large greystone house. He ran up the steps and tapped at the door. A smart maid, dressed in black with a white bib, opened to him. "Yes, sir?"

"I am Luke Vallette. I wish to see my cousin, Miss Barbara," he said, with a charming smile.

She gave him a dubious look. "Well, sir, Miss Barbara is having a party tonight. I don't recall your name on the invitations—"

He wondered if he would have to push his way in. But a pretty blonde girl came out into the hallway. "Who is it, Susie? Oh, my—who *are* you?"

She couldn't be Barbara, she just could not—

She beamed at him and looked him over speculatively, at the smart suit, the gold cufflinks, the emerald ring on his hand.

"Luke Vallette, at your service, ma'am!" he said, with a smile.

"Oh, Barbara's cousin! Do come on in. It's informal," she assured him, and put her long, slim hand on his arm. "Come along. You haven't been around before, have you? Cousin James has come, and Brother Rory, but not Cousin Luke." She grinned up at him.

He entered the large, pleasant living room to find it crowded. Over near the mantel he spied James Keane, beaming down on a girl who sat on a hassock at his feet, a cocktail glass in one hand, the other hand waving energetically to make her point.

The blonde girl dragged Luke in around the others to the girl. "Barbara, another handsome cousin. I would adore to meet all of them, you have such a good-looking family."

The girl jumped up. "Luke!" she exclaimed. Luke found himself looking down at a slim, rounded girl, with soft, brown curly hair and deep blue-violet eyes almost too large for her oval face.

"Hello, Freckles," he said, on impulse.

Color swept the clear pink and white face. The blue-violet eyes sparkled with anger. "You're just as nasty as ever!" she exclaimed.

James stepped forward. "Now, Luke, whatever did you come for?" he asked, plaintively. "I told you I'd look after Barbara."

"Why, I haven't seen my cousin for years. I thought I'd better check up on her." Luke coolly took the cocktail glass from her, sipped at it, and made a face. "God, child, you don't want this poison. Come on over here and we'll have a little chat."

She pulled back, but he was much stronger than she, and he effortlessly drew her over to an unoccupied sofa near the windows. The wind from the open window near them helped clear the air of smoke. She was eyeing him with disapproval—and something else, some wondering air.

"Sit down, honey. Now tell me, what's this all about?" He waved his hand at the party, the people now

329

talking, gabbling, laughing, drinking, smoking. Music poured from a Gramophone in another corner.

"My party, you mean?"

"I mean your party, and you living alone in Washington—"

"I am not living alone. I live with two other girls, and a housekeeper, and a maid and butler."

"Well, I'm glad to hear you are discreet," he said calmly. She certainly had grown into a beautiful woman. The violet silk of her long, straight dress suited her; her coloring was enchanting, her figure something to dream about, all curves and soft lines. He caught a glimpse of silver slippers on long, narrow feet under the hem of her dress. The silver matched the thin border of silver that emphasized the wide-bordered sleeves and the overdress.

She wore little button pearls in her ears and a matching creamy-white strand about her white throat. Her abundant hair was wound up intricately about her head.

"What are you doing here?" she asked, finally.

"I came to talk to some lawyers and some people in the army."

She gave him a quick, alert look. "I meant, at my party."

"Oh, that. James made me curious. And I meant to look you up and see what tree you were trying to climb this time," he said, with a mocking grin, and a slanted look at her.

Her mouth compressed. "I suppose you have heard from dad about me. Well, I'm in the movement, and I am serious about it."

"What movement?" he asked, though he thought he knew.

"The National American Women's Suffrage Association," she told him proudly, her head lifted like a dark flower on its stem. "We mean to have the vote soon, too. We have been oppressed and put down too long. Why, even dad won't let me vote my own stock in Vallette and Sons."

He reflected on that. "I didn't think you were so oppressed," he said, mildly. "Uncle John let you go to Oberlin, and now he lets you live in Washington—"

"Lets me?" she exclaimed furiously. "He kicked like a mule. But I have my own money, from mother's mother. They understand how I feel. Cousin Arthur thinks I'm terrible, but I think he is stuffy." She clapped her hand to her mouth. "Oh, I forgot. He's your brother."

"I think he is stuffy, too," said Luke. "I am glad we have something in common. What else are you doing? I hear you have a job."

"Yes." She gave him a wary look from her kitten-blue eyes. "I am working in the office of an insurance firm. I'm doing secretarial work now, but eventually they might let me sell also." She sighed deeply. "It's so hard to get into real work."

"Come back to Vallette and Sons, and you can be my secretary," he said.

"Dad won't allow women in the mills," she said, her pretty, pink mouth set. "You're just teasing me—"

"Well, maybe I am. Vallette and Sons is behind the times. I tell you, though, Barbara, you should come back for a month or two. Why don't you come this autumn? The countryside is at its most beautiful in the autumn, with the willows yellow along the Areuse. I have a new mare you would enjoy; she's just right for you."

For a moment her eyes were wistful, then she shook her head. "No, if I go back, I'll just fight with dad again."

"I'll stand between you."

"From what James says, you have enough with fighting him yourself," said Barbara sharply.

"James talks too much," he said, and glanced across to where James was staring hard at them, his mouth sulky. He looked downright cross, and anxious. "Does he come often?"

"Only about every two months," said Barbara, innocently. "He can't come oftener, he says, though he would like to live in Washington."

"Oh, really? I thought he was devoted to Vallette and Sons." Luke was thinking furiously. James had not said one word about seeing Barbara so often. He must be serious about her and didn't want John Vallette to find out, at least not yet. And he had kept mighty quiet about her, hardly even mentioning her to Luke. James must be crazy about Barbara.

"I must get back to my other guests." Barbara moved to rise, but Luke held her back easily.

"Oh, come now. I want to have a good talk with you. Meet me tomorrow for luncheon."

"I'm working."

"Evening, then. I'll pick you up at seven."

"I have a date with James." She was pulling against his arm. "Do let me go, Luke."

"I think you're up the wrong tree, Barbara," he said softly. "Come on down, now. James is not for you. He's too weak and easily led. You don't want a man like that."

Her eyes were suddenly dazed, a little afraid. She was pulling at him. He pulled her back, easily, and brushed her mouth with his hard lips. He felt her gasp against his mouth, felt an unusual tingle going down his spine at the sweetness of her lips.

She yanked back, and a slim hand smacked sharply on his cheek. "Don't you ever do that again!" she blazed. "I don't allow men to take liberties."

She jumped away from him and practically ran across the room to James. She took a drink from him and sipped at it feverishly. Luke watched her, a little amused, a little surprised at himself. How lovely she was, her slim, rounded body moving with such grace, her blue eyes flashing when she looked in his direction. She paid obvious attention to James for a while, then dropped him and sat beside another man, giving him the same rapt attention.

Luke was not alone for long. The blonde girl returned, curious and questioning. She sat beside him, teased him, waited on him, brought him drinks and food. She introduced him around, as "Barbara's

332

cousin," told him she was one of Barbara's roommates, and made sure he met the sedate housekeeper.

Luke finally decided to leave. As he picked his way through the thick group of young people, James said to him, "I was telling Barbara about your engagement, Luke."

"Engagement? What engagement? Appointments tomorrow?" asked Luke blandly.

"I mean, Jessie Randolph." James was red with temper, but determined to go through with it.

"Believe me, when I am engaged, I shall be the first to know it, James," said Luke, with a tight smile and a dangerous tilt to his head. "See me off, Barbara."

He took her hand and led her into the hallway. "Why not come back with me at the end of the month, Barbara?" he asked her with deceptive mildness. "I think you would enjoy autumn on the Areuse. And your mother would be happy to see you. You have rather neglected her, haven't you?"

She hesitated, then shook her head and turned her gaze from him. "Not now, Luke. I have my job, and we are working hard on a campaign for suffrage."

"I'll be over again," Luke assured her, seeing James hovering in the doorway behind them. "If you change your mind—I'll be glad to show you around, even help you climb the trees!"

She tossed her head angrily. "You always tease—"

"Not always." He bent his head down and kissed her mouth quickly, tasting the honey and wine of her drawn breath, her pink lips. "Goodnight. I'll see you again soon. Cousins should not be strangers."

He went out chuckling, aware that she was stirred and moved—and furious.

He was thoughtful on the way back to the suite. And he kept thinking about her. A pretty girl like that, active in politics and marching and protests and all that. It seemed a terrible waste. But Barbara was clearly serious about it. As for him—no arranged marriage for him, he thought, as he undressed for bed, stretched his lean arms, and yawned.

333

Jessie Randolph was pretty, and Uncle John liked her family. Arthur had hinted strongly that the Vallette family wanted Luke to marry a nice girl from a nice family, like Jessie, and if there was anything he could do to promote it—

No, thanks, Arthur, thought Luke. I'll choose my own bride, thank you.

Chapter 25

Sophia met Lionel out in the shaded garden, and caught at his hand anxiously.

"Do we go to see him today?"

Lionel nodded. His mouth was set, his gentle, vague, brown eyes unusually stern. "Yes, no sense putting it off. The rumor is around that we are seeing each other. I want to get it out in the open."

She squeezed his hand. "You make it sound like a terrible secret, Lionel." Her soft eyes adored him.

"I want to marry you, and I'm not afraid of Uncle John. We'll go to see him this afternoon, in the drawing room. He promised to come home early to see what I had to say."

"What does he think you will say?" she asked worriedly, her mouth puckering up enchantingly. He touched her lips lightly with his finger, in a soft caress. "Does he think you are referring to work?"

"Probably. I am on Luke's side. We think we should have more say in the board decisions, instead of being shut out."

That afternoon, about four o'clock, Sophia came down the stairs of her home to find Lionel waiting for her. Arthur, her father, had not yet come home from work; she was relieved for that. As his only child, she seemed always under his sharp observation.

Lionel had driven over in the carriage. He helped her carefully into the seat and arranged her pink skirts about her slim feet. Then he sprang up beside her and took the reins from the servant.

On the way, he explained, "I thought it safe not to say why we were talking to John. He may blow up at first, you know, Sophia, but we must just be firm. We love each other; we want to marry. And I do have my own money. And a college education. I can always earn a living."

She was silent, feeling uneasy again. Lionel had always dreamed of working at Vallette and Sons. He was intensely loyal, intelligent, proud of being a Vallette, looking up to Luke and Rory. He had always wanted to be like them when he grew up, he had confided to Sophia long ago. It had hurt him when Rory left the firm; he had wondered how Rory could bear to leave.

No one but the butler was in the entrance hall when they arrived at John's vast mansion on the hill. Sophia clasped Lionel's hand tightly as they entered. She felt like whispering, as they had as children, when entering this home. It was filled with the bullying, overbearing presence of Uncle John Vallette.

Lionel had told her John was as dictatorial at the works as he was at home. No decision was made without his suspicious thorough once-over. All must go through his pudgy, aging hands.

"Mr. John is in the drawing room, Mr Lionel," said the butler, quietly, and opened the great doors for them to enter. They started across the expanse of Persian carpets to the long sofa at the far end of the room.

John was seated in his huge sofa, stuffed against the cushions, his swollen feet propped up on a hassock. He had a tall, cool glass at his hand, a Havana cigar in his fingers.

The shrewd eyes watched as they approached, hand in hand.

"Well, children, what do you have on your minds? You're mighty mysterious," he said, jovially. The eyes did not smile.

They came to a pause before him, still hand in hand. Sophia's slim fingers tightened about Lionel's.

"Sir—Uncle John—" began Lionel steadily. "We have come to tell you—I mean, to ask you—I mean—"

Sophia squeezed his fingers harder, and he cleared his throat. Uncle John had this paralyzing effect on them all, with his small eyes staring at them intently out of the folds of graying flesh on his elderly face.

"You want to take a trip to Washington? Have a holiday from your work?" asked John, and took a sip of his whiskey.

"No, sir. I mean—yes, sir. That is, we want to get married." Lionel blurted it out.

John took a long, satisfying swallow and set down the glass. "Lionel, you want to get married? To whom?"

Lionel swallowed; his Adam's apple went up and down nervously in his slim throat. "To—to Sophia, sir."

"You're joking," said John, still mildly. "She is your first cousin. You have been raised as sister and brother. Now, tell me, whom do you want to marry?"

"He's—he's right, uncle," Sophia piped up, her voice sounding thin and unsure even to herself. "We—love each other—we—want to marry."

The small eyes turned to consider her. He looked her up and down. She tried to stand tall, but she was but five-foot-two, and small-boned.

"Nonsense. Does your father know about this?"

The two looked at each other. "We thought we would ask you first, Uncle John, because you are the head of the family," said Lionel, at last.

"You can't be serious. Still, perhaps Sophia is old enough to marry. Lionel, I should think you would be glad to be able to play around for a time. Give yourself a few years. Look at me. I didn't marry until I was forty."

Sophia took a deep, shaky breath. "We mean it, Uncle John. We wish to marry each other."

"Yes, we do," said Lionel. "We have loved each other for years."

"Puppy love," said John, and snapped his cigar onto an ashtray. His mouth set grimly. "Go away, and grow up. I have no time to consider such asinine requests. And you made me think it was serious business."

When Lionel persisted, John got angry. He roared at them, "You are being stupid and silly. If Sophia wishes to marry, we'll find her a suitable husband. We can't let the Vallette blood get drained. We need fresh blood in the family, in the company. Go away, both of you."

They gathered up their courage again and faced Arthur Vallette, and Henry, Lionel's father. By this time the whole family knew about it. Most were outraged. Why, Sophia and Lionel were first cousins, practically sister and brother.

Luke was thoughtful. He tried to talk to Lionel, but found the lad unexpectedly stubborn. "She is your first cousin, Lionel. Go out and look around. You're a shy lad—let me introduce you to some girls—you need to get more acquainted. There's a nice girl in the Stuart family—"

"I love Sophia." The hurt in Lionel's eyes reminded Luke of a puppy he had once owned.

Frantic, the two young ones attempted to elope. They were too inexperienced, and John and Arthur had them traced and caught at the railroad station in Washington, D.C. They were returned like truant children.

The two were kept apart for a time. Lionel was sent to work in New York, Sophia kept under her mother's thumb at home. Still they pined for each other. Each refused to go out without the other.

John had a series of talks with Arthur. "Your girl is ripe to marry," said John, leaning back in his ancient armchair in his office. "We'll find her the right chap and put them together. That will knock all the nonsense out of their heads!"

"Got any ideas?" asked Arthur, uneasily. "She's my only child. Her mother wants her to marry well, have a big social wedding, and all that. We could give them a house near ours—"

They put their heads together. As chance would have it, a man came to see them concerning the merger of his company with Vallette and Sons that winter. Rodger

Courtney was a southern gentleman, of an old fine family that had seen better days. He had fought his way up in a mining firm and was now one of the vice-presidents. He had married the owner's daughter, who unfortunately died in childbirth two years later. As a widower, he dated often, but discreetly, and kept his affairs to himself.

He was forty-one, graying, ruddy-faced, handsome, and wealthy. Arthur looked him over. John approved, though Arthur thought he was a bit old for Sophia, who was just nineteen. "Nonsense," said John. "Just the difference between myself and Ellen. Perfect match."

Arthur brought Rodger Courtney to his home as a business guest. Sophia was charming and polite, as one is to one's elders. Rodger was charmed. He cast his eye over her slim young form, her pink and white face, the soft brown eyes, the gentle manners, and was willing to be brought into the family circle.

Arthur broke the news to Sophia. He called the girl into his study, and said, "Well, Sophia, since you are set on marriage, we are going to agree to it, though you are a bit young."

Her face was incredulous, then radiant. "Oh, papa. You are so good to me. I shall write at once to Lionel—he will want to return home—when may we be married? I don't care about a big wedding—"

"How you do rattle on," he said sharply, uneasily, because he loved his only girl. "I don't mean Lionel, you know that is unsuitable. I mean Rodger Courtney. He has asked for your hand, and we told him—"

Her face went pale as death; she sank down into a chair and clasped its arms, still staring at her father. "You—are—joking—oh, papa, tell me—tell me you joke—"

"No joke. He is wealthy, a good match for you. He is older, and will settle you down. Besides, he promises to take every care of you—"

"But he is as old as you are!" she cried out. Her small hands clenched at the cloth of the sofa, her fingers ripped at it. "Papa, you could not be so cruel—"

339

He turned a deaf ear, convinced that she would be well cared for. John had given him a lecture about the evils of first cousins marrying, about how the blood went bad and the children were often defective. Sophia would give Rodger good and fine children. She would rebel at first, but she was a gentle girl; she would give in.

"I cannot—I cannot—" Sophia wept, and tried to enlist her mother's support.

None would listen to her but Lionel, who came home at once from New York. He was scolded vigorously, and so was Sophia. They were told the foolishness of their love, how they had misinterpreted the devoted love of a sister and brother.

Her mother took Sophia to Washington to shop for bridal clothes. Barbara took an interest, and told her she must fight for her rights.

"How can I, Barbara? They threaten to fire Lionel, to take away his stocks—his living."

"He can make a living at anything."

"At what?" Sophia's pallid face was drawn in agony. She had slept little; she had not seen Lionel for days. Rodger had been coldly impatient with her, a sad foretaste of their marriage.

"Luke would help you—" suggested Barbara. "He's tough as old boots. He'll help Lionel."

"He is already in trouble with father and Uncle John for advising them against Rodger. The firms are merging, you know."

"You mean, rather, that Vallete and Sons is swallowing up Rodger's firm," said Barbara shrewdly. "And Rodger will come to work for Vallette and Sons—he's marrying into the comapny. Quite a feather in his cap. Oh, Sophia, resist them. Don't agree to this horrible marriage. I don't like Rodger."

"I am—afraid of him," whispered Sophia, her brown eyes shadowed, dark lines below her eyes. She was thinking of the way he had kissed her one evening, when they were alone in the hallway. He had grabbed her, pulled her against him, and crushed her mouth under his. Then he had set her down on her feet and said,

340

"Grow up, girl, and grow up fast. I want a woman in my bed, not a wishy-washy girl."

She had told no one of that, for it haunted her dreams like a black crow of evil. He was cruel. Sometimes his fingers held her slim wrist and left bruises. His gaze would study her, going up and down her rounded young body as though he would strip the thin dress from her. She shuddered at his touch.

Sophia returned to the Vallette Washington suite with her mother, who was cross and tired from all the shopping. "We must speak of this, mother," she said in an attempt to be firm.

"Talk, talk, talk. I suppose Barbara is filling your head with nonsense about women being free. Well, let me tell you, girl, no woman is free in this world," said her mother with unexpected passion. "Sophia, you do as your father tells you, and be a good, obedient girl, and he will be pleased with you. If you make trouble, it will be the worse for Lionel."

"But if you would just listen—Rodger is cruel and hard—oh, mother, I do not want to marry him—" Sophia began to weep. Her mother turned and left her bedroom, slamming the door after her.

Sophia flung herself across the bed and sobbed. Was there no help in the world?

Someone came in quietly; she turned about, thinking her mother had repented and returned to her. She started up on seeing Lionel's pale face.

"Oh—Lionel—"

"Shush. I came in the back way. They don't know I am here." He sat down on the bed beside her and touched her cheek tenderly. "Crying? I couldn't keep from coming. Oh, Sophia, if only I could get you out of here." He drew her gently into his arms and she wept against his soft shirt.

"If only we could elope—"

"We tried that. They are more clever than we are. Let me see—we might enlist Luke—he is so smart—"

"If only Rory Vallette were here. He might help us. And Barbara—"

They whispered, exploring one plan and another.

"I love you so much, Sophia," he murmured. "I cannot bear to let you go—"

She shuddered, thinking of Rodger and his hateful touch. If she could not get out of his coil, she would be married to him; she would be his wife, and he would have every right over her.

"I love you, Lionel. I adore you. They won't understand how we feel—"

"I shall never love anyone else in the world," he vowed, his mouth against her wet cheek.

"Nor shall I," she said, more quietly. She turned in his arms and put her hands to his face. "I swear, I shall never love anyone else in this life. I love you—until death and beyond, Lionel."

"Oh, my God, my darling—" He turned her and laid her down across the bed, and lay with her, holding her. His hands stroked her, more and more urgently. She was so small and tiny-boned, like a frightened bird, soft and brown and sweet.

They had not done this before. They had meant to save themselves for their marriage. But the idea of the sanctity of marriage was grossly violated whenever they considered the marriage of Sophia to Rodger, the stubborn opposition of her father and mother, the quarreling within the family, the cold arguments brought to bear on them:

"You will make a wealthy marriage—"

"I'll settle more stock on you, Sophia—"

"Rodger is a wealthy, shrewd man—"

"You will have everything in this world. He is already building a smart new house for you. He promises a carriage—"

"Jewels—look at the fine ruby ring he gave you—"

Sophia could see the ring on her finger as she touched Lionel in love. The ruby glowed like blood, the blood draining from her heart at the thought of marrying anyone but Lionel.

She turned on the bed and flung the ring to the floor. She pressed her hands to Lionel's face frantically. "Oh, love me, Lionel," she whispered frantically. "I want you to love me—I cannot endure his touch—"

Lionel nodded, his face flushed. He got up and locked the door, moving the key softly in the lock. Then he came back to the bed. "We can have this, at least," he said. "They cannot take this from us—"

Lionel helped her remove the pink chiffon dress, then the dainty lace underclothing. As reverently as a bride-groom on his wedding night, he uncovered her and worshiped her body with his eyes, his hands, his lips. He lay with her a long time, on her narrow virginal bed, and made her his own physically as well as spiritually.

She shivered with delight at his loving touch. His hands moved over her body, his lips followed, to touch her small pointed breasts, the little pink nipples, the slim waist, the long thighs. She dared to touch him, moving her hands over his lean body, curling herself into his body, holding him to her without reservation. We can have this, she said to herself.

There was some pain as he took her. He whispered his remorse; she shook her head, the brown hair flying. "I don't care—I want *you* to be the one—oh, my darling, my darling—"

He drew closer yet and gloried in her bright, pink cheeks, her glowing eyes, the softness of her pink mouth under his lips. Her breath was his; they kissed again and again as they embraced. It was delicious, stolen, piercingly sweet.

They were resting, close together, under the covers when the tapping at the door became imperative. "Sophia? Sophia?" her mother called. Sophia held her breath, and shook her head in silent refusal. "All right, go ahead and sulk. But tomorrow, we shall go to try on the wedding dress." And her mother went away.

Lionel whispered, "Go along with her then, darling. We love each other, we shall find a way. And your wedding dress shall be worn when *we* marry."

"Oh, I love you, I adore you."

They whispered together, softly laughed, teased, and made love often before morning. He went away at dawn, promising to return again in two nights.

They met again and again. When Sophia had to return to her father's home, Lionel asked to be transferred back to the powder mills. They pretended not to care about what happened, and Lionel set to work in the laboratory.

They met secretly in the woods. They met in town. They met in a carriage and made love as the cold winds swept over the Areuse valley. Sophia was set to marry Rodger in the spring. But anything could happen. Miracles could happen, thought the two young people, wildly in love now.

It was enough to touch, to kiss, to embrace. They felt as though they were already married. She had her miniature painted at the studio of a famous artist and gave it to Lionel. He carried it everywhere. She wore his ring, a small silver ring, inconspicuous and set with a tiny amethyst for faithfulness in love, on her right hand. She felt covered with armor.

A miracle would happen by spring, thought Sophia. Lionel would rescue her. He must. But he must not be hurt, and she became anxious about that. John watched them both shrewdly, his small eyes always fixed on them whenever they were in the same room. Did he guess?

Rodger did not come often. He was engaged in moving his business effects from a town above New York down to Montgomery. By spring, his house would be built, he would be moved in—and the wedding would take place. He kissed Sophia possessively as he said this, and she held herself stiff.

"You're a cold one, but I'll soon warm you," he promised, with a possessive grin, his arm about her slim waist. "I'm looking forward to having my southern girl as fiery as I please."

She shivered and drew away from him. At times, she worried. What if the miracle did not happen? Lionel was trying to plan, but he was trapped in his work. He had no other source of income. She felt Luke watching them. Would he help them? But Luke was fighting his own battles; he would not have time for theirs.

And she did not want to get Lionel into trouble. By the spring, something might happen—she hoped, prayed frantically—and met Lionel every time she could manage. She lived for the days and hours in his arms. Only that mattered. Only his body next to hers, pressing hard, delicious muscles against her softness, his arms lean and tight about her, his voice husky in her ears.

Chapter 26

No miracle occurred to rescue Sophia and Lionel. Lionel lay awake nights, trying to think of what he could do. He tried to confide in Luke, but Luke was against the marriage of first cousins and told him frankly it would be a mistake. "But I love Sophia," Lionel said again and again.

"Would you want defective children?" asked Luke bluntly. Lionel turned away.

Sophia fought every way she could. She pleaded with her mother, with her father. They would not give in: Rodger would be "a fine husband."

So the Vallettes were summoned to come in May to the wedding of Sophia Vallette and Rodger Courtney. The business firms had merged; this marriage would cement the merger.

Rory Vallette came from Kentucky, and Angela Parrish from New York. Angela left a busy season, not admitting even to herself why she was so anxious to come to the Areuse.

Rory and Angela attended the wedding together. Angela saw Sophia's pallid face behind the bridal lace veil, saw the stark misery of the gentle brown eyes.

Then she looked again at the bridegroom, the heavy, fleshy face, the middle-aged plumpness, the gross jaw. "Good heavens," she whispered to Rory. "Whatever in the world—he is years older than she is—"

"Do you think that is a barrier?" Rory whispered

back. She looked into the flashing, dark brown eyes, and he was serious.

"She must be half his age," murmured Angela worriedly.

"She wanted to marry Lionel—"

"Oh, dear." Angela had heard rumors, but now seeing the wedding party, she began to realize. Lionel sat stiffly across from them, his lean face haggard, his hands clenching and unclenching. Sophia's mother turned to watch the bride come up the aisle, and she looked worried. Arthur looked placid; he beamed as he escorted his daughter.

Luke was not in the wedding party; he sat beside Lionel. Surely as one of the most imprtant of the younger generation he should have been best man—or did he, too, disapprove? One could not tell by the bland, courteous look on his tanned face.

Afterward, Angela compared notes with Rory. "Why did they force poor Sophia into this marriage? Surely she would have gotten over Lionel in time."

"I'm late in the news, having just arrived last week. It seems that Sophia and Lionel persisted in their attempts to marry. Also, Uncle Henry wanted Lionel to consider some other girl. And dad considers himself the head of the company; whatever he says, goes. He wanted to make the merger firm."

Angela, in a lovely blue silk dress, with a little blue-feathered hat on her head, looked toward the white-faced bride. She had not smiled once in that reception line. Mechanically she murmured her responses to any who came up to give her their best wishes.

As Angela watched, the bridegroom leaned to whisper to Sophia. At once, a mechanical smile came out, then remained fixed on the pale lips. His hand closed over her arm, and she seemed to wince.

"My God, not for me," muttered Angela fiercely. The man was a brute, anyone could see it, she thought; poor, dear Sophia.

"*What* is not for you—marriage?" murmured Rory in her delicate ear. "You're much too adorable to be a spinster. Aren't there any men in New York City to suit you?"

She looked up into his laughing, flashing eyes and thought he was the handsomest man she had ever met. "I've been busy," she said mildly. "What about you, Rory? No pretty girls in Kentucky?"

"Not as pretty as the ones here today," and his bold gaze roamed down over her blue gown.

"You turn a pretty compliment. Isn't Barbara lovely? One doesn't often see her at these gatherings."

"Sis didn't want to come to this, but dad insisted. I don't think she approves of the marriage. She tried to take Sophia under her own wing for a time in Washington."

Luke strode across the room to Barbara and took her hand in his. "Hello, Freckles," he said in a low tone, with a grin.

She grimaced pertly, her tomboyish look at variance with the soft lilac silk of her dress, the grayed mauve feathers drooping over her brown, curly hair.

"If you want a fight, go look for dad," she said, also in a low tone. "He's spoiling for one."

"Oh, I fight with Uncle John all the time," said Luke lightly. "I need a change. Come on out into the garden and let's fight."

"I've grown up," she said with dignity.

"So you have." The blue eyes laughed down at her. "How's the movement?"

"Don't make fun of it."

"If you land in prison, don't ask me to bail you out."

"I shan't. It would be an honor to go to prison for the vote for women. Mrs. Pankhurst has gone more than once."

"You're not serious, Barbara!" He lost his grin. "You don't know the conditions of the prisons. You don't want to get involved in anything like that."

"Then they should be ashamed to have prisons in such horrible, filthy condition, and we shall publicize what they are like."

Such a fierce jaw she had, and how her eyes sparkled

348

with anger. Luke looked down at her thoughtfully, at the toss of her head. She reminded him of the pictures he had seen of Granny Moira Vallette.

Rory and Angela came over to them. Angela looked very serious and drew Barbara aside. "Is it true— Sophia did not wish to marry him? I can scarcely believe they would force her against her will."

"Well, they did," said Barbara fiercely. "That poor child was crying and crying. They threatened to disinherit Lionel as well as her, and she adores the boy. I think they are mean."

Luke and Rory were conferring nearby. "What do you think this means for Vallette and Sons?" asked Rory in low tones.

"Bad. He's a cold-blooded bastard," said Luke, quietly. "He's all for efficiency, no matter who suffers. He has no concern for our workmen—and they have him in Personnel."

"More trouble for Vallette and Sons, then," sighed Rory. "You know, I think I shall have to return. Looks like a battle is shaping up."

"I would sure like to have you back, Rory," said Luke, eagerly, his eyes sparking fire. "There's more than one battle brewing. The one in Vallette and Sons, and the other in Europe. I think there will be war before many more years go by, and we need to be prepared this time. Your father won't see it, and he is bucking my ideas about building more powder mills. He won't approve any more money for experimenting with guncotton, either."

Rory looked to Angela eagerly speaking with Barbara. The family resemblance between them was keen—the rounded figures, the determined chins, the wide-spaced blue eyes. Angela's blue-black hair was fastened in a demure chignon, but it looked so thick it must be long, down her back to her waist. Rory mused briefly on how it would look spread out on a white pillow, the blue eyes soft and welcoming—

"If you think it would help for me to come back—"

"We'll talk tomorrow," said Luke rapidly, seeing Arthur coming toward them with a curious look on his face. "Meet me at my apartment. I'll fill you in."

The bride and groom were to leave before the end of the afternoon for the railroad station, where a train was to take them to Washington, then up to New York, where they were to embark on a three months' honeymoon in Europe. The bride had trunks of clothes, jewels, pearls dripping from her ears, and the unhappiest look Luke had ever seen on the face of a girl.

Lionel was drinking quietly, but determinedly, in the corner. Sophia turned to leave the room, but first took one long look at him. He raised his glass to her, with a smile that wrenched his jaw. She smiled at him, the first real smile that afternoon, and nodded her goodbye.

Luke bit out, "Dammit all. Those children could make me weep. It might have worked out—"

She was gone. They cried their farewells to the carriage. A white-lace-covered hand waved to them from the black carriage. Luke shrugged uneasily, then went to find Barbara.

The guests dug into the buffet of food and drank more champagne. Lionel left after a time, through the French windows. He was dizzy, dazed. It could not have happened. His thoughts followed Sophia to the railroad station and beyond. Would Roger be kind to her, and gentle? Would he guess that Sophia was no virgin?

Rory moved back to the Areuse. He and Luke had long talks, both in the laboratory and out. Lionel joined them; he was so miserable and lost that they took pity on him. They let him in on their plans and filled his days with work.

But the nights were empty for Lionel. He refused to go to any parties; he could not see any other girl in the world. He finally took to painting, because it filled his hours and made the nights pass.

He painted scenes of the Areuse. He went hunting with Luke, carrying a sketch pad instead of a rifle; while Luke shot, Lionel drew.

Later he went out west with Rory to look into sites for another powder mill. He was intrigued with the rough laborers in the railroads, the stout Irishmen who worked from morning to night, and with the Indians who appeared on the horizon to watch the white men. They were the last of their kind; many had been found roaming freely over the Great Plains, rounded up, and put into reservations where the government could take care of them. Lionel thought they would prefer to be outside the reservations and free, taking care of themselves.

Some people were born to be taken care of, others to do the controlling and directing—no matter how one objected. He tried to talk to Rory about this on one of their camping trips. The older man nodded.

"Right. Some are born to rule, others to be ruled. That's the way of it, my lad. I mean to be one of those who rule." And his jaw was very stubborn, in the manner of his father, John.

"But what if others don't want to be ruled? What if they just want to be left alone? I think the Indians would like to be left alone on the plains, even though they don't eat so well. Maybe they don't want to live in houses," said Lionel, sketching a fanciful scene of an Indian riding his horse across a desert land with only cactus and sand.

Rory gave him a quick look. "Lionel, the tough rule; the others have to give in, or fight, or die. That's the way of it. If you want to live your own life, you have to get out from under. Cut loose. Fight—or give in."

Lionel gazed down at his picture. "No other way," he said softly.

Rory leaned back on his elbow beside the open fire they had built. He was thinking of his long talks with Luke. There would be a showdown before long. Rodger's company wanted to close some plants, tighten up. Luke argued that they must expand or die. And he wanted more gunpowder stockpiled in the event of war.

Luke would be all for a big fight, thought Rory, with a feeling of excitement in his bones. He longed to fight alongside Luke. They would make a fine team. He gazed thoughtfully at Lionel. The boy was growing up; there were shadows under his eyes. But would he make a fighter? Probably not. Still, he would be useful; his lab work was excellent. He was a genius with chemistry; he was inventive. Quietly, Lionel plugged away at experiments, always dreaming up new ideas. He would often come into the laboratory in the morning with some new thought free in his mind, all fresh and ready to work it out.

If only dad would loose the reins, Rory thought, Vallette and Sons would expand and grow. Luke was right; it had potential. The chemical discoveries, the raw rayon that might make clothing, other fabrics that would mean whole new factories—

He talked to Lionel about it and saw the boy brighten up and take interest.

"I'd like to go in on that, rather than the black powder," said Lionel. "I hate wars. Do you think we will have another one? Father thinks not."

"Henry and Arthur and John are all hiding their heads in a basket," said Rory. "If they went to Washington and talked to the army, if they read the newspapers more carefully, they would realize we are headed for it. By the way, you want to learn to fly? I'm buying an airplane soon."

"I think not," said Lionel gently. "I would like to learn to drive Luke's motorcar, though. Do you think father knows about it?"

Rory shrugged. "I think they all close their eyes to what they don't want to know. So long as Luke doesn't drive near the works, they will ignore it. Get Luke to teach you to drive, Lionel. You'll like it. Maybe you'll soon want one of your own. Then you can take a girl out in it—"

He watched Lionel's face from under the shadows of his lashes. The boy looked down, sketched absently, and said nothing. But the obstinate look of his jaw was ominous. Still, it was early. Sophia was still on her honeymoon.

Sophia and Rodger had returned by the time Rory and Lionel got back from their trip west. Their house was finished, a grand mansion of marble and stone—cold as the grave, thought Rory. He went to the first reception there.

Rodger's new home was vast. Voices echoed through it. The hallway was covered with marble from Italy. The conservatory was stifling; orchids bloomed in spidery violet and mauve shapes against the green windows. The drawing room where they received guests was enormous. Persian carpets, a gift from John Vallette, covered the floor. Arthur had given them silk sofas and matching chairs in pale blue satin with fleur-de-lis design. The rosewood piano at one end of the enormous room was played by a hired pianist from Montgomery, accompanying a girl in white who played a harp softly. Portraits on the walls were of some of Rodger's relatives. He said he would have a portrait soon made of Sophia.

Rory was shocked to the core when he saw Sophia. The girl had been slim; now she was thin to the bone. Her face looked as though she had been weeping continously. There was a hardness about her, a brightness of rouge on the thin cheekbones. Her mother kept looking anxiously at the girl, as though afraid she would break down.

Rodger was grim, ruddy of face as usual, more hearty and loud after some brandy. His looks at his bride were not the usual tender glances of a lover. When she was asked about Europe, he said brusquely, "Tell them about Venice. You liked Venice."

The mechanical smile moved the pale mouth. The mechanical voice of a doll recited, "Yes, Venice was very lovely. The waters are quite blue. We took a ride on a gondola every evening. There was music in the square."

She did not look toward her husband. Her wrist was heavy with gold bracelets which seemed to weigh down her slim hand. Diamonds flashed in her soft, brown

353

hair. She wore a black chiffon dress—black on a bride, thought Rory.

Lionel didn't come to the reception. He had work to do in the lab, he had said.

Surely they would not be foolish enough to meet behind Rodger's back, Rory wondered. That would be the height of folly, considering the possessive way Rodger held her waist, the way he touched her arm, clutched her wrist more tightly than her bracelets. It was as though he were angry with her, determined to crush her to him.

"Show Rory your gift from Rodger from the diamond merchant's in Amsterdam," ordered Arthur, lifting her hand.

"Very lovely," said Rory, noticing the thinness of the fingers. She seemed to eat nothing that night; she drank only a sip of champagne. He wrote that night to Angela, "The girl is headed for a breakdown. It was a sad mistake to marry her to that brute. He had no appreciation of her. He is coarse and crude. My God, to see them together makes one ill. I was glad Lionel did not come. Even gentle Lionel would be ready to kill."

Luke left feeling as though he had been at an Irish wake: laughter and champagne, with tears not far from the surface. Arthur had gotten louder and louder as he drank toast after toast to the new couple. And Sophia—God, the look in her eyes, Luke remembered, the dazed, dead look. And Rodger—looking fit to kill.

Luke walked down the hill and out to his motorcar. He had parked it a discreet distance from the house. Rory followed him.

"I was getting sick in there," said Rory abruptly. "Do you think Arthur will ever admit he made a bad mistake with his only child?"

"You forget," said Luke grimly. "John and Arthur and Henry are incapable of making mistakes. Want a ride?"

"Yes, thanks. Put me up for the night? I don't want to go back home."

"Right you are."

They cranked up and sputtered off down the dirt road to Montgomery. As they passed the gates of Vallette and Sons, they noticed lights in the window of the laboratory.

"Lionel is working tonight," said Rory.

"Poor bastard."

"Why don't you take him with you to Washington next week? Get him out of here."

"He would hate Washington. It's noisy and dirty. Better to take him hunting and fishing."

"I'm going out to Pennsylvania in a month," said Rory.

"Take him along, then."

The two were silent for a time; the noise of the car filled the quiet country air. Back in Luke's apartment, they both moved around restlessly. Luke got out a bottle of whiskey and glasses.

"I have to drink to get that taste out of my mouth," he said, grimly. He filled their glasses, and raised his. "To bachelorhood. Long may it last." He drained his glass.

Rory did not touch his glass at first. He finally grinned. "To your bachelorhood, Luke, if that's the way you want it. The mighty Rory Vallette is about to fall."

"You're joking," said Luke sharply, setting down his glass. "Not that pretty Betsey."

"Nope. Not her. Another. I fancy we're going to have a battle royal again in the Vallette family. I'm going up to New York next week."

Luke stared at him. "You don't mean—Angela?"

Rory nodded. "We've been writing. I think it's time I paid her a visit and pushed some boyfriends off her neck. She shall look at me, not as a cousin, but as a suitor, my lad."

Luke nervously fingered a pattern on the table. Rory grinned.

"I have it all figured out. Angela told me right off. We are third cousins, once removed."

"What will your father say?"

"I'm not Lionel," said Rory. A stubborn set of his

355

jaw emphasized his words. "God help John if he interferes. Angela is no Sophia either; she is no meek miss to heed her father's words. There's a tragedy brewing with Rodger and Sophia, if I'm not mistaken, Luke," he said seriously. "Did you look at her eyes? I wonder if he has been—beating her?"

Luke shrugged uneasily. "There's something wrong. They hate each other. He is crushing her, of course. She is too mild, too gentle—"

"Well, let's think about something else," said Rory unhappily. "We can't do anything about that—except kill the guy. Have you thought about what you'll say in Washington? Are they determined to take us to court?"

"I think the lawyers can delay it for another month or two. Lawyers are good at delay. We might dream up some angle with the army also. I am planning to bring out another general or two to impress John Vallette." Luke flung himself onto the sofa and eyed the ceiling moodily. Talk of the company was an irritant, but it might help him forget the terrible look in Sophia's eyes. Like a small, dying rabbit.

Chapter 27

Events moved rapidly at Vallette and Sons once Rodger Courtney returned. He moved into his office, and into the board room, as though he had every right, even though he had been in the company less than a few months.

Luke, Rory, and Lionel attended the board meeting, uninvited, when they heard that John Vallette was considering the sale of Vallette and Sons to another company.

"He is out of his ruddy mind," said Rory incredulously, of his father.

"He has been for years—out of the century, at least," Luke told him grimly. "He is so far out of touch with the modern age he might as well be a medieval monk."

Lionel listened and said little, but when they asked him to come to the meeting, he nodded that he would. He was only distantly interested in the business. His laboratory work filled his days; he could concentrate on that and forget everything else for a time. He felt detached, floating somewhere in the ether. He dared not think of Sophia in that marble and stone tomb two miles away. He had seen her from a distance; that was all. They had neither written nor telephoned one another. Rodger was intensely jealous of her.

The board meeting started calmly. "John Vallette will present a motion," said Arthur, and nodded to the head of the company. He was placidly taking the minutes; no outside clerk was allowed into these sessions.

Minutes were taken in longhand, written into the board-minutes book in longhand, and locked in John's personal safe after the meetings. All very feudal, thought Luke, settling back in his chair in the back of the room. John, Arthur, and Henry had seats around the table, a deliberate arrangement. Everyone else sat in the back.

Luke was glad of Rory's presence, and Lionel's. The lad was quiet, but the fact that he dared to come was something. And his valuable work was recognized even by John Vallette.

John read from a paper before him. "Mars Powder Company has offered to buy the company of Vallette and Sons for the sum of eighty million dollars. After consultation with Arthur Vallette and Henry Vallette, I have come to the conclusion that it would be a good move to make. The shares would be reinvested in Mars Powder, while we would sit on their board."

Luke listened with growing incredulity. Uncle John refused to let Luke and the others sit on the board, but he would blandly sell to an outsider! What was his game?

He was soon to learn. John laid down the paper, and his shrewd, small eyes glanced about at the others, lingering thoughtfully on Luke's hard face.

"I am in my eighties. I have carried this company for years. I am growing tired, and my doctor advises me to let up. My wife and I should like to make a trip to Europe. So I have decided to sell the company and retain some controlling interest. What do you say, Arthur?"

"I'm for it," said Arthur promptly. "Rodger tells me that his company had been negotiating with Mars before they joined Vallette and Sons. A good, solid company, conservatively run. He has given me a summary of their assets—"

Luke and Rory glanced at the hard, fleshy face of Rodger Courtney, placidly making marks on the pad before him. He sat in the row with Luke, Lionel, and Rory, but a little apart from them.

Luke listened while they ran over the reasons for the sale. They would sell out to Mars, but receive in return certain stocks in exchange for Vallette stock. Vallete would become a subsidiary of Mars and concentrate on black powder. All other operations would move to the Mars plant in Missouri.

It would mean the end of the Vallette name and the company, thought Luke, furiously. And all without consulting the stockholders. Luke looked at John—he was quite ready to pass a motion without the least thought of those affected besides himself and his family. No thought for the New York Vallettes, to say nothing of Luke, Rory, Roseann and her family, Caroline and her family.

Another thought struck him at once. Of course! If John Vallette were ready to sell out, then he might consider letting Luke and Rory take over. Gradual excitement filled Luke as he only half-listened to the drone of voices—John and Arthur, with Henry echoing the other two. This was his chance. John admitted to being tired of running the company. He must figure out how to take it over.

They entertained a motion to sell; John made it, Arthur seconded.

"Just a minute," said Luke, getting up slowly, standing with his hand on his hip. "As a stockholder of some size, I have something to say."

John frowned at him and shook his white head impatiently. "Now, Luke, don't make trouble," he said mildly yet reprovingly, as to a child.

"It's my living also, Uncle John," said Luke, a gleam in his bright blue eyes. "These are my stocks you are talking about. I have about eight million in that eighty. That gives me a tenth right to talk, doesn't it?"

Rodger Courtney stirred and stared up at Luke calculatingly, but kept silent. Rory nodded emphatically. Lionel, on Luke's other side, sketched on a pad, as though he scarcely heard, but he listened intently. Was Luke about to issue a challenge to the old bull?

"Well, make it quick," said John, moving his hands impatiently on the table. His hands were old, covered with brown spots, pudgy with arthritis. But his small eyes were keen as ever.

"I object to the sale on the grounds that the owners have not been consulted," said Luke. "It would be illegal for you to continue with this action. If you want to sell out, sell to me. I'll buy all your shares—or a controlling interest, whichever you like."

"Nonsense, boy, you don't have the funds." John frowned at him. "Let's go on with it—"

"No, you can't do it, Uncle," said Luke, calmly and with authority. "You don't have the necessary votes. You have not asked my sisters and their husbands, you don't have any proxies. If this is to be a legal meeting, to consider selling you have to follow procedure."

"Dammit, I am the head of Vallette and Sons." John yelled at him, suddenly taking fire. "How dare you tell me what is legal and what isn't?"

"You've been running Vallette and Sons since my father died," said Luke tightly. "But that doesn't say you did it legally. I've been checking with lawyers. You made decisions on your own, without the approval of the stockholders. You don't own a majority—not by a long shot. You and Arthur and Henry together own only about 30 percent. And to sell out, to make a decision vital to Vallette and Sons—to decide to *kill* Vallette and Sons, which has existed for more than one hundred years—"

"You impudent puppy!" yelled John, pounding his fist on the old desk. "Your father would have whipped you for this! You dare charge into this meeting—"

"Father was not like you, Uncle John," said Luke softly, with a steely tone. "He respected the opinions of others; he thought of the workmen in the mills. Have you even considered what will happen to our workers if Mars takes over? They would close down three-fourths of our operations—that means firing three-fourths of our men. What will happen to them, to their families?"

Rory got up. "Luke is right about this, father," he said, mildly. "You have not thought through what this will mean to Vallette and Sons. The name will disappear—the name we have all been so proud of. Why, no Vallette is ignorant of our history. And we have never allowed outsiders to own stock in our company. Why have you tried to make this move now?"

John looked at his son, and his face was flushed and red. "You have no right to say anything. Sure, you came back. But you deserted the company when it needed you. And Barbara, your sister, refuses to live at home. Why should I consider what you want? Eh, tell me why."

"Are you doing this to spite me?" asked Rory, as though amused. His fist was clenched behind his back. "Selling out, so I won't get your stock and your position once you are—dead? That's mean and petty of you, father. I wouldn't have thought it of you."

Rodger Courtney stood up, his voice cool and rather disdainful. "I see no need to make this a family squabble, Rory. What is between you and your father—is immaterial. John Vallette is head of the company; he has a right to sell out—"

Luke turned to him. "Odd that you should want to sell out, Courtney. You just joined the firm. You are mighty anxious to get rid of the stocks you just acquired by virtue of marrying Sophia. Makes one wonder why you married her—why you joined your firm to Vallette and Sons—only to sell out to Mars—which you had decided wasn't good enough to join before."

There was a short, quivering silence in the room. John, Arthur, and Henry swiveled around to look at Rodger, who flushed and started to stammer.

"That's like you, Luke! To make this a personal attack on me!" Rodger managed to say, his fists clenching the chair before him—that of his father-in-law, Arthur. "Start smearing me and my motives and you'll have a fight on your hands, let me warn you."

"It is something to consider," said Lionel, in his calm, detached voice. "Why did you join Vallette and Sons, Mr. Courtney, if you want to pull out at once? You haven't even been around much. How do you know we are going under? Or is Mars paying you to sell out, and end Vallette and Sons?"

Arthur was on his feet, shouting over John's furious bellow. "Now, listen. This is not going to descend to personalities. We have got to consider this matter in a businesslike manner. I suggest that all those not on the board be dismissed from the room."

"And I suggest," said Luke, his voice rising over the roar of other voices, "that I should be on the board, and so should Rory, and so should Lionel—and all those who own stock, including the females. They resent deeply not being allowed to vote their stock. If they are informed that in secrecy their whole company was sold from under them, that their security has been tampered with—I predict you will have a petticoat war on your hands—if not a real war."

Henry, the coolest of those present, managed to calm them all down. After the voices quieted, he said, "I suggest that we table these ideas and consider them at a later date. Perhaps there is merit in the suggestion that those owning stock should be allowed to—ah—listen in on these discussions. I know Roseann and Caroline would probably be upset if they learned about Vallette and Sons being sold through some outside source—"

"Right," said Rory brusquely. "And so should I. I suggest that no action can be taken—legally—without our consent. Let's think it over, and come back—say in one month—and consider what action we *all* wish to take. After all, I own a large amount of stock, so does Luke, so does Lionel, so does my sister. We should all be informed of developments. And don't try to hold a board meeting wtihout us, father. We'll go right to court."

John glared at his only son, his fist raised over the table, his chin upraised. Rory glared back at him, his chin up. The other Vallettes watched with held breath. Courtney seemed about to speak; Arthur gave him an anxious, pleading look and shook his head angrily.

John banged his great fist on the table. "I declare this

meeting over. We'll talk it over, and see what happens." And he got up and stalked from the room.

Rodger went out after him, giving Lionel an ugly, menacing look. Lionel did not seem to see; he was sketching the picture of a bull buffalo charging an Indian on horseback, and seemed intent on getting just the right lines of the lance in the Indian's hand.

The older men departed. Rory said, "Whewwww!" and clapped Luke on the back. "First skirmish over, my lad. And how are all the children faring?"

"I think we have a chance," said Luke, wearily, wiping the sweat from his forehead with a white handkerchief. "My God. They would have sold it right from under us. The gall of them. I bet Rodger Courtney had a big say in that dealing. God, I don't like the man. Cold-blooded bastard!"

Rory punched him warningly. Lionel got up and went out, murmuring, "I'll have to get back to the lab. I left an experiment."

Rory and Luke went back to the small office they shared and began to figure. If the women were all on their side, and if John would sell some stocks to Rory, and Arthur and Henry consented, and if Rodger Courtney did not manipulate Sophia's shares, they could do it.

"But why the hell does John want to sell out, after all these years?" Luke asked Rory.

Rory shrugged. "He has been grumbling lately about his arthritis and the worry of running the company. I thought it was all talk to get mother's sympathy, though God knows she gives him plenty. But maybe he is serious. He wants to sell out, but he doesn't trust us to run his money and stock."

"But how can we buy? All my money is tied up in Vallette and Sons," murmured Luke, scribbling busily on the pad. He crumpled up the pages and tossed them into the wastebasket. "I've got to get my head clear. There are too many possibilities here."

363

John Vallette sent Luke back to Washington, perhaps to get him out of the way. "Tell those damn-fool lawyers and senators they aren't going to bust up Vallettes. If they want money, let me know. But we aren't going to court over this. I'll give them a long fight if they do."

"What do you care—if you are going to sell?" asked Luke, impatiently, to test his reaction.

John glared at him, his fingers tapping at the wood of his ancient desk, the one that Christophe Vallette had used many years ago to balance the accounts in his small, careful handwriting. Those books were locked in the safe behind John's desk, along with all the books of later years.

"What you know about business could fit into a pig's eye," burst out John Vallette. "And you want to run this company? If the trustbusters get to us, our stock won't be worth a penny. How can I give my wife and children security that way? I'm thinking of the future, my boy, the future."

Luke went to Washington and a series of rather fruitless conferences. He was tired and angry at the rumors that met him. One implied that as soon as the Standard Oil case was finally settled and some others were out of the way, they would take on the powder makers. And Vallette and Sons would be the chief target.

Luke talked to Colonel Trent, who was as gloomy as he. "We're sick about it, Luke, let me tell you. When war comes to Europe—"

"And it is coming?"

"Probably. This is 1910," said Trent, thoughtfully. "The pot is boiling. The Balkans are a hotspot, something might break there. Or those Germans are going to erupt. They want more of the land around them. I am going to England next month and hope to hear something more definite. They are closer to Europe, with ears to the ground. They are scared, let me tell you. England is too damn close to the Continent. If war comes, they will be hard put to stay out of it. And with the Royal House related to Germany and the sympathies all with

France and Holland and the little countries, God knows what will happen."

"If they do get into it, against Germany," said Luke slowly, "then Vallette and Sons will be more needed than ever. England does not make her own powder. And the shipping lanes must be kept open—they depend on supplies from America, foodstuffs, grain, cattle, to say nothing of the supplies from the South American countries."

"Right." They were silent for a time. When Luke got up to leave, he asked Trent to keep him informed and to keep working for them through the War Department.

"You may be sure of that!" said Trent warmly. "They are as worried as I am that the talk of breaking up big corporations will dry up the black powder supplies at the wrong time. Let me give you the name of the General I told you about—his address. You might make an appointment—or I'll make it for you."

Arrangements were made; the general was cordial and visibly anxious about developments. Luke left feeling he had a friend in high places.

But all this exhausted him physically. He went back to the Vallette suite to find it empty of any cousins. He was about to lie down after his hot shower when he thought of Barbara. Maybe he would go over there for the evening.

He dressed again, in his gray silk suit and wine-dark tie, and set out to get a carriage. He hoped there would be no big party going on tonight, and that Barbara would be home. She was lively and always busy. He smiled to himself, thinking of her enthusiasm for her many projects.

He was in luck. She was home with her roommates and the cozy housekeeper, and she was glad to see him.

"Oh, Luke, I have been thinking of you," came her spontaneous cry as he entered the room after the black-clad maid. She came forward warmly to take both his hands.

"Well, this is a nice welcome," he grinned down at

her. "And how beautiful you look. You're not about to go out, are you?"

She wore a silver-bordered green silk dress, with a round neck that showed off her white skin and soft, curly brown hair. Her arms were bare to above the elbows; a scarf had slipped down about her wrists. She pulled it up again, blushing as he looked her over intently. "No, this is an at-home evening, Luke. Come in. You know all my friends here—" And she got a drink for him, whiskey and lime, and a comfortable place near the fire. The October night was cooler than usual for Washington.

The two other girls soon drifted away. Only the housekeeper remained, clicking away with her knitting needles, rocking and soundlessly counting.

Barbara turned eagerly to Luke. "Rory has written about the big sound and fury on the Areuse. Do tell me what happened, Luke. I am so eager to hear. Did you really suggest that women should vote their own stock?"

He touched her pink cheek with his fingers, teasingly, and noted with wonder how soft her skin was, how silky. "I did, Barbara. And your father was furious. But he may come around. He sent me here to cool off and do his dirty work with the senators and the War Department. I guess he thinks I'll forget about his idea of selling Vallette and Sons."

"Mother is furious with him," Barbara confided frankly, sitting closer to him, her silver slippers drawn up beneath her hem. Her blue-violet eyes sparkled in the firelight. "Tell me about it, Luke. Mother dared not say much in her letters, and Rory was almost incoherent. What did you say, and what did Lionel say, that made Rodger want to kill him?"

Luke found himself relaxing into the soft cushions, happily recounting all that had happened to an intent and serious listener.

"I can't believe father thought of selling Vallette and Sons all by himself," confided Barbara, when he had finished his story. "I think it was that nasty Rodger Courtney. A more devious, tough skunk I have never met. I just hate it that he married Sophia. I think he wanted to get control of the company."

"And control of her," said Luke, in a low tone. "It isn't a pretty sight, Barbara. He is crushing her. I think they must be quarreling badly. Perhaps he knows about Lionel. He seems to hate the lad."

Barbara shuddered. "She has not answered my letters. I gave up writing. Poor Sophia. I should hate to be married to such a bully. If I marry, it shall be to someone I can respect and trust."

"I should certainly hope so, young Freckles! Or I'll forbid the marriage myself." Luke teased her, to bring a smile to her face. She did smile, and blush, and wrinkled her nose at him.

"Now, don't you bully me, Luke. You did enough of that when I was a child."

"That was for your own good," he said, with a grin. "You mean, you really didn't want me to rescue you from trees, and mean dogs, and rogue horses?"

She pounded his knee with her small fist; he captured it and raised it gallantly to his lips, with laughter in his eyes.

She snatched away her hand with a pout. The housekeeper looked up, smiled, then looked down again at her knitting, rocking placidly.

"Now tell me what you have been up to. How is the movement? What actions have you taken? I understand Senator White is on your side, and Senator Jenson is wavering—"

"Oh, yes. It is most exciting." Barbara sat up straight, her arms wrapped about her slim knees, and began telling him all about her activities, with her head turned to gaze up at him earnestly. He found himself watching the changing expressions of her vivid face, the sparkle in her blue-violet eyes as the firelight brought out the colors—like a deep opal, he thought, or a rare sapphire.

"And so we decided to enlist the President in our cause," she was going on, some half-hour later. "And we *shall*. If this President doesn't work with us, the next one will. We shall influence men to vote for us, and eventually the vote will be ours. It already is in some states—why not in all? And it is ridiculous that women of property should have to give it all into the keeping of their husbands when they marry. It is enough to set one against marriage forever."

"My God, Freckles, I hope not," said Luke soberly. "I think you would make a splendid wife and mother."

Halted in her swift flow of words, Barbara looked surprised, blushed, gulped. "Well—Luke—I don't know. I mean—I haven't had time to think about it."

The housekeeper spoke up mildly; they started as they realized she had been listening to everything. "If that young man hanging about you has his way, you will be whisked off to the altar before you know it, Miss Barbara."

Luke had a jolt. "Which young man?" he demanded.

"James Keane, his name is, and devoted. Always sending her flowers, and helping stuff envelopes," said the housekeeper.

Oh, indeed? thought Luke. So young James was still hanging around. James was thirty-eight, and had played around for years. Surely he was not serious about Barbara? But stuffing envelopes—that sounded serious.

Barbara looked at Luke uneasily.

"Well, I've been thinking, Barbara. How about coming back to the Areuse for a visit this autumn? I think you should be around to persuade your mother, and maybe your father, not to sell Vallette and Sons," said Luke, after a pause, as though he had forgotten James.

"Oh, do you think I could do anything?" She was doubtful. "I always put father's back up. He thinks I am silly. That's why I left home: he would never take me seriously."

Luke was about to answer her teasingly when he looked again at the flushed, serious face illuminated by the firelight. He touched her firm chin.

"I take you seriously, Barbara," he said quietly. "You are a Vallette. You've proved you are willing to work for what you believe in. And I'd like to enlist you in our cause. What about it? Come home with me when I go next week?"

She looked up at him; they measured one another's looks, and a funny quiver went through Luke. Barbara was twenty-one. She was a college graduate, had lived in Washington for months, and worked hard at a cause in which she believed. She was no child—no, she had grown up; and a very lovely lady she was, with a straight back and a firm look.

She finally nodded, and he felt a thrill of triumph. "Yes, I'll come, Luke. I have wanted to have a good, long visit with mother. When are you going?"

"Around Wednesday—it depends on my appointments. I'll come again tomorrow night—may I?"

"If you want, Luke. We can talk some more. Oh, I'm so glad you realize I am grown up," she added spontaneously.

He did not smile. "I realize it, Barbara."

Chapter 28

Barbara did go back to the Areuse with Luke the following week, planning to stay for a few weeks with her parents. Luke called for her in the carriage several times; they went back across the river, and took walks along its banks, and talked and talked and talked.

Barbara was suprisingly easy to talk to, understanding, and passionately sympathetic. And she was smart, thought Luke.

He found himself explaining the situation in the board room to her. She listened keenly.

"Why, they are being just like dictators," she exclaimed. "You are a director, by virtue of your stocks and your work in the laboratory. So is Rory, and so is Lionel. How can they keep you from speaking up and sitting on the board?"

He thought about it. It had been by force of John Vallette's will, he decided.

"They have no right," declared Barbara, firmly. "It is just like women's suffrage. They have kept women from voting for years. Yet we possess money, own land, own stock and bonds; we go to school. Some women are left to raise their children when their husbands die. Yet because of some stupid law, they cannot vote on issues which concern them vitally!"

Luke had never taken much interest in women's suffrage. Now, in response to Barbara's passionate interest, he began to consider the ramifications. It was not just women who were kept from voting and holding positions where their opinions could sway decisions. Bullies everywhere tried to gain control, by money or by power of will, and to prevent others from taking part in decision-making.

"Why don't you and Rory buy the others out?" demanded Barbara. "You could borrow the money on the strength of the future of the company. You said that the War Department has urged you to continue to make black powder in quantity, and to continue the experiments with guncotton."

"Borrow on the future," said Luke thoughtfully. "You know, Barbara, you're shrewd. That gives me an idea."

He decided to make a quick trip to New York City. He was gone four days, but in that short time he found bankers with a keen interest in Vallette and Sons. With the help of a smart lawyer, he came back with figures and ideas. Then he talked to Rory and Lionel.

And he talked to Barbara as well. They strolled along the Areuse on a bright November day; the river flowed gray-green, and the willows shed the last of their leaves down into the waters.

"According to what the bankers told me, I could borrow on the strength of Vallette and Sons, and its future. They were downright eager to give me favorable terms of interest. With that knowledge, I have a weapon with which to approach Uncle John and the others. If they will sell out to me, I can have the company on my own, with Rory and whoever else wants to go in with me. Or they could gamble with me on the future of Vallette and Sons, as the bankers were eager to do."

"How would that work, Luke?" she asked, her vivid face glowing.

"I would take all their stocks and in return give them notes against the stock's value. They would have income from that for, say, twenty years. Then I could either pay off the notes or continue them indefinitely. The income would come from the profits of the company. If they want to gamble with me, they could exchange their stock for stock in the new company I would form, which would really be a continuation of Vallette and Sons except with a new board of directors."

"I think that is terrific," she said, admiringly. "I wish you were in our movement; you would solve everything in a year."

He laughed, flattered by her confidence. He tucked his hand into her arm and turned her further upstream, past the latest mills, up into the countryside. Her sturdy boots kept pace with his big ones. They shuffled through the dried autumn leaves, scared up a small brown rabbit, and paused to gaze up at the nest of a robin.

"Oh, I do love it here," said Barbara, after a comfortable pause. "If daddy would just let me live my own life, let me come and go as I please. But he is always bullying me. I think he would arrange my marriage if I let him. So I stay away."

"Don't let him do that, Barbara," said Luke quickly. "You don't want a tragedy like—"

She nodded as he paused, her face sobering. "I went over to see Sophia while you were gone, Luke. Oh, her face has aged so. She is thin and tired all the time, and she can scarely force herself to smile. Have you looked into her eyes?"

"Yes."

"And he is so—so gross, and heavy, so brutally abrupt with her. He snaps at her if anything goes wrong and blames her for everything. The servants tiptoe about them. And she just smiles, and says, 'Yes, Rodger, of course.' I don't think she even hears him, and it makes him all the more furious."

Luke thought that Sophia would not last long—she seemed dead inside. But he did not say so to Barbara. Sophia had left them all mentally. She lived a secret life that no one could reach, and to all she was a cool, polite lady with few words. Even her mother could not reach her now.

What lay ahead for Sophia? Luke thought she would probably have a mental breakdown before long. Arthur was visibly worried about her, but unable to do anything. Rodger had been his choice. Rodger was in the company. Rodger was her husband.

Luke shuddered and glanced about at the lovely brown countryside, preparing itself for winter. Soon a snowfall would cover this land with a layer of frost and white. The trees would glitter with icicles, and ice would splinter over the Areuse.

"How lovely and peaceful it is up here," said Barbara, standing with booted feet planted firmly on a patch of brown earth. She was looking out over the hills, down at the Areuse, across to her parents' home on the hill beyond the Areuse. "Look—if you had a house here, you could have great windows overlooking the river and mills around. This is the highest hill about. And all these lovely trees—how they would shade the house in the summer."

"It is beautiful up here," said Luke, turning to look about as she did. "Yes, it is quite lovely. Well, Barbara, plan a house here," he added teasingly. "What would you like? Let's see—how about a dozen rooms, with a greenhouse for flowers over here, and a huge drawing room with your picture windows overlooking the river— let's stake it out."

She laughed and followed his lead, her cheeks glowing pink in the cool wind. She picked up a couple of sticks and began to draw in the earth, seriously. "The drawing room here," she said finally. "Yes, you could look out over the valley."

"And the master bedroom above that drawing room, the width of the house," said Luke, taking out a sketch pad and a pencil. He began sketching rapidly, with Barbara peering around his arm. Her pert ermine cap came about to his shoulder. She pointed.

"And a wide hallway here, with stairs dividing and meeting again on the second floor. And a comfy sitting room on the second floor near the children's room, so they can come to mama, and be private," she said cheerfully. "I would like that. Mama had a room where Rory and I could come and talk to her without daddy

373

knowing. And the nursery next to the master bedroom, with a room for the nurse beyond that."

Luke obediently sketched, a little smile emerging at the corners of his mouth. He sketched the first floor, with drawing room, French windows, a large dining room behind it, and along the back of the house a ballroom, with a conservatory for flowers off that toward the stables. There would be a smaller morning room, generous-sized kitchens, and pantries for cold goods and meats.

"And a third floor with a little tower room," added Barbara, enchanted with their make-believe. "I have always wanted to live in a place with a tower. Like a castle, only homey and comfortable."

"A tower you shall have, my dear," he said solemnly, and sketched in a third floor, with a couple of small bedrooms and a tower room overlooking all, over the master bedroom, with winding stairs ascending from the second floor.

"And I think a flower garden all about the house," added Barbara. "Do you think we might have a bed of roses? And a magnolia hedge—"

"Of course. Just what we need." Luke added all these, and made rapid additions as Barbara dreamed on.

They lingered until late afternoon, then strode down the hill to the carriage and the patiently waiting horses. He drove her back home, his mind full of plans. Barbara laughed and chatted. He watched her bright pretty face and made more plans.

There was a dinner at John Vallette's that night. Luke turned up early, hoping for another private talk with Barbara. He was disappointed. The entire clan had turned out, except for Lionel, who never attended these events any more.

The long table was full, from one end to the other, with aunts, uncles, cousins, and second cousins. They laughed and talked away animatedly. All except Sophia, who sat and smiled at them gently, her black chiffon dress setting off her creamy white face and gentle, dim brown eyes. She wore a cameo at her throat and, incongruously, a long strand of diamonds below it. Rodger's addition, thought Luke. She was so small, and now she seemed tinier than ever, her waist so slender he could have spanned it easily with his hands. She sat erect, chin up, eyes focused at some distance. Rodger would frown over at her, but she did not seem to see him.

The conversation after dinner turned inevitably to the future of Vallette and Sons. Thinking about it later, Luke realized that Rodger Courtney had turned it in that direction. He brought up idly the fact that another company was interested in buying Vallette, and it might be smart to sell as soon as competitive bidding made the price higher. The ladies gasped; the men had heard about this before.

"Sell Vallette and Sons? Never!" cried Caroline, in distress, turning to her favorite brother, Luke. "You wouldn't hear of it, would you, Luke?"

"He is not a board member," said Rodger, grimly. "He has nothing to do with it. It will be John Vallette's decision—along with Arthur and Henry, of course."

"Jumping the gun, Rodger," said Luke, in a sort of deadly murmur. His bright blue eyes were blazing. Barbara watched in fascinated awe. She had felt comfortable with him at times. Other times, she sensed the power of the man leashed behind the polite façade.

Rodger smiled, without mirth. "I don't think so. Oh, you thrash about, but you cannot do anything, really, can you? All you know is powder making."

"That *is* Vallette and Sons," said Luke. "Powder making. That is our beginning, our life, our future. Of course, you are new here. You may not know our history," he said, with the slightest emphasis on *our*.

"Odd you should say that," said Rodger. "As a point of fact, I have been studying the history of the Vallette family. I have studied the portraits of the Vallettes. In fact, I am amazed that you and your father, Brett, do not resemble the early Vallettes at all. You do resemble that Irish girl that Christophe married, that is all." He was still smiling, but it seemed more like a grimace.

There was a silence in the room. Arthur looked at Henry helplessly. The man was insulting them all!

Luke eyed him thoughtfully. Rodger could not know about the Indian blood—could he? Few knew of it. Brett had told Luke in confidence. Did anyone else know—or was it only a suspicion?

Barbara was furious, and finally spoke up when no one else did. "What a strange way you have of judging history, Mr. Courtney," she said, in a frigid tone. "You stare at a few portraits, look at some records, and decide that a long, respectable family line is—not respectable at all. Is that what you are saying, Mr. Courtney?"

"Not at all, Miss Barbara," he said, with a smirk in her direction and a long look over her low-cut pale green silk dress, his gaze lingering on her slim white arms and narrow waist as though appraising her. "I simply spoke my thoughts. In the family, you know. Luke does not resemble any of the first Vallettes in this country. Now Rory is the image of old Christophe, I believe. But Brett, Luke's father, is not at all like him. Antoine bears a strong resemblance to Etienne; Tristan does not."

Old John Vallette intervened at last, troubled, his face flushed. "Now, Rodger, you are judging hastily. If you knew Luke better, you would know he is much like Christophe. It was Christophe who really founded this company, for Conrade finally went off to New York to work in textiles. I can remember father telling about the old days, when Tristan and Antoine were learning the business. It was Tristan who understood the chemistry of it, and Antoine who went into the managing end. Always good partners. I miss Brett. He was the greatest powder man of them all." And John went on into an unusual rambling talk about the old days.

They were all quiet, listening to him, averting faces from Rodger. Caroline listened intently, her hand on the shoulder of her elder boy Foster. Her Joshua was listening also, sitting near his Uncle John, drinking in the stories of the old days.

Luke lit up a Havana cigar, safely away from the ladies. He was burning with anger, but he would say nothing. The trouble was, Rodger was shrewd. He had looked at the pictures and studied the accounts. Had he ever found anything about those lost four months in Christophe's life—the time when he was gone hunting— and returned with a pregnant wife, Moira? No, he was probably just guessing; but he was smart. Luke glanced at Barbara's flashing eyes and flushed cheeks. She was ready to do battle for him. He gave her a little grin and a wink as Uncle John went on, and she finally smiled back and began to relax against the cushions of the alizarin damask sofa.

John seemed unusually genial that evening. Perhaps he was really happy underneath about Rory returning to the powder mills, and about having Barbara back for a visit. At length, he asked about a family reunion at Christmastime, teased some of the girls about what they wanted for Christmas, and grumbled that he would not get away for a trip to Europe with Ellen until spring, but that he meant to go then definitely.

Luke was not really surprised to receive a summons to John's office three days later. He was engrossed in an experiment with Lionel, and he grumbled under his breath when Henry brought the message.

"Damn, I can't come right now. What about tomorrow?" he said. Henry's face mirrored his shock.

"But Luke—when John wants you to come and talk—" he began.

"I can finish this, Luke. You go ahead. Peter here will help me." Lionel nodded at the young powder man who was helping them, a keen young German boy who had worked with Luke for three years.

"Well, if you're sure—" Luke slipped off his grimy lab coat, changed to his gray shirt and suit, and went out into the yards. Once beyond the mills, he changed from the wooden-pegged shoes into his smart leather boots. He strode after Henry up to the small wooden office of the boss.

The office seemed unusually quiet that November afternoon. Thanksgiving was near. Luke glanced about and noticed that Rodger's desk in the outer office was neat and straightened, with no signs of current work on it.

John limped to the door of his office. "Come in, Luke, come in." John noted Luke's long look at Rodger's desk. "I sent him to Pennsylvania," he said, with a grim smile. "Henry, you watch out here. I don't want to be interrupted. Arthur is on his way to Washington."

He turned, and went back in. Luke followed him, rather dazed. Was John going to fire him? Would he go so far? But the old man did not seem angry, but rather thoughtful.

John said, "Shut the door." Luke obeyed, and sat down in the chair opposite the scarred old desk Christophe and Conrade had used so long ago. What stories that scarred, pigeon-holed wooden piece of furniture could tell, Luke thought idly. The scenes, the maneuverings, the plans, the quiet quarrels between the brothers and cousins, the heated arguments about what was best for Vallette and Sons.

"I've been thinking, Luke," said John. He sat forward, his elbows on the battered desk, his keen small eyes on his nephew. "You said a piece the other day."

"I guess I did," said Luke, noncommittally. He folded his arms and leaned back in the chair. He was ready for combat, or peace, whichever John wanted.

"I've thought it all over. Talked to Henry, not to Arthur. Arthur is too close to Rodger, his feelings are all mixed up in what he *hopes*, not what he sees with his eyes." John gave out a brief, gusty sigh, his broad jowls drooping. "Bad marriage. I should never have let them go through with it. Sophia is miserable. Rodger is a hard cuss."

Luke did not answer; his feelings were too strong for rational analysis of that situation.

"Well, they'll have to make the best of it," said John, and moved a couple of papers carefully. "How did you plan to pay for the powder mills?"

Luke started. John smiled grimly, pleased to catch the young panther off balance.

Luke soon recovered. He spoke briefly but thoroughly. "I have contacted bankers in New York. Several banks would advance me the money at a favorable rate of interest, and I could buy you out, at least enough to gain controlling interest. Or—Rory and Lionel and I could give you and the others matching stock, or due notes, with interest paid every quarter." He explained how that would work, as the lawyer and the bankers had explained it to him.

John listened, his pudgy, arthritic hands folded on the papers on his desk top. His small eyes never wavered. When Luke had finished and sat back, John said, "How soon do you want to take over?"

"Right away," said Luke, his blue eyes challenging.

"How much like Brett you are," said John softly. "Never realized how much. Even look like him, same Goddam-your-guts way of looking at a man. Well, you can have it."

"What?"

"The company. Vallette and Sons. I don't want to sell out to strangers. Goddam it, Luke, I'm an old man. I'm ready to retire. I want to take Ellen to Europe, relax, enjoy my grandchildren—if Rory or Barbara ever condescend to give me any!"

Luke drew a deep breath. "I'll be glad to oblige," he said, and John thought he meant just taking over Vallette and Sons. His forehead eased. He sat back, creaking in his chair.

"Good, good. Arthur wants to relax also, to take things easier. You going to stay on in the powder mills end?"

"We'll work it out," said Luke firmly. "Rory is coming in with me. I think Lionel will also. We'll parcel out the work among us."

"Rodger wants to stay on," said John, unexpectedly.

"I wanted to talk to you without him around. Luke, don't trust Rodger too much. I don't like fellows who are too clever for their breeches."

Luke did stare at the old man then. John nodded, slowly.

"You don't trust him? But you have him in the office."

"Oh, he's a smart man, a cool manager. He wants to use his stock, keep on here. But don't let him off the reins, Luke. Keep 'em tight on him. He'll go hog-wild and take over everything. And he isn't a Vallette, not even by marrying that child." John shook his head slowly. "Cold bastard. All he thinks about is money. He can help you or trip you up. But he'll want to stay on, I warn you."

To Luke's further surprise, John hauled out the precious record books and began going over them with him. Before Luke left the office that afternoon he was in possession of the safe combination, a key to the office, and John's old desk.

Rory went to New York the following day, at Luke's request, to put the situation before the New York Vallettes. He seemed very eager to go. He came back with their proxies, permission to proceed, and their good wishes on the venture.

Within two weeks, Luke, Rory, and Lionel had taken over the company. Through a combination of bank loans and exchanges of new stock for old, they took charge of Vallette and Sons. John retired, and seemed content. Arthur took a long vacation. Henry volunteered to remain on the board for a few years, to give advice if they required it.

The only real trouble they had was from Rodger Courtney. When he returned from Pennsylvania and found out what had happened, he raged and accused the new directors of acting behind his back, treating him like an outsider. He refused to consider selling out.

"Sophia is every bit a part of Vallette and Sons, and I vote her stock," he said emphatically. "When Arthur dies, and his wife, she inherits all of their stock also. I'll have you know, I won't be pushed aside!"

Luke eyed him thoughtfully, thinking of what Barbara had said about the votes of women. If Rodger did not have the right to vote Sophia's stock, he would have much less power than he now did. Luke told him mildly that he was welcome to stay on, and gave him a desk next to Henry's.

"Rory will be head of the office, I will be head of the laboratory," he said. "Lionel just wants to work in the lab, but of course he will be a director of the firm. We shall have open board meetings from now on, with any stockholder permitted to attend the meetings, except when personnel matters are considered."

Christmas and New Year's came, and the Vallettes observed their usual custom of visiting in each other's homes and taking presents to the women. Luke made a special trip to Washington to give Barbara a beautiful sable hat and scarf.

"Oh, Luke, it's too much! You shouldn't have!" Her cheeks bloomed with color. He crammed the hat on her head, laughing at her protests.

"It'll keep you warm in jail, if you're determined to go there," he said, with mock callousness.

She made a face at him; he swooped at her and kissed her pink mouth. She pushed at him. "Luke— don't."

"Between cousins?" he asked, laughing, eyes alert.

"You look like a panther ready to spring! I believe becoming head of Vallette and Sons has gone to your ego—it's bigger than ever," she said daringly.

For that, he kissed her again, squeezing her roughly in his arms. She squealed and kicked herself free.

Rory said to Lionel, quietly, "Why don't you go out west with me again, lad? I have to go for a couple of months this time, to see about the situation in Missouri. And I may go beyond to Colorado."

"I believe I will, if Luke can spare me," said Lionel slowly. There were great shadows under his eyes. He had seen Sophia with Ellen Vallette in Montgomery for a brief hour one day; they had all had tea, in a civilized manner, in one of the hotels. Sophia was pregnant, but not blooming. She looked drawn, old, tired. She scarcely spoke, but he had been conscious of her gaze on his face most of that hour. He could not endure much more. She was being tortured to death, he thought, and he could not help her.

Rory and Lionel went out west on the railroad, traveling long distances. They had continued by carriage into some remote areas. Rory was looking out for a new source of sulfur, and had heard rumors of finding some there.

Lionel sketched for hours on the trip, finding bleak satisfaction in improving his skill. He slept better in the open air, under blankets, with the night wind howling about their camp.

Rory confided in him, unable to keep it to himself. He had seen Angela several times in New York. "I think she likes me immensely. I had hoped in time she would come to love me. God, I'm not getting any younger!"

"What does Aunt Anna Moira think?" asked Lionel, sketching feverishly. Talk of marriage and love made him uneasy, as though some demon scratched at the hidden rooms of his mind.

"Oh, I think she likes me. But whether as a cousin or as a suitor for her beloved Angela, I don't know. Her brother Owen is interested in coming down here. He might join the firm," said Rory dreamily, his gaze on the dying fire. "Well, we better turn in. I could sleep ten hours!"

Lionel turned in also, but his sleep did not come so easily. He could see Sophia's great, brown eyes in the firelight, and the haunted look of her face. He heard her voice in the soughing of the night wind, the sobbing of an animal or in the shrieking of a bird.

Rory and Lionel returned in early March. Rory found Rodger sitting at Rory's desk in the main office, arrogantly in charge. He kicked him back without much ceremony into his own office, and set Henry in charge whenever he was gone. Arrogant bastard! he fumed, and went carefully over the books to make sure Rodger had not fixed them.

Lionel soon heard rumors concerning Rodger, and later saw for himself. Sophia was about seven months pregnant and had been ill much of the winter. Rodger was unsympathetic. The rumor ran that he had a mistress in Montgomery and kept an apartment there.

Ellen Vallette told her son Rory, "Sophia is indifferent whether he comes, or whether he goes. He calls her cold. She says to me that she lives in a marble tomb, why should she be warm? Oh, it is a terrible situation, Rory."

He shuddered, then gave his warm-hearted mother a hug. "And when do you and father take off for your trip to Europe?" he asked, to change the subject.

"In May, darling. Are you sure you can manage?"

"With nine servants?" he scoffed. "I shan't even have to boil my own coffee, as I do at Luke's apartment."

Lionel worked in the lab, mechanically, waiting, waiting. He was not sure for what he waited. He only knew that some heartstring that ran from his heart to Sophia's had been pulled drum-tight, and it would not let him rest or sleep.

Chapter 29

In early April Sophia began to go into labor. It was almost a month early, but she was so small that the heavy child within her was cramped.

A doctor was called and a nurse installed full-time, sleeping in her own bedroom. Lionel soon heard about it.

He went to Luke. "I know Rodger will not allow me near. Will you tell me about her?"

Luke put his hand on the young man's shoulder. "Of course, Lionel. Take it easy. Women have had children before, you know."

"Not Sophia. And she does not want to live," said Lionel, simply, and went back to the laboratory.

Lionel's remark made Luke uneasy. He went up the hill in his carriage. Barbara had come from New York. He consulted her. Barbara said at once, "I shall go over there to stay. I don't care how much Rodger growls. She should have some some family there. Aunt Ellen is too easily cowed."

Barbara moved in at once. She felt a strong distaste for that marble tomb, all the more because when Rodger came home he began drinking heavily in the drawing room. The smell of his strong cigars was everywhere, with the smell of whiskey overlaying it.

Barbara took a bedroom near the master bedroom where Sophia lay. During the long hours of the night she took a pillow and blanket and sat in a chair near the girl's bed.

Sophia looked like death. Her cheeks were sunken, there was no color in her face, her great brown eyes were wide-open, staring at the ceiling. When the pains came, she gave a little moan, then stifled her cries with a stiffening of her body.

The nurse pleaded with her. "Let yourself relax, ma'am. You have to relax. Cry out, scream if you want. It'll help the baby come."

The brown eyes flickered. "I never scream," said Sophia, politely.

There were dark bruises on her arms and legs. Barbara had noticed them, the nurse also, but they said nothing. It was too late for words.

"If she lives," thought Barbara savagely, "I'll get Luke to do something. He must let them separate; he could get Sophia away. That great hulking brute—oh, God, this poor child—"

The labor went on and on. Sophia's mother was no use in the sickroom; she sat sobbing bitterly in the corner, visibly distressing Sophia. Barbara urged her to go home and rest.

"We'll call you when the baby comes," said Barbara firmly.

Arthur came several times and stared down at his daughter's face. At first, she acknowledged him with a faint smile. Later she seemed to have withdrawn to a dream world, seeing no one.

Rodger slept in the drawing room, sprawled drunkenly across the silk sofa, with cushions under his head. His valet had put a blanket over him, and a fire was kept going at all times in the huge marble-topped fireplace. The place was stifling hot that warm April day, as Luke came again to see how Sophia did.

He went up the stairs. Barbara came from the room, closing the door softly behind her. All color had fled from her clear young face; the distress in the blue-violet eyes hurt him.

"How is she?" he whispered.

Barbara shook her head. "The baby finally came—stillborn. She doesn't even care. She turned her head from—it. The nurse has sent for the doctor to come again."

"Rodger knows about it?"

The young pink mouth set grimly. "He cursed, and went back to sleep."

"God. Is there anything I can do?"

He had caught her arms and held her lightly. She was swaying with weariness. She had not slept much for two days and nights.

"Yes, Luke. Would you get Lionel; see that he comes up here?"

"Lionel?" Luke went silent, staring down at Barbara.

She nodded. They stood quietly there; she half-leaned on him. It had been a bad night, with the baby born and dying at once. There had been no life in it, still and waxlike, like a doll, so tiny and fragile.

"She has asked for him, him only," said Barbara finally, in a thread of a voice. "No one else, not even her mother."

Luke bit his lips. "All right. I'll get him."

"You could come in the back door," she suggested.

"No, the front," said Luke grimly. "And if she dies, by God, that bear downstairs gets kicked from here to South America."

"I'm afraid it's too late for that," said Barbara. "But if anyone can persuade her to try to live, it is Lionel."

Luke left and went down to the laboratory. He found Peter working quietly about the lab and Lionel sitting on a lab stool staring blankly at some papers, not even moving them.

Luke went up to him. "Come with me, Lionel. Sophia wants to see you."

The eyes lit up for an instant. "She is awake—all right?"

There was no use trying to fool him. Luke said, very gently, "The baby died at once. Barbara—thinks you should come. I don't know how Sophia is doing, but it isn't good. Anyway, she wants you to come."

Lionel started for the door. Luke found the lad's coat and went after him, draping it about his shoulders. He did not change from his leather shoes with the wooden pegs, he did not change his white lab coat. He just went out to the carriage and climbed in. He was green under his tan acquired on the trip west.

Luke drove the two miles back to the marble and stone mansion sitting grandly in the midst of tangled vines and neglected flower beds. An empty swimming pool was filled with autumn leaves. No one cared what happened there, evidently.

They went in the front door. Rodger Courtney was stirring in the drawing room. He staggered to his feet as he saw them enter. He came to the door, his face covered with a stubble of beard, his eyes bloodshot, his breath heavy with drink. He glared at them both. If he had said a word, Luke would have knocked him down.

He said nothing, breathing heavily, leaning against the door frame. A servant came forward, then backed away at the sight of Luke's set, hard face.

Luke went after Lionel up the long, winding stairs. On the second floor, Barbara came from the bedroom at the sound of their heavy shoes. "Oh, Lionel, come in," she said, almost casually. "Sophia wants to see you."

He nodded and went in. The nurse straightened up from leaning over the slim, frail body under the white covers. The room had been cleaned; all traces of blood and agony had been swept away. The drapes had been opened to the morning sunshine, and the golden rays glowed over the white covers and pale gold carpet.

Sophia's long, brown hair hung over her shoulders in two plaits. Her long, slim hands, so small and fragile, lay open on the coverlet. On one, the massive diamond ring seemed too heavy for her fingers and had slid forward to her knuckle.

As though sensing Lionel's presence, she opened her eyes. The faraway look was in them, as though she saw beyond the present, beyond the room and the silent people in it.

She turned her head slowly as Lionel came to the bed. Quite naturally, he sat down on the edge of the bed. The nurse darted forward nervously. Luke caught her arm and drew her out of the room.

"Watch for the doctor," he said tersely, and shut her out of the room.

Luke went over to stand near Barbara, his hand on her shoulder as she seated herself in a rocker near the window. Lionel had bent over and taken Sophia in his arms. One arm was under her slight, frail body, and his other hand went to her shoulder, slowly stroking over her arm, soothing her.

"Oh . . . Lionel . . ." murmured the ghost of a voice.

"I am here, darling, where I have wanted to be," said Lionel with quiet assurance.

She smiled up at him, her eyes suddenly radiant. "I had . . . a horrible . . . dream . . ." she whispered.

"It's over now. All over. We are together again," he said.

Barbara's voice caught in a sob. "Oh—if that doctor would only come—" she whispered to Luke. His grip tightened on her shoulder till she thought vaguely she would be bruised. But it was reassuring. Luke was strong. He would do something about this. He was the one person who could kick Rodger out of here, clear to South America if he chose.

Lionel and Sophia talked together, so quietly that even in the still room they could not be heard by the others.

"My love," he said to her. "How I have longed to be with you again."

"Thought you . . . might forget . . . me . . ."

The brown eyes pleaded for reassurance.

"Never in this world and the next," he said.

"I . . . love . . . you . . . so . . . Lionel . . ."

"And I adore you, Sophia. My love, my only love—"

She was quiet then, her head on his shoulder, a half-smile on the pallid lips. Her slim hand reached vaguely for his arm. She clasped him, then her fingers fell away.

The others at the window waited quietly. Sophia's hoarse breathing was suddenly loud in the room. Lionel bent over her and kissed her forehead and cheek gently. He held her, stroked her arm, and then clasped her fingers strongly in his.

They waited.

When the doctor opened the door and entered, it was resented as an intrusion. Lionel frowned, but did not turn from his patient posture on the bed, holding Sophia closely to him. The doctor went over to them, then around the bed to the other side. He took her wrist in his fingers, scowled, then finally let it down carefully.

"But she is dead," he said, his voice harsh in the still room. Barbara jerked involuntarily. Luke drew a deep breath.

Lionel looked at the doctor, but said nothing. Finally he drew back and let the doctor lay Sophia down carefully on the pillows.

Luke said to Barbara, "I'll come back for you in about two hours. You'll want to move back to Uncle John's." She nodded, her eyes blinded by tears. He bent over and kissed her cheek gently.

Then he took Lionel away with him. Outside in the carriage, he waited as he saw Arthur and his wife approaching in their carriage. In the bright April day, in the sunshine with the smell of early jasmine on the air, he waited. Luke felt wrung out with fury. He wanted to kill, to lash out with a knife, but at Arthur's haggard face, and his wife's anxious whiteness, he could not.

He went over to them and helped his sister-in-law down. "I have sad news for you," he said, the conventional words stiff against his tongue. "Sophia is gone."

"Gone?"

They begged for reassurance. He cursed the euphemism he had used. "She is dead," he said baldly.

Lionel spoke up, unexpectedly calm and rational. His eyes were the only living thing in his face, like burning coals of darkest brown.

"Would you—bury her up on the hill, with the Vallettes?" he asked. "She doesn't want to be buried with the Courtneys. I promised to make sure she was buried near granddad."

Sophia's mother broke down weeping. Arthur put his arm about her shoulder, his old face working strongly as he tried to repress his tears. He nodded. "I'll make sure—of that—" he said, and turned to enter the house.

Luke and Lionel drove away. "I'll go back to the lab," said Lionel, as though they had been away on a brief outing.

Luke let him out down there, then drove back for Barbara. He was not sure he could keep from punching Rodger in the nose, but he wanted to make sure Barbara was taken care of. Rodger was shouting as he entered the great marble house, shouting drunkenly about Sophia. "She is not dead, she is not dead. You are all goddam fools. Let me see her, let me see her, I'll make her get up. She is shamming again. Little cheat—little cheat—"

Luke got Barbara away from there. She was shivering in her blue cloak. "God, he is horrible," she said simply, leaning thankfully against Luke's shoulder. "No wonder she didn't want to live."

She began to cry then. Luke turned the carriage off the road into a cornfield, took her in his arms, and let her cry it out, soothing her with his hand stroking her hair.

"It's so unfair; she was so sweet," wept Barbara. "If only she had been stronger, if only she had defied them all—"

"You have to be very strong for that," said Luke, remembering his own battles with John and Arthur and Henry. "Poor child. She is at peace now."

Barbara finally drew back and wiped her eyes with Luke's handkerchief. "I'm sorry, Luke, I didn't mean to weep all over you."

"I am honored," he said.

She gave him a sharp look, to see if he was sarcastic. He was looking down at her with a tender, gentle look she had rarely seen on his hard, lean face. "Thank you, Luke. I used to be afraid of you. But you do have some softness under that scary exterior," she said, trying to laugh a little.

"You are not afraid of me, are you?" he asked with some surprise. She was twisting the handkerchief in her fingers.

"Well, not really. Only I never know if you're going to pounce," she said frankly. "I'd have to be really angry to fight against you."

"I hope you never get that angry, Barbara. I should not like to fight you. I can think of much more pleasant things to do with you," and he gave her a slow grin.

Barbara returned to Washington after the funeral. Luke escorted her, and Rory and Angela also went along.

"Sophia has not looked so calm, so peaceful, in years," said Angela. "Poor darling, how thin and tired she looked."

Rory looked at his sister. "I could kill that Rodger," said Barbara. "She had bruises all over her poor body. God, he is a beast."

"I blame the family," said Angela, with some anger. "Why didn't they stop the marriage? How criminal can it get? If anyone tried to marry me off, I'd kill them!"

"They aren't trying, are they?" asked Rory sharply. She gave him an innocent look.

"Not just now," she murmured.

Luke hid a grin. Rory was fighting against his desires, his longing for bachelor freedom warring with his love for her. And what would the family say? Another marriage between cousins? But they were more distantly related than poor Sophia and Lionel.

He was having his own struggles. In Washington, he was balancing the army men against the senators, his own lawyers against the sharp lawyers who thought to break up Vallette and Sons. It was his company now, and the trustbusters were more suspicious than ever. Yet the country would need the black powder should another war come. Even if America did not get into it, England would look to America for supplies of ammunition.

391

James Keane was already settled in the Vallette Washington suite when the others arrived. He looked intensely annoyed at seeing Luke arrive.

"What the devil are you doing here? I thought you didn't have to come this month."

James was nattily dressed. Luke exchanged a significant look with Rory. They had left Barbara and Angela at Barbara's house and made plans to return to take them out to dinner.

"Am I answerable to you?" asked Luke, in a dangerous murmur. "I thought I was a director of Valette and Sons now; in fact, I believe I am in line to be President. Are you questioning my doings?"

"Oh, come on, Luke, don't act the big boss with me. We have known each other all our lives. If you think I'm going to bow down to a kid I used to roll down the hill like a hoop—"

Rory raised his eyebrows. Luke put his hands on his hips and surveyed his cousin coldly. "You don't have to bow down, not like everyone did to Uncle John," he said finally. "But goddamit, I am the head of Vallette and Sons, and if you don't like it, you don't have to remain. Get it into your head that the situation has changed. You are a stockholder, yes, and I value your work in the lab. But dammit, nobody is indispensable."

"Well, damn your eyes," exclaimed James, in real annoyance, and went off to his bedroom.

Rory clapped Luke on the shoulder in a friendly fashion. "Hold your horses, Luke. You can't expect instant respect. We have worked and played together for years. Sure, you're the head of the company, and major stockholder. But James is used to speaking his mind to you. You're not going to start acting like dad, are you?"

Luke made a grimace and eased his stiff shoulders. He had flared up instantly. But it was not just the company. It was James's attentions to Barbara that were getting to him.

Luke and Rory took the girls out to dinner and had a happy time of it. They drank some fine white wine with their fish, some red wine with their steaks, and finished up with champagne and flaming crêpes for dessert.

"I think this is the restaurant where I came with James last month," said Barbara, leaning back with her coffee. "He was fuming when they refused to serve the crêpes—they said the chef had fallen sick and gone home."

Luke's mouth tightened. Rory grinned at him and kicked him under the table. "Seems to me, sis, you're seeing a lot of James."

"Oh, he is always in Washington," said Barbara. "I thought it was for Vallette and Sons. Isn't it?"

"Not on *our* business," said Luke, tightly. "I handle the contacts at the Washington end."

She raised her delicate eyebrows, then gazed out through the window over the Potomac, as though losing interest in the subject. Luke eyed her broodingly. She was so lovely in the shimmering mauve silk with the low, round neck setting off her white shoulders and arms, and with the sable scarf set back from her brown chignon.

The next day, Luke confronted James sharply. "Why are you coming to Washington so often? Barbara is under the impression it is on Vallette business. I never assigned you anything of the sort."

"You aren't the only one in Vallette and Sons," said James furiously. They had faced off in the suite's drawing room. "Rodger Courtney and I think we have the right to make contacts with politicians. He is thinking of running for Representative from our district. It helps to get contacts in the right places."

"Oh, indeed," said Luke in a low deadly drawl. "You and Rodger. So you're putting your heads together to make plans for Vallette and Sons. And without my knowledge and consent."

"Come off it, Luke. John knew what we were doing and never objected. It pays to make friends in Washington, you should know that," he added in a patronizing tone, his face flushed.

"I do know that. And I also know that John is no longer in charge at Vallette and Sons. *I* am the boss. You are answerable to *me*. When you shirk your lab work and come traipsing off to Washington—without informing me or getting permission—you are making trouble for yourself, James. You better get that straight. Now, you'll tell me what contacts you are so fondly making, and what you have done about it. I won't have you and Rodger Courtney going behind my back to make deals."

Rory had come in quietly and sat, listening to and watching the showdown he had been expecting for some time.

"What contacts?" Luke repeated sharply, his blue eyes blazing, his lean face intent. The panther was unleashed. "The names, tell me."

James told him, reluctantly. Luke flared at him.

"My God, you utter ass! Crooks, all of them! What kind of deals did you think to make with them? Vallette and Sons is damned well not going in for bribes. We do business—honest business. We have no need for bribes—whatever happened in the past. And what in the name of all that's unholy did you think to get out of those rotten politicians? Washington is a swamp, and they're the kind of rotten creatures that make it smell to high heaven."

"You have no right to criticize. Rodger and I think—"

"By God, you can stop thinking, if that is a sample of your great ideas. Stop it at once. You'll make no deals for Vallette and Sons. I'll send our word—and believe me, I'll make it stick—that nothing either Rodger Courtney or James Keane can say or promise has any validity at Vallette and Sons."

"You're a cur, Luke! You're a dog in the manger. Just because Barbara likes me better—"

"Leave her name out of this. This has nothing to do with her," Luke blazed at him, his fists clenched. "Just get this straight, James—and I'll inform Rodger of the same: You have no authority—absolutely no authority—to wheel and deal for Vallette and Sons. And don't think you are going to take company money to pay your damned bribes."

James bit his lip and blushed, making Luke peer at him suspiciously.

"So—you've already been at the till, have you?" he added ominously. "I'm going to order an audit of the company books at once. And you'd better be prepared to account for every penny issued to you. Now, get out of here. Find yourself somewhere else to live in Washington, if you mean to stay. And I warn you, if you stay long, you'll be out of a job when you go back to the Areuse. I won't have slackers about."

James raved incoherently, waving his hands. But Luke was implacable, and James moved out that day.

Rory drove over in a carriage that evening to pick up Angela. "My God, I couldn't move from my seat. I was riveted. I thought Luke would kill the man. I've seen him furious, but never like that. And God help Rodger and James if there is any discrepancy in the audit. Luke shot off a telegram at once to a firm of auditors to move in on the company today—*today*, mind you—and get busy auditing the books. They have authority to commandeer every scrap of paper in the place."

"Good," said Angela, with intense satisfaction. "I hope Rodger Courtney has been embezzling funds."

Rory glared down at his pretty cousin, with her chin in the white fur of her coat, which made her look like a very pretty angel. "What in the name of—why do you hope we've been embezzled?"

"So you or Luke will slug Rodger and throw him out of the company. I cannot abide him," said Angela firmly, her round button nose deliciously pink from the cool April breeze that blew about their carriage.

"Good heavens, you're bloodthirsty," said Rory, and flung back his head to laugh. "Just when I think you are a meek, gentle, sweet creature—"

"I am not!" she cried.

Rory drew up the carriage in a strategically darkened place overlooking the Potomac and fastened the reins around the post. Then he turned to Angela. "What are you not? Bloodthirsty? Or gentle and sweet?"

"It was the way you said it," she said apologetically, in her soft voice.

The long blue-black hair was wound around her head, making her round face look even smaller and more delicate in the dim lamplight. Rory gazed down at her intently. "Angela," he said, in a deeper tone.

"Are you going to make love to me? I don't want it," she said, firmly. "I promised mama I would not get into trouble here in Washington, or she would not have let me come."

"Darling," he said recklessly, throwing caution to the winds. "I love you, I adore you, there is no one in the world like you. Marry me."

"Did you have too much wine tonight, Rory?" she asked in a deceptively soft drawl. "You don't really mean—"

"I mean, I love you, I want you, I shall marry you, though all the devils of hell and father included try to keep us apart. We aren't all that closely related—"

"Third cousins, once removed," recited Angela. Rory swept her up against his chest and hugged her tight. She squealed.

His mouth sought her cheek, and found it cool and scented and marvelously soft. He traced it down to her earlobe, nibbled at it, felt her shiver, was encouraged to try his luck with her throat, and up again to her cheek. Then, greatly daring, he turned her head with one big hand, and held her firmly so he could kiss her mouth.

Her lips were scented and sweet, gentle, innocent. He pressed his mouth softly to them, then more firmly when she did not resist. His head swirled with the delicious sensation. He turned his head and tilted it so he could find her mouth more deeply with his. Her lips parted—in protest? or in longing? and he kissed her, touched her tongue with his, held her closely, his arm lean and hard about her softness.

"Oh—Rory—" she murmured when his lips traveled

396

to her forehead, to the soft, blue-black hair swirled about her head. "Oh—Rory—darling—"

"I love you, I love you—" he whispered.

"Oh, Rory—really?"

He drew back a little. "Really," he said wildly. "Really, completely, devastatingly, thoroughly, madly—I love you, oh, Angela, you are so sweet—Do you think I am too old for you?"

"Oh, I thought you would never ask me," she sighed.

He buried his mouth against her hair, opened her coat, and put his arms inside. He was caressing the rounded swell of her breast over the silken dress when a policeman came up.

"Sorry, mister, you better move on. Take your lady somewhere else," said the cop, looking rather sympathetic, as Angela pulled herself out of Rory's embrace. He blinked at her radiant face, the lovely round face with scarlet cheeks, and scarlet mouth, and bright blue eyes.

"That's all right, we're going to be married," said Rory, happily. He tossed the man a silver dollar, unwound the reins, and they drove on, slowly, with Angela clinging to his arm. "You did say so, didn't you, love?"

"I don't remember," she said dreamily.

"Just in case, I'll repeat it. Will you marry me, right away?"

"Oh, yes, Rory, of course, darling," she said. They went back to Barbara's, found the drawing room blessedly empty, and went right back to where they had been interrupted.

There was some grumbling from John when Rory told him he wished to marry Angela. But John was tired and impatient to go off to Europe with Ellen. And the death of Sophia had shaken him badly.

"Are you sure this is what you want, Rory? She is your third cousin. Not such a risk, but nevertheless a risk. And her mother—have you talked to her mother and father?"

"I shall, sir," said Rory. "I think they like me."

"As a son-in-law?" asked John drily. "Well, let me know. I'll be gone by May, and I'll not be back until July or August."

"Good excuse to get married right away," grinned Rory. And so he arranged it. They were married within a month, just before John and Ellen departed for Europe. It was a quiet family wedding in the church the Vallettes had attended for a century.

The bride was radiant, the groom proud. Luke stood up with him, Barbara with the bride. Rodger did not come, and was not missed.

James tried to claim Barbara's attention during the reception. Luke cut him out, to Barbara's disapproval. "You're being downright rude to James," she told Luke.

"I'll do worse than that if he tries to take you away again," said Luke in a low tone, his eyes blazing. "We're having dinner together. And if you stand me up the way you did last week—"

"I had a meeting—"

"From which James drove you home at two in the morning."

"You had no right to wait around."

"My girl, you're asking for trouble."

She met his eyes, and finally turned away, flushing. "Let's keep peace, Luke," she said, at last. "I don't want trouble at Angela's wedding."

"Neither do I. So behave yourself." And he put his arm possessively through hers, and held her there at his side.

Chapter 30

The auditors discovered that about $100,000 had been paid to Rodger Courtney and James Keane over a period of two years.

Luke fumed, then finally called a meeting of the full board. Rory protested that it would be humiliating for the two men. Luke was adamant.

"They're going to have it all out in the open. With any luck, they won't be forced to pay it all back."

Rory studied the fury in Luke's face and finally nodded. "Okay, Luke. I'm behind you all the way."

The full board meeting was called. Luke sat as President; Rory was Vice-President, Henry; Treasurer. They used the large office of the company, and Luke formally welcomed them. "I hope that all of you will continue to take an interest in the operations of Vallette and Sons. This will be an open company," he said, firmly. For the first time the women had been invited. Barbara had come, and Angela with Rory, John and his wife, Arthur and his wife. Rodger came, and sat in the back sullenly, beside James.

Luke presented the leftover business quickly, then came to the present business. One of the auditors was present and read his report. There was a stillness when he finished.

Luke finally spoke, his tone chilled. "James, do you wish to account for these sums you have spent?"

"I told you, it was for Vallette and Sons." James remained seated, and his tone was rude and angry.

Caroline spoke up. "Oh, James, however did you spend so much? Was it on bribes?" Her tone was sweetly reproachful.

James colored angrily. "Ask John. He authorized it."

Luke looked toward his uncle. The older man, looking fit and tanned after his ocean voyage, nodded. "I admit I told them to go ahead and see what they could do to help our cause in Washington."

They discussed it for a while. Then Luke said, "From now on, I shall be doing the contacting in Washington. James has no further authority along that line, nor has Rodger Courtney. Any funds they draw out from Vallette and Sons must be set against their own personal accounts." He spoke dispassionately. Rodger was furious, his red face set and grim.

Luke did not give them time to argue. He went on to other business, then explained briefly the present position of Vallette and Sons. Because it was his first meeting as President, he told them what he intended to do.

He would build up the powder mills against the possibility of another war in Europe. He intended to build a new mill in Pennsylvania, which Angela's brother Owen would manage.

"Futhermore, Foster and Joshua have expressed an interest in joining Vallette and Sons when they finish college. I am advising them to go to MIT for their training, and to work with us in the summers to learn the powder trade."

He briskly outlined his plans concering the antitrust case of the federal government against Vallette and Sons. "We are watching the outcome of some cases now in court that will give us guidelines for the future behavior of our company. Rory has some ideas about going into the textile business with artificial fabrics. Rory?"

Rory got up and explained tersely what he intended to do in the way of directing some research and possible development. His new wife watched him with glowing, admiring eyes. Barbara was also listening intently, taking some notes as they spoke.

The meeting lasted over three hours. They adjourned to take coffee that afternoon in Arthur's house, the old Vallette homestead. They chattered about the old days, about Granny Moira, and about old Christophe who had founded the company more than a hundred years ago.

As John and Ellen prepared to depart, Ellen said, with pleasure, "This has been almost as nice as a Christmas reunion, Luke. We must do this again."

Barbara was giggling as she departed with her mother. Luke gave her a resigned look. The new generation of females could be serious about company business. It looked like the older generation was interested, but not as intent upon business details.

Rodger and James had not come to the coffee session. Luke went off to Washington the next week for further conferences. When he spoke with Colonel Mark Trent, he was disturbed to hear that both James and Rodger were in Washington, staying in Rodger's Washington flat.

"And I think he is conferring with some Representatives. I don't know whether it is about his own political career, or whether he and James are stirring their fingers in the Vallette pot. At any event, they are making the most of their Vallette connections," said Colonel Trent thoughtfully. "I heard someone say that they were high in the company, and that whatever they did had the appproval of the head of the company."

"I'll stop that rumor fast," said Luke furiously. He pounded his fist on Trent's table. "Damn them, I just warned them!"

Trent sighed. "Well, that's all about that. Now, about the gunpowder. We are going to need more than I told you before. The War Department is convinced that we shall be drawn into the war in Europe when it breaks out. The Mexican incident last spring is over, but we might get drawn in again, and it did use up too much ammunition."

Luke spread out the papers he had received from his lawyers. "Do you know anything about this?"

Trent picked up the papers and read them thoughtfully. "Dammit, they are really after your hide," he said, laying them down again. "Well, all I can say is I'll get my General to say a word to them privately. We can't have you ripping up the company to please the fanatics who hate business corporations, just when we need the gunpowder you can provide. I'll see what I can do, Luke."

"They say these are preliminary to a court case," said Luke, folding the papers and putting them into his briefcase. He felt very tired. He wished he could go back to the laboratory and work a fourteen-hour day—it would be more restful.

"Well, show them the books. You have just had them audited; it should all be clear and open."

Luke thought, yes, except for that $100,000 James and Rodger have been spreading around like manure. That should show someone that all was not open and aboveboard. Damn those two, anyway.

Luke was in no placid mood when he went out to Barbara's house that evening. He had showered, rested, and changed to a navy suit with a light tan tie under his high white collar. He wanted a quiet, peaceful evening with Barbara. She could be stimulating or gentle, sweet or fiery. But she could always make him forget business for a time.

He frowned when the carriage drew up and he heard music and saw lights blazing from the opened windows of the house. It was September, and a light breeze ruffled the trees and bushes. The sky was a mild blue, and stars were beginning to pierce it with brilliant sparks. Barbara was having a party.

Luke went in. The maid beamed at him, took his tall hat, and led him to the drawing room. "Mr. Luke is here, Miss Barbara," she said to the room at large.

Barbara detached herself from a group near the windows and came over. Her blue eyes sparkled, the color matching her blue-violet silk gown which slid down over her lovely, rounded figure as though it loved to caress the white skin. Her brown, curly hair was worn low, about her shoulders, the long hair turned and fastened up under the fall of shining hair. Her shoulders were bare except for a long necklace of pearls, their milky pink color matching her pink cheeks. Long earbobs of pearls swung against her face.

"Hello, Luke. I am so surprised to see you. James assured me you were working hard in the lab."

"James is often wrong," said Luke harshly, his gaze swinging to where James stood defiantly facing him. The blonde face was flushed with drink; he held a glass in one hand and a cigar in the other.

Barbara slid her bare arm into the curve of Luke's elbow. "Well, come in and make yourself comfortable," she said lightly. Then she hissed in his ear. "And don't be difficult and sullen, or I'll be angry with you. I don't want you fighting with poor James tonight. He was so humiliated by you."

"Was he? How sad." Luke came forward, accepted a drink from a young blonde person in a silvery bob and short silvery dress that revealed her slim ankles in silver stockings. Her green eyes sparkled up at him. He lingered to talk to her, concealing his fury at James and at Barbara.

Barbara returned to her other guests, circled about, made sure there were drinks and cigarettes and cigars, and drew them to a buffet set out on a long table. Luke ate mechanically, stoking himself. He had eaten nothing since the long, tiring dinner with Trent. He liked the ham sandwiches, ate two, and then ate some of the little crackers with caviar on them. After his third drink, he felt more relaxed.

The little green-eyed blonde lingered with him, obviously admiring him. It was some solace, but Luke wanted to talk to Barbara, alone. He wanted to talk to her seriously, to tell her his problems, and to be soothed by her attentions. And instead she was flitting, like a gay butterfly in her blue-violet moth wings, from one man to another, never staying long with any one.

By eleven o'clock, most of the guests had thanked Barbara for a gorgeous evening, and departed. Luke stretched out his feet to a hassock; he was quite comfortable in the large, masculine, brown chair. He accepted another drink from silver-bob, smiled at her, and asked her about her work.

"I'm a worker in the cause," said the silvery girl, confidently. "We're going to get votes for women in a year."

"I would vote for you anytime, darling," said Luke. He earned a very frosty look from Barbara.

"Oh, would you? You're really sweet."

Luke lingered, his feet up. He was quite comfortable. James glared at him, as more guests left, and Barbara looked from one to the other of the men with more than a hint of exasperation.

James sat on. Finally it was midnight, and only the two men were left of the guests. The housekeeper yawned in the corner, and Barbara finally said, "I should so like to turn in. We have a big day tomorrow."

"It was very pointed, darling," said James. And he came over, lifted her chin, kissed her, and turned to Luke. "Coming, Luke?"

"Not just yet, James," drawled Luke, still seated. He looked at James under his lowering dark brows, and the blue eyes gleamed like fire. "Oh, don't miss the papers tomorrow morning. If you think you'll sleep late, ask Rodger to run out and get them for you. You'll be interested in an item."

Barbara said, on a caught breath, "What item, Luke?"

James stood, on the verge of leaving, but curious as hell. "What are you talking about?"

"I had an interview with a reporter this afternoon. I gave him quite a long story, for which he was grateful. And then I asked him to put in something I had written out." Luke stuck his hand in his coat pocket and drew out a scribbled paper. "Want to hear?"

"Don't be tormenting, Luke," said Barbara, quite sharply for her. "Tell us or not, as you please."

"Of course—*darling*. It reads like this, 'To whom it may concern: This is to notify everyone in Washington, D.C., and the rest of this great country of ours, that one James Keane and one Rodger Courtney have no power to make any decisions regarding the company of Vallette and Sons, powder makers of the Areuse valley in Virginia. I, Luke Vallette, President of Vallette and Sons, am the only one with power to make contracts, approve the sale of stock, authorize dividends, and pay out money for services rendered. Anyone who accepts any stock or money from the said James Keane or the said Rodger Courtney may be sued by Vallette and Sons for the return of such funds. Signed, Luke Vallette, President of Vallette and Sons.' This will be in the morning papers, the reporter assured me." Luke returned the paper to his pocket.

James had turned quite white, and his hands holding his tall hat shook with rage and fear. "You cad, Luke. How dare you do such a thing. Everyone will ridicule us."

Luke stood up slowly and walked toward James. James began to back up hastily. "What do you think I meant? I am going to stop your bribery if I have to do worse than hold you up to ridicule. I told you I would not have you and Rodger playing around with the Vallette name and reputation. To say nothing of the money! And you can tell Rodger he is risking his position in the company if he persists."

James stared at him, then turned and fled. Barbara drew a deep breath. The housekeeper watched curiously.

"Oh, Luke, that was cruel—cruel and horrible," she cried. "You were terribly rude to him."

Luke stared down at her, grimly. "I won't have it, Barbara. You will not take his part. He is wrong, and well you know it. Do you want the Vallette reputation smeared with mud? Do you want someone like Rodger Courtney making deals in the name of all of us? Well, do you?"

"I think I'd best turn in, Miss Barbara," murmured the housekeeper, and scuttled past them. "You'll be coming right up, won't you?"

The other scarcely noticed her. Luke shoved the door shut after her, that was all. "Let's have this out, Barbara," he said.

She backed away from him nervously. "James says you are jealous of him—over me," she said, in a low tone. "You should not take it out on him because of—me."

Luke gave a curious smile. "Perhaps I am jealous," he said calmly. "However, I shall let nothing interfere in the way I run Vallette and Sons. We are going to run a clean and open company. Don't you realize the danger? Trustbusters are after us; they would seize eagerly on any rumors of corruption. It would prove their point—that Vallette and Sons should be broken up, that we are not worth salvaging. I have been fighting for years to keep Vallette and Sons together. Will you let a money-hungry man like Rodger and a greedy pup like James rip us apart?"

"That is not what James says," said Barbara, uncertainly, backing away further as Luke slowly approached her. "Luke, we are cousins, I value your opinion," she added hastily. "But you should talk it out—with—with James—not humiliate—and you were rude, staying on when I want to go to bed—"

He backed her up against the back of the sofa, and there she stayed, hands out to hold him off. He caught her roughly to him. The long day of work and the evening of waiting had made him furious with her as well as with James.

"Luke—" she said, muffled, against his broad chest.

His mouth was on hers, ruthlessly, hurting her for a moment before he eased up. Then his lips were teasing, pleading, and his hands moved up and down sensuously over her silk-clad body. She shivered, and yielded to his touch. She had wanted this, yet feared it. He was like a panther, prowling around and around, then pouncing—

He held her hard against his lean body, and her softness seemed to sink into him. One large hand held her hips against his, so she felt the hardness of his thighs, the leaping passion of his body against hers. His mouth sucked at hers, wildly, with desire and honey-sweetness, as his tongue flicked into her open mouth. His other hand was behind her head, holding her hair in his long fingers so she could not twist her head away from him.

His kisses were longer, and more passionate, violent, as he felt her yielding to him. He had bent her back until her body seemed about to break under the force of his passion. Her hands went up to his shoulders, clasping him to hold herself erect. One hand slid to his neck, the fingers feeling the crisp rasping of the short hairs there, the softness of his blue-black hair, so like hers.

His mouth slid over her hot cheeks, down to her bare shoulders. He nuzzled against the soft flesh of her neck until shivers went up and down her spine. No man had ever touched her like this, no one—ever—

She had not dreamed of such violent caresses, such need, such desire, drawing from her an answering passion.

His head lifted; she uttered his name. He looked down at her, the blue eyes dazed and slightly out of focus with his blind desire for her. He lifted her, and carried her over to a sofa, and dropped down with her on his lap.

He began nuzzling at her neck again, hungry for the softness and perfumed warmth of her neck and breast. His fingers went to the rounded breast; he stroked over and over again the curves there. She caught at his hand.

"Luke—don't—please—oh, Luke—please—stop—"

He finally lifted his head, caught his breath, and tried to recover. He held her closely against him. His voice, when it came, was husky and low.

"I love you, Barbara. We're going to be married."

"Luke! We can't—"

His fingers were stroking intimately the pointed nipple of her breast, swollen under his touch. "Yes, we are, darling."

"But—dad will never let us—we are cousins—you know how he feels."

"I'll convince him. I'm not—Lionel, and you are not Sophia."

His words sounded hard, implacable. She sighed, and leaned against his shoulder, turning her face wearily from his seeking lips. "We can't, Luke."

"We are second cousins only. Barbara, the important thing is that I love you madly. I think you love me also. Don't you? Do you—"

His mouth touched hers, then released it to hear her.

"Oh, Luke—"

"You love me?"

"Oh, Luke—"

"Tell me," he whispered.

"Oh, Luke, I do love you. But I'm afraid—"

"Never be afraid, darling. Love is meant to be happy, joyous. I'm going to make you the happiest woman in the world."

Drawing back, she studied his face seriously. She saw the purpose in his gaze, the firmness of his mouth that had just conquered hers, the hard leanness of his chin. Tenderly she touched that chin; he turned his head and kissed her fingers.

"You're going to marry me," he said again, with a ring of conviction.

"Oh, Luke, it is crazy—"

"Tell me you are—"

And he would not leave her that night until she had promised. In the morning light of the next day, when she wakened in her virginal bed, she wondered at herself. Had she been mad that night? Luke had literally swept her off her feet. But she felt so happy, so quietly, beautifully happy. Luke loved her, he was strong, nothing bad could ever happen to her, for she was secure in his love.

Before Luke left Washington that week, he had a ring on Barbara's left hand, a sapphire surrounded by pointed diamonds that made the whole ring sparkle with more light.

He went home to the Areuse to find he had stirred up two hornets' nests. James and Rodger had come before him, complaining bitterly to John and Arthur and Henry.

Luke went to see John, on the old man's summons. He told him frankly what he had done. He said, "James and Rodger were meddling about for two or three years. They could undo all the good I was trying to do, to convince the army men to step in and aid us in our cause against the trustbusters. One hint of any wrongdoing, the bribes given and received, and it could all come apart at the seams. Rodger is in it for the money, and maybe a step up into politics. James will do anything to spite me, especially since Barbara has promised to marry me."

The old man sighed deeply. "Luke, Luke, what have you done?" he said sadly. "Barbara is your cousin—"

"Second cousin," said Luke, and gave him a hard look. Did the old man know that Brett was James's father as well as his own?

"Of course, James's mother and your mother were sisters. He and Barbara are no relation. But he has always lived with your family, just like one of you. That is why I allowed him to escort Barbara about Washington. Nice fellow. She likes him a lot."

Luke drew a deep breath. "Uncle John, did dad tell you the truth about us?"

"The truth?" John looked blank, bewildered. He looked his age today, with trembling, pudgy hands, the brown spots larger. He sat with his legs propped up to ease his swollen feet.

"I think we had better call James in. Father said I could tell him if I wished. And I think he had best know now."

Luke felt hard and cold as he thought of how James had tried to block him at every turn. Let James have a taste of it! When he learned he was not entitled to the money from the Keane family which had eased his path everywhere—

James came, chin jutting out. "Rodger wants to come also, he is in this with me," he said, as soon as he came into the drawing room at John Vallette's home.

"Not in this," said Luke bluntly, and shut the door after him. "This is just in the family, just between the three of us. I'm going to tell you a long story, and I want you to keep your mouth shut while I tell it, and I think you'll want to keep it shut afterward also."

John said plaintively, "I don't think you need to be rude, Luke."

"I don't feel one bit polite, uncle, but I'll try," Luke said, taking a deep breath.

"I warn you, I'm going to block your attempted marriage with Barbara. I don't think cousins so close should marry," said James, furiously, his fair face flushed again. He sat down opposite John, his underlip stuck out firmly.

Luke gave him a thoughtful look. "Best hear my story before you make rash statements, James," he said ironically.

He paced up and down the room as he spoke. John leaned forward incredulously as Luke went on and on.

He told them about Christophe's hunting trip, and how he had returned with a pregnant bride, Moira, but that the baby of that marriage was not Christophe's, not the first baby.

"My great-grandfather was not Christophe Vallette," he said. "He was an Indian chief, of the Cherokee tribe, known as Red Hawk. Christophe traced him later. He was moved out to Oklahoma, where he lived for a good many years with my many half-relations," said Luke ironically.

"Then—then you are not a Vallette," gasped James, with triumph. "You have no right here!"

"Guess again. Christophe adopted the baby, named Tristan. He had every right under the law. And Tristan put his brains and sweat into the works. He was a great powder man, and he ran the company along with Antoine, John's father."

"Uncle Tristan was half-Cherokee?" asked John, rubbing his head. "Then that accounts for so much— the portraits—the likeness—oh, if I had known—"

"Tristan knew. Christophe told him, or Moira did. Someone. Granny Moira told Brett, my father, and left it up to him whether he ever told anyone else. He told only me, because I was so like him. Arthur and Henry and the others, most of them resembled mother," said Luke, thoughtfully. "Though I can see something of Brett in Henry at times, and certainly in Caroline."

"But what has this to do with me, except it proves you have no right to run Vallette and Sons," said James, excitedly.

John gave him an ironic look. "Guess again, my lad. Luke has inherited more than Indian blood. He inherited the temper and strength of his fathers and mothers. And their stock. He owns the stock he needs to run Vallette and Sons, and he has the necessary knowledge of gunpowder making. Go on, Luke, I think you have more to say."

Luke had been listening with a half-smile on his face, watching James and his fair face. "Yes, more. This part you won't like, James. Father told me more. It seems that your mother, Julia Vining Keane, was a very attractive woman. Brett married her pretty young sister, Cecilia, my mother. But Julia kept chasing after him. She married Frederick Keane, but could have no children by him. So—she had an affair with father—"

James leapt up, his face greenish-white. "My God, you will not slander my mother."

"Listen to me, James. It is the truth," said Luke, more gently. "Father said that Julia swore to him on her deathbed that it was true. He had guessed—he had relations with her about the time mother was carrying Caroline. And you were born about that time also, just a few months later. Julia would not admit it when he confronted her wtih it. Later on, when she was dying, she told him the truth. Frederick probably guessed it. He left you with us—"

"Oh, God, will you shut up? You have got to be lying. You're jealous of me—Barbara favors me—you're jealous—"

"No, it is not a lie. If you had kept straight, I would not have told you," said Luke, sternly. "I wanted you to know. Because, you see, if your straightlaced Keane relations ever find out the truth—which some of them guessed, by the way—they would go to court and cut you off—and try to take away the money and stock your father Frederick left you. He knew, probably. He may have left some evidence—"

"You're just jealous of me," said James, blindly, groping, holding onto the back of a chair. He turned to

411

John appealingly. "He's jealous of me. Why, I'm not a Vallette!"

"Neither was Brett Vallette, except by virtue of his father's adoption," said Luke, gently. "You resemble your mother, not Frederick Keane. And I resemble my father, descended from an Irish girl and an Indian chief. Welcome, my half-brother, to the illegitimate Vallette clan!"

James gave a choked cry and sank into a chair, his face in his hands. His shoulders heaved. Luke surveyed him dispassionately, then turned to John.

"You swear this is true, Luke?" asked John, pulling at his lower lip.

"I swear it is all true, John. But I think we should keep it to ourselves," said Luke. "I don't care who knows about it, but I think James cares. And Arthur would care, and bitterly resent it, as would some of the others."

John nodded wearily.

"The point is," Luke added, "James has no more right to marry Barbara than I do, if you consider second cousins. For we are equally related to her. And we are related to her only through Granny Moira, not through the Vallettes. It is not much of a risk, I think, John. Do I win your consent to our marriage?"

"Oh, God, you—you utter cad," James cried out, and stormed away, slamming the great door after him. Luke waited until the echo had died away before repeating his question.

"You are a tough one, Luke," said John, shaking his head. "All right, I consent. And God help us all. I think you will rule with more of an iron hand than I did."

Luke held out his hand, with a ghost of a smile on his hard face. John shook Luke's hand. "Are you going to tell Barbara the whole story?" he asked, as he rang for a servant to bring sherry.

"That depends partly on James. I'll see if he spills the story," said Luke, thoughtfully. "Meantime, I want the site up on the hill behind Arthur's house, John. Who owns it now?"

"Well—up on the hill, you say? I think it is common Vallette property. You want to build there?"

Luke grinned, relaxing into the big chair, his lean body stretched out like a lazy panther after the kill. "I'm going to build Barbara a big new house, just what she designed."

He arranged to take over the property within a week, and had workmen digging ground before the deal had gone through. He had the plans made out by a good architect, and hoped to have the roof on by Christmas. It would be just as he and Barbara had planned it, with a round tower on the top and a beautiful view over the Areuse.

They would entertain, for she did it beautifully. They would bring back paintings from New York and Europe, rugs from the Orient, and ivory and jade from China and India. And they would have room for the big family he wanted. Barbara was fond of children, she would be a good mother, and he meant to keep her too busy to get into the mischief she could easily find.

Barbara was a lively, spirited, healthy young woman, with more ideas in her young brain than her father had been able to understand. Luke meant to understand her, love her, adore her, and keep her within his arms, sheltered and protected. She was too reckless for her own good.

With a young family growing up around her, with much work to do on the Areuse, with the workingmen's families in her care, and all the good works around that she could find time to do, she would forget about Washington and the outside world. Someone else, thought Luke, could fight for women's suffrage and go to prison for it. He would not endure to have Barbara go through that.

So he made his plans, and kept a wary eye on James and Rodger, now back in the powder mills. They were both sullen and brooding. They would act someday, probably against him. He meant to stay prepared.

Chapter 31

Barbara and Luke were married in March of 1912. The house was completed on the outside. Rory promised to keep an eye on the workmen while the newlyweds honeymooned.

And Angela promised to go on with furnishing the interior. She and Barbara had held long conferences on the color schemes and the types of furniture, some of which had been ordered. Angela had worked out a floor plan, room by room, and would see to the work while they were gone.

"No problem," said Angela, radiantly. "This will be a life saver for me. I adore Rory's dad and mother; they gave us a choice of rooms, and are terribly considerate. But there is nothing for me to do there!"

She was already pregnant. Soon she would have plenty to do, Rory reminded her, and she smiled. "I know. But I want to fuss with the curtains and draperies, Rory, and change the furniture around. And in your home, there is nothing to change. It is quite perfect!"

He had offered to build her a new house. But Angela, mindful of Rory's wistful parents, had refused. They would have that mansion eventually for their own. Meantime, she could ease the path of her mother- and father-in-law.

Before he left, Luke sent James out to Texas and Rodger to Missouri to see to work there. "Keep them apart, and out of mischief," he told Rory grimly. "I gave Rodger the job of organizing a whole new mill.

That should keep him busy. If you have any trouble, write to me in Rome. I think we'll end up there for a time."

"For God's sake, Luke, you'll be on your honeymoon. Give Barbara your whole attention," Rory teased him.

"Don't worry about that!"

Barbara and Luke spent a week in New York, partly taken up visiting relatives there. They did not feel completely alone until they boarded the ship to France. They paced the deck, arm in arm, sat in the bar, idly made a few friends, but spent most of the time together. Luke was weary; there were new lines around his mouth, and a new network of crinkles around his deep blue eyes. Barbara often felt protective toward him. This past year had been especially hard for him, fighting the elders, taking over the company, organizing everything.

They danced a while one evening and retired early. Luke wanted some sleep, he said. Barbara found her pretty new violet nightdress and brushed her hair into two braids before sliding into her single bed near the windows of the luxurious cabin.

Luke promptly slid from his single bed over to hers. She caught her breath. She was not by any means accustomed to the sight of the bare brown chest bent over her, of the large hands reaching to stroke her. She wriggled, and finally sat up.

"Luke, you are not going to rip this nightdress, too! That makes three you have torn. I won't have a single one left by the time we get to Paris."

"I'll buy you a new one," he said, reaching out to pull her down again. "A slinky black number with lace in all the right places."

"Luke!" She was blushing vividly in the dim light of the windows opened to their private section of the first-class deck. "Please—Luke—"

"Okay, take it off," he said, and lay back with resignation as she slid from bed. She removed the nightdress and came back to sit on the edge of the bed. He leaned over and began to trace a lazy, purposeful line with his lips down her spine to her rounded hips. "Come here, honey—you're too far away."

She settled into his long, hard arms. He bent over her and his mouth nibbled at her soft shoulder, down her slim arm to her elbow, then over to her waist, and up to her round breast. He settled against her breast, nibbling at the nipple which had risen up, pink and taut, to his lips. She stroked her hands over his lean, muscular shoulders, down his hard back, feeling him, learning him as he learned her.

"Luke?"

"Ummm?"

"Have you had—lots of women?"

He jerked up his head and gazed down at her in the dimness. "What a hell of a question," he said, with a laugh in his voice. "Are you jealous?"

"Well, no," she said, not very truthfully. "I just wondered."

"Well, sorry to disappoint you." He drew her to him and lay back, caressing her soft skin with his rough fingers. How very soft she was, softer than silk velvet. "I didn't play around much. I was too busy working. I spent sometimes fourteen, sixteen hours in the lab. When you do that, you don't have much time for playing around."

"Really?"

She sounded skeptical. "Really, honey," he said firmly. "Oh, I've had a few girls, enough to know my way around. But I never went in for it. For one thing, I am too vulnerable to blackmail. Any wealthy man is. It pays to be careful."

She was silent.

"Disappointed?" he asked softly, tickling her round chin.

She shook her head. "Surprised, I guess. Luke—why didn't you, really?"

"Guess I wanted to wait for you, darling," he said, simply. "I want love and sex together, and that is a rare combination. Then I found it, in you. No other woman mattered."

"Oh, Luke." She turned impulsively and bent over him as he lay back. Her long braids swung onto his hard chest. He stroked his hand lazily over one long braid. "I do love you. I always will. I can't believe you really love me—you could have had anyone."

"You flatter me. Who would put up with my tempers and tantrums? Who else can talk to me intelligently about the powder business, and listen while I rave about the corruption in Washington? You know, honey, years ago, I read something—"

"What?" She cuddled down against him, loving this aspect of their relationship. When he would confide in her his real thoughts, murmuring in her ear, holding her gently, really talking to her. "Tell me."

"I read that some of the ancients believed that on birth, a soul is parted into two different halves. One searches the world for the other half of himself, the part that will fit perfectly into his half, to make one soul again. Until he finds it, he is incomplete. If he tries to mate with the wrong half, he is forever rasped and irritated by the ill-fitting mating. But we two, Barbara, we met and became one whole soul. I truly believe that. You are the one I was destined to find, to complete myself, as I complete you." He drew a deep breath. Would she laugh, or mock him? Surely not, not if she was the way he believed.

She was silent. He traced her face tentatively with his fingers, and was surprised to find tears on her eyelashes.

"Darling—crying?"

"Oh, I am so happy, Luke. I am so happy. That is the most beautiful thing you could have said to me. I love you so much."

She clasped him, and they began to make love, and it was deeper and more passionate than it had ever been. They fell asleep in each other's arms.

The ocean voyage was long, but they were content, together, aloof from the world. No mail reached them, no telegrams. No message awaited them when they reached the impressive hotel in Paris where Luke had made reservations for them.

They wandered through the streets of Paris, hands clasped, looking in shop windows, taking a few tours, gazing upward at the spires of Notre Dame, idling along the Left Bank, and lounging in small restaurants with red-checkered tablecloths and the most heavenly food they had ever eaten. They drank bubbling white wine in the shadow of the Eiffel Tower, often ate fish freshly caught, and developed a special fondness for a spinach dish creamed and made unrecognizable and delicious.

Finally, after two weeks of touring and walking, and talking, and some shopping, they went on. Barbara had to protest to keep Luke from buying everything she admired, but he did purchase a set of sapphires from a jeweler and some alluring, see-through black night-dresses, as he had threatened to do. The fragrance of the expensive French perfume Luke bought her subtly filled their rooms. And they laughed like two children when she modeled some brief underclothes for him.

They took a train down to the Italian Riviera, lingering for a week on the warming beaches in the spring sunshine. Then they went on to Milan, toured it thoroughly, then journeyed down to Venice and admired that aging courtesan of a city. Then they went on to Florence.

"Oh, I love it," breathed Barbara on their first evening's stroll. "These high walls, the soft, seashell coloring of the Tower of Giotto, sitting in an outdoor café in the evening, the smell of coffee, the beautiful violets from Parma—"

"Want to stay for a while?" Luke asked, holding her arm closer to his as they strolled along the narrow, cobblestoned streets. "We have all the time in the world."

"We said we would wait for mail in Rome—" She hesitated, visibly reluctant.

"We'll wait and see." Luke wrote from Florence and told Rory where they were. Barbara enclosed a note for Angela and her mother and father. That duty done, they went on forgetting the world.

The treasures in the Uffizi and the Pitti held their rapt attention. In a search of the back rooms of antique shops, they found some old marble and alabaster sculpture. Luke bought the ones they liked and had them shipped home. He did the same when Barbara chose some deep-hued paintings, a portrait of a medieval lady, a gay of a fiestas, a tender Madonna and Child, a subtle scene of an Italian cavalier with his lady, and a musician in austere colors and subdued lighting.

April in Florence was heavenly. The sky was a deep purple at night, and dotted with stars, and the whole city was enlivened wtih mellow laughter and singing in the streets until midnight. At night they slept in each other's arms, in a wide, deep featherbed, and wakened each morning to the sound of more singing as a chambermaid brought them coffee in bed on a silver tray.

It rained; the skies opened up and poured. But still they enjoyed it, sometimes splashing around, running from shop door to hotel door to café door. Sometimes they sat in a café watching the rain stream down the windows facing the piazza, enjoying the sight of the elderly Italians gravely playing chess in the corner, puffing on their pipes and arguing fiercely about some long-ago war. They drank the creamy-white coffee, and ate lavishly of the crisp rolls and butter and jam.

Barbara bought an Italian costume—a long, red skirt and a green and white embroidered blouse—and wore them along with a flower in her hair. Luke refused to wear a costume, but did manage to add a red cummerbund to his smart black silk suit when they went out at night.

They peered into dim old churches, venturing in after services and wandering about the faded walls, studying the frescoes to make out the figures of Christ, fishermen, the Madonna, Mary Magdalene. When paid a coin, the custodian would follow them about with a branch of candlesticks, hold up the light, and recite solemnly in Italian what the scene depicted. Luke knew a little Latin, and sometimes he could understand and translate what the man said.

419

They had no word from home. When Barbara saw that Luke began to become restless and frown, she suggested they move on to Rome, and he agreed at once.

"This has been great, but we might have mail there," he said. Reluctantly, she packed, with the help of the friendly chambermaid, and they moved on.

Rome was big, nosiy, overwhelming. Luke went down to Cook's, where the American mail was supposed to arrive, and Barbara waited for him in a café nearby. She ordered her favorite coffee, proud that she could make herself understood in Italian. In the sunlight, shaded by a big umbrella, wearing the blue and white dress she had bought in Paris, she felt quite smart and cosmopolitan. The Italian men thought so also, pausing nearby to make complimentary sucking sounds with their teeth and tongues. She felt rather embarrassed by the time Luke returned to her. He gave the men a comprehensive scowl, and they scattered, lifting their hats.

"Can't leave you a minute," he growled, sitting down opposite her. "No wonder, you look so beautiful," he said more softly, and put three letters into her hand. He was already tearing open a thick envelope with the Vallette letterhead on it.

Barbara smiled at him and nodded to the waiter who brought fresh hot coffee. She poured some for Luke before opening her first letter, from her mother. Luke was deeply absorbed in the sheets before him, scanning them rapidly.

Barbara smiled over her mother's letter. It was so typical of her; she rambled from one topic to another without much sequence. She had missed Barbara immensely. Several letters to Barbara from Washington concerning the movement had arrived: when was she coming back to work? Angela had raved about the furnishings. The sofa and chairs were *dear*. Would Barbara like a piano for a wedding gift, John wanted to know, and what kind? Dear Lionel had come to dinner with Rory; he seemed so absentminded, he worked very hard, and his socks did not match.

Barbara sighed and smiled over the letter, folded it, and took out Angela's letter. Luke was still absorbed, going over the lines with fierce concentration.

Angela was more to the point. The house was coming along beautifully. The beds and dressers had arrived and been set in place. Rory and Angela had bought sheets and blankets—she did hope Barbara would like them. Angela had heard of a couple who wanted work, highly recommended; would Barbara like a butler and cook installed? Enclosed were some fragments of velvet; would Barbara like to choose now what she wanted for draperies in the large drawing room, or would she rather wait until she returned?

By the time Barbara was opening the third letter, from one of her co-workers in the women's suffrage movement, she was beginning to worry about Luke—he was scowling so, and tossing the pages about with an impatient hand. She read quickly, then laid her letters aside.

"What is it, Luke?" she asked quietly, when he had finally set down the thick sheaf of papers.

"Trouble, I think, Barbara." He picked up the coffee cup, and drained it impatiently. The waiter hastened to fill his cup again. Luke gazed out at the bright, sunny, Roman May day, with the crowds hurrying here and there on their lunch breaks which stretched out for three hours. Flower vendors paused at their table; Luke shook his head and they went on.

"Can you tell me?"

His gaze came back to her. "Of course, Barbara. I was just trying to plan what to do. The army contract work has slowed up; we are six weeks behind in supplying gunpowder to them. And I had promised solemnly we would keep to the schedule." His tone was savage; he ruffled his hair with a hard hand.

She caught her breath. "Why are they behind schedule?"

"Rory found that there was some misunderstanding in the Pennsylvania mills. Some orders got botched up. Bad paperwork, I guess. Henry is trying to straighten it

421

out—he went up two weeks ago to examine their books. But dammit, that's not the problem. He should get after them to increase the supply, not worry until later how it happened."

Luke seemed to find relief in talking it out. He went on and on, referring to Rory's letter as he went.

Finally Luke calmed down. He turned to Barbara's letters. "What news do you have?"

She told him lightly, concluding, "Angela wants to know about details on the curtains and draperies. I think maybe we ought to get back and look after business, don't you, Luke?"

The relief in his look rewarded her. "I meant for us to stay on here in Europe for another month or two," he said.

"I know, darling. But we both want to get home, don't we? I adored Florence, but we must go back sometime. We could stay for years without seeing it all."

Luke was already planning quickly. "I'll see to a couple of tours in a private carriage with a guide. We should see Rome. Over at Cook's, I'll see if we can get a ship from Naples early next week. That will give us time to see Naples a bit, then get on our way."

The honeymoon was over, she thought regretfully. Luke was claimed again by his work. But she would not have him any other way—hard, responsible, worried about Vallette and Sons for them all. He was mature, tough, the man she wanted, the man she had, the man who was now part of her, in her fiber and under her skin.

They sailed early the next week from Naples and enjoyed the long, slow voyage home. They arrived in Washington in early June, and were home two days later. The house was not completely furnished, but it was inhabitable. The excellent servant couple had been hired and were firmly in command.

Rory met them at the railroad station with a carriage, and Barbara sat silently while he and Luke talked busi-

422

ness rapidly from the time they met. Luke turned once, apologetically.

"Darling, I am sorry—"

She shook her head. "Why don't we let you off at the works, and I'll go on home?"

"You don't mind?" His eyes expressed his gratitude. She smiled back at him.

"Just so you come home in reasonable time for dinner," she said gaily.

He laughed with Rory. "Just like a wife," said Rory. "Angela is always after me to keep some decent hours—"

"How is she?"

"Fine, looking forward to the baby. Healthy as can be, she says," he told them proudly, his face glowing.

Barbara went on to the house after Rory and Luke stopped off at the mills. By the time Luke came home that night, she had unpacked some of their clothes and become acquainted with the new cook and butler. The cook had a cousin who needed a job; she would make an excellent maid, the woman assured Barbara—an Irish girl, cheerful and hardworking, with nine younger brothers and sisters. Barbara told her to have the girl come up the next day.

The next day, Luke spent all day in the mills. He came home tired, grimy, scarcely speaking. Barbara laid out his clothes, rather troubled.

"Darling, do you feel up to going over to dad's tonight? I told mother we would come, but if you—"

He straightened his sagging shoulders and passed his hand over his face. "No, I need to see John anyway. A shower and rest will fix me up."

It worried her that already he was so tired. But that evening she found out why. Luke had been firing off telegrams to Henry, to James, and to Rodger, with orders to speed up production of black powder in all their mills. He had gone over papers with Rory and examined the results of experiments with Lionel without pausing for lunch or coffee.

She dressed in one of her pretty new Parisian gowns—for Angela and her mother's benefit, she admitted. She thought the men would scarcely notice them, and she was right, although as they were dressing her gown of pale blue silk trimmed with lace received a nod of approval from Luke. "You look nice, darling. How about the sapphires?"

She fastened them on, with a little grin.

He did notice that, peering over her shoulder at the mirror in order to fasten his high white collar and thin blue necktie. "Smiling, love?"

"I had a bet with myself that you wouldn't even notice what I had on!"

He ducked down and pressed a kiss where the lace of the dress met the creamy white of her throat. "Asking for trouble, are you, love?" he murmured. "Don't count on my being so tired that I won't give it to you."

And he laughed at her blush. They took the carriage over to John's place, as it was still called, though Rory had taken over much of the management of the mansion. Angela met them at the door, radiant and blooming in her advanced pregnancy.

"Oh, how lovely to see you. Darlings, do come in. How was Paris? Didn't you just love Italy?"

Dinner was a happy occasion. They told of their travels. Barbara promised to give a special showing of her gowns for her mother and Angela. The men soon became absorbed in their own conversation. Barbara was surprised at what Luke was saying.

"Talk in Paris was of coming war," he said. "They hope they can keep out the Germans. I don't share their hope. And in Italy, the men I spoke to were worried about the Balkans. They feel the trouble will ignite there."

The women fell silent as the men talked war. Luke was drinking rather heavily for him, four glasses of wine with the meal, and brandy afterward with his heavy black cigars. The ladies talked in Ellen's sitting room for a little, then Barbara said, "I want to hear what the men are saying, mother."

"But darling, the men are talking business," Ellen protested mildly. Barbara insisted. The women drifted downstairs, pausing to admire a painting Angela had added to the hall collection, then entered the drawing room.

The air was blue with smoke. John looked shocked to see them, but Rory stood up to show them to chairs. "Getting bored, darling?" he asked Angela lightly.

Luke gave Barbara a wink and brought her a glass of sherry. Then they went on with their talk. It was of the contracts not completed, the work that needed to be done. They would need to hire more men, training them as they worked.

"No, I can't see opening another mill at this time," said Luke, decisively. "We don't have time to train men for another whole operation. We must expand the mills we have—additional buildings, more manpower. What about the Missouri plant? What do you hear?"

Barbara listened in silence, but she understood what they said. She also realized that Luke was grasping the reins of the company with a firm hold, and that John was giving them up. Rory headed the financial part of the firm, but he deferred to Luke.

Luke worked like a demon during the next weeks. He spurred on the Areuse mills, added more men, and sent wires across the country urging on the others. Under his leadership, the mills turned out more thousands of barrels of powder, and the contract work began catching up with the schedules. He paid for it in long, hard days that left weary circles under his eyes. He fell asleep as soon as he lay down in the large bed at night.

Barbara accepted all this with resignation. She had known all along that he drove himself harder than any of his men. But when he calmly announced at breakfast one morning that he was setting off for Washington that day, she rebelled.

"Luke, you're not."

"Yes, I have to, honey. Business." He drank his coffee, and shot back his cuff to glance at his watch.

"But you know I wanted to go to Washington. I could be packed and ready—"

He turned to her, with understanding showing in his eyes. "Look, honey. I don't want you to go. I know you want to get involved in the movement again, but I don't want it. If I take you to Washington with me, you'll be stuffing envelopes, or writing passionate declarations, or even giving speeches. Send them money, all you wish, and let them hire help. But I don't want you personally involved."

"Luke!" Her mouth was trembling; she covered it with her napkin. She felt hurt to the core.

"We can't discuss it now—I'll be late. But I need you here, honey, more than anybody else in the world needs you. Take my word for it, and help me. Knowing you are here, safe, keeping the home fires warm for me—giving me aid and comfort when I stagger home—" His mouth twisted a little. "Sounds like corn, but I mean it. I need you here, my darling."

He bent over her, gave her a hard kiss, and was gone. She felt a little better, thinking over his words. But a little sting of resentment was still there. And she found it difficult to settle down to hemming curtains and showing the maid how she wanted the velvet draperies hung.

She had great pride in her new home. It would be comfortable as well as a beautiful showplace for entertaining. The drawing room was arranged in conversational sets of sofas and chairs; the mantlepiece was of marble from Greece, veined with gold. They had set the lovely pieces of sculpture from Italy about on tall, greenish marble stands from Vermont. Paintings hung in the hallway, in the drawing rooms, and in the bedrooms that were finished. There was much yet to be done, and Angela helped every day. Barbara was not lonely. Yet—had Luke ever really told her he was cutting her off from the women's suffrage movement?

In Washington, Luke left his suitcase at the Vallette suite, and drove at once to Mark Trent's home. The

Colonel was not at home yet; but Lucille let Luke in and chatted politely with him until her husband arrived.

"We are all so curious to meet your new bride—I hear she is beautiful, Luke."

"She is that, Lucille. Beautiful inside and out, a real gem," he said with a smile. Mark came in, shed his coat with relief, and held out his hand.

"Good to see you. I had hoped you would come at once."

The men shook hands. Mark turned to Lucille. "Darling, would you send sandwiches to my study? We need to talk in private—sorry, darling."

Lucille grimaced, but agreed, and went off to give the orders. In the study, Luke sat down, accepted a cigar, and lit up.

"You sounded urgent."

"It's a bad situation. Delicate. I don't know how to start." Mark sounded unusually upset. Someone tapped at the door; he let in the butler with the tray of sandwiches and glasses of wine. "Oh—bring us a big pot of coffee, will you?"

"Yes, sir."

The door closed, and Mark paced up and down. "Luke, I can't say this more discreetly. If I'm wrong, no one will be more relieved than I am."

"Go ahead."

"Are you experimenting with a smokeless powder for high-powered rifles?"

Luke caught his breath. He laid the cigar aside carefully. He looked at Mark and nodded. "Yes. And I thought I was the only person in the world who knew about it," he said, with deadly softness. "The experiments are not complete. I haven't had time to work on it for months."

"God." Mark rubbed his head frantically. He waited while the butler brought in a pot of coffee and two cups and withdrew again. Mark poured out the coffee. Neither man had touched the food.

"How did you hear?" asked Luke. He felt curiously

cold, as though something had stopped inside him. His pet project, his work of years—

Mark finally sat down and shoved the tray of sandwiches toward Luke. "A colleague of mine was approached by a man from a rival company of yours," he began cautiously. "The man had a formula for the smokeless powder. But my colleague became suspicious when he offered to sell the formula, to be made up by any company he wished. Usually a gunpowder factory wants to get the contract to make up the powder themselves. But the offer was for half a million dollars, outright."

"Go on."

"Then the man could not explain what experiments had been conducted. He could not tell him if or when the army could come and watch tests. My colleague knew I had some dealings with gunpowder, especially with Vallette and Sons, and so he approached me with the story, in confidence. He said he didn't know whether he had a tremendous bargain or a pig in a poke."

"A pig, I would say. The experiments are not completed in the laboratory. I haven't figured out anything about mass production," said Luke thoughtfully. "I set the stuff aside, put the papers away in the safe in the laboratory office, and forgot it for a time. I had no time to work on it. It needs refining—the proportions are not quite right yet."

"Could you recite your most recent proportions to me now?" Mark reached into his pocket, drew out an envelope, and took a paper from it. He looked down at the paper as Luke recited the figures and chemicals. He nodded. "Right. That's what we have here. Peculiar, isn't it?"

"Damn strange." Luke finally reached for a sandwich, though his stomach was churning. "Someone obviously has unauthorized access to the safe and is trying to sell our industrial secrets. I wonder what else is missing?"

"What do you want me to do about this?"

Luke's chin hardened, his eyes blazed. "Give me the paper. Tell your colleague that you have heard it is stolen goods, and that the army is not interested. I'll deal with it at my end."

"I bet you will." Mark looked much more cheerful. They talked on for a time about it. "Do you think you would have time to work on it, refine it, work out production? When war comes—"

Luke promised to do what he could. He went back to the Areuse after three days of fruitless conferences with two senators about court cases.

Luke was determined to find out who was stealing material from the company safe. So far as he knew, only a few company officers had access to the safe in the laboratory. And he had his guess about who had done this. But he had to have proof.

Barbara greeted him cheerfully. He was glad for that, remembering how they had parted. He had bought her a string of pearls and some new earbobs for her small ears.

"Consolation gift?" she asked drily, with a pert grin.

"Cheeky girl," he said, and kissed her hard. "Love me?"

"I don't know why, but I do—like mad," she said.

She had her own secrets to hide. James was home from Texas and had come over, knowing that Luke had gone to Washington. He had been sullen and disagreeable. She had wanted to be a cheerful, undemanding friend with him, but he would have none of it. He had wandered about the first floor of the new mansion on the hill, sneering at the paintings, the velvet draperies, the sculpture.

"Is this going to console you for not being able to call your soul your own, Barbara?" he demanded. "Luke won't let you do what you want, you know. Has he put his foot down yet about your women's suffrage work?"

"I don't think that is any concern of yours, James," she said coldly.

"That means he has. I could have warned you. Luke

has to be top boss of everything, including his wife. His wife, his company, his house, his possessions. God, I am sick of him."

"You always were sick of him, as I recall, James," she said, with fake cheer. "You have been rivals since you were children."

"You'll get tired of him too, Barbara," James warned. "Has he told you about his flat in Montgomery, and about the women he takes there? And of course, he doesn't want you with him in Washington."

"Don't be nasty, James," said Barbara, calmly. "How about some coffee?"

She could smell the wine on his breath. All she had to do was ring for the butler, so she was not afraid of James. But she did worry about the nasty look in his eyes, and the sneer in his voice.

She thought, the higher a man climbs, the more enemies there are waiting and hoping for him to fall. Her loyalties were to Luke. She would not bother him about this. She cajoled James, made him laugh a little, and sent him away. She would not tell Luke—he would be furious. And he had enough worries on his mind.

Chapter 32

Angela's son was born in October of 1912. Rory was proud and happy. But even his happiness could not exceed that of his father. John Vallette whipped out pictures of the baby boy at any excuse. There was no grandfather so proud as he was.

The birth was not difficult, though Angela confided wryly to Barbara, "It does seem difficult at the time, let me tell you, Barbara. There is no pain like it. But it is worth it all, every scrap, when you first see the little mite of a baby you have made with the man you love."

Barbara kissed her cheek. "I can hardly wait until I have one," she said, "and Luke wants one also. Though he is so darn busy and tired, I wonder how long it will be."

Angela chuckled, rocking the baby in her arms. "You'll find a way, love. I did. Rory might be busy, but the nights are mine."

Barbara grimaced. Luke was still so furiously busy that he often did not come home for lunch and was late for dinner. If she planned entertainment, she notified him in advance, left a note for him on the breakfast table, and told Peter in the laboratory to remind Luke again at five o'clock. Sometimes even then he was the last guest to arrive for dinner.

Arthur had not recovered from the death of Sophia. He rarely came to the works. He finally decided to purchase a vacation home in Miami, and he and his wife

Hazel went down for the winter, leaving Lionel alone in the house that had been the old Vallette homestead.

"I feel sorry for Lionel," Luke told Barbara. "He isn't eating properly. The servants stay in their quarters, and no one cares whether he eats or not. I think he goes off to his room and paints most of the night."

"He needs someone to keep an eye on him." Barbara was thoughtful. "Luke?"

"Ummm?"

"What about the west wing of our house? The second floor has half a dozen bedrooms and that suite of rooms. We won't need it for years, except for guests. Couldn't Lionel—"

"Darling, that's a lovely thought. Are you sure you wouldn't mind having someone else about?"

"He is so quiet, we shall scarcely know he is here," said Barbara frankly. "I just hope I can get him to meet our guests, then perhaps he'll get interested in some girl."

"You can try." Luke shook his head. "I don't think Lionel even knows it when we are about, much less a pretty girl."

"He is in a daze all the time. Is he like that at work?"

"Oh, absorbed in his job, he is a wiz."

Luke approached Lionel about the move. Lionel looked surprised, momentarily coming out of his daze. "But you don't want me hanging about the house, Luke," he said gravely. "You and Barbara are just married—"

"Nonsense. The house is huge. Barbara and I thought you would enjoy the suite in the west wing. Why don't you come up and look it over?"

Lionel came, looked at the grand rooms, the suite of bedroom, sitting room, and bath, and shook his head in wonder. "There is four times the space I have," he said, "and the light will be great for painting. Are you sure—"

"You only have to promise to come and join us for dinner, Lionel," said Barbara firmly. "Luke here is bad enough, deserting me and leaving me to entertain the company half the evening. Maybe you can reform him."

432

Luke laughed, and a sort of wry smile tipped the corner of Lionel's mouth. "You want me to change Luke?" he asked. "Ask me to move an iron mountain."

But he was glad to move in. He had been more and more uncomfortable living with Arthur and his wife. He was a constant, galling reminder to them of Sophia. And he could not sit in the drawing room in the evening without gazing at the portrait of Sophia. He felt numb inside emotionally, as he had since her death. But he knew they ached also.

He moved in on a gray November day and set up his easel and drawing stand near the north windows at the end of the west wing. He felt distant from the others in the house, yet he could join them anytime. Barbara had thoughtfully left a strip of bare boards near the windows so that he could paint and not worry about drips. The rest of the drawing room floor was covered with a rare Persian carpet, and the furniture was new and comfortable. A soft, gray-green sofa faced the fireplace, and was flanked by two large armchairs in deeper green with gold cushions.

He set up the paintings he had framed, and felt at home for the first time in years. When he went to bed that night in the vast four-poster, he felt comfortable and warm. Barbara and Luke had been so welcoming, as though he had done them a favor to move in. Perhaps he might be godfather to one of their children, he thought, as he lay there, wooing sleep.

He would never have children of his own. The woman he loved was dead. He could not endure even to touch another girl. They did not understand, Barbara and Luke, talking as they did about introducing him to girls. They did not realize how he flinched from the thought of someone else. Sophia had his heart, and he had hers. It was all he wanted. Someday he would join her in death, and until then he would work, and paint, getting through the days and nights somehow. In the life after death, no one could part them.

As he did every night, he took the small miniature from his pocket before retiring and set it beside him on

433

a small night table. There he could gaze at Sophia's gentle brown eyes, study the soft curls about her throat, the curve of her neck beside the white lace, and the hint of the blue gown she wore. She went with him everywhere; sometimes he talked to her when no one was about. How could they believe he was alone? Sophia was always with him now.

Luke sent Lionel out to Texas after Christmas, to study the powder there on which they had had complaints. Lionel was glad to get away. Christmas and New Year's, with the family visits, the gaiety, the remembrance of times past, were always painful to him. He took his sketch pad, and traveled slowly. He took the train to Dallas, hired a horse, and rode for miles before turning up at the powder mills.

He slept alone at night under the stars, listening to the chomping of his horse on the thin grass nearby, or to the wailing of a dingo, or a coyote as the Americans called them. He mused briefly about the Australian book he had been reading. He might go to Australia one day; the Outback was something like this, but it was even wilder and more untamed.

He carried a gun as protection against snakes. He did not worry about bands of Indians from the reservations or the wild "badmen" of the West. If he were killed— he shrugged. He carried little in coin, only enough for his needs along the way. Vallette's name was good for credit anywhere.

He was untroubled, one day, when a band of outlaws came up out of the brush and sat their horses around him curiously. He had set up a small portable easel on the sagebrush, and was sketching out a scene of a waterhole with a couple of cows about and the gaunt outline of a cactus nearby.

"Howdy," said one of the men finally. They did not wear guns sticking out of holsters, but Lionel knew the guns were there, under the opened coats. And rifles stuck out from their saddles.

"Howdy. Get down and I'll fix something to eat as

soon as I'm done here," said Lionel, in his calm Virginia drawl. He went on sketching.

The men looked at each other, and finally slid down. This tenderfoot was a different species, either very cool or very stupid. They looked around his small camp, and a tall man picked up the unloaded rifle leaning against his sleeping bag.

"Nice weapon," said the tall man.

"Thank you. It's a new one—we're testing the gunpowder in our works," said Lionel, finally laying down his charcoal. "Want me to show you our new powder?"

The men stared at him. "What are you talking about?"

"I'm from Vallette and Sons. My name is Lionel Vallette. We make gunpowder. I brought some of our new stuff with me. The cartridges are specially made. If you'd like to set up a target, I'll show you how straight the bullets can shoot."

One man pushed back his wide sombrero and scratched his red hair. "Well, you're a new one to me," he finally exclaimed. "You mean, you're that Vallette what has the blasting powder when we buy powder, and you're on the label?"

Lionel nodded and took the rifle from the man holding it. He opened his bag of bullets, and showed them the cartridges, concisely explaining the difference between his bullets and theirs. His face livened up, his brown eyes glowed. The men did not really understand his talk about the chemicals, but they did understand that this man in a brown frock coat and hat knew what he was talking about.

They set up a target. Lionel lifted the rifle, aimed, and fired. A small black spot marked the exact center of the target.

"Whew," said the redhead. "Let me try that with my rifle."

"Try your bullet, then try one of mine," suggested Lionel, pleased.

The redhead first hit the target on the outer edge. Lionel said, laying down his rifle, "Let me show you

435

how to hit center. Here, load it with my bullet. Now put your rifle against your cheek, sight down it. Don't fire yet. The rifling in the barrel must be slightly high. Now, draw the rifle down just a speck, just a little—that's right—" The man hit almost dead-center, the small black spot hitting just to the right of Lionel's. "Well, there you are," said Lionel, nodding.

The men eyed him with even more respect: a man who knew rifles, knew shooting, knew bullets. He might be a dude from the East, but they liked him.

They experimented, tried his rifle, tried his bullets. Finally they got out skillets, shot a half-dozen rabbits, and cooked them along with some dough. Lionel ate with them, explaining what he was doing out in Texas.

"We best escort you through to Houston," said one man seriously.

Redhead nodded. "Yeah, we better do that," he said. "Mr. Vallette, you don't know what hard, tough hombres there is hereabouts. We'll escort you on your way."

"Oh, I plan to go slowly and sketch along the way," said Lionel, mildly. "I do appreciate your offer—"

Redhead shook his head, firmly. "You don't know what you're up against. Why, we had a ruckus just a day or two ago. Bad men about. We'll take you on your way. No harm done if you want to stop and draw things."

So they had their way, and Lionel rode to Houston with a pack of outlaws "riding herd" on him, making sure this valuable gentleman reached his destination. They left him on the outskirts of Houston, telling him to be more careful and to ride the rails back home, or he might get hurt.

Lionel enjoyed these rough, hard men who treated him like a precious piece of merchandise. He parted from them with regret.

"Gentlemen, I shall miss you," he said, shaking each one's hand. "I have never heard such fine stories about the campfire, and your adventures are truly exciting. I wish I could pay you for your escort, I am sure I have brought you far out of your path—"

"No, won't hear of it," said Redhead, in spite of nudgings from one friend.

"Besides I didn't bring much cash with me. However," said Lionel, "if you would accept a box of cartridges with my thanks—"

They accepted with pleasure, and cantered off swiftly. Lionel received some questioning looks from some men who had seen the parting, but he went serenely on into town and put up at the best hotel. From there he sent a messenger to the Houston plant.

He went in the next morning, shaved, brushed free of dust, and relatively clean again. He was greeted with great respect. James Keane came down to greet him.

"Well, Lionel, glad to see you. The lab is all ready for you," said James, warmly. In spite of his friendship with Rodger, he had always liked Lionel. The mild-mannered, efficient chemical expert had earned his respect as well.

Lionel shook hands with him and smiled. "I am early—I did not expect to come until next week. However, I had some friends escorting me, and I went more rapidly than I planned."

"Actually, we were worried when you didn't come on the train. Luke wired us to expect you three days ago."

"I rode," said Lionel. "Fine horse."

"God, you took a chance," James told him, as they wended their way through the plant toward the laboratory. "There's a bad lot of outlaws about, led by a man called Red Mike. He's a killer. You might have met up with him."

"Is that right?" said Lionel. "What kind of trouble have you been having with the powder? Too wet?"

James began to explain, and forgot to question Lionel further. Lionel examined the powder, nodded, and then went outdoors along the river to the mills. He examined, poked about, then set to work.

The procedure was too hasty, he thought. They must

be more patient in letting the powder dry thoroughly before packaging it. The process was longer. James complained that when Luke had speeded them up, they had cut down on the drying.

Lionel worked there for three months. Then, satisfied that they understood the importance of the drying process, he took his leave—on horseback. This time he occasionally saw men at a distance, but none approached him. He was rather sorry for that. He did sketch on the way, and took the train from Dallas to Virginia.

Spring on the Areuse. It wakened painful memories in Lionel, and he walked along the river, thinking, remembering Sophia, and their short time together. How she had clung to him, how her face had turned radiant and pink under his caresses, how her soft body curved to his, and the sweetness of her kisses against his lips. He picked some spring flowers in a grove where they once had lain, and brought them back to his suite. He set them in a china vase on his desk where he could look at them.

Barbara and Luke were delighted to have him back, and insisted on having a dinner, with Rory and Angela, Owen and his wife, young Foster and Joshua. "Another time we'll have the older ones," said Barbara. "Lionel, I am sure you must have had some adventures out West."

"I did work in the lab, and I did some sketching," he said mildly, with a smile for his lively hostess. "Thanks for taking care of my paintings. I must buy some more tubes. The colors of the desert at dusk are incredibly beautiful."

Lionel liked Foster—the lad was eager and smart. He had started in at MIT and was doing well. Owen was grave and looked much like his sister Angela in a masculine fashion; he was taking hold in the laboratory very well. He was inventive and practical all at once. He wanted to talk to Lionel about going more into fabrics.

Lionel enjoyed the evening, his cousins, their talk, and the quiet way in which they made him feel comfortable. There were no long, unhappy silences, as there had been with Arthur, no pained glances at the portrait of Sophia.

The next day Luke filled him in on an event which had occurred while Lionel was in Texas. In the drawing room after dinner, Luke and Barbara and Lionel sat to talk.

"I told you about the rifle powder incident," Luke said, gravely, lighting up one of his strong Havanas.

Lionel nodded. "Did you change the safe combination in the lab?"

"Yes. But something else has been stolen. I filed patent papers for the new process we were working on, for coating the seats of motorcars. The patent application was shot back to me, with a stinging rebuke—someone else patented the exact same process three months ago."

Lionel drew in his breath sharply. Luke's face looked like one of those Pharaoh's heads, with hard lines about the cheeks and eyes. Barbara looked troubled, but had evidently heard about this before.

"Any idea who did it?"

"A rival company," Luke shrugged. "They probably bought it from someone who stole it from us. The chemical formula was exactly the same, I was informed."

"We could improve it," said Lionel thoughtfully. "I think the seats will smell soon. It's a strong chemical smell. Why don't we work on something with a more pleasant odor?"

Luke's laugh was a short angry bark. "That's just like you, Lionel. You don't give a damn about the millions of dollars we just lost. You just think of improving the product!"

"He's probably right, Luke," said Barbara, gently. "No crying over spilt milk. And with an improved formula, you could get the business anyway."

"The problem is to keep the next formula a secret," said Lionel. "Do you have a safe here in the house?"

Luke nodded, brushing back his black hair wearily. "Behind the portrait of Barbara on the wall." He indicated the painting.

"Perhaps we should bring the papers up here every day after work and put them in the safe. It is large enough, I presume?"

"Good idea," said Luke, immediately more relaxed. "Lionel, you are a smart man. What are you working on now?"

"Nothing Peter couldn't take over," said Lionel. "The saltpeter experiments. Why don't I start in on the fabric tomorrow?"

They discussed it for a time, then went to bed. Lionel lay awake for a time, thinking. He counted the people who had access to the safe, and nodded. He thought he knew who it was.

Several days later, he had a further indication that he might be right. Peter said to Luke late in the afternoon, "Mr. Luke, Mrs. Barbara said to tell you that you have company for dinner tonight. She would be very pleased if you would not be very late."

Luke did not look up from the table where he stood, his white lab coat stained with grit. "Tell me again about five, Peter."

"It *is* five o'clock, Mr. Luke."

Luke groaned. "Oh, God. Why do I agree to these things?"

Owen grinned at Lionel and gave him a wink. "I'll finish up for you, Luke."

"No, no, this is a stopping place. I'll continue tomorrow. Let me see—Peter, put these papers in my briefcase, I'll take them up to the house."

"Doing lots of homework?" asked Owen idly.

"Right," said Luke briefly. He then changed his coat, packed the rest of his papers, and departed. Owen left about an hour later, and Lionel sent Peter home.

Lionel was still in the laboratory about seven o'clock, finishing up an experiment. He was brooding about the results, poring over a paper, when the lab door quietly opened. He glanced up, into the dimness, to see a man come in quietly and walk directly over to the closed safe.

Lionel watched him. The man reached for the safe's

440

combination knob and twirled it about; the knob came to a rest, and he pulled. Nothing happened. Lionel cleared his throat. Rodger Courtney whirled about.

"Who's there?" he asked sharply.

"Lionel," said the young man, clearing his throat again. It was the first time he had spoken to Rodger since the death of Sophia. He felt a little sick inside. "Can I get you anything?"

"Where is Luke?" Rodger came forward briskly, frowning as though over matters of importance.

"He went up to the house. Barbara is giving a dinner."

"Why aren't you there?"

"Not invited," said Lionel, mildly. In fact, Barbara had hinted she would like very much for him to come; she had invited two very charming sisters, unmarried and very sweet. Lionel had told her he must work.

Rodger hesitated, glaring at Lionel. Lionel clicked off some operations on an adding machine, wrote down some figures on a pad, and mused over them. He felt a sort of deadly calm.

"I have to get some papers from the safe. Would you open it for me? I have to write a report tonight."

"Can't," said Lionel, untruthfully. "Luke changed the combination while I was gone. He hasn't given me the new figures."

"Oh—yes?" Rodger teetered uncertainly, then turned and left the lab abruptly. Lionel finished his work, closed up and locked the laboratory, and departed with his papers in his pockets.

He pondered whether to tell Luke about this. After all, he had no proof that Rodger was going to examine the results of new experiments. He guessed that Rodger was the one selling company secrets—but that was not proof.

He brooded over what to do. He went up the hill, entered Luke's house by the back stairway, and went on up to his rooms. He heard the sounds of laughter and music from the main hall. The party must be in full swing. He sat down in his favorite chair before the fire, and thought and thought.

He felt really too detached to do anything tonight. He must warn Luke—but Luke was smart. He had probably guessed already. The changed combination might keep Rodger out for at least a while. And the really important secret papers were now safely behind the smiling portrait of Barbara in the drawing room.

The maid came. "Mrs. Barbara, she says as how you should come and join them, Mr. Lionel."

"I'm too grimy and tired, thank you. Please give her my apologies."

The maid hesitated. "Then I should bring you a tray of hot food. Mrs. Barbara says I must."

"I would like some coffee," Lionel said, with his gentle, absent smile.

"Yes, sir, I'll bring it up at once."

He ate a little, without knowing what he ate. But the knowledge that Barbara thought of him, worried about him, and sent him food and coffee, helped to melt that little cold feeling in his heart. She was a sweet person, and Luke was a happy man with her. He was glad they had a good marriage. Too few good marriages in the world, thought Lionel, as he went over his papers once more.

Barbara wakened that night and peered with one eye at the clock beside the bed. Two-thirty. What had wakened her? She groped across the bed for Luke, but did not find him. She opened both eyes.

He was standing at the window, in his pajama bottoms, the broad chest bare, his hair ruffled. He was looking down the hill toward the mills which glowed even in the night. They were working two shifts, one day and one night, six days a week.

Barbara watched him lovingly. He could scarcely forget his work day or night. He drove himself harder than he drove anyone else.

"Luke, aren't you coming back to bed? You'll get cold."

He turned and came back to sit down beside her. "Sorry I woke you. I was thinking."

She touched his face gently. "Doesn't that head ever turn off?"

"I wish I had switches there, I'd get you to flick them and turn off the problems," he said, with a grim smile.

She put her fingers on his temples. "Click—click—" she said. "There, they're off."

He bent over and kissed her lingeringly on the lips, then pressed his face to her breasts with a tired sigh. "Oh, darling—"

"Come into bed, you're cold," she urged. He lay down again and drew her into his arms.

"Are you glad about the baby?" he asked, softly, into her masses of dark hair.

"Ummm, very happy, love. Are you?"

"You know I am. I just hope things calm down so I will be able to spend more time with the baby. I remember how dad used to take me down to the mills and show me around, and take me fishing and hunting. Arthur and Henry were jealous—they said he never bothered when they were young. I think a boy needs his father."

"So does a girl," she said, twisting her fingers in his hair and giving it a gentle tug. "What if I have a girl? Will you cast me off?"

"Fat chance. You're hooked for life, girl, just don't try to get away from me." He turned and pressed his mouth to her throat, then to her shoulder. But he was weary—she could feel it in his tense muscles, in the tightness of his shoulders when her hands caressed his back.

She stroked her hands over and over his back and felt him begin to relax. She talked soothingly about the baby, about what the doctor had said, about the nursery room she was preparing. And gradually he moved about, sighed, and settled down to sleep again, his arm still hard about her.

She lay awake for a short time after he fell asleep. Luke had said he needed her. She had thought at the time, early in their marriage, that it was a ploy to make sure she did not go back to Washington, to the women's suffrage work. But now she was beginning to believe he had said just the truth. Luke was a direct, straightforward man in their emotional dealings. Whatever cunning he had he used in business. He *meant* he needed her.

And he did. She alone could soothe him and make him forget and relax and enjoy life for a time. She alone could command him to come from the laboratory, and he would come. She alone could make him laugh, when the grim lines along his mouth were hard and stern and his eyes flashed fury. He loved her, he adored her, but more—he did need her.

She filled an emotional need in him, deep and timeless as the world. Wife, mother, confidante, friend, his other half. She wished they could go away again together. But the work held him here, the exasperating, demanding, backbreaking, mind-twisting work of the laboratory and the control of Vallette and Sons. Rory depended on him, smart as he was. Lionel constantly asked his advice on lab problems. Owen turned to him. The young lads looked up to him adoringly. He was like Brett, said Arthur, with a sigh. The strong one, the one they all leaned on.

She must see that he did not break under the strain.

Chapter 33

Luke came up the hill early that September day in 1914. He was eager to see his baby girl again. How that little thing with the big blue eyes drew him! He went into the house by the kitchen, paused to scrub his hands at the sink, teased the cook, and sniffed hungrily at the huge pans warming on the stove, then strode up the stairs to the second floor.

He went directly to the nursery. Barbara always fed the baby about this time. He went in softly.

Barbara was sitting at a low rocker near the window. She lifted her head as he came in and smiled at him. Her face was rounded and serene, her eyes glowed. How lovely she was, even lovelier in her security, her motherliness. She held the small girl close to her.

"Feeding all done?" Luke bent down to kiss Barbara lingeringly on her pink mouth. Then he bent closer to see the baby. The sleepy blue eyes opened wider; the baby saw who it was and gave a small crow of pleasure. The dimpled hands reached out to him. "Hello, darling. What a big girl you are now."

"She's growing by the day," said Barbara proudly. The tiny hands grabbed for the big, tanned fingers; she caught one and drew it right to her mouth to suck it. Luke grinned. The touch of that small hand was incredibly moving. Such a wee hand, such tiny fingers, such pink fingertips. "I hate to leave her even for an evening."

"That isn't what Angela says," said Luke, in a soft

murmur that would not disturb the sleepy girl. "She is glad to get away from her boy. She says he is teething and he screams half the night."

"Oh, dear, that's too bad." Barbara looked fondly down to the mass of black fuzz on top of the baby's head. "Serena is good as gold—at least so far."

"I'll hold her while you change." Luke held out his arms, and Barbara reluctantly let him take the baby. "It always takes you twice as long as me."

"You don't have to wear a girdle," said Barbara.

"God help me, no." Luke sat down in the chair, still chuckling as Barbara departed. He smiled down at the little one, rocking her gently, his hard face softened. "Hi, sweetie," he said, when Barbara had gone to their bedroom. "Blink your blue eyes, love. What a bit of a darling you are."

He had never dreamed what nonsense he could talk to a baby. But she was so sleepy and sweet, gurgling up at him, waving her fists vaguely at him. He captured one and put it to his lips; she was faintly scented with baby powder, and as silky as a toy lamb.

She settled down into his arms contentedly; her eyelids, so tiny and just fringed with dark lashes, began to close. Luke rocked her slowly, thinking back over the day.

The war in Europe had started in August. The gunpowder orders had promptly multiplied ten times, and all the new mills were in full operation. All other work was by the board. The gunpowder must come first.

Thank God, he thought, that he and Rory had set their stubborn course and held to it. James had fumed that it was a waste of work for the new mills to be turning out black powder at such a rate. Rodger had told them they were fools and had threatened to pull out. Yet he sang a different tune last month, as word came in on the start of war.

Would America get into it? He hoped not. Rory was restless. He had kept up his flying lessons and now owned his own plane. He was crazy to speak of going over there to volunteer to fight. The war would be over in a few months, said Rory, and what an opportunity to fly!

Angela was worried sick. Rory needed calming down. No matter how long or short the war, there was no need for him to go to France and fly. The thought of Rory going into battle, flying those fragile wooden-and-canvas winged ships, tossing bombs out onto the ground scared Luke, too. Rory was almost forty. Let the young fellows, reckless and foolish, do that kind of fighting. There were plenty of them eager to get into action. Rory was needed in the offices of Vallette and Sons.

The nurse came in softly, took the baby, and laid her in the crib. Luke thanked her and left after a long look at the sleeping baby. He could not endure to leave her; nor did he know how Rory could think of leaving his fine young son and Angela.

He went into the bedroom. Barbara was fastening the huge pearl buttons of a smart new gown of green shot silk. Pearl earrings and a long pearl strand lay on the dresser. She gave him a keen look.

"Did you talk Lionel into coming?"

Luke grimaced. "I think so. When he heard that Rodger Courtney would be there, he wanted to back out. However, it is the last time we will be together before Arthur goes back to Florida. And he is really fond of Arthur. If only—"

"Yes," sighed Barbara. She reached for the earrings, fastened them carefully, and slipped on the large pink pearl ring and the strand of matched pearls. "There, how do I look?"

"Gorgeous. Let's stay home and make love."

She giggled like a girl as he came over and kissed her cheek. "Oh, Luke. We haven't been out for a week!"

"I know. I'm mean to you."

"You're mean to yourself. The works won't fall apart if you take off one evening a month."

But she spoke mildly, with a smile. He could be pushed just so far. And she knew that the deeply graven lines beside his mouth were not there just from work. He worried a lot.

447

Rory and John were having all the family over for one last big bash, as Rory put it. Arthur and Hazel would be returning to Miami for the winter. Anna Moira, Stephen, and Rose Marie had come to visit Angela for a few weeks. Stephen and Rose Marie were up in years—he seemed especially fragile. Stephen and John were the same age. When they talked about "the war" they usually meant the War Between The States.

It was a lively group, talking, gossiping, laughing, reminiscing about years past. From Stephen and John down to the youngest member present, one of Caroline's brood, they had a grand family reunion. They dined on turkey, for they would not all be together at the holidays.

Angela started the meal with fresh shrimp in a cocktail sauce; and white wine accompanied the fish course of fine sole in a cream sauce. Then the turkey was brought in, golden brown and puffy with bread and sage dressing. The sweet potatoes were tart with pineapple sauce. Mashed potatoes and gravy was the favorite of the younger ones, along with cranberry and orange relish, corn fritters dripping with butter, and biscuits with jam. And then the dessert was brought in while they groaned: plum puddings, pumpkin pies with whipped cream, and angel food cake with strawberries.

The men made their way to the drawing room after dinner. The younger boys followed them, Foster and Joshua tagging along to hear the business talk even though they could not share much in the whiskey and cigars. They sat with small sherry glasses glowing brown in their hands and listened eagerly to the talk of the European war and the business—how much gunpowder had been produced the past month, the expansion of the cooperage sheds.

"Smart of us to plan ahead this way," drawled Rodger complacently, crossing his neat gray legs and eyeing his boots with pleasure. He took his third glass of whiskey neat. "We'll be sitting pretty when the profits come rolling in."

Even Arthur looked at him with distaste. The others

448

had noticeably stiffened. But Rodger was impervious—he has the hide of an elephant, thought Luke.

"Actually," said Luke carefully, noticing the appalled looks of Foster and Joshua, "war is not profitable. Oh, our business increases, with the gunpowder, certainly. But we try to sell at a level just over cost. And after the war is over, we'll convert to other products, including fabrics. The war is delaying our experiments. The fabrics should be much more profitable than the gunpowder. Still, we must do it—the Allies need all the gunpowder we can furnish."

"Don't be a sanctimonious bastard," said Rodger. "You know we stand to make millions out of this goddamn war."

Stephen lit another cigar, eyeing him thoughtfully through the smoke. John grumped and shifted. Rory finally said, "You haven't looked at the profit sheets lately, Rodger. It shows our profits down. We have expanded the mills, and put on more men who need training. Our expenses are eating up any profits from the gunpowder."

"Nonsense. I figure to finish this war as a multimillionaire. I'll retire and go into something more interesting."

Lionel moved the sherry glass around in his long, clever fingers. There were times when the hate rose in him and choked him. He longed to fling the sherry in the man's face.

Luke changed the conversation by asking Arthur about his winter home. Arthur was glad to describe the swimming pool and other advantages of the warm climate.

Rodger rumbled on to John about how much money he planned to make, how he would enlarge his home and buy more paintings. "Paintings are a safe investment; they increase in value every year. Why, my broker told me—"

Rodger was more obnoxious the more he drank. He seemed unable to control his tongue. The ladies had hardly joined them before he insulted Angela and Barbara, saying how plump they had become with their children. "Not that I mind a bit of fat on my girls," he beamed at them, looking them up and down.

"I noticed," said Rory. "She was quite plump, the one with you in Washington. But her hair was rather— unnaturally—blonde, don't you think?"

The men laughed; the women looked severe. Rodger got red, gobbling like a turkey cock. Rory did not laugh; he was fuming inside.

They were all glad when the evening was over, much as they enjoyed the New York Vallettes and most of the others. Rodger was enough to spoil an entire company, like a bit of poison in a tasty dish.

Luke had been listening thoughtfully all evening, saying little, his lean face expressionless. A few days later, he asked Rory to stop by the house, and Lionel came also.

When they had lit up their cigars, he began abruptly, "I think we had best get rid of Rodger."

"How?" asked Rory promptly.

Lionel looked at them both. "Can you? He controls—stock. And will inherit Arthur's stock when he goes."

"There's a way around it," said Luke. "I strongly suspect Rodger is the one who was stealing company secrets. His talk about making money on the war is a coverup. I watched his eyes. He means to make that the explanation for becoming a multimillionaire. But I happen to know he is buying diamonds, paintings, gold, and stock in blue-chip companies. He is spending money hand-over-fist. I think he is the one who has stolen formulas and sold them."

"To get back to the beginning," said Rory. "We have talked before about Rodger stealing company secrets. We can't prove it. However, what about his stock? He inherited Sophia's, and he'll eventually get Arthur's."

"No," said Luke. "I had a long talk with Arthur. He is not obligated to leave his stock to Rodger, and he owns much more than Sophia did; so does Sophia's mother. I persuaded them to change their wills. He's going to leave it all to the children of Caroline and Rose-ann, they have so many."

Lionel laid his cigar carefully in the ashtray beside him. "Does he know yet?" he asked quietly.

"Arthur is telling him before they leave," said Luke, with calm satisfaction, a fierce light in his blue eyes. "I told them that in no way will I permit an outsider like Rodger to gain so much control over Vallette and Sons. He would sell us out in a minute. Arthur finally agreed, and made up his new will last week. It is all signed and registered."

"Bully!" said Rory, leaning back with a sigh of satisfaction. "I admit that was an irritation to me."

"Do we agree that I should do my best to get Rodger out of Vallette and Sons? I can offer to buy his stock. He may refuse. So I may have to use force," said Luke, unconsciously flexing his lean fist.

The other two men looked at the fist, and at the hard face. "Will he leave, even then? He is a director in the company," said Rory. "My God, what a relief to get him out if he will go. I hate those meetings, with his sly suggestions about his friends in Washington and greasing people's hands."

"He is no asset," said Luke. "Are you with me?"

"Of course," said Rory.

Lionel nodded. "He keeps trying to get into the laboratory safe," he said quietly. "After work, he comes over when he thinks Luke has left. I think he has been able to get into it, also. He may have found out the new combination."

"When did he get in, do you think?" asked Luke, with surprising calm, drawing on his cigar fiercely.

"Last Saturday night."

"Good," said Luke. "I hope so."

The others stared. Luke grinned, and amplified his remark.

"I left a dummy formula in the safe. Then I left the combination and my wallet in the main office for an hour on Saturday. When I returned, Rodger scolded me for leaving personal effects around and said I ought to be more careful. I thanked him and left." He chuckled. "Took the bait, then? Well, we'll soon see."

"What will we see?" sighed Rory. "You're too devious for me."

"We'll see if the copyright office notifies us that someone is trying to patent a type of fabric coating for which I received a patent last month."

"The car covering—that new one?" asked Lionel.

Luke nodded. "We should know in another week or so."

The proof came through two weeks later. Luke had been like a lean cat on hot bricks. When it came, he whooped, waking up the baby. Barbara scolded him, but laughed when she heard about it. "Good. Throw him out, Luke. I have longed to hit him over the head with a skillet."

"That's my girl," he said, and patted her shoulder. "Wish me luck, Barbara. I want that guy out of here, without a scandal. But with it or without it, out he goes."

After much thought, Luke asked Rodger to come to his study on a Saturday afternoon, and asked Rory and Owen to come as well. He asked Lionel to stay out of the way. "He hates you, as you know," said Luke, with unusual gentleness. "And you him. I'll let you know what happens."

Lionel nodded, his gaze faraway and aloof.

When Rodger arrived, Luke greeted him.

"Ah—Rodger, come on in. We're going to have a rather brief session, hope you don't mind," said Luke, formally drawing up a chair for him.

"Going to expand somewhere, eh?" asked Rodger, genially. "We ought to have James in on this. Why did you have to send him off to Texas again?"

"The Texas operations need his steady hand," said Luke, seating himself and drawing some papers before him. He glanced over them. "Rodger, for some time we have suspected that you are taking Vallette material and selling it to our competition. For that reason, I am ask-

452

ing you to resign, sell your stock to me, Rory, and Owen, and leave the company."

Rodger gaped, like a fish out of water, his face slowly reddening. "You're mad," he finally gulped out.

"On at least three instances, I have traced the loss of material, most recently a valuable formula, to your activities. Now, I don't particularly relish having the Vallette name smeared across the front pages in a scandal which this might bring on. Nor do I imagine you want to be accused in court of selling stolen material. So I thought we might compromise."

Rodger looked into the steely, hard, blue eyes and gasped, "You can't mean this. You can't throw me out of Vallette and Sons. You have no power to do anything—"

"As the head of Vallette and Sons, I have the powers invested in me by the Board of Directors. That includes doing what I think best for the future of the company. And the future does not include you, Rodger." Dislike filled his voice. "You are a greedy, double-dealing bastard, and the sooner you leave, the cleaner the air around here will be."

Owen stifled a muffled word; Rory was silent, keen-eyed. Rodger looked fit to burst. Luke had never pulled his punches, and he wasn't doing so now.

"You'll have a tough time throwing me out," burst out Rodger. "You may have conned Arthur into changing his will, but I'll soon tell him he owes me that. I married Sophia, his only daughter. I am entitled to that stock—you can't take it from me. And he owes me—"

"His daughter's life," said Luke gravely. There was a slight shocked silence in the room. No one had ever said it aloud in Rodger's presence. "But for you, she would be alive. You killed her, with your brutality, your beastly ways. She was a gentle girl, we all loved her—"

"Yes, all her *cousins* loved her," sneered Rodger, now purple-red in the face, his hands shaking. "My God, you stick together, you even marry each other, rather than let any outsider—"

"That's enough," said Rory sharply. "Stick to the point. What price for your stock?"

"You'll never get it."

"I think so," said Luke. He named a price. "That is above the market value. You can buy into some other company. But I won't have you here—"

"There's my house, my property, my pool—" Rodger was stammering with fury. "You can't just throw me out. I won't go. I belong here—"

"You never belonged here," said Luke, rising. "I have evidence that you tried to sell a formula about two weeks ago. The company you sold it to did not know I had already taken out a patent on the material. I have evidence, signed statements; I can take you to court. Do you want that?"

"You have no proof of any damn thing."

Luke lost his patience. He strode over to Rodger, lifted him out of his chair by a fistful of jacket material, and jerked his face to within an inch of his own. "You'll get out, and sell out. I won't have you around here another day. Name your lawyer—and your price."

"Damn your eyes, I will not. Damn you for a bastard—" The words had scarcely left Rodger's mouth when Luke knocked them back in. The blow echoed throughout the room. Rodger staggered, then fell back into the chair. But he jumped up again, aiming a blow at Luke.

Luke's eyes gleamed. He stood the heavier man off, toe to toe, and traded punches with him. Rory restrained Owen from stopping them. "Let them go, I've wished for this moment," he said gleefully.

Luke knocked Rodger down again; he bounded up, blood streaming from a cut on his cheek. Luke hit him again, then again. Rodger groped for him, furiously mad, like a wounded bull trying to charge. Luke sidestepped him and struck him again, the blow echoing around the room of fist against fleshy chin.

Rodger's head snapped back and he fell to the floor. Luke stood over him. Owen finally went over and knelt to examine him. "Knocked out," he said gravely. He took his handkerchief, wet it with brandy, and wiped Rodger's face.

The man came to in a few minutes. He staggered to a chair and sank into it. "All right, damn you," he said bitterly. "I'll sell out to you. But you'll regret it."

"Not this," said Luke. "Sign these papers." He shoved them at Rodger across the desk.

"I won't sign without my lawyer."

"You'll sign before you leave this room, or I'll knock you out again," said Luke. "Sign. The price is fair, and I'll buy your damn house, though I mean to tear it right down."

Rodger finally signed, then stumbled away. Rory said, "He may contest this in court."

Luke was looking over the papers with calm satisfaction, a blue-green bruise appearing on his right cheekbone. His knuckles were bloody, but he ignored them. "He can fight all he pleases. He is out, and he stays out. I'll file these right away. Rory, you want some of the shares?"

"I'll take a third," said Rory. Owen nodded that he would take another third. Luke paid for the rest.

Rodger left the Areuse valley and went right to court. He slapped all three of them with a lawsuit, claiming they had coerced him into selling his stock. News of the scandal filled the papers—and it was big news, as it concerned one of the biggest industries in the country. But war news soon crowded it out. Luke hired some excellent lawyers, explaining he didn't care what they did so long as Rodger never got back into the company again. He would fight in every court up to the Supreme Court of the United States before he would let Rodger back in or pay him a cent in damages. He had already paid enough for the stock and the house and property.

But to his surprise and disgust, company secrets were still leaking out. Colonel Mark Trent in Washington kept him informed when patents relating to gunpowder came up, while a lawyer kept a close eye on the Patent Office for fabric items.

James had returned immediately from Texas upon

hearing about Rodger's departure and had bitterly denounced Luke for his actions. "He's a good, strong company man; you were wrong about him, Luke. He did his damnedest for the company, in spite of the way the family treated him like a dog."

James refused to return to Texas. Luke finally sent Owen out, and was pleased with the way he took hold and improved production. The powder was now of excellent quality, and fewer complaints came in from that region. Luke gave James another job in the company, sending him to New Orleans and St. Louis on sales junkets to keep him out of mischief. James returned every month or so to work at the main office and write out reports.

But Luke wondered. Had he misjudged Rodger, as James claimed? Secret formulas still leaked out. Luke changed the safe combination again and kept the most important papers at home. He noted that none of the formulas kept at home got out—only those from the laboratory. He mulled the matter over and considered the workers there, but he would have staked his life on Lionel, on Peter, on Rory, and on any others familiar with that work.

He could not find a clue, now that Rodger was gone, as to who was still stealing Vallette's formulas. However, he was not sorry that Rodger had left.

Chapter 34

Rory enlisted in the French Air Force. He wrote jubilant letters at first. "These are great chaps. You should know their courage, their daring. I would not change my position here with any in the world," he wrote to Luke.

To Angela, he wrote tenderly, reassuringly. "The war will soon be over, darling. Meantime, I am having the time of my life. Flying every day! We get up at dawn and are out in the sky before daybreak. The sky before daybreak—how beautiful! And at dusk, the sun sets in the crimson clouds—"

Then his letters began to change. They were briefer, scrawled hastily between missions. The newspapers told more—of the air battles, of the brilliant German pilots, of the French who had been shot down. And the Germans marched relentlessly into one country, and then another.

Angela came over to see Barbara and Luke often, her pale face telling of sleepless nights. They did not speak much of the war, but she showed them Rory's letters and hungrily read the ones he wrote to Luke. "He didn't tell me that Jean Dupres had died in battle," she said slowly, one evening, her eyes filling with tears. "I think more of his friends have died or been gravely wounded than he ever tells me."

In May of 1915 the British liner *Lusitania* was sunk by a German torpedo. More than a hundred Americans were killed in that terrible action. All America seethed.

Many of the men in the Vallette works wanted to volunteer at once and go off to France to fight the Hun. Luke had to stop his own work for a time to persuade them that making gunpowder was every bit as telling a blow against the Germans as fighting in the trenches of France. A few went anyway, and their families were both proud and anxious.

Luke refused to allow the powder making to be speeded up. Again and again, he told the men patiently, "The powder must be dried for the right amount of time. If the Allies' guns have wet powder in them, they will explode. No, the powder must be made right."

They were working seven days a week now, night and day. The fierce light from the mills shone for miles around. The men worked a twelve-hour day every day of the week, proud that they were exceeding the amount of gunpowder they had ever before produced. It was packed into their own kegs and shipped off on special trains to Washington, and then to Europe.

All that summer, they wondered if America would enter the war along with France and Great Britain. But in October, Germany finally apologized for the *Lusitania* incident and offered reparations. Entry into the war was averted.

Luke subscribed to New York and Washington newspapers, and also to two British publications and one eminent French one. Barbara spent her mornings poring over the French one, quickly translating, thanking God she had studied French, and leaving a translation of the contents for Luke to read when he came home. Angela wanted to read them also, but some of the action was so bitterly tragic that Barbara wished she would not.

Then Rory's letters abruptly ceased. They waited, almost paralyzed with fear. Luke shot off letters, wired congressmen, talked to his army friends. Finally a stiff telegram arrived. Rory had been shot down and gravely wounded. They would send word of his condition as soon as possible.

Frantically, Angela begged Luke to do something. He brought Owen back from Texas and sent James out there again. He talked it over with Owen. They were about to set off for France themselves to rescue Rory when word came that he was being returned on a liner. He would arrive in New York, with luck, in about a month.

"A month," moaned Angela, wiping her face with her wet handkerchief. "He could die on the voyage. Why won't they tell me what happened?" Luke finally learned that the liner was in a convoy and might be in New York in about two weeks. He made reservations at the Waldorf-Astoria, and they waited.

Early in March, having no word about the liner, Luke, Barbara, and Angela went up to New York, leaving Owen instructions to wire them at once if any message came through to Vallette and Sons.

Luke took the women out to dinner; Angela had scarcely eaten for weeks. Both women were pale and worried. He offered to take them to a play; they shook their heads no.

"I cannot endure anything but to have Rory home," said Angela.

Angela's mother, Anna Moira, came over to stay with them. She was a tower of strength, the age indicated by her graying hair belied by her brisk, firm step and the snap of her eyes. Three days later, Luke came rushing in, his cheeks red from the brisk March wind.

"The liner is coming in. I'm going down to the pier with the motorcar, a driver, and some cushions. I'm getting him out, come hell or high water," he said.

"Oh, let me come with you," Angela begged him, her face paper-white.

"No. Prepare a room for him, Barbara, get hold of that nurse who promised to come. I don't know what condition he'll be in. And get the doctor on the telephone, we'll want him to come up."

Luke went out again and was gone the rest of the day. The women agonized. Anna Moira made pot after pot of tea, forced them to drink some which she had doctored with brandy, and then they waited until dusk.

Finally the telephone in the room rang. Barbara

jumped for it. It was Luke's crisp voice, weary but strong.

"Barbara, is the room ready, the nurse there?"

"Oh, yes, Luke—is he—"

"Listen to me. Keep Angela in with you; don't let her out of the sitting room. I've got to talk to her before she sees Rory. I mean this, be strict, Barbara!" And he hung up.

Barbara swallowed, turned to the anxious Angela, and clasped her hands. "They are coming up. Angela, you are to stay here with me until Luke has talked to you."

"He is dying," said Angela faintly, and collapsed onto the sofa, almost out of her head with grief.

"Nonsense, he said nothing of the sort," cried Barbara.

For the next half-hour Anna Moira applied wet towels to Angela's face and brought more brandy. Then they heard the light clang of the elevator doors, then nothing more in the silent hallway. The rugs kept all sound from reaching them. Angela clasped her hands, her head bowed in prayer.

Luke opened the door and came in. He looked so hard, so strong, his mouth grimly set, that Barbara went to him and clasped his arm in her hands.

"Rory—is—" she faltered.

He closed the door and went to sit down. "Would someone kindly fix me a drink? Then we'll see to the patient's meals. He is starvingly hungry, or so he says," said Luke, lightly, with a grin at Angela.

Angela burst into tears. "I thought—I thought—"

Luke turned more grave. He nodded his thanks to Anna Moira as she handed him a stiff drink. He drank down half of it, then set the glass on the small table beside him.

"You'll take this well, Angela," he said, rather sternly, his blue gaze fixed on her wet face. "Rory needs your help, rather badly. He is—upset and unhappy, afraid of how you will take this."

"What?" she breathed. "Just so he lives—just so he lives!"

"He will live," said Luke. "He is in better shape than I had dared to hope. But—he has lost his right leg."

The silence in the room was profound. Luke was watching Angela keenly. Color finally returned to her cheeks. "Oh, Luke, is that all?" she whispered.

"All?" he barked. "Don't you know what that means? He will have to have an artificial leg. And there are other wounds, deep scars. His face is scarred—"

"Oh, Luke, let me see him," she said. "I cannot wait." And she darted past him and down the hallway in a flash.

Luke drank the rest of his drink. Angela knocked lightly on the door of the bedroom where her husband lay and went in. The nurse turned, warily. "I have just put him into bed, Mrs. Vallette," she said, in that cool, professional way. But Angela's attention was only for Rory, lying there, thinner than ever, his scarred, tired face turned toward her.

She flew to his bedside, dropped beside it, and reached out to clasp his hands convulsively. "Oh, Rory, darling Rory, I was so worried. But you have come home!"

The nurse went out quietly and shut the door.

Rory's hands clasped Angela's strongly. "Oh, my love. I have lost my leg," he said.

"I know. Luke told me—I'll walk for you, I'll run for you. Only never leave me again." And she put her wet face down on his dear, tanned hands.

"Don't cry, Angela. The other chaps—I was lucky," he said painfully.

"I know—I have read in the newspapers—I was so afraid—but you got away—"

"My plane went into a tailspin, burning. I thought I was a goner. I thought I would never see you again, nor my son."

"He's waiting at home for you. Oh, darling, darling—"

They stayed a few days in New York, until Rory had

recovered enough strength to travel on by railroad to Montgomery. A stretcher was waiting for him, and two husky men to carry it. But it was still a long, anxious journey until they had him into a motorcar and up the hill to his home. John Vallette met them at the door.

"You crazy boy," said John Vallette to his forty-one-year-old son. "You might have been killed. Don't you ever do such a fool thing again."

Rory laughed along with the others, with tears not far from the laughter. He was confined to bed for a time, but the good food, loving attention, and home life served to get him up in two months. He was fitted for an artificial leg, and went back to work in the office

Angela worried about it, coming over to talk to Luke and Barbara. "Should he work so soon?"

"He feels useful; he has perked up amazingly," Luke reassured her. "And he is invaluable to us. His knowledge of the works, his new knowledge of mechanics he learned in France—all that is great. And we tell him so. Don't worry, Angela. Owen won't let him overwork. At the first sign of strain, he goes home."

"How can I thank you, Luke?" Angela bent over and kissed his brown cheek. "Without you and Barbara, I would have collapsed. Now I feel—I can manage." Her thin shoulders straightened, her lips firmed. "If Rory can start in again, as strong as ever, so can I. When is the next board meeting?"

"Good girl," said Luke, and patted her cheek and grinned down at her. "It's on Tuesday, and I want you and Barbara to come and vote. John and Henry are acting up again, going all conservative on me. I want the approval for Lionel to continue to work on textiles. Perhaps we don't need them now, but we will when the war ends."

The board room was full that Tuesday. Nine of the women had come, along with a dozen men and boys of the company. Luke presented his plans, and talked about the future of Vallette and Sons.

"This will probably be the last war fought with black

powder," he told them, his keen look going over those present.

"The last war, period," said John Vallette quickly. "We will never have to go to war again."

"I wouldn't count on it," said Luke, drily. "But nevertheless, the experiments with dynamite and smokeless powder are showing that black powder will probably be consigned to work with mining and other uses, such as quarrying. And dynamite may replace that. So I want Lionel to continue his work with plastics and fabrics. That is our future direction. When the war is over—"

"We cannot think about that now," cried Henry. "All our endeavors must be focused on producing gunpowder. We must think of nothing else."

Luke ignored him and said, reasonably, "Lionel's work is far in advance of production. He is an experimental chemist, our finest—one of the country's finest. It is wasting his valuable time and his even more valuable brain to confine him to supervising black powder production. Others can do that, even the foremen of the works."

Rory spoke up, shifting his artificial leg painfully as he moved in his chair—he was not used to it yet. His wounds pained him, the chest wound especially. But he was home, in his beloved home, and with the work he enjoyed and his family about him, he could endure the pain.

"I have been discussing Lionel's work with him. He is coming up with some valuable results. It would be disastrous to take him from that work just when he is coming up with products we can convert to after the war. I figure the war will be over as suddenly as it started. And we must be ready. Remember how it was after the war with Spain. The government needed no more black powder and canceled their contracts. We had thousands of barrels left. Oh, thank God, it was over. But if we had not been ready to convert to peacetime industry, it could have meant the end of Vallette and Sons."

Luke said, "Remembering what my father told me, and the way the company almost sold out, it could have meant the end, yes. Vallette and Sons must not be allowed to go under for lack of foresight. We must spare some time, in the midst of our work for the war effort, to consider what Vallette and Sons will become in the years to come, for our children to carry on."

He spoke forcefully in this vein for some time. Barbara's heart swelled with pride. He was the most brilliant of the Vallettes, she thought. Oh, Lionel was the brightest, smartest chemist, but Luke was the best all-round man, thinking ahead, working for the future as well as the present. He caught her glance, as Henry took the floor and spoke ponderously, and gave her a slight wink.

She gave Luke a bright smile and quick nod of approval, her pride shining in her face. James looked at her, then down again. He had come in from Texas especially for this meeting, but found he was allowed to say little. He felt as though he had been left in the background of the war effort, stuck way out West, just flogging it out to produce as much powder as possible.

James resented it deeply. He was older than Luke, yet he was not considered important to the firm, just because he had the name of Keane. He had always admired Luke—they had played together much as children, and the younger boy had more than held his own. In later years, their rivalry had torn them apart. Was Luke really his half-brother, as he had told old John Vallette? He stared at Luke, mentally comparing the image he saw every morning as he shaved with the lean, hard face before him. They did not look alike, yet their mothers were sisters—and they might have had the same father. James scratched his blonde hair and shifted impatiently in his chair.

"Let Lionel tell us about his experiments and let us judge for ourselves," James finally spoke up. "Then we can vote on whether to let him continue."

There was a little murmur of approval, and some nodding from Caroline and Roseann.

Luke gave James a bleak smile. "Our competitors would love to get hold of Lionel's ideas," he said bluntly. "That is just what we don't want. Sorry, you'll have to trust us and let us give Lionel the go-ahead. The formulas will be kept secret until we are ready to patent."

"That sounds like you don't trust us!" said James, his fair face flushing red. "That I don't like. You ask us to give you a vote of confidence, but you don't trust us with information."

"All you need to vote upon is the decision to let Lionel go ahead on his research, and give him Peter and another man to help in the experiments," said Luke, with unusual patience. "I have talked to him about the work he is doing; so have Owen and Rory. The four of us know about the work; it is practical and smart, and in the direction we want to go. Too many should not know about this."

Barbara spoke up in the short pause that ensued, as the Vallettes all looked at each other and shifted about uneasily. The sound of her own voice startled her—it was so firm and sure, as though she were addressing a group of women about women's suffrage instead of a mixed group of stockholders.

"I think it is the Chinese who have a saying: When more than two know a secret, it is no longer a secret," she said. "The fewer that know about this, the better. You all know that some formulas have disappeared from the safe and turned up in attempts to patent the same processes. I don't think Lionel should be asked to work so hard just so someone can steal the information from Vallette and Sons. I move that the request for Lionel's funds be granted."

There was a rather aghast silence. John Vallette and Henry stared and frowned at the bold young woman who had spoken. John could scarcely believe his daughter had had the gall to speak out in a stockholders' meeting.

Caroline, who admired Barbara deeply and silently, cleared her throat and murmured, "I second the motion," and sank back, blushing deeply.

Luke, hiding his surprise and pleasure, briskly called

465

for discussion, cut that short, and called for a vote on the motion. It was passed, eleven to three, with several abstentions.

"Then Lionel shall have the funds to carry on his experiments," said Luke. "Now we move to consideration of the problem in Missouri . . . "

After the meeting, John Vallette growled at him, "I would have had just three of us meet, and pass what I want. Goddamit, Luke, you had all of us there—and you still got what you wanted. How do you do it?"

"The will of the majority, Uncle John," said Luke, gathering up his papers.

"And your wife!"

"And my wife, a stockholder in the company," said Luke. "Any other questions?"

John went out, muttering, followed by Henry and James. Luke watched them go, thoughtfully. John had been fretful recently, talking of regretting his retirement and how the young people might be leading them wrong. Their stock might be worth nothing at the end of the war, said John Vallette.

At dinner that evening, the two of them alone, Luke said to Barbara, "Thanks for the help in the meeting, darling. I think your work in the women's suffrage movement has helped us both."

She blushed with pleasure, and her eyes sparkled. "Do you really think so, Luke?"

"Of course. I think when the war is over, women's suffrage will be considered the right thing. Women are working in factories, holding meetings to raise funds for overseas, rolling bandages, helping in the Red Cross."

"Yes. We decided it was best to wait until the war is over to try again for the vote," said Barbara, with a sigh. "When they see that we mean to be considered full citizens, in good times and bad, they may grant us the vote—I hope so, anyway. Or we'll have to start over and fight it all through again." Her chin was set firmly. She had been corresponding with friends, now that she had time again. "I want my baby to grow up and have the vote."

"She'll have it, all right," said Luke ruefully. "Serena is a strong-willed young woman."

Lionel, in his rooms, with a cigar and a tray of hot food, was going over his notes. He kept them now in a safe in his own suite. No one came there but the cleaning woman and a girl to bring his food and drink.

He leaned his head back wearily after he had gone over the notes. He took out Sophia's miniature, set it before him on the table, and spoke to her.

"We're getting somewhere, darling," he said. "I think I'll work more on the formula that I tried last winter. That was right, I feel it in my bones. If I could just alter the formula slightly, it might work this time, and not stick."

He mused on her beautiful face. Was there a slight smile on her lips tonight? How beautiful she was in the firelight.

"Tomorrow," he confided, as he often did. "Tomorrow I'll try again."

The maid knocked and came in for his tray. "Any more coffee, Mr. Lionel?" she asked respectfully. She was sure she had heard his voice before she entered. She saw the miniature before him.

"Nothing more, thank you."

She curtseyed, took the tray, and departed, thoughtfully. Such a nice man, gentle and quiet. But perhaps he was not entirely sane. She had known a man once who talked to himself all the time, not making much sense either. Still, those who should know did say that Mr. Lionel was a genius. Maybe he was. Geniuses were often not sane, everybody knew that.

Chapter 35

"I can't agree," said John Vallette, puffing strongly on his black cigar. "Rodger and Arthur have talked to me about this. It seems to me you need some older, steadier heads in the active management of Vallette and Sons."

He picked up his glass of brandy and drained it. His old face was flushed, his small, brown eyes eager and shrewd. Luke sighed to himself. It was bad enough that Arthur had returned from Florida, full of vim and vigor, and decided he wanted back into Vallette and Sons. Bad enough that Rodger had enlisted Arthur in his lawsuit against the Vallettes. He had enough troubles with the war effort—and now this.

"I'm going to court tomorrow," said Luke wearily. "It's going to take a lot of valuable time to fight this. You really want Rodger Courtney and his tricky ways back in Vallette and Sons? He sold formulas, stole from the safe—"

"You have no proof of that."

"Yes, I have," said Luke, bluntly. "We traced it back to Rodger. He is the man who sold the formulas. Now he can't get into any respectable company, no one will take him on—"

"Because you won't give him a good reference," snapped John.

"Hell, no. I tell them the truth—that he just about wrecked Vallette and Sons, that he stole from us while

468

working for us. And it is a matter of public record, his dealings with Mars stock—"

"What I can't understand," said Rory, stretching out his artificial leg and rubbing his thigh in that motion that was becoming automatic with him, "is why Arthur takes up with him again. After all he did to Sophia—"

"If we had treated him more like a member of the family—" muttered John.

"He is a pig. He was born one, he remains one," said Luke, forcefully. "No family connection could have changed that. He killed Sophia. Why should we embrace him and let him stab us in the back again?"

James had been sitting silently, resentfully, his underlip stuck out. "The way you talk, Rodger was a cheat and a fraud," he said at last. "He is a damned good manager."

"You can't trust him an inch," said Luke, flatly. "I don't like to have a man about whom I can't trust."

The ladies joined them then, and the conversation turned to lighter matters. Barbara came to sit near Luke. She was heavy with their second child, and her gown flowed about her like that of a Madonna. Her cheeks were pink and her smile sweet as Luke leaned to tuck a cushion behind the small of her back.

"That better, honey?" he asked in a low tone.

"That feels good, thank you."

His big fingers touched her cheek gently in a light caress. His face softened. "We'll head for home shortly. You need your sleep."

James watched them, then turned abruptly away to stand at the French windows and gaze out at the wintry gardens. The bushes looked ghostly white in the moonlight. The roses had been cut back and tied up. He remembered how green and fragrant had been the gardens the night of the ball here when he had first met Barbara, home from school for the holidays. She had worn a violet dress with silver trim and narrow silver slippers on her slim feet. Her laugh had been like silver bells, he had thought, entranced at the change in the tomboyish girl he had known as a child. He was seventeen years her senior; she had made him feel young and hopeful again. And there was Luke, leaning over her, with the right to care for her, to look after her.

James had never married. He had kept a mistress for a time in Washington and had later acquired a girl in Texas whom he still saw occasionally. Yet he felt if he never saw either of them again—small loss.

He had loved but one girl, and Luke had gotten her. Why? Why was life so unfair? Rodger had sneered and said that the money did it, and that brute way Luke had of riding roughshod over everyone. "Women love the male brute," he said. "Knock her around a bit, she'll love it."

James had flinched, remembering the taut, suffering look on Sophia's face. It was the one thing which he had held against Rodger. Otherwise, he thought the man clever and smart. He knew how to work things. Or—did he? He was fighting Luke, and losing. Even in court, Luke could make him look a fool. Just giving the facts in his cool tone, Luke could make them respect him, and believe him.

Back home, Luke ordered Barbara right up to bed. She made a pert face at him. "What about you, Luke? You're as tired as I am. You're not going over those papers again, are you?"

"I'm due in court in the morning, honey." He kissed her hair, turned her about, and kissed her full on the lips, the slumbrous look on his face a warning. "If you weren't so pregnant, daring—" he said.

She blushed hotly. He could still make her blush just by looking at her or touching her with his big hands. She went on up to bed alone and listened for Luke to come to the small room next door where he slept in the later stages of her pregnancy so he would not disturb her.

He worked late and went up to the room at two o'clock. The facts were firmly in his mind. He moved restlessly about the room, trying to be quiet.

Barbara came in, tying a warm robe about her

swollen body. "Luke, aren't you settling down yet? Do you know what time it is?"

"You'll catch cold; go back to bed, honey."

"When you do," she said.

He came over, ruffled up her hair, smoothed it again, kissed her. "If I just knew it was the right thing to do," he said, restlessly. "Maybe we should divest ourselves of some of the stock—we are a huge company. But we can make the prices low for the gunpowder, the government admits that, by having our own sources of sulfur and saltpeter—"

"Luke, you are right," she said firmly. "Remember that, when you go in tomorrow. Don't have doubts about it. Think how the French and the British need the gunpowder. And we need your organizing ability here. Rory is good, but he can't stand up against John and Arthur. Henry keeps pushing, pushing. You have to stand firm. Don't let the doubts creep in. They are wrong, you are right."

He laid his cheek against her hair and held her carefully against him. She was going to have a child in a couple of months; he did not want her upset. Maybe—maybe this time it would be a boy. He adored his small upstart daughter; she was willful, sweet, adorable, cunning, and devilish all at once. A little handful, like her mother. But a son—a son to carry on the Vallette name, the Vallette company—with any luck, a strong son, to start the next generation of Vallettes—

And if their son had the courage and strength of his mother, and the intelligence and shrewdness of his father, he might have a chance of being the next head of Vallette and Sons. Luke thought, I hope I have the guts and wisdom to step aside when my time comes, and not impede the next ones.

"What are you thinking, love?" she asked, her hand against his rough cheek. "Not still worrying?"

"Thinking about our baby," he said, with a smile. "He's getting pretty big, isn't he?"

"Nancy thinks I'm going to have a boy, he is so big and so low," said Barbara, returning at once to the most

471

fascinating topic in the world to her, the child. "I'm going to have to get a wheelchair and ride about in it if he gets much bigger!"

He laughed a little and said, "And now, off to bed, you and my child! You have to take care. It's chilly in here. He moved her off to her room, saw her into bed, with the covers up, kissed her again, and went off to his own narrow bed.

He found he was smiling, thinking of Barbara and his child. A son! Might he have a son—

And he fell asleep, contentedly, on that thought.

The court case was set aside for more urgent matters, and the lawyers told Luke they thought they might be winning. The government was being pressured by the War Department to let up on Vallette and Sons. They needed the gunpowder.

And by March, the War Department needed it more than ever. Word came that German submarines had torpedoed three American ships. On the *Laconia,* many lives were lost.

The country was in a furor, demanding that something be done to punish the Germans. The armed forces were ready to go; many American boys were already overseas, serving with the British and French. President Wilson addressed Congress and asked for a declaration of war—and it was granted.

Luke was busier than ever. Telegrams shot back and forth between him and the army generals. They would need huge quantities of black powder now. Could he supply more powder for rifles? What about the new formula—would it be ready? They needed high-powered rifles, and gunpowder to match. Luke promised to speed up work on that.

Luke went back to the laboratory late one night. He had not had time to finish work on a final experiment. He was weary, yet he must work. If he could have four clear hours to work, he might get done.

He would not ask Lionel to work on this, and Lionel was the only chemist he would trust with the delicate

472

precision work. Lionel was busy enough with his passion for the plastics; he was making great strides in the experiments.

Luke spoke to the night watchman in the corridors before he went to his lab. "I'll be working until about four o'clock, Paul," he said.

"Yes, sir, Mr. Luke. You ought to get some sleep, though, sir. Begging your pardon for mentioning it," he said, with the familiarity of long acquaintance.

"When the war's over, Paul," he said, with a tired smile, and went into his office at the laboratory to get some papers. He glanced over them, closed the safe, and sat down at his desk. He would read these, then go to the lab—

He heard a sound in the next room. Instantly, he tensed. A dim light shone there—a flashlight? He started out of his chair and headed for the next room without a thought for his own safety. He had not thought much about spies lately—he had been too busy. And the grounds were heavily guarded, with wire fences all about and guards every few yards.

He stared to see James and Rodger, papers scattered before them on a lab table. The lab safe was open. Both men stared at him in the light of the small flashlight that James was holding to the papers. Rodger was examining one after another, to judge by the way the papers were laid out.

"What the devil—my God, Rodger, at it again? And James with you—" Luke was almost speechless: James to have turned against them! Thank God, the important papers were in the safe at home.

"Damn you to hell, you would come in!" said Rodger, coldly. His fleshy face was pasty white; his eyes blazed.

"Put those papers down. I'll call the guard—by God, James, I should have suspected you before. You were always about, the formulas and secret information were still going—but somehow I trusted you—" Luke was scathing, furious. That James had fooled him! Stupid, weak James—a poor manager, a lazy man—or was he?

473

Had he deliberately slowed down production out there in Texas?

"James, get to the door, guard it. I don't want to be interrupted." Rodger ordered, and before Luke realized it James was standing at the door, one hand in his pocket, the other hand holding the flashlight steadily on Luke. Rodger was in the shadows, the papers still scattered before him.

Luke went cold, his anger dying as he realized his position. These two men were desperate; they had little to lose, and much to gain, if he never left the room alive.

"Don't be fools, both of you," he said crisply, backing slightly from the table. Rodger was circling the table slowly, one hand in his pocket, his eyes strangely glazed. "I'll call the guards. You have gotten away with this for too long. You might have expected to get caught."

"We haven't been caught—at anything," said Rodger, with deadly softness. James was looking anxiously from one to the other, the flashlight wavering. "Keep that light on Luke, damn you," Rodger ordered.

"You can't—Rodger—" James began.

Rodger's big hand came from his pocket, and a clasp knife snapped open. The long, deadly blade was pointed at Luke. James began to move, without knowing he had stirred.

Luke backed up, his hands up before him in a boxer's stance—but what chance had he against a knife? And Rodger could throw that knife—James had seen him.

"Rodger—don't fool around—" James said breathlessly. The flashlight was shaking in his hand. He came up beside Luke. "Don't do anything—crazy—"

Rodger flung himself at Luke. The knife blade came up in a slashing motion. James crashed against Luke, knocking him aside and down to the ground. Luke hit the cement floor, then shook his head wildly to clear it. James fell on top of him, blood gushing from his body.

Rodger was shaking with rage and hatred. He

leaned down over James and yanked out the knife. It was poised at Luke again.

Luke yelled, "Paul! Guard! Here, guard!" He rolled over and over, out from under James's heavy body, kicking out at Rodger's feet. The big man stumbled, but still came after him.

The lab door crashed open. The guard stood there. "What is it—oh, my God—" He flicked on the lights and stared in horrified dismay.

Luke kicked out again as Rodger came after him. Rodger tripped and fell down over Luke; Luke grappled with him and grabbed for the hand holding the knife. Rodger was large and heavy, but out of condition. Luke was lean and hard; he caught the hand with the knife and hit it again and again against the cement floor until Rodger howled and the knife fell to the floor with a clatter.

Then Luke went for the man's throat. They fought fiercely. He punched Rodger in the nose until blood streamed down. The guard had gone to James.

Paul bent over the unconscious man. Blood gushed from his stomach. Paul tried in vain to stanch it with great cloths from the lab table. The two men had fought themselves into a corner and were punching, grunting, rolling over and over.

"Mr. Luke—I got to get a doctor—" The guard realized they did not hear. He leaped for the wall and sounded the alarm. Men came running, their boots sounding heavily in the corridors.

Rodger heard them. The instinct for survival, strong in him, took over. He gave Luke a vicious kick, which connected with Luke's leg. He fought free, leaped up, and ran. He was out the open lab door, pushing past the bewildered guards who gave way to him.

Luke got up. "After him—get that man—"

Two men took after Rodger. Luke staggered over to James.

"He needs a doctor bad, Mr. Luke," said Paul, anxiously, towels in hand. Blood stained the towels about them on the floor.

James opened his eyes slowly as they worked over him. Someone had sent for a doctor; the guards were ready to help. Two burly men lifted him to the lab table, among the scattered papers. Another guard hastily swept the papers out of the way, and stuffed them into the lab safe.

James's face was pasty-white, as though all the blood were gone from him. He flicked his gaze about the room, bewildered, and finally saw Luke bending over him.

"Luke . . ." he muttered.

"Here, James. Keep quiet, the doctor is coming."

"Too late . . . sorry . . . about. . ."

"Mr. James, who knifed you?" asked Paul, leaning to him. "We got to give a statement about that."

"Rodger . . . Courtney . . . knifed . . . me . . ." muttered James, his words clear. "We were . . . were . . . Luke found us . . . at the safe . . . Rodger . . . knifed me . . . was after Luke . . . hated him . . ."

One guard returned and stood in the doorway, appalled. Luke glanced toward him. "Well? Did you get him?"

"No, Mr. Luke. He got away in his motorcar, damn his hide," said the guard. "The other man, he went after him, but I figure that motorcar is too damned fast to catch."

Luke nodded curtly. "I'll get a warrant sworn out for him. We'll get him. And if he ever dares show his nose around here, I'll put him in chains." His voice was savage. When he bent to James, the touch was tender on James's forehead.

James was moving restlessly, the pain reaching into his vitals.

"Easy, James, easy. The doctor will soon be here." The tone had softened. "You stepped in front of that knife. Why, James?"

A ghost of a smile twitched over James's white lips. "What you . . . told me . . . was it true? . . . about . . . father?"

Luke nodded, then realized that James's vision was

blurring and he could not see him. "Yes, it was true, James. Quite true."

"Glad . . ." muttered the dying man. He gasped; his hand moved toward his stomach. Luke caught it gently and held it in his hand. The pulse was fluttering weakly.

"Luke. . ."

"Yes, James." The room was very still; the guards did not move, their fascinated gaze on Luke and James. What had happened they did not quite comprehend. But they knew the man was dying.

"I was . . . jealous . . . horrible . . . of you . . . worked with Rodger . . . let Vallettes . . . down . . ."

"Don't try to talk. The doctor will soon come—" Luke could not let anger rise now. The man was going, and he could think only of the early years: the stocky, handsome James laughing and teasing the younger boy, rolling downhill in the grass, tussling and playing; the time James had let Luke ride his own horse; the time he had come home from college and taken Luke hunting with him, when Brett was too busy to do so.

The face was gray, aged. His hair was thinning on top. But James would never grow any older now. Luke realized it, and was curiously sorry, pitying. The man had betrayed him, for the oldest of reasons, envy.

"Luke . . ."

"Yes?"

"Will you . . . put me . . . up on the . . . hill?"

Luke was puzzled for a moment. Then he remembered. "You mean—with the Vallettes—in the—" He could not say "cemetery."

James moved his mouth, slowly, and managed to say, "Yes. Beside . . . Brett . . . or nearby . . . if you . . . would. . ."

"I promise," said Luke

The doctor came in. They had been there for almost an hour. James was sinking fast; he had lost a great deal of blood. The doctor worked on him, but his face was grave. Within another hour, James died.

Luke left the bloodstained laboratory and walked slowly up the hill toward home. Lights blazed in his house. Barbara must have been awakened with the news. Barbara, expecting a child within a month.

"Oh, God, why, why, why James?" he muttered to the cold night wind. "To betray us—when dad raised him, was really his father—"

He tried to comprehend how James could coldly, systematically work for years to help pull down Vallette and Sons. Work with Rodger Courtney—

"By God, I'll get him one day. He won't be able to show his face for a thousand miles, but I'll get him—"

But Rodger did not surface. A warrant remained in effect for his arrest, the ports were combed regularly, descriptions sent out, but he did not show up anywhere. Years later, a man died in Brazil, and his effects were sent back to a distant relative. That was the first anyone knew he had gone down there, changed his name, and worked in a sugar mill and then on a coffee plantation, as an assistant manager, until his death. He had not dared come back even to claim the fortune he had built up so cunningly on the bodies of two wives and much betrayal.

Chapter 36

James was buried on a cold, rainy day, near Brett Vallette. Luke refused to let Barbara attend the funeral. It would be too much for her, though she wept over James.

She was there when Luke came home, waiting in the drawing room with a tray of hot coffee ready. Luke went straight to her, bent over, and kissed her.

"All right, darling?"

She nodded. Her eyes were somber, the lids pink and swollen from weeping. "Poor James," she whispered. "If—if it had been any different—"

Luke shook his head. She poured coffee for him, and the maid brought in sandwiches. Luke went to the mahogany bar in the corner and poured some brandy in his coffee. "Damned cold, over there," he said absently, thinking of the bleak funeral, the canvas over the grave, the water running into it. But James would not know that now. He was beyond the reach of all earthly matters.

Within a month, Barbara bore a son. They named him Matthew. He was big and lusty, bawling when scarcely out of the womb. He had black, curly fuzz on his head, and his eyes were a vivid blue.

"Looks just like you did when you were born, Luke," pronounced John Vallette, who had come over to see his new grandson. "If he turns out like you, God help us all."

They all laughed; John had a grin on his tired, old face. He raised his glass of brandy high. "To the next generation, especially young Matthew John Vallette," he pronounced, and they all drank to the young baby asleep upstairs.

Luke was radiant, though very tired. He had raced back from Washington when told Barbara had gone into labor. When they were alone, and she had rested, he opened a box he had brought back with him.

The jewelry case was made of purple velvet, lined with gray silk. It set off the sprakling set of diamonds: a small flowered tiara, a gleaming bracelet, earrings that sparkled with pointed light, a huge ring set with sapphires, and a magnificent pendant on a silver chain, a great, pear-shaped diamond surrounded by more sapphires.

She gasped, and gasped again. "Oh, Luke, you'll go broke!"

He grinned. "Not a chance." He set the tiara on her mussed black hair as she sat up, the pink bed jacket echoing the pink of her cheeks. "There. And you've got your waist back, just as you wanted."

"Isn't he beautiful?" she sighed, looking toward the blue-netted crib nearby.

"He is beautiful, and very clever. John told me that Arthur has decided to drop the court case. The elders have given in at last, Barbara. They are really making way for the next generation."

She clasped his hands weakly in her slim ones. "Oh, Luke, the best news yet."

He bent over and tenderly kissed her cheek. "Not the best—Matthew is the best. Everything else I can handle. But you managed to bring forth Matthew. I adore you, know it?"

She brought one of his big hands to her face and kissed it. "And I love you—so much, darling—" Her voice was weak. Gently he removed the tiara, shoved it carelessly into the case, and eased her down on the pillows.

"Get some rest, darling; you've earned it," he joked a little, watching her anxiously. The birth had been hard on her, for the baby was so large. "Rest, and sleep. Call me when you want me—I'll be nearby."

He had other news, but it could wait. He sought out Lionel, and talked with him in his study.

"The government has finally stopped the trust suit," he told Lionel, jubilantly. "I was told in Washington that they just can't afford to jeopardize the production of gunpowder. And the case has weak points. The lawyers were smart enough to see them and realize we just might win, especially with the war continuing as it is."

Lionel smiled at him gently. The brown eyes seemed far away, though his brain was as keen as ever. "Good news, Luke. I knew you would manage it. But you look tired. Get some rest, you can afford to slow down a bit now."

"I told them about the gunpowder for the high-powered rifle," Luke said, and rose to pace restlessly about Lionel's study, pausing to examine the china vase with a few wilted flowers in it. "They are sending several observers next week. I'll take them out on the range."

"Get Owen to do it. He is very capable. Smart young man—goes right after details," said Lionel. He raised his glass to Luke as Luke turned about. "And here's to your new son. I didn't congratulate you before."

"Thank you." Luke grinned, a brief flash lighting up his tanned face. "I'm very happy—I wanted a son—"

"The next generation," said Lionel. "You and Rory will do well. He says that Angela is expecting again."

"Yes. Great. Our children will grow up together." Luke hesitated, on the verge of teasing Lionel, encouraging him to marry. Lionel would never marry, said Barbara. He was withdrawn, except for his work. He cared nothing for society. Arthur had given the large portrait of Sophia to Lionel, and it hung in his rooms now. Luke turned from the gentle gaze of the brown eyes. They made him feel guilty, somehow, and ill at ease.

"I have heard that Arthur has given up," said Lionel, as Luke glanced back at the portrait of Sophia. "He

481

came and told me he is going back to Miami. He regrets tying in with—with Rodger Courtney." He was able to say the name with level tones. "Didn't realize he was such a scoundrel. But James's dying—that convinced him."

"It is a pity that it takes a death to make people learn and understand the truth," said Luke savagely.

Lionel smiled vaguely and looked back into the heart of the red fire near his toes. He stretched out one white hand to the fire. Death? Did they not understand that it could be the entrance to another life? Perhaps not. Luke had never struck him as a religious man. He and Barbara went to church regularly, but faith in an after-life did not seem to occur to Luke. Perhaps it came only to those who so desperately wanted to believe in it.

After Luke had left, Lionel continued to muse about the afterlife. Was it real—was there a place to go when the body was weary of the strains of earth? He believed because he could not endure not to believe. He had to know that one day he would be with Sophia again. It was all he had left.

He leaned his graying head against the cushions of the tall-backed armchair. He had papers to study, but he left them on the small table near his hand. He wanted to remember the days with Sophia, the sweet spring days, the green summers, the hazy autumns.

The summer and autumn were strenuous and exciting. The war in Europe moved at a suddenly more rapid pace, as fresh, eager American troops were moved to the trenches of France, where they fought, some died, and still others struggled out of the trenches to push the Germans back.

Funds were raised for the war effort. Barbara wrote letters, addressed groups of women earnestly, and came home only to take care of Matthew and Serena. Women were working in factories, turning out blankets, suits, helmets, gas masks. Horrible stories of German atrocities appeared in the newspapers, and these stories made the Americans all the more angry at the brutal enemy.

482

German-owned factories in the United States were seized. Owen was sent to manage one for a time, borrowed by the government. Foster came home from college to work. It was more important than finishing his training, he told Luke. Luke accepted him gladly. The boy was old for his years, very responsible.

He put Foster under Henry in the office, then transferred him to the laboratory under Lionel, after he had learned the fundamentals of the way Vallette and Sons worked. Joshua, envious of his brother, begged to join them also. Luke said yes, and put him in the office. Two of Roseann's children wanted to join the firm. The next generation was already here, thought Luke ruefully, but with pride.

In November, New York State's decision to grant women the vote was greeted with much excitement and jubilation.

"This means the federal government must grant us the vote soon," cried Barbara, waving the newspapers in both hands and doing a jig in the drawing room. "It has to come, it has to come now!"

"You'll win your cause, Barbara, I know it," said Luke, watching her with a smile of pride. Her determination, her courage, her intelligence, were a source of great pride to him. "With women like you about, the country will be better and stronger. Think of Granny Moira, how strong she was, how she held the family together."

"And Rose Marie, and all the others," said Barbara, pausing to perch on the edge of his chair and give him a quick kiss on his rough cheek. "And all the women pioneers. And all the women in factories across the country, doing men's work—"

It was a tough but exciting winter of 1917–1918. The newspapers were full of accounts of battles in France. Rory read them silently, longing to be in the action, but Angela could not hide her relief that he had come home. If he had stayed—she blessed his wounds, ashamed of herself, yet unable to regret it—if he had stayed, he would have been shot down, killed, she knew it.

Christmas was quiet. It did not seem right to celebrate when so many were fighting and dying in the trenches of France. Rory and Angela came over with their children for the day, and Lionel came down to join them, unexpectedly. He seemed to enjoy the young children. One of them was continually sitting on his lap, and he would drawl out one of his stories about travels in the West, or he would draw something for them on a pad. Uncle Lionel was the greatest uncle ever, they thought. He had a tender, gentle touch, his smile was sweet, and he always listened gravely to their chatter.

Foster came in the late afternoon, after the others had departed. He seemed flushed and embarrassed; his motorcar sat shining red in the driveway. Quite a young man now, thought Luke, with some secret amusement.

"Uncle Luke, could I talk to you alone, in the study?" Foster stammered, after a few minutes in the drawing room. Luke exchanged a quick look with Barbara; her blue eyes were wide with curiosity.

"Surely, Foster, come along." Luke led him back to his study and sat down at the desk. "Problems at the laboratory? Advice on some experiment?"

Foster turned redder and squirmed in the chair. "Well, no, Uncle Luke. I should not bother you with this, but everyone says you're the head of Vallette and Sons now, and you know the world, and you—well, you're the smartest man I know—"

Luke leaned back, faintly amused. What in the world did the boy want? To return to college? Surely not to enlist? His mother Caroline would have a fit. Luke thought about ways to persuade the boy not to go. He was exempt from the conscription because he was involved in vital war work.

"You see, there is this girl," Foster finally blurted out, and his brown eyes grew radiant. "She is from Montgomery, and she is very lovely—I think she likes me quite a lot. I adore her, and I wondered—"

Good grief, thought Luke, appalled. Foster was going

to ask his permission as patriarch to go courting! Whatever would he say? He listened with becoming gravity, remembering his own anger, rage, jealousy, and uncertainty over Barbara. But the lad was so young, scarcely twenty-four—no, only twenty-three.

He had much work before him; he wanted to get a master's degree in chemistry; he might go on for a Ph.D. Should he consider marriage now?

Foster went on and on about the charms of the young lady.

"How old is she now?" asked Luke finally.

"Well—eighteen," said Foster, blushing again. "She has completed high school. She wants to start college next spring. However, her parents want her to go to a finishing school. And they have their eye on another man for her, someone in her father's business—"

Luke thought about it. Love affairs were not much in his line. What would Barbara say? That gave him the inspiration.

"I tell you, Foster, why not bring her around, in a sort of casual way, with her parents. We could give a dinner next week, over the New Year, and you could invite them all. Barbara could talk to her, maybe give you some advice on her. She's a smart woman. If the girl doesn't seem mature enough to know her own mind—"

"Oh, she loves me—I think," added Foster, dubiously.

"Well, it won't hurt to get the families together and get to know them," ended Luke. "Now, how is your experiment going on motorcar curtains?"

They discussed that for a little time. Foster was enthusiastic about it, even more than he was about the girl, thought Luke. Maybe he was just in the throes of youthful adoration and would recover in time.

But it made Luke feel very odd, later, as he explained to Barbara what had happened. "Made me feel like old John, passing judgment on the family," he said ruefully.

"Well, you're one of the senior members of the Val-

485

lettes," Barbara teased him. "Your advice is valuable. Shall she fit into the family, do you think? Shall you forbid Foster to see her again?"

Luke's face changed abruptly from light teasing to sorrow. "God, no. When I think of Sophia and Lionel, the tragedy—it could have been handled better. I still think they should not have married; they were first cousins, and the children—it wasn't safe. But to put her in the charge of that brute, Rodger, that was a horrible thing to do. I hope I never become so arrogant in my judgments that I let common sense be overridden like that."

Barbara touched his hand in silent sympathy. As long as she lived, she thought, she would never know Luke completely. He had so many sides to him. She had known first the older boy, the teasing, laughing companion. Then the man, strong, arrogant, sure of himself, riding roughshod (she had decided) over all his elders. Then she had married him, loving but not really understanding his needs, his passions. He could be lover, husband, tender companion, stirring her to wildest desire for him. He could be the hard-faced, coldly subtle man who directed Vallette and Sons, the largest gunpowder company in the United States.

He could be the gentle, thoughtful man who was so careful with Lionel and the younger ones. The father who held his daughter and kissed her small, waving fist. The tough competitor who dared Rodger Courtney to take control from him. The image of the tired, white-lined face of the overburdened man haunted her. She had to soothe him, help him; she rejoiced when she could make him relax and smile.

She studied his face now as he frowned over the evening newspaper. He said, absently, "With the Russians out of the war and the Italians about licked, the Huns will turn their full attention on France and England. I look for worse battles toward spring." He sighed heavily and laid down the paper. "That means more gunpowder. I had best send word to Henry in Missouri to increase production there; they have room for two more mills."

He was already busily planning. She left him to his thoughts, silently sewing a new little nightrobe. With Matthew but a few months old, just eight months now, she was pregnant again. Barbara thought ruefully, I had planned to have but one or two children. But Luke can't stay away from me, and I don't want him to. He was so tenderly ardent in bed, so sweetly demanding, that she would go wild with him. It was her fault as much as his.

The war dragged on. With spring, the battles increased fiercely. As Luke had predicted, as the army had expected, the Germans directed their full attention to France. They were thrusting toward Paris.

The Allies rallied and fought back fiercely. The American General John J. Pershing, sent to aid French Marshal Foch, won an important victory at Château-Thierry. The Germans were thrust back along the Marne in July and August. The summer was waning; still no end to the war was in sight.

Lionel, in his laboratory, felt far removed from all events. He had been thinking so much of Sophia this summer that it was as though she called longingly to him. The summers were so beautiful along the Areuse. The wildflowers bloomed in shady patches among the thick trees and bushes.

He strolled there sometimes on Sundays, his only day off. He would lie down in the hollows and dreamily watch the serene, puffy white clouds sailing in the clear blue sky—such a bright, clear blue. Sophia would have loved such a day, with the heat bringing out the fragrance of the grasses and herbs, the roses and the phlox.

He was working in the laboratory one Saturday evening, absorbed in an experiment. The men had gone home, calling goodnight. The mills flared with light all night, but in the laboratory it was peaceful. He could dimly hear the roll and crunch of the heavy powder-grinding machinery. It was part of his life, that sound in the background.

He finished the experiment, took off his white lab

coat, and set it aside. He would go home, to gaze at the full-sized portrait of Sophia, to dream. Perhaps to drink a little. He dared not drink much—it blurred his brain, and he must keep alert, for his work was important, the only important thing left on earth.

He put the papers in the safe and locked it. Then he glanced about and gave an exclamation of impatience. He had forgotten to clear out the pans of chemicals.

As he emptied one, his hand jerked—he was thinking of Sophia. When he set down the pan, he realized his mistake at once. But it was too late. He had knocked over one pan, and its contents spilled down into the sink where the other chemicals still lay, not having been rinsed down the drain.

The explosion blew the roof off the laboratory and echoed for miles in every direction. Lionel knew nothing of it. He lay where he had fallen, on the cement floor, his hand clasped tightly around the miniature of Sophia.

"He could have known nothing, no pain," the doctor reassured Luke two hours later when the men had been able to get into the laboratory. A fire had started, but it had been quickly doused. Lionel's suit was singed, no more. His face was peaceful once the bloody streaks were washed from it.

"What is in his hand?" asked Rory. He had come at once, limping down the hill, too impatient to wait for a carriage.

"Sophia's miniature," said Luke. "I tried to get it out, but his hand is too tight about it."

"You'd have to break his fingers to get it away from him," the doctor advised.

Luke shuddered. "No, let it be," he said sharply. "You're sure—he probably felt no pain?"

"He must have died at once," said the doctor.

They buried him up on the hill, on a bright August day, with a clear, warm sun shining. Luke directed that he be laid to rest beside Sophia, despite a weak protest from Lionel's father, Henry.

"They were parted in life; they shall not be parted in

death," said Luke, and that was the end of the matter.

"He should have forgotten the girl and married," said John Vallette brusquely. "He could have had sons himself. Forget all that youthful nonsense."

"He loved her, dad," said Barbara softly. "No other girl in the world meant anything to him."

She had insisted on going to this funeral, and in her dark outfit her clear face was sad. She was heavy with their third child, due next month. She thought of last year, when James had died so terribly, when the rain had poured down. "I'm glad it was beautiful today," she said, hanging on to Luke's arm as he helped her down the hill from the cemetery and into the carriage. "And the flowers were beautiful. Sometimes flowers help." She and Luke had brought floral wreaths of bright yellow and red roses.

"He enjoyed flowers," Luke said. "And he was a damned good chemist, the best in the business." Luke felt savage and beaten.

Lionel. His best man. His close friend—quiet though the man had been.

Gone.

Luke's second son was born in September. A quieter son, with vivid blue eyes and a lean, long body like Luke's. "Look at that chin," said Barbara, leaning over her new son as they lay together in bed. "I never saw a chin like that except on you, Luke. He'll be you all over again."

"Poor tyke," said Luke, but he bent to gaze with interest at his boy. When the baby yelled, he did so with such command that the nurse came running. He cried only when he wanted something. The rest of the time he was quiet, content, even placid. But that chin—!

"I'd like to name him after Lionel," said Barbara, looking at Luke questioningly. "He never had a son of his own. Yet he loved children. I would like to think there was someone named for him."

Luke nodded, his throat too choked for words. Barbara understood how much he missed Lionel. He was training Foster in the laboratory; later they would take on more young men. But Lionel—how do you replace genius?

"Lionel—Christopher—Vallette," he said finally. "To remember the old man, the company's first Vallette. All right with you?"

"Fine with me—grand with me," said Barbara, contentedly. She yawned. "Oh, I am sleepy yet. Do you think I shall ever get enough sleep?"

Luke bent over and kissed her, then drew up the covers about her. She was so sweet, so motherly; he adored seeing her with a baby in her arms, with the younger children about her.

He left her to sleep and went down to his study. Over a pipe, he studied the papers Lionel had left in the safe. He had made great strides in the past two years, almost as though he had known not much time was left to him.

Luke had more time now, with the trust cases dropped and the courts leaving him alone for a change. He would continue Lionel's experiments, he decided. When the war was over, they would convert at once to plastics—for a start, there would be the motorcar curtains that Lionel had worked out so well. The chemical formula looked good. Luke decided to spend more time in the laboratory and bring Owen back to handle the office. Henry was doing well in Missouri. Texas was in the charge of a new manager, a man who had married one of Roseann's daughters. It looked in good order.

Over the papers, an image came to Luke, of small Lionel Christopher, sleeping in his crib, the clearly defined eyebrows striking in his small face, and that chin—that firm chin. Luke smiled. It was a fine thing to have a daughter and two sons!

Chapter 37

The Armistice was signed in November of 1918. After the wild celebrations at the powder works, Luke collapsed and rested for several days and nights. Refreshed, he set about planning for the future, canceling government contracts for war supplies and turning his full attention to the work on plastics begun by Lionel. It seemed clear to Luke that plastics would play a large part in the future of Vallette and Sons.

That Christmas of 1918 the Vallettes had a great family reunion. Some of the New York Vallettes came down to the Areuse Valley and stayed at various homes. Stephen and Rose Marie were not there—they had died of influenza during the violent epidemic that had broken out that October. Stephen had died first, and Rose Marie had followed within a week.

But Anna Moira came especially to see her children Owen and Angela. Her husband, Martin Parrish, had retired, and they were thinking of building a home in Palm Beach. Darcy came with his family, and it was the first the others had seen of him in years. And Chloe, vigorous and in good health, arrived with two of her children.

Henry came back from Missouri. Owen returned from his government assignment, happy to be released, happy to start in with Vallette and Sons again. During the week before Christmas they held long conferences, planning how to change Vallette and Sons—debating which factories to keep open, and which to close and remodel. Luke was anxious to start right in with peace-time products.

On Christmas day Rory and Angela held a huge feast at the great mansion on the hill. The ballroom was open all day, with a small orchestra playing much of the time.

Luke looked about and was much amused at the sight of the Vallettes of all ages. He stood near the huge, long buffet table laden with a chocolate Yule log decorated with red and green icing in the form of holly leaves and berries. Along with the Yule log were immense fruitcakes and pumpkin pies, as well as sandwiches of ham, chicken and turkey. More turkey lay in slices on great platters. A salad bar along one side held a dozen bowls of potato salad, fruit salad, and greens.

The young people danced vigorously in the afternoon, partly to work off all they had eaten. Luke noticed that Foster had a new young girl in tow, a pretty little thing with brown hair and great brown eyes, dressed in a stunning crimson gown. Luke looked further and spotted Barbara, radiant in her azure gown, daringly showing her slim ankles, her tiara slightly askew on her dark, curly hair, with a diamond and sapphire pendant shining brilliantly, reflecting the glancing lights from the chandeliers. She turned her head, saw him, and smiled as radiantly as the diamonds that swung from her ears. She made her way over to him.

"Noisy, isn't it?" he said into her ear.

"Yes, but such fun," she sighed. "Isn't it great so many could come?"

"Do you think you could endure my stumbling through a waltz?" asked Luke. "I don't think we've danced together since!—uh—"

"Not for years," said Barbara, positively, putting her hand on his shoulder. "I wouldn't miss this dance for the world!"

He grinned, swept her into the waltz, and managed to get through it without disgracing himself. Then he glanced about the room. He noticed his niece Elizabeth with her husband; maternity had made her serene, and a little plump. Then he noticed with a smile the dancing couples: Foster and his new girl, Joshua and a cousin, and Anna Moira and her son Owen. They were having a great time, despite the children darting in and out, just managing to keep from underfoot.

Luke kept a sharp eye out for his small Serena, who had insisted on coming. Her two little brothers slept—peacefully, he hoped—back at the house. Then he spotted Serena playing in the corner with Rory's son. She seemed to be bossing him about. Luke shook his head. Such a cheeky, adorable girl, his Serena, she twirled everyone around her small, pink fingers.

When the music grew louder, Luke and Barbara withdrew to the great drawing room. There they found elderly John Vallette, wrapped in a blanket, before the huge fireplace. Rory and Angela, hands clasped, sat on a sofa nearby. Rory had white wings of hair against his cheeks; he seemed to have grown much older during the war. Angela was lovely in a rose maternity gown.

Presently Anna Moira came in with Owen and her husband Martin. "Here they are, all the sedate ones," she mocked lightly, sitting down beside her daughter Angela. She patted Angela's hand. "And are you talking business again?"

"Haven't gotten started," said Luke, with a grin, as he leaned back beside Barbara on the sofa across from them. "Where shall we begin?"

"Where you like. You know I'm interested," Anna Moira said, her dark eyes sparkling. How much she was like her mother, Rose Marie, Luke thought—the same liveliness and gaiety, the same seriousness beneath.

"Well, you know about the motorcar curtains. Before Lionel—died—he had completed work on the chemical formula. We've been trying it out. He did his usual thorough job. It's workable. We could go into production with it by the spring."

"Good, good," said Anne Moira. "Poor, dear Lionel. I often pray for his soul. Though he probably doesn't need it. A better, kinder man there was not. Such a dear man."

Barbara's hand clenched tighter on Luke's; his big fingers folded over hers.

"Tell me about the dress fabrics," drawled Owen.

They discussed the possibilities for developing synthetic fabrics, and so turned the conversation from Lionel's sad death, which still haunted them. Henry came in, dropped down into a chair near John, and listened keenly.

They all accept Luke as the boss, thought Barbara, as the conversation went on. They look up to him, they seek his advice, they respect his judgment. There was no more family feuding, thank God. He knows what is best for Vallette and Sons. He knows how to plan for the future.

Others drifted in, to listen, to chat, to compare notes on their children. And presently all returned to the ballroom, to eat again, to drink again, and to laugh and gossip and exchange news of the more far-flung members of the family. One of Darcy's sons was going clear to India to climb a mountain. Whatever for? asked Angela, in wonderment.

Then finally, as dusk approached, John turned to Luke. "Luke, you're the head of Vallette and Sons. Give us a toast, lad, a toast for the future. Go on, now."

They had done this in past years, toasted the future of Vallette and Sons, only the toast had always been given by John, or Henry, or Arthur. Luke cleared his throat and reached out for the glass of champagne offered by one of the white-gloved waiters. He waited, collecting his thoughts, while glasses were taken in hand by all the Vallettes except the children. Serena gazed up at her father with shining eyes. Barbara looked at Luke, and so did all the others.

Luke lifted his champagne glass and announced in a loud voice: "To Vallette and Sons! May we keep to the traditions of family loyalty, integrity, and honor that have sustained us in the past. May we build so that our future generations will be as proud of us as we are of our ancestors. To—the future of Vallette and Sons: *Together—Forever!*"

494

Many of them murmured "Amen," before tossing off their champagne gaily, with excitement and pride. Then the talking resumed, and the laughter, and later the dancing. It was a grand evening that lasted until four in the morning for many of them.

Luke and Barbara had left long before then. She was concerned and anxious about the boys, especially about young Lionel. And Serena had begun to yawn often, though she tried to hide her sleepiness from her parents.

It was a happy week for the Vallettes. They visited from house to house, exchanging gifts; and someone was always dropping in for tea or coffee in mid-afternoon, in addition to dinners and luncheons. They caught up on news, reacquainted themselves with cousins and aunts and uncles, and learned of plans for the future.

On New Year's Day, Lionel Christopher was baptized in the church the Vallettes had attended since Christophe's day. Many of the Vallettes remained for that ceremony. Luke had intentionally delayed it so that they might attend. Rory was godfather to the boy, Elizabeth godmother.

Luke's thoughts wandered as he gazed into the face of his son lying so still, so wide-eyed and wondering, as Elizabeth held him while the blessings were pronounced over him. What would be this lad's future? What would happen to him in the years to come? Would he, Lionel Christopher Vallette, be the future head of Vallette and Sons? Or would it be laughing, rambunctious, lusty Matthew, now kicking up a fuss in the arms of Anna Moira behind them?

As the minister prayed over his infant son, Luke bent his head and prayed also, for Lionel Christopher, and for them all. They, the proud Vallettes, had weathered many a crisis over the past one hundred and more years. From the early beginnings of Christophe, from his experiments in the laboratory, from his building of the first powder mills . . . Through the wars in which Vallettes had fought, had made gunpowder, had met crucial deadlines, had gallantly given their lives both in

495

combat and on the home front . . . Through explosions and fires in the mills . . . Through family crises, heartbreak, and tragedy . . . Through all, the Vallettes had endured, prevailed, their hopes steadfast . . . Triumphant!

The future was theirs, to do with what they would. God help us, prayed Luke, to do what is right and good for all of us, for our company, for our America.

SPECIAL PREVIEW

Here are the opening scenes from

THE VAN RHYNE
HERITAGE

The exciting second book
in
THE AMERICAN DYNASTY SERIES
Coming in February 1979

Staten Island, New York, 1830

Pieter Van Rhyne steered the great clumsy periauger with the skill of long practice. It was like the old Dutch canal scows. Loaded with rough lumber, it still rode the shallow, treacherous waters, the marsh flats of New Jersey, because it was of shallow draft. Its single four-sided lugsail caught what little wind was raised. It could not go rapidly, but tonight Pieter did not care. He had other matters on his sharp mind.

A small fortune, he thought. His uncle Pieter, his mother's brother for whom he had been named, had died and left him a part interest in some canal boats. What could he do with it? Canals were the future, his father had said, remembering his days in Holland. America had finally gotten smart and started building canals, now they would see some progress!

Pieter's large attractive mouth tightened in the darkness. He was young, and he was out in the world—the bustling world of New York, and he was no longer confined to a farm on Staten Island. He had listened, watched, and picked up information when sharply dressed businessmen rode across to New York on his periauger. He had heard, and he had thought about what he had heard. Yes, the canals would be good for business, but the real future lay in something quite different.

He let the boat bump gently into the dock. Then he sprang ashore and tied it up, his large sturdy body moving rhythmically. He was six feet two inches tall, as stocky as his Dutch ancestors, and as strong as a young bull. He had worked hard all his life, first on the family farm, then on the periauger he had earned and paid for with his own money. Now he was ready for grander affairs.

"Hendrik!" he called softly, yet imperiously, into the darkness. There was no answer. It was past midnight, yet Hendrik had promised to wait.

He sighed and began to unload the lumber himself, tossing it into neat piles near the dock. He had the boat unloaded and secured for the night and was on his way to the sturdy Van Rhyne farmhouse by one o'clock.

When he arrived there, he let himself in, quietly, to find his mother rocking beside the dying fire.

She was large-boned but thin, and her face was worn. Their father's illness had wearied her more than had the births of four children and the stillbirths of five more.

"The soup is hot," she said briefly, not pausing in her rocking. Then she looked into the Bible once more, her mouth moving soundlessly with the words.

He had taken off his heavy wet boots at the door, and he now walked in his stocking feet to the kettle. He dipped out some soup, then found the bread and cut off a large piece. His mother had set out some cheese covered with a wet cloth. So he sat down now at the trestle table to eat and drink hungrily. It had been a long day, beginning at four in the morning.

When he had finished, and had set aside the bowl, his mother finally let the Bible rest in her lap. Then she pushed her hair back wearily.

"You should not anger your father," she said placidly, yet with a warning evident in her tone.

"He is no better?" asked Pieter.

She shook her head. He came to stand before the fire, tall, broad-shouldered, straight, his blond head gleaming, his vivid blue eyes sparkling in spite of his weariness.

"He thinks only of the past," said Pieter, showing the harsh judgment of the young for the old and feeble.

"He is furious that you do not think of buying another boat. Hendrik needs one to increase our marketing of produce."

"Hendrik does not help me with this boat," said Pieter. "He did not come with me tonight, and he did not meet me at the dock to help me unload. Shall I fling away the money on a boat for him when he does not work with the one that he has?"

His tone was flat, precise. His mother sighed again. Pieter had grown up, and he was now twenty in this year of 1830. He had always worked hard and he could not understand his younger brother, who liked to laugh and run off with his friends.

"He will grow up if given more responsibility," his mother said.

"No matter. That is up to him," said Pieter, with a shrug. "I have my own plans for the future, and I shall carry them out. This inheritance but brings my plans closer to the working out of my destiny."

Wilhelmina Van Rhyne looked at her eldest son in a puzzled manner. He had inherited her shrewd mind, but he had gone beyond her understanding. His father was solid, hard, a farmer who had been grateful to have her dowry of a few acres of farm land. But Pieter was different: he longed for boats, and for a life beyond Staten Island. What did he dream of, that made his blue eyes shine? Where would he go, that made him glitter with bright promise, and set his will against his father's?

She herself had taught him to read and write, and he did both indifferently but well. He had caught on to mathematics much more quickly, not on paper, but in his mind. He cared nothing for reading books, yet he would draw by the hour on any scraps of newspaper or butcher paper. And draw what? Engines, and tracks, and more boats!

Strange, foolish matters, she thought.

"Your father is ill. I will not have him disturbed by these arguments," she said firmly. "You are only twenty, but you owe it to us to help out. We raised you; now you must help your family."

He bowed his blond head, and thought. "I will work on the canal for two more years," he said finally. "Hendrik must do his share, however. At the end of that time, he may have the periauger as his own—if he has worked hard. And I shall go off on my own when he is able to help the family. I will send money back to you, but I will not be bound."

"Be bound! Is that how you think of your own family?" she flashed, in a momentary anger. It stirred her plain face and showed the spirit she had had once, as a girl. She had once been pretty, some twenty-five years or more ago, when she was first married. Now her hair was gray, her face worn and thin, her hands reddened and rough. "You are ungrateful!"

"I must be off about my own business," he repeated. "I have dreams, and no one must stop me, mother. I do not forget you and father and my family. Yet, I will do what I must."

She looked at the hard inflexible mouth, and shook her head. "The farm is not good enough for you," she said sorrowfully. "You work at it, but your heart is not in the land. No, you had to go off about the boats, and work until you could buy a boat. Now you work all day on the land, and in the early morning and the evenings, you work your boat on the river and the flats. You will drive yourself to death, and for what?"

"For the future!" he laughed, his shoulders shaking a little. "Does not every young man dream of the future!" He stretched, then yawned mightily. "I will sleep now. Waken me at five, if I am not awake before."

She did not need to waken him. He was up long before five, and had eaten and left the house in the darkness before she was up. She roused herself, and then got Hendrik up. "Your brother has already left, Hendrik. You must rise, and help me with the farm work."

Hendrik yawned and rose reluctantly, shivering in the cold darkness of the early spring. He splashed cold water on his face, shuddered, then wiped it dry. He pulled on his shirt and pants over the underclothing he had worn all night.

"Did you speak to him, mother? Was he angry with me?" he asked eagerly as he sat down at the trestle table for his breakfast of hot tea, eggs and ham.

"Yes, he is angry, but firm. He has his plans, as you know. Why did you not go with him last night?"

"Oh, I went off with the boys," he said, quickly sullen. "Pieter can work all night, if he wants! I worked fourteen hours yesterday, that is enough!"

She compressed her mouth, looked at his handsome features, and knew him weaker than his brother. She sipped her tea and said, "He has promised to stay on two more years. However, you must work with him. At the end of that time, he leaves, and you may have his periauger. If you work well, he said."

"Two years!" flashed Hendrik. "But I want a boat now! He earns money for poling the produce across to New York, and the lumber and straw. I know he has some stuck away. Why does he begrudge me the money for my own boat?"

"He earned the money for his own. I suppose he feels that you should also!"

Hendrik finished his breakfast in silence and stamped out of the house. Nevertheless, his mother soon noted with relief that he, hoping for that boat, helped more on the land and was more courteous to Pieter.

The two years slid past, then Pieter said, "Hendrik, you may have the boat. I shall be off. Take care of the family, and I will send money from time to time."

They had talked a little about his plans. "Let me come with you," said Hendrik eagerly. "You will have adventures! I don't want to be stuck here with the family!"

"They need you," said Pieter firmly. "Father may not last long, and mother and the two girls need you. Take care of them, and I will come and see how you do. If you wish to marry, as you said, then you must learn

503

to take care of the weaker ones. You cannot start a family and be off to adventures!"

Hendrik flushed, for he was already fond of a girl on a nearby farm. The girl had no brothers. Her father had said warily that if he showed promise, the girl might marry him, and Hendrik could have half his farm as her dowry. Hendrik scratched his head. How could a man marry a sweet girl, and have her farm, and be off on adventures at the same time? He reflected sadly that he did not know how to plan his life so well as Pieter did. Heart-whole, Pieter had made up his mind, and his iron will would not permit any changes.

Pieter had been carefully dividing his money, the money he had earned over the years with the extra work on the boat. Now he left half of it with his mother, advising her to put it carefully away where it would not be seen.

"For Hendrik would immediately think of a dozen ways of spending it, mother," he said. "You will need it for the girls' dowries, and for father, as he is so ill. I will come to you and see you when I can."

She touched his cheek when he left. They did not kiss, they were not sentimental people. But she looked after him wistfully, standing a long time on the dock, in the chill wind, as Hendrik poled him away from the farm where he had lived all his life.

Hendrik left him in New York. "What will you do, Pieter?" he asked for the hundredth time.

"My business, brother," grinned Pieter. He felt as free as the sea gulls above them lazily wheeling about in the air. But he was no bird, he was a man of money and promise!

He had been looking about these past two years, and he had been thinking soberly for longer than that. He had gone to see the canal boats left him by his uncle, and he had directed their use on the canals. But he had had no intention of becoming a canal man. He had had enough of boats, at least for now.

He rented a room at a boarding house near the docks. He had stayed there overnight at times, when he had been detained on business in New York. Now the landlady asked, "And how long will it be this time, Mr. Van Rhyne?"

"I don't know, ma'am. I'll let you know in a day or two."

He washed, then changed into his good suit of dark green wool and tossed a yellow muffler around his neck. He still wore his boots. He brushed his hair until it lay down, though some curls still rose about his bronzed neck.

Then he went directly to the office of the Grimes brothers. He knocked at their door and stepped in. The two men were seated at their identical mahogany desks. They looked up impatiently when their clerk showed him in.

"Yes, what is it? Foreman or laborer?"

Deliberately Pieter closed the door after him, on the clerk's quiveringly curious nose. "I came to see about some stock in the railroad. I heard it was for sale."

"Stock?" Their eyebrows rose high. They looked him over, in his hard wool suit, his high boots, with his cap in his hands. "Stock? Huh, how much you want, one share?" said one brother, and the other one laughed gruffly.

"How much per share?" asked Pieter. He was still standing, for they had not invited him to sit down in one of the hard chairs opposite the desks.

"One hundred dollars per share," said the other brother promptly.

"I heard it was sixty-two dollars per share," said Pieter, his voice very gentle.

The men looked at each other again. Then they looked back at him. Was he a greenhorn, or no? They looked at the sharp blue eyes, at the big burly build.

"Sit down, Mr.—ah—?"

He sat down on the hard chair. "Pieter Van Rhyne," he said.

"Mr. Van Rhyne. Ah—where did you hear it was sixty-two dollars per share?"

"On the street, maybe," he said, his face impassive.

"Hum. Well, how much did you want to take?"

"How many shares do you have for sale?"

They did not know how to take him. Businessmen had manners, and they wore high stocks and carried ivory-handled canes. This man looked like a laborer; he seemed to be a tough businessman, it was true, but he was obviously a hardworking man, judging from the look of his big red hands.

"We've got plenty. How many you want?" the quieter brother asked. He pulled a pad to him, picked up a pen and dipped it in the ink, and looked up, ready to write.

"At sixty-two dollars per share, I'd like one hundred shares—to start," said Pieter, casually, his boots squarely before him on the wooden plank floor.

Both men stared now, jaws agape. Pieter would have been amused under other circumstances, but now he only felt impatient. How much time men wasted!

"Do you have the money—with you?" they asked.

"I don't carry that kind of cash. If you care to come to the bank with me . . ."

They cared. They both went with him after closing the office. At the nearby banking office of a merchant, they went in with Pieter and watched as he was greeted with respect and shown into the office of the merchant. They saw him ask for his account, waited while a clerk filled out the forms, and watched as he signed his name in a painful scrawl.

Then he hesitated for a moment. "Ah—I believe I'll take two hundred shares," he said, still as casual as could be.

Both of the Grimes brothers felt rather dizzy. The man must be wealthy! Much more respectfully, they signed over two hundred shares of their railroad stock to him and took him to dinner. It warranted at least a steak and oysters, with beer to wash it down, to have sold such a large block of Grimes Railroad Company stock that day.

Pieter questioned them over dinner, asking short,

brisk questions that went to the heart of their operations.

"How far along are you? Where is end-of-track? How much do you pay the foremen? How much for the men? What kind of food? Where do they live?"

They returned to the office with him and took out charts and crude maps and showed him how far along the railroad lines were.

"We mean to join up with the Erie to the North," they said. "That will make our line important, you see."

He saw that and much more. "How much do you pay the foremen?"

They told him. He said, impassively, "I'll take a job as foreman for that pay and one more share of stock per month. I'll live out at end-of-track, and oversee the operations. I like to see where my money is going."

They did not like it much, but he had his way. He was a big solid Dutchman, and they could see he knew what he was doing. And all that money—!

Pieter bought a horse and moved out the next day. He rode to end-of-track with his gear, including a new tent, rough blue workclothes, a pistol and powder horn, and a sharp knife he carried always. Then he got to work.

He was at end-of-track for a year before he went home. He had sent notes back to his mother from time to time. One man he trusted, and with this man acting as a courier, he was able to send some money to her along with the notes. Other than that, he worked from one end of the week to the next, and took Sundays off only because the men insisted on having it.

He lived out of doors except at night, which he spent in the tent. He became even browner, tougher, harder. He swung an axe with the men cutting ties, and he swung a pick with those digging in the hard earth.

His quiet voice directed the workers even better than did the yells and oaths of other foremen. They knew that when Pieter Van Rhyne said something, he meant it. And he could outwork them, outthink them, and out-figure them any hour of the day.

Most of the men were Irish but a few were German, and this led to fights every Sunday. Pieter watched them curiously. To use up such energy in such a wasteful fashion! And he stopped them with a few curt words when they went too far.

"You got so much vigor and strength, tomorrow you'll dig those roots out with your picks," he said once, separating two combatants, one Irish and one German.

"Listen, he called me a son of a—" began the Irishman.

"Words! So they make scars, do they? You'll make holes in the earth tomorrow, they're the scars you'll make," said Pieter.

"I'm a foreman!" Joe MacSweeney blustered. "I direct the men, I don't do no work like that!"

"You do what I tell you, that's what you do," said Pieter, staring him down. He was taller and broader than the Irishman. MacSweeney hesitated, then flung himself away to drink from his bottle and grumble in low tones to a friend.

That night, Pieter kept the flap of his tent open. He always slept lightly, with one eye open, as Hendrik used to jeer at him. Now, about midnight, he heard and saw the shadow that came to his tent.

When the figure had got right inside his small tent and was about to bend over him, he said, easily, "What do you want? The pigs got loose again?"

The man started, yelped, and ran out. Pieter grinned to himself and lay back, loosing the small sharp knife in his hand and laying it carefully beside him on the blanket.

Pieter went home again after a year and a half. He went first into the office of the Grimes brothers and reported their progress and corrected their maps. Then he took a boat out to Staten Island.

As he approached the dock he looked over the farm

land. It didn't look bad, and the corn was coming along well. He tied up and went slowly up to the house.

One of his sisters came flying out to meet him. "Pieter! You came!" She clasped his hand and beamed at him affectionately.

"Well, Marta, all goes well?" he asked, clasping her hand in return. She was his favorite sister, for she was quiet, and hard-working, and good to their mother.

She shrugged. "Oh, Sadie, she is crazy over a boy, and Hendrik grumbles about his work. And father—he is ill," she said, and her face shadowed.

He saw his mother working in the fields and strode out to her. "Where is Hendrik?" he asked furiously, without greeting her. She was standing, with hoe in hand, her face under the sunbonnet looking drawn and brown.

"He is out courting a girl, Pieter. It is good to see you. I will stop now and come in to fix your dinner." She showed no surprise, only her fingers went briefly to her cheek. "You look good, Pieter. So much bigger and stronger. You are happy, yes?"

"The work goes well," he said. "How is father, worse?"

She nodded. "I think he will not live another winter," she said simply.

They went back to the farmhouse together. He listened more than he talked, and learned much. Sadie was crazy about a city boy who had been visiting with relatives on a farm nearby. Marta had been going with a young man, the second in his family, who helped on the Van Rhyne farm at times. Hendrik often came home late, flushed, with the odor of drink on him.

His father lay in bed, thinner than ever, his gaunt face upraised to the ceiling, his eyes sunken. He brightened a little when Pieter bent over him. "Son," he whispered. Theodoric Van Rhyne had always been big and husky, and it was a shock now to see him so wrinkled and crumpled there, like a husk of himself. "You come home to us, eh?"

"For a few days. But the work goes fast, and I will be

509

needed again." He listened to the old man's vague complaints, and noted the way his hand pressed feebly to his bowels. He was sick unto death, thought Pieter, compassionately. Already his father's mind wandered.

In the kitchen, he talked to his mother quietly. "What does Hendrik do all day?" he asked mildly.

She looked uneasy. "He goes to help at the farm of his girl. He is too tired to help us much here."

"And the boat?"

"He said it was too much work to haul lumber and produce. He sold the boat, and bought a ring for his girl, and some suits for himself, and a bonnet for me. I did not want the bonnet," she said apologetically.

"Will the girl have him? And her father, does he approve?"

The old woman looked relieved at Pieter's mild tone. "Yes, he likes Hendrik, they laugh and play cards together."

"Well, I think all can be arranged." Inwardly, Pieter was furious. "Hendrik needs to be married, I think. And what of little Sadie?"

"She is too young to marry, I told her so."

"And Marta?"

Wilhelmina Van Rhyne looked sad. "She loves a good man, but he has no land, Pieter. He has but his own two hands."

Pieter looked thoughtful. They talked a while longer, then they went to bed. He lay beside his brother in the old bed, and thought. He never needed much sleep. By morning, his plans were made.

He called on the family of Marta's young man and liked them. There were eight children, sturdy and strong, of Dutch descent. Her young man was shy, but eager to work, and his look went often to sturdy Marta.

"You will walk part of the way home with me, Lars?" asked Pieter as he took his leave.

The women had gone ahead in the carriage, with Hendrik driving. He liked to show off his skill with horses.

"Ah, yes, Pieter. We become acquainted, ya?" Lars was eager, hopeful.

Pieter got quickly to the point. "You like my sister, Marta, and she likes you much, I think, Lars." They were striding along the river, and Pieter looked back at the fields keenly. They were well-kept, in neatly plowed rows.

"Ya, very much, I like her. She is—the kind of woman I wish to marry. If only—"

"Lars, you marry my sister, you will have the land. Only I wish you and Marta to make a home for my mother and father, and for my young sister Sadie until she marries. You would do this?"

Lars gaped at him, his honest face shocked. "But—but the land belongs to Hendrik! He says so!"

"It would have, but he does not work the land. Lands belong to those who would take care of them. He cares more to work the land of his girl's father," said Pieter drily. "I will look to Hendrik. What do you say?"

"I would work my fingers to the bone for Marta. However, I do not wish to cause the bad feelings in her family. Whatever will Hendrik say? And the good mother?"

"Say nothing now. I will arrange all before I go. Come tomorrow, it is Sunday, and we will visit. All will be good, Lars. I like you, and you will make a good husband for my fine sister. Let us shake hands on this." And he held out his burly, bronzed fist.

They shook hands heartily. Lars drew a deep breath, and began to beam. "I could never believe it would happen! I thought all my life to work for my father and brother—"

"You will care for this land, you will work it well. I make pretty good money now, I will send money for the care of my father and mother. If aught goes wrong, send for me, at once, and I will come. I depend on you, Lars."

"May you never regret your trust in me!" he said fervently, his face glowing.

"Go home, now, and come tomorrow with your parents. Perhaps at three o'clock?"

They agreed on it. Pieter went home, to tackle his sister, then his mother, and finally his brother. Hendrik was furiously angry.

"The land is mine, all of it! You said so! It is mine, and you cannot take it back!"

"You pay more attention to the land of your girl's father than to ours," said Pieter calmly. "I come home to find mother working the land. She will do so no longer. You will marry your girl, if she will have you, and that land is yours. This land goes to Marta and to Lars, who will care for it, and for our parents and sister."

He was inflexible. Hendrik fumed and fussed, and tried to get his mother to take his side. But she had had enough of him and his ways. She had quietly saved money, and Pieter agreed with her that Hendrik should have a sum of one thousand dollars to take to his new father-in-law.

So it was arranged. Before he left, Pieter saw Hendrik married to his girl, and Marta married to her Lars. Lars was installed as head of the household in the Van Rhyne home, and Pieter knew that his parents would be cared for.

And Pieter finally set out on his own business with a sigh of relief. Later, he would find a good husband for Sadie, for he had warned Lars to let him know if she began to show interest in someone unsuitable.